Anger Child

Manuscript

Roy Tomkinson

This book is a work of fiction. People, places, events, and situations are the product of the author's imagination. Any resemblance to actual persons, living or dead, or historical events, is purely coincidental.

Published by Globe Publications
United Kingdom

Printed and bound in Great Britain by
CPI Antony Rowe, Chippenham, Wiltshire

ISBN 978095597360-4

Globe Publications Limited
PO BOX 85
CF37 7WW

Dedicated to the person who started me
on my journey as a writer.
Forever grateful
Thank you.

This bed thy centre is, these walls, thy sphere.

John Donne, The Sun Rising

Chapter one

The clouds were low and grey, the wind slowly gaining strength as it rained lightly, just enough to chill the bones with a feeling of dampness. The weather was about to change for the worse a harbinger of things to come as Colin walked home through Cwmparc to his house that was at the very top of terraced houses, before the road abruptly ended and the mountains began. These were no ordinary mountains, but black unstable mountains; manmade, spewed out of buckets from the colliery over the green fertile grass like volcanic craters continually changing, as the slag heaps grew ever larger. Covering forever the true splendour of this little part of Wales with no feeling for the occupants or the beauty this Welsh valley had trapped in its grove for thousands of years.

Colin had been to see his grandmother in Chepstow Road when he should have been at school and was now on the pavement of the main road walking home. He stopped and looked into the hardware shop between the chemist and fish and chip shop his parents regularly frequented. They were hardened fans of newspaper fish and chips eaten with the fingers with lashings of salt and vinegar. The window of the hardware shop was full of different tools; hammers, drills, levels and saws of all sizes marked for sale. There was also a picture of a man in working clothes with a saw in his hand, smiling, and a boy by his side about the same age as Colin.

This image hit him like a bullet; fast and furious it penetrated his mind. The person could be his father; the father he loved but no longer respected. As a child everything seemed so simple, to be born, to grow up, to follow his father's ways and beliefs, not to the pit but into an apprenticed trade "to better his prospects," his father's words.

He was getting older, more rebellious, starting to resent the world he was born into, blaming his parents for everything that he saw wrong in his life.

"Why are we so poor?" He would cry looking at his father, who had his pipe in his mouth. "Why can't we have a big house, lots of other people do?"

"Things are what they are my boy," his father would reply lighting his pipe as if not a care in the world, which made Colin angry and would say not another word, but the bitterness was in his thoughts, his mind was shifting to blackness.

He had forgotten the warmth, the love and understanding of his parents, saw only two middle-aged people with little formal education and no prospect of betterment; to his mind losers because they readily accepted their situation in life. His feelings were out of control; to his young arrogant mind, they were to blame for the degradation in the valley because they had accepted the situation as if it were normal and this made him bitter.

He could see no way out of the pit way of life, tethered as everyone was to the power of the black lump and all it represented. As a young child he was proud to call his father a miner but now felt ashamed and wished his father were different.

He no longer lived in the black and white world he knew as a child, the simple straightforward world of right and wrong. His mind was transforming, shifting and shaping in the maelstrom of life.

A dreary repetitive hazy mist that could chill the warmth out of a summer's day had descended into his mind and was starting to strangle his heart. The only world he could see was the world of his parents that stood for hard monotonous grafting in a never-ending circle of automated movements without end, reason or logic.

This was not for him. He needed adventure, excitement, not the drab way of his parents. Their way of life was a poison to him. How could they be so happy knowing they had so little?

Knowing what you need, or think you need is one thing; to achieve, or how to achieve what you think you need is another. He was starting to dream about success or what he thought was success and he wanted it, so wanted it, no matter what the cost.

He sought, so desperately sought, what he could not have; living in a small terraced house sharing a room with his two brothers meant failure. This is my parents' fault; why don't they move to a bigger house, get a car, and go away for long holidays? They must be very bad people not to give me these things, he reasoned.

Everyone worked in the pit; hard manual labour was a way of life. Wages were poor; there was talk of redundancies and the fight for jobs. Fight for what! To remain poor and have an ingrained black face and broken limbs through years of hard work? To have lungs full of black powder that chokes out life and denies air. This is a fight for fools and clowns, Colin believed.

Some things are not worth fighting for, to chase a rainbow at the end of which is no more than a black lump and even that belonged to someone else would not be for him. He would not go into battle to fight for the right to die a horrible lingering death clogged to the throat with the foul black dust the collier breathed every day of his life. The miners suffered pneumoconiosis, dusk, lung disease, black and deformed knees; constantly fought to breathe the air we all take for granted. Lungs black, disfigured, scarred through breathing the dust given out when they mined this black treasure. It is a curse as bad as any curse the pharaohs could inflict upon disturbing their rest for thousands of years.

He could identify with these people no longer. They were talking about fighting for their way of life; to Colin it was valueless. Nothing more than the right to remain poor, stay destitute in a valley where death and suffering were the routine.

Where is the sense in this? The community spirit, the solidarity of the valley was for accepters, society's losers. He was angry, resentful, a troublemaker. The more trouble he became the more the teachers were convinced he was an agitator and not worth trying to educate, one of life's failures.

He had all the makings of a modern day terrorist, felt deeply the only way out was to use violence, after all, that is how the system was attempting to train him, or so he believed. Spare the rod, spoil the child, the harder the beating the more compliant the child so the reasoning decreed. The system taught him this way; tough love would be the justification name for this behaviour or so the theorist would have you believe. For every demon they were trying to beat out of him another two immediately replaced them far nastier than the one they expelled, it was an exercise in futility.

He had a few days left in his present school before moving next term to the senior school but would not be going back to complete those last days. He had run out a few hours earlier and went to his grandmother to tell her what he had done. She lectured him on conformity but how could he conform and learn if everyone believed he was not worth teaching, caught in a dichotomy of his own making.

"Say your tables' boy," the teacher shouted, walking towards him cane in hand, looking straight at him. He knew what was coming; the teacher held the cane above his head, waiting, ever waiting for him to hesitate, and of course, he always did, and paid the price.

The cane came down on his hand resting on the desk as the teacher shouted. "You are a stupid boy. What is he class?"

"A stupid boy, sir," the class repeated.

This angered him and in temper shouted. "You are a stupid teacher and I hate you."

The teacher's face turned red with anger; next came a sharp slap against the back of Colin's head. The teacher grabbed him by the collar and at the same time marched him out of the class into the head teacher's room to extract retribution.

The head had the same amount of apathy to education as her teacher and approached the children in a similar manner. "Hold your hand out boy," she instructed, looking at him as if he were dirt under her feet.

"No, you old bag," he replied in temper and pushed into her trying to get away from her clutches. She grabbed his hand and held it out trying to hit it with a cane simultaneously but missed.

"I hate you all, and this school," he shouted and ran out the door knocking over a table as he hastily retreated.

The teachers tried to run after him but were not fast enough; yet again his temper had the better of him. Every teacher he ever encountered over the last twelve-months thought he was stupid. If this is what they believed, that is what he would give them and live up to their expectation.

He so much wanted to learn but had no idea how, needing understanding and help, not more discipline. An illness had kept him off school for a term; he was academically behind, way behind, and was unable to catch up or make any sense of the lessons. Teachers told him to copy off one of the other children, which infuriated him to distraction. He blamed his parents, school, teachers, anyone and everyone equally for the way he felt.

He tried to discuss this with his mother who did not think it important. "You are being silly, school is school, if you want to learn you will," she stated dismissing his feelings as an irrelevance. He felt the lack of importance in her words and pursued the matter no further; instead, he went deeper into his world locking the door against reason. From that moment on, whatever his parents or authority thought, he thought the opposite.

He studied the small house into which he was born. The lack of money, the material things his parents didn't possess, the way he was dressed, spoke, behaved, made him feel cheap, worthless, accentuated further the more he fell behind at school. His parents' values were no longer his values, school no more than a waste of time. He would fight for what he needed and win; take what others had earned, let them suffer like him. If they had it, he wanted it and would get it at any price irrespective of the consequences. If he hurt other people so what? To exploit was to have, to give to remain poor, be exploited. He wanted revenge on the world and would take it no matter what the cost.

He had so much energy in his young body, a keen brain, both lacked direction, a lethal combination as he erupted into adulthood. Pictures of large houses, cars, televisions, clothes, boats covered magazines, materialization had arrived, but not for the likes of him. Leave school, go down the mine or become an apprentice, work hard, drink hard, smoke if you like, don't try and be educated or get above your station in life, would be the words etched into his memory by the attitude of society at large.

Chapter Two

The talk in the valley was of redundancies; demand for coal was on the decline and would get worse. New forms of energy, cleaner energy that did not pollute the environment was taking over; colliery closures were inevitable.

"I've been in the pit for over thirty years since a lad, at my age will never find another job." George, Colin's father, stated, his face etched with concern.

"You and everyone else in the pit, we are all in the same boat," Albert his brother responded. "I've worked in the pit for the last twenty eight years as you know George. What are we to do? There are no jobs around."

They looked at each other for a moment and then at the floor. George was the first to break the silence. "It's the dole for us both then," he added lighting his pipe with a match as if putting a full stop on the matter and sat on the garden seat beside his brother.

Albert would not let it rest and in a raised voice replied, "I intend to fight for the right to work, we can't allow those bastards to grind us down we owe it to our forefathers."

George contemplated this statement, weighing his words carefully. "The police are ready for a long strike, have been for a while, Gwynfa told me. I'll not fight we can never win. The government is against us, we have very little sympathy from the country," pipe now in full steam with the smoke going for once in a straight direction.

"What does Gwynfa know, he is in the police force and cannot be trusted, he is one of them," Albert responded in an angry voice that sounded unusual, normally he spoke quietly.

"Come on Albert, the police have always been against us and for authority, it can be no other way, think what happened in Russia, authority overthrown and look what replaced it. They have their job to do and would do nicely out of a strike. There'll be plenty of overtime keeping us all in line. Is that what you want to give them more money?"

"Well no, not really."

"That's what will happen if we strike. The country will always need coal but is not prepared to pay the full price for keeping us warm. We must accept the inevitable Albert. They intend to break the power of the miners and we are falling into the trap," George said in a low voice.

"If the police need a fight, by damn, we'll give them one and win. We are strong together, if need be we'll take on the police and government and drag them down into the dirt. They need us more than we need them." Albert responded feeling agitated as the resentment started to build against his brother's pacifist attitude.

"Win or lose, things will not be very different for the likes of us. I see no value in fighting for my sons to go down the dark hole," George replied sharply.

Both men knew things were about to radically alter, a harbinger of insecurity. The drudging monotony of the valley was to alter forever; the wind of change was sweeping over the endless rows of terrace houses sending a chill into the occupants as they sat next to their coal fires. The pit was a central part of their lives and went back generations, now there was talk all this could soon be at an end.

"What are you two up to; you both look like monkeys waiting for nuts." They turned their heads to the sound knowing the voice but not the direction. "Throw over a match would you George," Henry shouted as his head popped up over the garden fence.

"Keep the box I have another one," George shouted throwing the matches over the fence.

"Thank you," he caught them with both hands. "I'll be with you in a minute," and true to his word was over the fence in a jiffy.

"Nice to see you again," Albert remarked. "What shift are you tomorrow?"

"I'm working afternoon shift; what shift are you Albert?"

"Tomorrow is a rest day for me, I'm working the day shift next week, for how long it's anyone's guess; things aren't right, not right at all," Albert replied.

Henry responded to this remark with a sharp twist in his voice. "They think we are like old pit ponies to be put out to graze and forgotten about."

"The slag heaps more like, we are to be thrown out like lumps of slag," Albert vehemently responded feeling angry.

"We are pawns; they play with us as if they were gods, declaring this, decreeing that. They are the puppet masters and we are expected to follow the string," answered a contemptuous Henry.

The entire time George sat quietly listening, puffing his pipe. "Gods or not, the situation will not change, coal is no longer profitable, if there is no upturn for coal the pits will close." George decreed knocking his pipe against the bench, the sparks flying in all directions as if they were the start of the fire, which shortly was to follow.

"Shall we go down the pub? I'm thirsty and could do with a pint." Henry remarked his eyes lighting at the thought, lifting the tension.

"You are always thirsty," George replied and chuckled. "There again so am I, come on, let's go and have a few. What do you think Albert?"

"I'm all for it George, let's go."

They all trotted out of the garden and a few minutes later were in the pub standing at the bar. "Three pints please," were the first words spoken by Henry as he looked around. The large stove in the middle of the room was glowing with heat and sitting to the left of it was Bill.

He was a large round type of fellow who always wore loose trousers, an open necked shirt and Wellington boots. Both garments looked un-pressed. Bill's clothes and an ironing board were alien to each other and could not speak the same language, indeed, it was rumoured by the locals they were not even from the same planet. He was a bachelor. His clothes creased, dishevelled, and well worn but in his defence always clean. If they were dirty, he would call it clean dirt less than twenty-four hours old. On the corner of the table rested a walking stick with a large curved handle. Bill didn't really need the stick but it suited his image as being a little eccentric and gave him the air of being a farmer.

"Will you have a pint Bill," Henry shouted hands outstretched as if to magically will the almost empty glass in Bill's hands to jump out and land on the bar without human intervention.

"Thank you Henry don't mind if I do," he replied finishing the contents of the glass quickly.

"Give me the glass," Albert remarked and walked over to Bill who, still seated, handed him the empty glass. Albert walked back to the bar placed it on the top to wait refilling. He paid for the beer and the three of them moved from the bar and sat around the table with Bill.

"What do you think of all this talk of redundancy and pit closures," Albert said directly to Bill getting straight into the subject.

He took a sip of his pint. "Not a lot, only that coal is not as profitable as it used to be, why do you ask?" Thinking there were far more exciting things than the price of coal.

"I mention it because if the pits do close we will all be out of work. I thought that was obvious," Albert said, turning to George and Henry for agreement.

"Is that such a bad thing boys, look at the number of friends we have buried over the years? You'd need forty hands to count them. A lot of them would be with us now if it wasn't for the pit."

"We all need to eat Bill," George responded in justification.

"If it comes to a fight it will be an uphill battle." Bill remarked not caring much for the conversation.

"Uphill or not we will fight and win, Bill," Henry responded reproachfully thinking him too casual.

"Now, now Henry, there are more important things to think about than a rumour of pit closures," Bill replied taking a sip from his pint.

"What can be more important than losing your job at our ages?" Henry remonstrated looking indignantly at Bill.

"Have you heard about the two people who died recently in Maerdy?" Bill replied thinking it more important to steer the conversation away from the pits.

"No! What happened?" George jumped in, thinking there had been a pit accident.

"Two women died of the smallpox yesterday," Bill replied, gaining the moral ground.

This produced a sudden shock in the three people; George was the first to speak. "That is one sod of a disease and highly contagious."

Albert showed concern forgetting the pits for a moment. "Did they have any children?"

"Yes, five between them, all still at school. What are the symptoms George? You are a trained First Aider," Bill enquired.

"A headache followed by backache, vomiting, rash and finally delirium and in a number of cases death, but it can be vaccinated against, this must be some new strain, all viruses mutate over a period. Those that survive are normally pox marked for life," George answered.

"Let's hope the two cases are the only ones and the disease doesn't spread over the valley to us," remarked Henry.

“Come on drink up it’s time to go,” George stated drinking up his pint and placing his glass on the counter.

Chapter Three

Colin could barely read and write and felt strongly school was not for him. In junior school for the last year trouble followed him wherever he went, like a trusted dog. He was written off as a duffer, marked down to go into the colliery or some other manual job, school little more than a place to wait out time until old enough to start work.

Arriving at his new school he felt nervous and lost, but hid it well, already a master at keeping his feelings from the world even from himself. Outwardly, he portrayed confidence, inwardly he felt alone, misplaced, as if he should be somewhere else and was not expecting this school to be any better than the last; he was there because he had no choice.

At the entrance to the school, a voice came from behind him; turning his head in the direction of the sound, his eyes fell upon a small friendly person smiling at him.

"You're new here?"

"Yes, first day," he replied unconcerned puffing out his chest.

"Keep out of the way of the snake gang, they try and push the new boys around," he warned.

"No one pushes me around," Colin replied sharply, clenching his fists.

"Have it your way, but be careful," he responded. "I'm only trying to help."

"What is your name?"

"Tim, my name is Tim," he repeated proudly. "What do they call you?"

"Colin. Let's get into school before we're late." Both entered together. Colin had made a friend.

One school can be any school. All schools to Colin looked the same, drab, boring, well-worn floors, grey walls, large ugly windows, and doors to match the uniformity of an institution that he thought is nearer to a torture chamber than a place of learning. It was his concentration camp, the walls his barbed wire, the teachers his jailers.

The hallway in the centre of the school was the first meeting place of the day where they all met as one large group for morning prayers each class arranged like sheep in a pen in strict order, according to age and class status. Colin was the fresher and told to go to the front and sit on the wooden floor and cross his legs.

The floor was full of splinters, hard to touch and uncomfortable on the bottom. Pain and discomfort did not matter, it was reputed to be character forming and educational or so the local council and teachers believed. The greater the distress the greater the learning, pain and education went hand in hand, no pain no gain, and pain there was in abundance, so somewhere there must be gain but Colin had just not found it, but there would be time, plenty of time, and time was the one commodity he had in plentiful supply when in school.

Colin was ripe for teaching and desperately wanted to learn, the bravado on the outside a mask hiding his insecurity and uncertainty of the place he now found himself in as a pupil. He was a part of the establishment but the establishment did not wish to be a part of him. It seemed as if he were there without an invitation but convention decreed he could not be turned away, so some means of punishment would need to be found to make him pay for wasting the time of this hallowed institution and conform to their rules without questioning.

After the morning assembly, teachers directed them into their classes and the brutalisation of these young minds would quickly get underway. That lunchtime in the school play area, the snake gang introduced themselves to Colin. One of the older boys accosted him and asked him for money.

"I have no money, sorry," Colin honestly answered shrugging his shoulders.

"Well get some if you know what's good for you or the gang will beat you up," the boy called Evans replied looking as tough as he could through two missing teeth.

"Where do I get money from?" he answered perplexed not really paying much attention.

"That's not my problem, get it by tomorrow," he emphasized and walked away crunching his fists.

That afternoon Colin informed Tim what had happened and how he did not intend to pay money to the gang.

"Most of the boys do, or give something else instead," he was reliably informed.

"How many are there in the gang?"

"Five, the two to be careful of are Hopkins and Barry the rest are just along for the ride and are nothing without the other two. It's easier to pay and keep out of trouble. They can be very nasty if crossed."

"I have nothing to give, especially money."

"Well you're in for a hiding."

"I won't take it off the teachers so I'm definitely not taking it off them," Colin said defiantly.

"How will you stop them?"

He shrugged his shoulders. "I'll think of something."

The rest of the afternoon went without incident and the final bell rang bringing to a close the school day. All the pupils got up and darted for the door wedging into the doorway all trying to be the first out of the room as the teachers shouted instructions to walk. Colin and Tim walked out together talking about Bumble

Head the teacher who had just taught them. They ambled through the schoolyard in no particular hurry to get home.

Tim asked. "Are you really not going to pay?"

"Yes!" was the short sharp retort. "Why should I?"

"On your head be it," he pronounced. "Make the excuse that you'll pay them later."

"We'll see."

The following day at school, Colin had forgotten all about the incident with Evans until he approached him at lunchtime. With him were Hopkins, Barry, and two other members of the gang who asked again for money.

"I've already told you," Colin stated politely. "I have no money for myself let alone for you. I'm sorry but that's how it is, no money."

To this remark, two of the gang grabbed Colin and forced him against a wall struggling and kicking all the while.

"My, you're a tough one," Hopkins laughed as he pinched him on the cheek.

"Leave me alone," Colin screamed, "or you'll be sorry."

"I'm quaking in my boots," Barry laughed as he pulled Colin's hair until his eyes watered.

He struggled and kicked out at Hopkins catching him on the leg but before he could kick again, Barry hit him in the stomach knocking all the wind out of him. The two other members of the gang searched him for money but found nothing.

"Tomorrow you'll get worse if you have no money," Hopkins screamed and left. Colin, winded, leant against the wall feeling hurt and angry, bent on revenge.

It took him a few minutes to recover; he felt used and abused by the snake gang, and determined to get his own back. He took off his school socks, looked around for two stones, placed one in each sock, and waited in a hidden corner of the yard for the rest of the afternoon missing all his lessons. He was determined to surprise Hopkins and Barry and attack them before they knew what was happening.

The school bell sounded and the classes started to drift through the door, he saw his two targets walking together. He held the socks one in each hand. He'd had all the afternoon to brood upon how he would go about the attack and decided to come up behind them and hit them as many times as possible, gaining the advantage.

He ran at them from behind one sock in each hand swinging them wildly, he hit one on the back of the neck and the other across the head, they turned, and hit again directly in their faces. Blood burst from both noses as Colin hit them repeatedly with the socks knocking them off balance. All the while Colin screaming, "I'll kill you, I'll kill you." His eyes glowed crazy as if possessed by an evil demon.

They both fell over but Colin was unable to stop and hit them indiscriminately over all their bodies. They tried to scramble away using their hands but he hit them again across their backs and they collapsed to the ground. Tim ran up and shouted at Colin to stop and to come to his senses before he killed them.

"No one hits me," Colin kept screaming over and over again in a frenzied voice, "and gets away with it."

The two bullies, on the floor, whimpered and asked Colin to leave them alone. The other members of the gang came running ready to pounce but when they saw what Coin had done they stopped, frightened, the two were covered in blood.

"Come on," Colin shouted, "search me now, you bastards," swinging the blood soaked socks in the air.

"You're mad," the two cowering on the floor covered in blood whimpered. "Leave us alone," said one spitting out a few teeth.

"Yes," Colin grinned. "Mad enough to kill you if you ever touch me again," he screeched, demented. The other boys held him back, sure if not stopped he would carry on hitting them until he killed them.

"Don't worry we won't, keep your money." They both mumbled in reply.

"And you'll keep your lives," he shouted and they knew he meant it.

"You should be locked up." One of the boys in the crowd shouted quickly slinking away before Colin had a chance to see who it was that spoke.

The three other members of the gang went to aid the two on the floor as they staggered to get up unable to stand let alone fight. It was lucky they were not both killed as Colin stood his ground with the two socks still in his hands. Tim took the socks off him and emptied out the stones. They both walked away as the snake gang looked on in dismay. They would not be asking Colin for money again.

"When I first met you," Tim emphasised. "I didn't think you would take the snake gang on but the next day you nearly killed two of them," he laughed. "You're very dangerous Colin," he said jokingly and smiled but really meant the words.

The snake gang from that point on did not trouble Colin again, whenever they saw him they gave him a wide berth believing he was mad and too dangerous to bully. There were plenty of other people in the school to get money out of without the risk of having a stone smashed over their head.

He might have been a local hero in the school with a reputation for fighting but the way Colin went about this task showed a total disregard for himself and other boys. He could have killed the two boys. They were bullies granted, needed taking down a peg or two, but cudgelled and battered with a stone spoke volumes of what was to come if Colin did not learn to stay his hand in the future. He had spent the whole of that afternoon hiding, waiting like a leopard to strike at these boys, bent on revenge, not the action of a normal boy's second day at a new school.

Colin got away with this assault, the two boys refused to report the incident. They told their parents they were in a fight and the school accepted this explanation. The teachers were aware of these boys, knew they were always in fights and bullies, and said nothing more on the matter, to Colin's great relief. These were tough boys, and the last thing they would do was to brag about the fact Colin beat them with a sock, albeit with a stone inside, so the incident was laid to rest.

The headmaster graded Colin into the B class as you would grade eggs, some good, others just all right the rest broken. He was at this stage in his school career meeting the grade of all right; if the school knew of the fight incident they would relegate him to the broken category and expel him.

Tim and Colin, over the next few terms, became good friends and met in the schoolyard most lunch times. Many of the other boys gave Colin a wide berth glad he had the better of the snake gang but at the same time not wishing to spend time in his company because of his reputation of being revengeful.

Colin paid little attention to schoolwork, the teachers did not go out of their way to be helpful, and he expected little or no support from his parents. It was not as if he could not do the work, often, when he concentrated, he accomplished a task to a high standard. On a few occasions, he received top marks but his mind was too frequently somewhere else instead of where it should have been, on schoolwork. This behaviour did not endear him to the teachers, even the good ones, some cared for the welfare and education of their charges, but Colin was never prepared to meet them half way.

He found spelling difficult and could not see why words were spelt differently to the way they sounded and put this down to teachers deliberately making the words difficult to spell in order to show how clever they were to the pupils. He did enjoy one thing in school, the sports lessons and always excelled in that area whether it was rugby, running or swimming, and came out somewhere near the top of the class on most occasions.

Colin left for school every day but often did not arrive or went for the first lesson but did not stay for the rest. Habitually caught and punished, to him this was just part of the risk and played the game to the best of his ability repeatedly taking other pupils from the school with him. He had leadership qualities in abundance and it was not long before he had his own gang, running his own racket at school, which proved far more effective than the snake gang ever managed to achieve.

Frequently he was in fights and had a fierce reputation, fought with the tenacity of a bull terrier, kicking, biting, clubbing, using any method at his disposal to win. Winning meant all to him and would often kick his opponents after they fell to the ground even after they conceded defeat, with little remorse for his actions or the unnecessary pain inflicted upon them, until eventually few would challenge him and was given the nick name Mad Dog, MD for short.

Chapter Four

Redundancies were starting; one pit after another shed labour, they were waste paper, written on, used, and now to be recycled. Miners, who knew no other type of work but the pit, were told to take a hike, and thrown unceremoniously, out to graze. They fought; going on strike for months to try to reverse the closures but it was in vain. There would be no turning back. The pits were to close and close they would.

George, Albert, Henry, Bill and the rest of the workers were surplus to requirements and thrown out of work. They would be entitled to redundancy payments but this money would last less than two years with little prospect of future work.

They spent more time in the gardens, in anticipation of being out of work; every miner knew the score, and it took their minds off the reality of being unemployed. Digging and planting did not cost money, supplied vegetables for the table in abundance. Broth was one of their staple meals. Vegetables, cooked together with a shoulder of lamb would give the family several nourishing meals at little cost.

George was sitting on his bench in the garden when Henry approached, looking concerned. "I didn't sleep last night." If he had something on his mind, would always sound out his friend George and have a chat about what was troubling him and this was no exception.

"What's wrong Henry?" George asked seeing the tiredness in his eyes.

"The smallpox has killed another three people in Treherbert; I worked with one of them for years. I thought it was contained in the other valley but it's with us now. I don't understand, I thought we could cure this with vaccinations."

"Yes, but strains change, another few cases have already been diagnosed in Treorchy. Forget what we're told, the disease is already out of control." George stated. "I think it's been underplayed."

"Inoculation should have been carried out months before the disease had a chance to spread."

"Better late than never Henry," George responded but felt the same as Henry, there should have been quicker action.

"What can we do to try and stop it?"

"Not a lot, it may just fizzle out in the next few weeks, only time will tell," George optimistically answered.

"Let's hope we've heard the last of it. I'm not letting Sophie go on trips and insist she is straight home from school. The baby we're not taking over the door until this is all over," Henry stated, concern cracking his voice.

"How is the young one anyway, he's not been too well of late so my wife says?" George enquired but realised too late he had said the wrong thing as Henry's face darkened.

"A cold, just a cold George," he emphasised emphatically in case George was alluding to something else. "He's sleeping soundly again now so the worse of it is over, it gave us a scare I can tell you. It's your boy you should be concerned with, continually in fights, showing no respect, totally out of hand so I've heard."

"That's a bit strong; growing up pains that's all; remember the fights we used to get into, we were trouble at that age," George replied laughing, minimising his son's exuberant behaviour. He had heard as much from several people and intended to have a word with Colin before his actions got out of hand but did not let

Henry know he was concerned, feeling it was a private family matter.

"It's a bit more than just fighting. I've heard he attacked two boys with a stone and they were off school for a few weeks. Fighting is one thing but to use a stone in the fight like a knuckle duster is another matter, he could have killed them." Henry further elaborated irritated that George was taking the incident far too casually.

"Leave it for now Henry! A lot is exaggeration, if I hear anymore about it I'll have a word with the boy," George said trying to placate but felt uncomfortable about the whole issue.

They sat for a few minutes not speaking, looking at the garden cognisant only of the thoughts in their head. A miner was good at closing off, letting his mind wander out of his body as he toils in blackness, taking him into exotic places. Green fields, sun shining down warming his body, it's their way to escape the drudgery and monotony of the work.

The first to break the silence was George. "Are you going on the march to Cardiff about the pit closures?"

"Yes! Why do you ask? Everyone is going." Henry replied, perplexed that George even asked the question. Henry was one of the main organisers, as far as he was concerned, it was a duty for all to turn up and march.

"I'm not. What's the point?"

"We've had this discussion before George," Henry answered exasperated. "I say you should go."

"Do you honestly think it'll make any difference," George responded.

"I'm going. We'll never agree over this so there's no point in discussing it. Just turn up or you'll lose a lot of friends," he answered annoyed and left in a huff.

Chapter Five

In school, Colin had replaced the snake gang, becoming an acknowledged leader. Even though he was one of the youngest in the group, he still dominated it with his personality and his resounding lack of fear in all he did. This lack of fear frightened many pupils, a large section of the school kept well away out of his orbit of influence, avoidance being the best policy. His reputation was that he was a callous, uncaring, determined person, and would strike with the speed of a cobra if threatened and just as deadly.

If he applied these energies to his schoolwork, all would have been fine but his behaviour was destructive to the school, the people he associated with, and himself. He was intelligent, picked things up quickly but passionately believed that schoolwork was not for him and paid no attention to what the teachers tried to teach. All types of punishment were to no avail; he did not respond to anything they tried and some of the teachers tried very hard to make him change his behaviour. He wrote them off and they eventually wrote him off, the lines were drawn. The battle between the two sides continuous, one punishment followed another, he persisted in his ways to the dismay of all concerned.

The headmaster called Colin's parents to the school many times, but to no avail, the worse his behaviour became, and they were at a loss where to go next. He was punishing his parents just for being his parents, blaming them for his behaviour, thus, absolving himself from his own actions because they were poor and uneducated. He was bitter to the core, found any type of authority oppressive and dictatorial no matter how benign.

His peers refused his challenge to fight; even if he lost, and in the early days he did a few times, he never forgot or forgave. He would wait silently in the shadows to get his revenge. On one occasion, he even followed one boy to his home and when the family were out broke in, destroyed all the items belonging to the boy, and ransacked his room leaving the rest of the house intact. The police were involved and they interviewed Colin but there was no evidence and he got away with it reinforcing his belief he was omnipotent. He could not let his triumph die; he mentioned it to the boy a few weeks later giving away just enough information to let him know he was the one.

"You're crazy in the head Colin," the boy replied.

"Yes," he grinned. "Crazy enough to stop you listening to music," Colin laughed back in a mocking taunt.

"If you try that again Colin…" the boy straightened up as if to hit Colin but just walked back into class saying, "you're not worth the effort." Colin was delighted and felt elated in his victory knowing he had conquered yet again.

Tim, who Colin considered his friend, whenever possible tried to keep away from him but they often bumped into each other in the schoolyard and Tim felt obliged to talk with him always careful what he said, never sure if Colin would turn on him.

"Look Colin, you need to be careful," Tim said in a pleading manner before Colin had a chance to speak, "or you'll end up in prison. You're my friend but even I'm afraid of you sometimes when your eyes glaze over."

Colin laughed. "Don't worry we're friends. I'll never hurt you."

"When the madness is upon you it's as if you are another person."

"You're ridiculous. Are you coming with us?"

"Where?"

"Bunking off school tomorrow of course, you want to come?"

"No, nor should you."

"Come on Tim don't be such an old bore," Colin taunted. "It's more fun over the park, school is boring."

Tim shook his head. "If you don't change your ways there will be trouble ahead for you. I can see it."

"Yeh! Yeh! This school is one big trouble. I intend to spend as little time as possible in it," Colin replied in a laughing manner. "We'll come for the first lesson and slip away, even if caught, what can they do?"

"Expel you," Tim said seriously. "That's what'll happen. They'll throw you out."

"Big deal! That'll mean… save me bunking off then. We can spend more time in the park, please yourself. If you want fun, you'll know where we'll be, don't be a pansy all your life. Live now, sod tomorrow!"

The following day after the first lesson four boys met at the end of the school playground waiting for Colin. A few minutes later he turned up and they all disappeared over the wall and were gone heading for the park. They passed a few shops on the way and Colin lifted a few apples that were stacked outside one of them then knocked over the stall to delay the shopkeeper before he could give chase. Apples rolled over the pavement as the shopkeeper clenched his fists and shouted after them as he scrambled to pick up the fruit. Colin gave a gesture back with his fingers and just laughed, another mug for the taking he thought.

They arrived at the park entering at the back to keep out of sight. The local whiper'in frequently watched the front entrance, and if caught, he would march them back to school. They were wiser than this and always kept to the bottom of the park in the trees out of the way and unseen. A river ran by the side of the park and they would spend a lot of time playing under a bridge over which the road traversed. They built a den near the bridge unseen from the road and anyone who entered the park. They spent time inside plotting and planning new adventures.

"Why don't we rob old farmer Evans' chicken hutches, sell the eggs in the evening around the doors?" Colin said to the other boys all busily eating the apples he stole.

"How can we get into the sheds they're always locked, chickens make a lot of noise. We'll get caught," replied one of the boys. "I'm not…"

"Not what!" Colin interjected. "Not scared are you?"

"No!"

"Well then, I'll go in through the chicken flap and hand the eggs out to you. We'll hide them for a few days and then sell them around the doors, the farmer will never know. It's easy money, don't be wimps."

Another member of the gang spoke to show he was no wimp. "Colin I'm smaller than you. I'll go into the sheds and collect all the eggs, you stay outside and watch." Demonstrating he was up to the job.

"It's settled then, we go now. Why wait?" Colin stated and off they all went heading for the farm on the other side of the hill. Two of the boys were not happy about robbing the farmer but Colin soon put them right. "If you're chic - chic - chic chicken run home to mammy, cluck, cluck," he said as if talking to a baby.

This immediately had the desired effect; no one wished to be a baby especially a chic, chic, cluck, cluck baby so the dissent stopped. Colin was rarely overruled and off they went to the farm. A few adults shouted to them they should be in school, they just ran on regardless turning their faces away not to be recognised.

A while later they were there, hiding behind the cowshed looking to see if the farmer was anywhere to be seen. They were lucky, a tractor moved in an adjoining field. The coast was clear they would be in and out in no time. They ran across the yard to the back of the farmhouse and into the chicken pens.

There were rows of chicken pens, like a line of small houses, a plank leading up to a small door through which the chickens entered. Inside were perches from one end to the other and a number of nesting boxes with eggs still warm.

One of the boys wriggled through the little door with just enough room to get his shoulders in and pulled the rest of his body inside with his hands. He went to the boxes, started to collect the eggs passing them through to the rest of the members crouched outside waiting.

They realised they had nothing to carry the eggs in and started to panic but Colin held them together, went off, and found a few old corn sacks. They collected many dozens of eggs and crept out of the chicken coop still unseen. A few would almost certainly have been broken but this did not matter they had plenty; they ran past the cow shed down the mountain. There would still be many left to sell and were already spending the money in their thoughts, totally unconcerned they had just committed a robbery.

"We could do this every week," Colin, carrying the eggs, suggested and laughed. "It's easy."

"The farmer is bound to notice after a while and it won't be so easy then," one of the gang replied.

"There are other farms, stop being a namby pamby and get real," Colin contemptuously replied. "Follow me and you'll get rich."

They stayed away from the main roads and travelled the back way along the lines of terrace houses until they arrived on an old allotment. They hid the eggs in an abandoned shed under an old rusted piece of roofing zinc intending to collect them a few days later to sell door to door. It was now near the time when school would finish for the day and they split to go their separate ways, making sure they arrived home at the correct time in order to give the impression to their parents they were coming home from school.

A few days later Colin went back to the allotment, the farmer did not realise any eggs were stolen, or if he did it was not reported, so Colin felt relatively sure the eggs could now be sold with impunity. To his horror, the place was a mess; broken eggshells littered the shed floor. There was not one egg unbroken, rats had gotten into the shed and ate their fill. The smell attracted some of the local dogs and they made short work of the rest.

Colin was annoyed, felt cheated at the loss of profit, but not down hearted. It would mean going back to the farm again and risk the farmer catching them but that was part of the fun. He didn't wait but went straight to the farm. The farmer was in the farmhouse, and as bold as brass Colin went into the chicken pens and had his fill of eggs placing them all carefully into strong bags he brought along for the purpose. He hid the eggs in a safer location this time placing them on a high shelf in a tin box, covering the top to protect them against further attack.

This time the farmer did report to the police someone had raided his chicken pens and the village was on the lookout for any one selling cheap eggs. Colin had to take the eggs further down the valley in order to sell them and the profit was not what he expected. Colin distributed the proceeds according to his formula, which meant he kept the lot, telling the others dogs had destroyed the eggs.

A few days later on his way home after school the farmer's son approached Colin and asked about the eggs. Colin denied he knew anything about stolen eggs, looked startled at the audacious approach, and felt affronted, the anger built in him as the conversation progressed.

"Why were you selling eggs a few days ago? Where did you get them from?" the farm boy accused Colin.

"That's nothing to do with you."

This did not deter the farmer's son. "Look, we're missing a lot of eggs, what's more, the pens were all left open and a lot of the chickens were spooked by a fox.

"That's not my problem," Colin answered his eyes gleaming hatred towards the farm boy. "I'll beat you to a pulp if you call me a liar," Colin indignantly answered feeling his anger rise higher.

"Where did you get the eggs from then? The ones you sold, tell me. If I'm wrong, I'll apologise. That's fair isn't it?"

Colin pushed him. "Be careful! I don't like being called a liar."

"I'm not afraid of you so don't push me."

Colin jumped at him but he was ready and hit Colin hard as he attacked knocking him back suddenly. Colin came in again and grabbed the boy around the neck locking his arms over his windpipe. They fell to the floor and rolled over again and again, Colin holding him tight around the neck.

He rolled again forcing Colin to release his grip. The farm boy was strong and hit Colin hard in the face, instantly his nose split, blood trickled down into his mouth.

Colin tried to claw at his eyes but he moved and his fingers hit the ground. The boy jumped up and kicked Colin in the stomach and he curled up in agony, holding himself tight, feeling an intense pain in his stomach.

"Leave it Colin," the boy cried, "I've had enough," and started to walk away. Colin jumped up and hit him on the back of the neck knocking him down to the ground. He rolled and Colin caught him again with his foot on the side of his back but he managed to crawl away before Colin could inflict any serious damage. They locked into each other again but two of the teachers, who were on their way home, separated them and held them apart until they cooled down and told them to report to the headmaster first thing the following morning.

Colin was in pain; his punctured pride hurt more than his smashed face. He walked away seething, hell bent on revenge not considering for one moment that he was the one at fault. His self-importance damaged, he was determined to settle the score at the earliest opportunity. His mind locked, closed to all reason, a cannon waiting to go off not caring what damage he would inflict, determined to blast his mark on the object of his hatred or anyone that got in his way.

Chapter Six

Colin wasn't totally bad; it was a delight to watch him with Sophie; his bullying ways, and his arrogance not seen when he was with her. He would play games and tell her stories. To see them together made the heart warm, he was a completely different person in her company.

"Come on Soph, I'll race you to the end of the garden," Colin laughed pretending to run off. The little girl ran after him and he slowed down to let her reach the other end of the garden first.

Sophie smiled. "I'm the fastest," she shouted back at Colin who was coming up behind her.

"Yes! You sure are a good runner. You outdid me."

She ran at Colin and hugged him around the waist and said, "I love you Colin, you are… you can be my daddy sometimes if you like, only when he's not around mind but you can still be my friend."

Colin laughed. "Seems fair to me Soph. You are my friend as well," Colin answered, "and I love you too."

"Look!" she said jumping up and down with delight, "Colin, a capitillar," looking into a bush of nettles.

Colin smiled. "Be careful those nettles will sting you," and cautiously picked off the caterpillar, handed it to her placing it in the palm of her hand and both studied it crawling over her fingers.

"Be careful you don't hurt it," Colin said in a loving voice.

She was thrilled. "I… careful, this will be my pet. I'll keep it in my room."

Colin shook his head. "If you do that it will die and won't turn into a butterfly," he answered gently.

"Where can I keep it then?"

"You can't, you must let it go and set it free. Look! There are others all over the bush; it will be lonely and pine if you take it from its friends."

Sophie's eyes registered disappointment; slowly she tilted her hand and carefully placed the caterpillar on the leaf turning her eyes to Colin for him to acknowledge her as a good girl. To watch these two playing together, one, many years older than the other, a delight, and would warm the heart of the hardest tyrant. This was the other side of Colin, the side that made him human but very rarely shown, a gentle side he was ashamed of showing, but when with Sophie it did not matter.

He really liked playing with her and she with him; often he would seek her out and be together for hours at a time. A bond formed between these two young people, the angry Colin was nowhere in sight. It was not even in the next street, extinct when the two played together. Colin held her hand and led her back into the house where her father Henry sat by the fire.

"Daddy, daddy, we've got capitillers in the garden."

"Don't you mean caterpillars," he laughed. "You are always smiling when Colin is around. I'll ask him to move in with us if you like," Henry joked.

"Yes, yes please! Oh! Can we daddy?" jumping up and down with excitement.

"No, I'm only teasing, Colin's daddy would be very sad."

"I'll play with you every day if you like," Colin said mildly.

"Oh yes! Will you read to me? I like stories. Please!" Sophie exclaimed.

This caught Colin somewhat by surprise, reading, any type of schoolwork was very low down in his scheme of things. He had never learned to read very well, now Sophie asked him to read to her.

"Later," he replied procrastinating trying to get out of it.

She persisted. "When later? Shall I get a story book now?" Off she went into the next room and returned with a picture book to Colin's great relief. There were simple words which Colin had little difficulty in reading and they spent the rest of their time together looking at the pictures with Colin making up stories about the characters in the book until it was time for her to go to bed.

He left determined to learn to read correctly. He could not let little Sophie down, went home, and started to read his father's newspaper. He found it difficult as he poured over the words and underlined the ones he did not understand. He then borrowed a dictionary from one of the neighbours and looked up these words. He was busy at this task for the rest of the evening until his mother shouted it was time for bed.

The next morning Colin was up early and started again with the dictionary finishing off all the words he underlined the day before. He then copied them in spidery writing onto a sheet of paper intending to learn them off by heart. Before he went to school he called over Henry's and asked Sophie if he could borrow her story books making the excuse that he needed them to read to his younger brother.

Sophie's mother handed five books to Colin with instructions to return them in a few days.

"You can read me the stories when you bring them back," Sophie said excitedly.

"Yes of course but it won't be for a few days, is that all right?"

Sophie's mother smiled. "Of course Colin," turning to Sophie. "You will have to wait. Do you hear? Colin has other things to do not just read stories to you."

"That's all right I'll return the books in a few days, and, yes, I'll read all the stories to you," Colin said to Sophie whose face beamed.

He left, took the books and concealed them in his bag, together with the dictionary, and went to school. Mid morning, not saying a word to anyone, he crept out of school and went to the park near the river to keep out of the way. Making sure no one was around, he read the books in his bag.

He could manage most of the words but found quite a number difficult and looked them up in the dictionary making a note on a pad going over the word several times before moving to another. He stayed there the whole afternoon and still only on the first story but was determined to know every word even if it meant not sleeping for the next few days rather than let Sophie down.

Colin noticed a few of the boys walking towards him and quickly hid the books in his bag.

"We wondered where you went. Why didn't you tell us you were going? We would have joined you," said one of the boys.

"I just went without thinking," Colin lied. "Can't stay now must go."

"I thought we were going after eggs," another of the gang stated.

"Yes, later, must go now, see you tomorrow at school," and off Colin ran carrying his bag. He went straight to his father's garden, into the shed, pulled out his pad, and started to go over the words once more. The following day he did not go to school telling his mother he felt ill and spent the whole day and the next reading the storybooks. Before the end of the week, he had learned all the words and could read the stories as if presenting them on radio. He was now ready to fulfil his promise to Sophie.

That Friday evening Colin returned the books, thanking Sophie's mother for the loan but before she could say a word, Sophie ran to him and gave him a big hug.

"I've missed you, where have you been this very long time."

"Not very long only a few days Soph."

"Seems like forever."

"All she's done is talk about you and her stories," Sophie's mother said.

"Will you read to me now, you promised," she implored.

He grimaced at her. "Yes, I did, didn't I?"

"Yes you promised."

"Perhaps Colin is busy just now," her mother answered.

"That's all right, come on then Soph, I'll read them all to you every one," he replied smiling feeling confident.

They sat together; Colin read each story many times before she was satisfied. Sophie's mother in the next room could not but be impressed with Colin's reading skills and the way he narrated the stories to her daughter with many actions. She had a lot of time for Colin, could not accept that he was a troublemaker and always fighting, believing the stories exaggerated.

To see him sitting next to Sophie reading would have melted the hearts of Colin's hardest critics. If his gang saw him they would not believe their eyes, he was the most disruptive, manipulative boy in the school, here he was reading to a five year old for hours on end enjoying the experience as much as Sophie, if not more so, until her mother shouted it was time for bed.

Colin left with another promise extracted out of him that he would go to the library, borrow a number of books and read to her every week. This suited him, he had time to study each book beforehand and understand them before each reading session.

That weekend, Colin and his gang returned to the chicken pens, barbed wire protected the top of the fence and the doors locked. The farmer was taking no chances, they watched from a safe distance hidden from view, they could see the farmer with his son near the chicken sheds. Colin hated this boy and was determined to extract his revenge at the earliest opportunity but in a fair fight the farm boy could win and this rankled him deeply. The boy had bruised him badly in the last fracas and Colin was determined to be cleverer the next time they met.

"We'll wait until it goes dark and get in under the fence," Colin whispered.

"I'm not happy about it Colin," one of the gang related. "That barbed wire looks awesome."

"Wimp, wimp, wimp. We'll crawl underneath the wire and take all the eggs. It'll be easy," said Colin determined to follow through with the plan more to thwart the farm boy than for the eggs.

They waited for some time until they were sure the farmer and his son were in the farmhouse and slowly crept towards the wire, loosened the bottom with a stick, breaking the wire in the process. They made a hole large enough for them to crawl through weighting the wire with large stones littered around the fence. They found all the chicken flaps covered and the sheds locked.

Colin wedged his stick into the small door but it held solid. He went and got a nearby stone and started to knock the door trying to break the hinges but they held fast. The chickens were getting restless; Colin looked over to the farmhouse. They could see the kitchen light going on; someone heard them.

"I think the farmer is coming," one of the boys shouted, "quick or we'll be caught, we've been rumbled."

They ran to the fence and started to go through one at a time. They heard shouts from the direction of the farmhouse; a shotgun went off above their heads startling them. They struggled to get through the hole in the fence quickly, running away from the farm as fast as their legs would carry them. They heard another blast from the shotgun but were now far away and would not be returning, frightened in case the farmer would shoot them. The farmer had enough and was determined to protect his chickens at all costs. Colin was feeling frustrated, angry, but even he was not stupid enough to go up against a shotgun.

Chapter Seven

The men were out on strike. The price of coal had fallen again and the miners still in employment asked to take a pay cut in order to protect jobs, or so the officials of the colliery related to the assembled men. It was obvious they were looking for a fight. They did not accept and promptly walked off the job. A few did go back to work to the great annoyance of the majority and they were jeered and booed, called blacklegs, scabs, and worse and would forever be known as traitors, shunned by their fellow workers until they died. A few of the striking miners surged forward, checked by a line of police, the crowd held back as the blacklegs filed past flanked on both sides by police.

"Pigs! Scum!" people shouted from the crowd.

"You might as well move out from the valley now, you're finished here. You'd better keep you letter box locked, or…" A police officer looked at the striker who didn't finish the sentence.

"Scabs! Scabs!" The crowd roared. "Blacklegs! Blacklegs."

There was another surge by the crowd. The police line held, just; more workers filed past, the striking throng was turning nasty. Someone in the crowd threw a stone catching one of the blacklegs on the shoulder knocking him to the floor, the crown roared with delight.

The striking miners shouted loud obscenities as the blacklegs ran the gauntlet of hatred closing around them. More police arrived holding their truncheons, not yet pulled for action, but ready, they were nervous. Another stone flew over hitting one of the policemen breaking his nose, he fell to the ground holding his face, blood hosed through his hands as he tried to stem the flow.

The truncheons were out of their pouches ready for action, the police had enough. The crowd surged again; the blue line buckled; the living mass moved forward; the police hit back; the crowd dispersed a little but then turned on the police like vicious tigers hungry for a kill, their anger whetted, vented towards the line of blue that stood before them.

The police hit back truncheons moving this way and that way; beating, hitting, striking out in a frenzy of hysteria; the hard object thudded into flesh smashing bone and breaking skin. The crowd started throwing any object they could lay their hands on as the fight intensified. No one wanted this; the police were part of the same community but the divide was deep, and getting deeper, one side fighting to retain law and order the other to keep food on the table. It was a conflagration, the match lit, sparks everywhere, and the bonfire raged.

The battle went on for many hours; more miners arrived followed by extra police. Ambulances were full of the injured on both sides. A number of the police had brothers, fathers and other relations in the mob. They were fighting their own people, in a never-ending spiral as the violence escalated out of control. Many received more than an injury that day, the psychological scars would last a lot longer, for many a year, some forever, and never heal; a community that had stayed together for generations, ripped apart.

Each striker was a law-abiding citizen but when together became a hammer of brute force. They felt justice had ignored them, passed them by, and would now set their own standard ruled by sickle and scythe each side caught in a shocking cesspit of thuggery.

As the mob surged forward, a few of the miners fell to the floor under the pressure, followed by others falling on top of them. The police moved back, as sick of the violence as the miners, and the hullabaloo started to ease. Officials asked people, through loudspeakers, to disperse. The police retreated further, trying without success, not to directly challenge.

Four people lay on the ground motionless. A few people rushed forward to help; the police noticed the bodies on the floor and a few ran over leaving their helmets and their truncheons behind to show their non-violent intent.

One of the police officers recognised the face before him and ran back into the police line to look for Sid Davies. He came running dropping his truncheon as he ran bending over his father's limp body; tears ran down his face, his eyes wet as he held his father's head in his hands.

"God no, please no, dad wake up, wake up," he shouted shaking his head. The fight had gone out of the crowd; the police took their helmets off and walked over to Sid sitting on the ground with his father's head cradled in his hands. The other three men's injuries were non-life threatening, one nursed a broken arm; the others bruises, and had passed out under the weight as they fell over.

No one expected a death but a death there was, both sides responsible, yet no one individual to blame. It started to sink into the assembled mass that actions have consequences, this consequence resulting in loss of a life. The father on one side the son on the other, each doing what they thought was right but one no longer alive.

John Davies was proud his son entered the police force and often bragged over a pint of beer how well he was doing. They had disagreed over the way the police were handling the strike resulting in a heated quarrel between them but no one expected it to end this way. Sid hadn't spoken to his father in over two months the acrimony deep. Both believed they were right, one now dead, the father, and reconciliation too late.

Henry, one of the main agitators in the group, came forward. He was a work colleague and friend of the family. It flashed into his mind the time they spent the evening together when Sid was born, how they could hardly stand, John now lay dead, his son next to him on the floor cradling his head.

He looked up. "Why Henry? What did my father ever do to deserve this?" he cried. Henry was speechless; there was no answer, any response, other than remorse was futile.

He was the main instigator of the demonstration and had to persuade John to attend. His son was in the police force and he wanted to stay away but Henry believed it would be a coup if he came and faced the police knowing his son was on the other side. By the evening, they would all be having a pint and a laugh together after having made their point. The only point made now would be the funeral and Henry felt responsible.

George had also turned up on Henry's insistence, but felt no satisfaction in seeing him racked with guilt and tried to console him.

"What have I done George? God! What have I done?" Henry kept repeating to George in disbelief. "This shouldn't have happened. How can I ever face the rest of the family, damn this strike, damn the authorities, damn the pit and damn me for allowing this to happen."

George stood, looking at the dead man, "you couldn't have foreseen this; no one could."

One of the police officers walked over placed a blanket over the body and helped Sid to his feet as an ambulance arrived.

"Come! Henry it's time to go, it's over," George stated.

Henry was inconsolable. "I should have listened to you George, this should never have happened, never. Why John?"

"Why anyone! No one could foretell this would happen. In my eyes violence never achieves anything except further violence."

"It could have been prevented George, it could have been prevented," Henry stammered feeling deeply it was his fault.

"As I said earlier, violence never achieves anything, it can't be measured, things get out of hand, people get hurt, it happens,"

George said trying to make Henry feel better. He would not do it by giving total exoneration to his friend, Henry was not blameless, and George did not intend to lie to him to make him feel better.

"If… if I listened to you he'd still be alive," Henry replied.

"Look Henry, if you hadn't organised the strike someone else would in your place. If the blacklegs hadn't crossed the picket line; if he wasn't standing where he was; if the police reacted differently; if the crowd hadn't thrown things; if the police behaved better. If… If… You can't blame yourself for the 'ifs,' but I did warn you it could get out of hand. Come, let's go and have a pint, we can't do any more here."

They walked together to the pub both feeling disconsolate. The only thing achieved was the death of their friend, claimed by the pit all be it indirectly, but the pit nevertheless.

"Sophie is really taken with your lad," Henry said still thinking of John but trying to talk about something else.

George smiled. "Yes, Colin thinks the world of her, plays with her for hours. Normally, he comes home with his clothes in tatters fighting, it is nice to see him coming in still tidily dressed every time he goes over your house, makes a change I can tell you."

"You know he spends hours reading to her and telling stories," Henry said.

"What! I've never seen him reading without someone pushing him. He hates school; we are forever being called to the headmaster to answer some trouble or other, the latest being bunking off."

"Well I've listened to him reading and he knows every word. That boy has talent if he applied himself instead of courting trouble," Henry stated.

George looked surprised. "He seems angry at the world, thinks he can just take what he wants, I tried to talk to him on a number of occasions but nothing seems to work. If he's in any more trouble at school they will expel him, he's had his last warning. I thought it would happen last week when the headmaster asked to see us but he has been given his last chance, I'm not holding my breath about it."

"I know he's always in trouble but I'm inclined to put it down to his age. I thought at first he was going off the rails, now after seeing my Sophie and him together, I think differently."

"I hope you're right Henry but he has a chip on his shoulder the size of a tree and he does not get it from us."

Chapter Eight

The strike was still going on but the guts of the fight had gone out of the men. Hundreds of people attended John's funeral, including a number of police officers. George was right; the pits would eventually close no matter what fight the miners put up. The world was changing; heavy industry was on the decline all over the world, the buzzword around all the job centres and in the offices of the colliery was 'retraining,' a new age had arrived.

No one thought how to retrain a miner full of dust, bones twisted and bent through years of toil and hard labour, but everyone who was anyone, except the people who really mattered, placed all their reliance on retraining and self-employment. The men would receive generous redundancy packages so there should be no problem, everything will be all right again. No one could answer the main question. Where were they to find meaningful work?

The buzzword covered all eventualities, a catch-all word. Whenever the miners tried to get any sense out of anyone the old bumblebee would always come through buzzing here, buzzing there, offering false honey, meaning nothing, saying everything. Go quietly, say nothing, don't cause trouble, take your redundancy like good little workers but we will stop all government benefits until the money is spent. We'll give with one hand but take back with the other.

The country needed them once, but no more, they could now join the slag heaps, a waste product of a bygone age. Discarded like old soldiers who helped to make Britain great and had won the war but now, task complete, no longer needed. Once they were the mainstay of the economy, enriching, enhancing commerce, increasing the country's wealth and economic well-being in the same way the soldier protects the country in time of war. Now, in time of peace, old soldiers are not trusted to keep a bullet let alone a gun, but told to go quiet, quiet, into that good night. Their usefulness spent, value depleted, war over, now dispensable.

Colin was oblivious to all these feelings running through the valley, far too young to understand what the changes meant. He saw no value in the old ways; felt he was only part of the environment because of his parents, nothing more. He intended to get out as soon as he could, take what he wanted from what he considered society's losers, irrespective of the consequences to others. He would be a man of tomorrow, forget yesterday, but he forgot one thing. All men of tomorrow came from yesterday and must learn from what went before.

Colin had not forgotten the farm boy, and intended to even the score at the first opportunity. In his eyes, the boy had insulted him. He did not have to wait long for the chance. Colin was walking by the side of a stream and noticed him on the other side. He quickly ducked out of sight and waited until the boy was in front of him. Colin quietly crossed the stream, picked up a small branch, and crept up on the boy.

When a few paces behind him, he ran and hit him forcefully across his back with the branch. The boy stumbled, turned, and Colin struck him again across the front. He fell into the shallow water dazed, Colin jumped after, hitting at him in a mad frenzy; one punch followed another until the boy was unconscious. Colin was a rabid dog out of control; he grabbed the farm boy by the hair and thrust his head under the water shouting all the time. "Now hit me, hit me now," pushing and pulling the farm boy's head in and out of the water. His voice howling to the air like a wolf baying at the moon after a kill, his mouth foamed with madness, out of control.

He was just about to push the farm boy's head back under the water to complete the drowning, when his hands stayed, held as if in a vice. The harder he tried to move the head under the water the stronger the force held him. The grip drained his energy paralysing his actions. He tried and tried again but the power held, forcing him eventually to let go of the farm boy. He stood up and felt himself compelled to drag the limp body to the bank, no longer in command of his own actions.

Their clothes were soaked through. One of them semi-conscious, the other over conscious with anger ingrained deep in his heart. He tried to hit the farm boy again but his fist stopped suddenly as if there were a metal plate in front of him. He howled in agony as his hand made contact with an invisible object around the farm boy protecting him from further harm. Frustration set in around Colin. He wanted to kill this boy but something prevented him from concluding this final act of madness; he turned and walked away leaving the object of his hatred on the floor, helpless.

He ran, not aware for how long or to where and stopped only when he could run no further and dropped to the ground exhausted. The reality of his actions started to dawn, the warm sweat on his face turned into a cold sweat of fear. If his hand had not been stayed he would be a murderer of that he was sure, condemned for the rest of his life. Something stopped him, his actions stayed by an invisible force he didn't understand, which saved him from himself.

Colin looked up at the sky, clouds rolled over his head, and he felt a cold wind on his face and sighed. He was young but knew, as young as he was, if he had killed the farm boy was destined to spend many years in prison. It was this and not the fact he would be a murderer that made him breathe a sigh of relief, repentance an unknown force in him; he still wanted revenge on the farm boy.

The incident blew over after a few weeks; the farm boy did report the occurrence to the police but they took no action. There were no witnesses and they put it down as a fight between two children. The farm boy had bruises over his face and body, prompting the farmer to speak to Colin's father about the incident but that was as far as it went. George had a serious chat with his son but Colin lied to cover his tracks saying that the farm boy hit him first with a stick and he retaliated in self-defence and was sorry.

Several more terms passed, other than a few fights at school, Colin stayed out of serious trouble only because no teacher caught him. To go back to the same farm and steal was now far too risky. Colin and his gang did visit other farms further afield, stole eggs, and got away with it. The nearest they got to being caught was one of the boys being bitten by the farm dog. They also started to steal other things; on one occasion even breaking into a house and stealing money. The gang believed that with Colin at the helm, they were invincible, and no one would catch them. Each step took them a little deeper into crime where there was only ever one outcome.

Colin's grandmother was one of the last to hear about his exploits and bad behaviour. She always tried to be positive about what would happen and was beginning to believe her dead husband William had been mistaken, but the incident with the farm boy had confirmed her greatest fear. When she heard what had happened from her daughter she knew Colin had not told her the whole truth. There was now no doubt, it was happening, the madness had started. The battle with his conscience had begun, and prayed for his soul.

He was already well known as a troublemaker, many of the parents would not allow their children to go anywhere near him. This he considered as a compliment, "the parents are afraid of me," he would gloat to his gang.

Colin used to visit his grandmother regularly and spent hours listening to her telling stories about the past and the old ways. He was in a dichotomy, wanting to know about the old ways but hating the values that came with those ways.

His grandfather had died a few years previously and Colin still missed him more than he was prepared to admit, even to himself. He spent most of his younger years with his grandfather and they used to go for walks on the mountains or in the forest and sat many hours in the garden watching birds. Many people thought that Colin's behaviour change stemmed from the loss of his grandfather. He cried a lot when he died and was angry with his parents and the world for not making his grandfather better.

"Gran, why did Gramps have to die?" Colin asked. "I wanted him to stay with us."

She smiled lovingly at him. "We all did love, but he was called."

"Can we call him back?" he asked, knowing this impossible.

"It was his time to go, to move on. I miss him also, every single day; we had a good life together; when I'm called we will be together again."

"No Gran, I don't want you called. You must stay, please, I need you," Colin pleaded unable to imagine life without his Gran.

"It will not be my decision. I'll have no say in it; when my name is called… enough of that, what have you been up to?"

"Nothing Gran," he innocently replied knowing he was lying.

"Don't give me that young man; of late trouble follows you around like a poodle," his Gran sternly said. "Well I'm waiting!"

Colin looked at his Gran then at the floor unable to speak but she stayed silent waiting for him to talk.

A minute past and Colin became agitated. "I've been in fights, nothing serious."

"It's a lot more than that from what I've heard."

"Yes b…"

"No buts Colin, you've been up to a lot of no good and I won't be having it. Your mother and father don't know where to turn and quite frankly neither do I; if you keep on with this behaviour you'll end up in prison or worse."

"I'm working hard at school," Colin interjected trying to change the subject, but could not sidetrack his Gran.

"That's what you should be doing; don't expect to be tapped on the back for that. What are you going to do about your behaviour, is what I want to know. Now!" she said with finality placing both hands on her hips and looking straight at him.

"I don't know Gran," he cried and meant it, tears showing in the corner of his eyes.

"Well you'd better before it's too late," she replied sternly. "Whatever demon possesses you, making you fight, you must expel it; expel it before it is too late."

Colin's mind went back to the incident by the river and realised he was more than capable of killing and his Gran knew. In his blind rage, he intended to kill the farm boy, wanted to kill, felt compelled to kill, but was prevented. His grandmother's words hit a home cord but he dare not say that he nearly killed someone. His grandmother already knew what he was capable of in his madness and she shuddered, Colin picking up the vibe.

Colin was on the hook, his Gran not letting the incident go until she heard the right words.

"I'll keep out of trouble, promise," he said not really meaning the words but wishing he could have answered honestly.

"Good, let's hear no more bad reports about you. I'm visiting your grandfather's grave this afternoon to put flowers on it. We would have been married sixty years today."

Colin could not imagine sixty years. He only knew he loved his grandfather and asked if he could also go along. They had lunch together; his Gran pottered about in the other room, returning a little later wearing a black hat and coat.

"Are you ready, young man, or it'll be tea time before we leave," his Gran said and off they went hand in hand.

They arrived at the cemetery a little while later both carrying flowers purchased in a shop nearby and placed them in a vase on the grave. The inscription stated, 'William John Phillips died aged

79 years beloved husband of Maria May Phillips. May God's wings fly you straight into heaven.'

"Gran," Colin said disturbed. "I never knew you had a name."

She laughed, everyone called her Mam or Gran. "You have a name, what is so strange about me also having a name."

"It just does not sound right. Maria May Phillips," Colin spoke looking at the inscription on the gravestone. "Gramps called you 'His Light.' Why is that?"

"We were light to each other," she said kneeling at the graveside; Colin knew his grandmother wished him to be quiet.

Colin stood next to her and noticed her white hair and frail thin neck, her tiny hands and wrists. She was a very old woman and for the first time he realised she did not have long to live in this world. A shudder went through his body petrified of losing her.

He knelt next to her, she reached out and held his hand, but her mind was below the ground in the coffin with her loved one. Tears started to lightly fall down her face, more in happiness of the good times they shared together than sadness. She wiped them away with her hand and closed her eyes to pray. Colin was just about to do the same when he noticed a movement in front of him.

They had been totally alone in the cemetery a moment ago but Colin could see coming towards him a young man, but walking slightly off the floor as if weightless. As the figure got closer he smiled directly at Colin, a warm radiant smile as if the sun shone out of his eyes. Colin thought he knew the person, blinked but when he opened his eyes, the person had vanished.

His Grandmother opened her eyes and looked at Colin. He was just going to mention the figure but decided against it as he looked into her face. She was serene, her age lines seemed to have melted, her eyes sparkled giving off a glow like diamonds. She placed her arms around Colin and kissed him gently on the cheek. As they stood, a little robin perched on the gravestone, chirped twice, and went on its way flying into the sky and disappeared.

"Why are you so happy Gran?" Colin inquired. "You were sad when you started to pray."

"Because my prayers have been answered," she replied. "I felt your grandfather was near filling me with his love. He's waiting for me to join him, told me as much."

"Join him where Gran?"

"In paradise, where the sun shines all day, he is there waiting for me," she quietly replied with a happy voice.

"But Gramps is dead," Colin said mystified.

"Only dead to this world love," she replied exuding an inward glow of contentment "only in this world."

"How many worlds are there Gran?"

She looked at Colin. "This one the temporal, the other eternal and goes on forever. Come, it is time to go."

They walked out of the cemetery his grandmother's arm through his making him feel grownup. He loved his Gran with all his heart. They had tea together and his grandmother started to talk about when she was young and how life had changed over the last eighty years.

It was difficult for Colin to imagine his grandmother as young; even his mother was ancient by his reckoning. However, reason dictated that they must have been young at one time or they would not be old now. Old to his mind meant anyone over the age of thirty so they were both already ancient in his eyes.

Colin was a strange mixed-up boy, full of contrary emotions; one side of him hating all that was about him and the values of his parents and their way of life, the other a caring and loving person sensitive to emotion far in advance of his years and wanting to know about his past and feeling proud of it.

He was at a cross roads, the path he would follow over the next few years would determine his fate. His conscience, his sense of right and wrong nonexistent in many respects, destined in the future to be an ardent criminal or worse, on the other, as sensitive as a new born baby's skin aware of what was right and what was wrong. One continually fought the other for supremacy in the age-old battle that has raged since time immemorial, good over evil, the prize, his soul.

Tea over they sat back letting the food settle when his grandmother asked if he would like to look at some photographs. She went into the next room, returned with a box full of old pictures, and started to show Colin photos of when she was young. Frills and petticoats were the order of the day when she was a young girl; long flowing dresses almost touching the ground.

They looked at pictures of his great-grandparents; the photos were grey but the pictures still clear. They made him laugh. Straight faced, unsmiling were the images looking back at him. Colin saw his mother as a girl and giggled at her serious expression and the pictures went on mostly of people long dead but captured forever for that brief moment in time for eternity.

Inside was another smaller box and she opened the lid stating they were his grandfather's folks. "There are pictures here of your grandfather as a young man. Oh, he was such a dandy."

"What is a dandy Gran?"

She smiled. "A word that is not used much nowadays, it means he was smart, a fine upright man, my man," she giggled as if still a schoolchild.

She handed Colin a few photos to prove the point. A ripple of cold ran down his back; instantly he knew that the photo was the man he had seen in the cemetery.

His eyes opened wide and he stuttered. "Gran he was at the cemetery today."

She smiled. "Yes of course he was love; this is a picture of your grandfather, William John Phillips."

"No! I know, but there was a man that looked exactly like him walking towards me when we were kneeling at the graveside," he stated staring at the picture.

"Colin, stop it now. I told you your grandfather was with me in spirit, he is never far away, but to say you saw him alive is very wicked," she replied sternly, "and I'll hear no more about it. Here, take a look at a few more you must be mistaken, we were alone.

The only living things there were us and the birds," handing him a few more pictures of his grandfather.

As Colin studied them, there was no doubt in his mind, the person in the cemetery was the person in these pictures. That is why the figure was familiar to him. It looked like his grandfather only much younger. Even the clothes he wore were similar, if not the same, as the photos.

Colin wasn't about to let it rest. "Gran, Gramps was at the cemetery I saw him walking toward me, he was there… I know he was, please Gran you must believe me. I know he was…"

His Gran interrupted before he could finish. "Yes, I know love," she reassuringly said, changing her stance. "I spoke to him in my prayers as well and he answered. If you saw him, and I believe you did, it was in your mind. It happens to me all the time, I close my eyes and I can see him, he is there protecting us, love transcends death."

"No Gran, you don't understand, he was there in the cemetery alive, he walked towards me, I saw him. Gramps was there Gran," Colin kept repeating.

"I felt his presence, he was there with us today, his spirit is looking out for us, for you Colin. He is dead but his presence grows on us.

"The photos, it was Gramps I know."

"If you felt him near he was there, you did see him in your mind," trying to placate. "After all death is but another room."

"But b…"

"Please Colin enough!" the firmness back in her voice. "Come have a cup of tea," she stated changing the subject. Colin could sense she did not wish him to speak about his grandfather any more, but knew what he knew and it felt like no dream to him.

His grandfather had died a few years ago an old man but the man at the cemetery was young, his grandfather as a young man. Colin had no explanation and tried to look for alternative answers but none came. The more he looked for alternatives the more convinced he became; it was his grandfather or he was hallucinating but decided to say no more on the subject.

"Come, your mother will wonder where you are, let's get you home."

"Yes Gran," Colin answered meekly his mind still on his grandfather. A warm glow came over him as he thought of the many happy times spent with him, the love still fresh, real and warm.

"Take this cake for your mother and straight home."

"Thank you Gran," taking the cake. "I love you and Gramps and miss him lots."

"We all miss him love, now let's be having you home."

Chapter Nine

There were further cases of smallpox, a few more people died mostly the old and very young; everyone was worried, this was a new strain and the authorities were desperate. The social life in the valley was non-existent. The churches and pubs were empty, all social gatherings banned. It was work, home, work, people kept out of each other's way as much as possible. The schools were empty; children kept at home only mixing with the immediate neighbours often not even them. Fear was around every corner as the inhabitants were trying to come to terms with the disease that gripped their valley.

It was enough to survive in a valley where collieries were closing, but now, to contend with this new pressure meant everyone was near breaking point. This did not stop Colin, he was still up to his old tricks pilfering whenever he could and fighting whenever anyone disagreed with him. His schoolwork did show a marked improvement, the teachers were starting to accept he was intelligent, especially his comprehension of and increased interest in literature, but he was still disruptive. "A loose cannon waiting to go off at any time," one of the teachers remarked. "If only I could get through to him."

Colin was at Henry's house, reading to Sophie whenever he could, helping and encouraging her with schoolwork. She thought the world of him and he of her. He was not the hard fighting thieving Colin to her but a true friend encouraging her to read and write, assisting her time and time again with her lessons.

Colin spent hours studying and reading, not for his own sake but in order to regurgitate the information for Sophie. He was the big brother she never had, and just as close, if not more so. A bond of steel had developed between them of tensile strength but tempered by love. Yes love, a true, pure, untainted, deep love that would last throughout their lives; a rare kind of affection. Their souls had met, embraced, and found a home in each other. They revelled in and seemed to live for each other when together. As young as they both were, they knew they had something special and wonderful. All who looked on thought the same and could not help but smile when they saw these two young people playing and interacting together.

The redundancies had started; the valley was downbeat, reality hit home. Smallpox was gaining in strength; every day more people were going down with the disease, worry clouds were all over the valley, gathering pace for the thunder and lightning to follow.

George and Henry arrived at the pit for their final shift, a poignant time for them both as they descended deep into the hole for the last time. Generations of their family had worked in the mine, many dying long before their time; tradition dictated; they were from mining stock, working class men hardworking and proud of it, now the stock was sold out, the shop about to close.

The cage hit pit bottom; out they streamed in silence. No one felt like talking, locked in their own thoughts as they silently walked along the dark narrow passages to their place of work. Their torches flickering, lighting up the darkness for a brief second, the coal sparkling as the light beams ricocheted off the black surface.

George picked up his shovel and started to move the coal out of the seam one spade full after another throwing it into a nearby dram. Henry next to him, pick in hand, striking the coal seam in ritualised movements, one, two, three, strike, the coal cracking under the strong pressure as the pick found its mark time and time again. They had done this work all their lives starting together when they were fourteen years of age. Henry in the first ten years on underground explosives, and considered an expert in that area. Human moles in a manmade hole and still together, older, wiser and on the last shift they would work in this colliery.

"How is your lad, George?" Henry asked sweat ran down his brow and glistened on this forehead as the pick struck the coal seam.

George stretched his arms and smiled pleasingly in the darkness. "His school work has improved by leaps and bounds but trouble still follows him like a dog a bone," and bent to shovel a spade full of coal into the dram.

"He's a good boy really, you should see how he and Sophie play together, the lad's a first rate reader."

"Yes but we are at our wits end to know what to do next. I tried keeping him in, talking to him, stopping his pocket money and keeping him busy in the garden, what more can I do?" George said exasperated. "But at least he's taking more notice of school that's one thing I suppose."

"It's his age, he'll grow out of it, you'll see as he gets older."

"I hope so Henry or there's no telling where he'll end up," George dejectedly replied.

"The way my Sophie is with him and he with her it won't surprise me one bit if they get married when they are older."

George smiled. "They both have a lot of growing up to do first," another shovel full of coal followed the last.

A whistle sounded and they stopped work and sat by the side of the coal seam. George unscrewed a bottle full of water gargled a mouthful and spat it out to clear the coal dust from his throat and drank deeply of the contents. Handed the bottle to Henry who followed the same pattern but using two mouthfuls of the water to clear the dust out of his mouth and throat before drinking.

Henry opened his lunch box and offered some of his cheese sandwiches to George who did the same only he had jam sharing two each.

"Well we won't be doing this again down here," George remarked, his blue eyes shining in the dim light against his black face.

"Yes the last lunch," Henry replied drawing on the reference to the last supper.

"Not a bad thing Henry but I can't help feeling that a large chapter of my life is coming to a close. I'm happy and sad at the same time, happy I'll not be going into this black hole again, yet sad to be leaving this part of my life behind," George said poignantly.

"Yes I know the feeling. I was in the shaft this morning thinking of my father, wondering what he would make of all this. He's been in my thoughts a lot of late; funny when change or tragedy is afoot we fall back on what we know and yearn for, the cradle of our parents, the safety of home." Henry reminisced.

"My parents are long gone only the wife's mother is left in Chepstow Road."

"Yes I know we are the next to move forward waiting to be called to the happy hunting ground. It seemed but yesterday we were kids," Henry said through a black smile as the whistle blew to restart work. "Where have all those years gone?"

"Hold on a minute. We both have a good many years left yet. Come, let's give this last shift all we've got," George stated as he stood up placing his lunch box and water bottle in his bag hanging from a roof beam out of reach of the rats, any food left on the floor would soon be snaffled by the vermin.

They worked, fevered moles, with sweat pouring off them by the bucket full. They would go out in a blaze of glory, proud hard men apprehensive of what the future would hold, but for this last shift, they were still colliers and by God, they would go out as colliers, head held high with pride.

The shift over, they walked back along the tunnels waiting their turn at the pit bottom to be taken to the surface. The only sound was the creaking and groaning of the timbers holding back the millions of tons of earth above their heads as it pressed down trying to close the unnatural manmade hole in the ground.

One of the men started to sing, a deep rich voice could be heard in the black wilderness followed by other voices as they joined in harmony; hundreds of voices sang together; they would go out in a glory of voices true Welshmen to the end. The strong pealing sounds rang and reverberated off the walls as the voices rose in a crescendo of sound and movement.

George and Henry stood together singing, full of pride, true to the values they both held sacred. Proud miners, singing as if their very lives depended upon the song, streams of light bounced off the dark walls as they waited for the lift to take them to the surface.

Chapter Ten

Colin got worse; it would only be a matter of time before the police caught and imprisoned him. There were no doubt in people's minds this would be sooner rather than later; it couldn't be soon enough for many. He would not listen to his parents or his teachers; he was out of control. The only people who had any influence over him were his grandmother and Sophie. His schoolwork improved but this was more down to his determination to help Sophie than a genuine interest in learning. It was more by luck than judgement that he had not already killed someone as young as he was, so the future did not bode much hope for him unless there was a dramatic change in his behaviour, which seemed unlikely.

Colin's parents bought him a dog in the hope that this would help to calm him. He took to the animal immediately like a duck to water. When he was not at school, the dog was constantly with him even when he was playing with Sophie. The dog would always be at his feet or running after them barking and wagging its tail in delight.

"You've really taken to that dog," Henry remarked one afternoon to Colin when he was reading a story to Sophie. The dog was under the table watching every movement, tail wagging whenever someone looked at him.

"He's my best friend," Colin answered.

Sophie's face turned into a scowl. "I thought that was me," she said indignantly.

"You've done it now lad," Henry laughed.

Colin backtracked. "Yes, you are my best friend and Sandy," pointing to the dog, "is my best dog friend."

Sophie smiled accepting the explanation and asked him to carry on with the story. Henry turned and walked away grinning quietly to himself they really are like two peas in a pod he thought.

Colin left Sophie; it was time to go home he had been with her most of the afternoon. The dog followed behind, the two were now inseparable. He felt proud, very grown up now he had his own dog.

Colin was spending an increasing amount of time with his dog walking the mountains. He was a loner, he had his gang, but still he spent most of his time alone his thoughts growing ever darker as each day passed. Many children were afraid of him, their parents had warned them to stay clear of him, "a bad egg in the making, rotten to the core," one of the parents commented to another when they saw him walking by with his dog. These comments didn't worry him, he was proud of them, wore them as a badge of honour. He cared nothing for other people's opinion, their life or their property, taking it whenever he thought he could get away with it.

The community locked their doors against him and he locked his heart against them and the world. Each day a little more compassion left his being, hardening his heart; "he is the devil's child," people muttered more than once behind closed doors. The only exception to this hardening was his grandmother, Sophie and his dog Sandy. He loved these all dearly and behaved differently towards them, he was always polite, affectionate, and caring. Colin's schoolwork continued to improve; he spent hours alone learning in order to help Sophie, his one selfless act in his ocean of selfishness.

He often thought of his grandfather and the figure he saw in the cemetery. He knew from the photos it was his Gramps. His mind reasoned it was impossible, his heart told him different. He had looked at the photos many times over the last few months when at his grandmother's house and felt his grandfather coming out from them, trying to reach out and communicate with him as he stared at the pictures. They stared back at him; the eyes seemed to move and he had to look away to gain his composure but something compelled him to return repeatedly to them. He felt warmth from the photos; they soothed his troubled mind.

One warm and hazy afternoon, coming home from his grandmother's, Colin walked over the mountain and stopped by a large fir tree and sat on the floor resting his back against the trunk, Sandy by his side. He closed his eyes and drifted into sleep.

He awoke and sitting next to him was the same figure he saw in the cemetery. He was startled, more with shock than fear and tried to get up; his whole body paralysed.

"Wh… What do you want?" Colin asked feeling no fear.

The figure stayed silent and smiled.

"Gramps, it is you!"

The smile disappeared. "Yes Colin."

"You are dead Gramps. You look different, have you come back to us? Gran will be so happy. You must let me take you to her."

"I'll be meeting Maria shortly; it's you I've come to see. There are things you need to know."

"Will I be rich?" he quickly added excited, thinking only of himself.

"Not in the way it matters," and he touched Colin on the shoulder.

He was moving. Faster, faster, he spun; suddenly, he stopped and stood holding the hand of the spectre. In front of him stood a large detached house surrounded by a well-kept garden, two expensive cars stood on the drive.

The spectre pointed at the house. "Look! This all belongs to you Colin."

"Wow! I will be rich, thanks Gramps," Colin answered his eyes gleaming at the wealth that stood before him. "Everything belongs to me?"

"Yes, everything."

"This is brilliant; I knew I was different, better than the rest of them, thank you."

The apparition turned to face him. "Don't thank me, these are but trash in the game of life."

"I'll take all the trash you can throw at me, including that gold medal on your chain," he answered fastidiously not caring for anyone's feelings but his own. Colin was full of excitement.

"It already belongs to you."

The door of the house opened, a white haired lady, advanced in years, bent double with arthritis, face contorted through years of pain, came out and closed the door and walked towards them. Colin was going to move out of the way but she was unable to see them standing in front of her. Her face old and worn as if wearing a sad clown's mask to a ball, haggard, not just with age, but full with pain through constant crying; wrinkles deep, pitted, brown with age, wearing her pain for all to see.

The apparition's voice was deep. "Look close at the face Colin what do you see?"

"A horrible old woman, with a sad face. Is this house the one I'll live in when the old hag is dead?" he replied dismissing the old woman contemptuously.

"Yes, this is the house you'll live in. It will belong to you Colin," the apparition replied.

"Brilliant! I'll be rich?"

"Yes Colin, you will be very rich. I'm here to show you the price you must pay."

Colin's exuberance got the better of him. "Price? Money is happiness. I'll give anything to live in a house like that Gramps."

The apparition shook his head. "And you shall live in that house if that is what you want. But there is a price."

Colin felt frustrated. "Want! I want it more than anything in the world and do anything to get it."

"Then you shall have, first you must see what it will cost."

"Boring!" said Colin and blinked his eyes, when he opened them he was back by the tree. Sandy by his side sleeping, I must have been dreaming he thought. That house, that's what I call living. That old hag should hurry up and die so I can move in, pity it was only a dream. "Come Sandy let's get home."

That night Colin dreamt about the house and cars, it was all so real. He pictured himself living there among all the splendour, servants on call to his every whim. He woke, the picture of the house locked firmly in his mind and wondered if Sophie would be there with him and smiled. Why not he reasoned, I'll be rich and can have what I want, pity dreams can't come true.

He determined to tell his grandmother that he dreamt of Gramps and about the large house. A few days later, he went to see her and told her of the dream. She was intrigued at first and feigned surprise.

"What will you do with a house that big, you'll get lost?" she teased.

"You could come and live with me."

"I'll be long gone, love," she answered poignantly. "Of late I've felt your grandfather's presence more; he's waiting for me to join him."

"Come off it Gran, I want you to live forever."

Her eyes opened wide. "No! Don't wish that on me even in jest. Let's have no more of that, sometimes wishes can come true."

"I wish then to live forever and ever with loads and loads of money."

Sandy jumped up on the chair. "Get that dog off the furniture," pointing at Sandy starting to snuggle down.

"He's tired Gran."

"Well tired or no, he can do it on the floor, shoo, off," she shouted as Sandy jumped off the chair onto the floor.

"Can I see the photos of Gramps again?"

"You know where they are kept, go and get them."

Colin went into the next room and a moment later returned with the box and laid all the photos on the table. He picked up all those of his grandfather and started to look at them.

"Why is Gramps not wearing his medal on his chain," Colin asked pointing at the watch chain hanging from his grandfather's waistcoat in the photo.

"He hasn't worn that medal on his chain since we were marr… how did you know about that? Even your mother does not know about the medal, it was our secret. Who told you?" she demanded.

The force of her words flummoxed Colin. "I don't know, in my dream he was wearing it, that's all."

"You must have seen it in another one of the photos, let me look." She took every photograph of her husband and looked very closely at each one in turn; not one of the pictures showed him wearing the medal on his chain.

"Gramps said the medal belongs to me," Colin innocently added.

"Yes when you reach twenty one, wait a minute…" and stopped and sat by the table not saying another word. No one knew about the gold medal, not even her children. They made a pact together on their wedding night that the gold medal would be placed in a box and deposited with the local bank in Treorchy with instructions that when the first grandson reached twenty one he would have the gold medal as a present, if he survived the madness.

They would be long dead, they reasoned, but they wanted to pass this gift, their legacy, to the eldest grandson, the gold medal had resided with the bank ever since. Neither of them had seen the medal since deposited there, the day after they were married over sixty years ago; the medal once belonged to her husband's grandfather and passed to him on his twenty first birthday.

The only reference to the gold medal was in her will that she had only recently deposited, sealed, with her solicitor. Not even the solicitor knew, and would not know, until he read the will after her death. She was the only living person who had knowledge of the medal's existence, except now for Colin.

"Are you all right Gran?" Colin enquired concerned.

Her hands trembled. "Gramps must have mentioned the medal to you when you were little and you forgot about it until you saw his photos," she remarked racking her brain that this could be the only explanation.

"No Gran, he was wearing it on his chain, the one he keeps his watch on," Colin naively replied perplexed his Gran was making such a big issue of the medal.

"But how did you know it was for you?"

"I asked him for it and he said it already belongs to me," he replied.

"Yes but that was a dream love, how would you know that if you had not been told?"

"I don't know," he said shrugging his shoulders. "Gran, have I said something wrong… are you angry with me?"

She composed herself. "Angry? No. Wherever did you get that idea? I'm just interested in how you knew about the medal, Gramps never told me he told you that is all."

"If I see him in my dreams again I'll ask him for you," Colin innocently replied.

She smiled, "yes love, of course, you do that for me," she answered looking at him eyes filled with love. Keeping the dark secret away from him locked deep in her mind, she wasn't sure about it in any event. "It's time you were on your way home, here, give me the pictures I'll put them away."

Colin rose from the table, kissed his Gran on the cheek, and left. She looked at the photos again, love radiating out of her face warming the little room they shared together for all those years. She was waiting to follow him, she was ready, felt strongly her dead husband's presence especially when she was at the cemetery with Colin a few weeks ago.

He was the sun in her life, she the light in his. She had loved him from a child, never wanted anyone else not even in her dreams, even her fantasies were about him. They had a rare type of love; some say they even shared the same soul. The little room glowed bright as her thoughts reached out to him past death and beyond; death is but another room, she believed, a little tear fell onto the pictures held in her hand.

"You're an old rascal William John Phillips," she shouted at the pictures laughing, "not telling me you told Colin about the gold medal. If you were here now you'd get a mouthful off me I can tell you."

Her voice went quiet; she closed her eyes and her mind drifted. How much longer are you going to leave me here without you? I'm ready William, you are my sun and I want you to call back your light, it is dim here without you. I'm ready, please come shortly, mend my broken soul and make it whole again.

She opened her wet eyes. "What a silly sausage I am," she said out loud, placed the photos back into the box, got up from the chair and put the kettle on the fire to make herself a cup of tea. Her thoughts changed back to Colin and prayed to the Lord he would come through the ordeal. Already, she suspected, he was on the path and she powerless to help.

Chapter Eleven

Smallpox had taken hold; everyone was worried. Four streets away in Vicarage Terrace there were two confirmed cases; a girl aged fourteen and a young man of twenty two. Doctors had rushed them to hospital into quarantine, but there was not much hope. The girl dying the following day confirmed this almost immediately. The other person was critical but stable, the hospital thought he would pull through, but a few days later he also died; everyone gripped in a paralysis of fear, human contact shunned wherever possible.

Everyone hoped the contrary but knew these cases would not be the last; the valley was bracing itself for the worse. A week later, doctors confirmed another case this time in Chepstow Road the very street where Colin's Grandmother lived; it was creeping up the valley street by street, the march relentless. This worried Colin. His Gran was the one person in this world he still respected. His mother went to bring her to live with them but she refused to leave her home.

"If I'm going to die it will be here in my own bed," she decreed.

"But mam, you…"

She was resolute. "Mary Ann, no," she butted in not letting her daughter finish the sentence. "This is final."

"Let me stay with you then for a few days. George can manage the children now he's out of work," she pleaded knowing it was futile to pursue the matter further.

She smiled, knowing what her daughter was up to but kept the thought to herself. "Your place is with your husband and children not looking after some old woman. I've had my life and more, don't you go fretting about me. Do you hear me?"

"Yes mam."

"There then, that's the end of it."

She tried one last time. "Be reasonable."

She scowled at her daughter. "The smallpox is all over the valley no matter where you'll go, it's no safeguard against the disease so I might as well stay. Come, stop worrying, what will be, will be, and pass as such."

A dog scratched at the back door, a minute later Colin entered. "I've come to stay with Gran, is that alright mam?" he said apprehensively playing the advantage knowing his mother would be there.

"That's preposterous." His mother's face looked shocked. "No! I want Gran to come home with us," she answered indignantly.

"Good! I'll help you pack Gran."

"Hold on you two, don't I get a say in this?"

"Only if you say yes," her daughter replied trying to force the point home now her son had arrived.

"Well I'm not, and there's an end to it, my last words on the matter, no, no, no. I've lived in this house for over sixty years; you were born here, and neither smallpox nor anything else is forcing me out. Have I made myself clear?"

Colin pleaded. "Can I stay with Gran, Mam? Please!"

His mother didn't know what to do for the best. Her preferred solution wouldn't hold water; she could not change her mother's mind. An outbreak of smallpox was only a few houses away from where she lived, it was all over the valley, could strike anywhere, no place safe; one place as safe or as dangerous as another.

She did not wish her mother to be alone in the house that was the reason she was trying to persuade her to go and live with her for a few months. There was no further point in trying to make her change her mind. If Colin was staying, they could look out for each other so reluctantly she agreed. Additionally, she reasoned, with school suspended until the epidemic was over it would keep him out of mischief looking after his Gran.

"If there's a whiff of trouble you're back home," she sternly stated. "I'll bring some clothes for you." Still feeling very uncomfortable about the situation but knowing there was no more she could do. She had to let it go and left to return later with clothes for Colin.

Colin had acquired an aptitude for reading, enjoyed losing himself in a book, and would read for hours. His Gran would also spend hours reading; together in that little room sharing the same space, one life nearing the end the other only just starting, was a scene that could be displayed on any postcard and be proud to put on view on the mantelpiece at Christmas depicting warmth, contentment and happiness.

"It's getting late, bed."

"After this chapter Gran, five minutes."

Colin put the book down a few minutes later and walked over to the sink, cleaned his teeth, washed his hands and face kissed his Gran good night and went off to bed. The bedroom was small but cosy and it was not long before he fell fast asleep.

His thoughts drifted, he was with his grandfather standing in the street with his dog Sandy and asked about the medal.

"Tell her you were talking to me in a dream."

"Is this a dream? It feels so real."

"Come Colin, I need to show you something," he said ignoring the question.

"The big house, can I see it again?" his mind could never get past material things.

"Later! First, come with me."

His grandfather grabbed Colin's hand and in an instant was at the farm inside the house. Colin recognised the farmer and his son, the same person he nearly killed in the fight by the river. The boy was sweating heavily the father bent over him his mother in another room sobbing silently in a corner and praying quietly so as not to be heard.

"What's happening?" Colin asked feeling rather disturbed.

"This is the person you killed. He's dying of smallpox."

Colin felt nauseated and started to shake and wanted to be somewhere else, anywhere, but this room. "B… but killed… you said I killed him," Colin stuttered unsure.

"Yes, he was drowned," the apparition replied staring hard at Colin and pointed to the sick boy. "You remember the stream and what you did?"

Colin froze with fright. "It never happened! I dragged him to the side of the bank and left him, alive. I didn't drown him he's still alive; he is still there alive. He has a cold, a cold that is all." A chill ran through Colin's body. "Why do you say these things to me that he drowned."

"He is alive only because you couldn't drown him, your hand was stayed from killing, the past once changed will always reassert itself, it can be no other way only postponed to a future day, now he must die and all will be as it should."

Colin was confused, he knew he didn't kill the farm boy but the apparition was telling him he did. He did try in his rage to drown the boy but failed, something prevented him from doing it. "I didn't drown him, this has nothing to do with me."

The apparition shook his head. "Oh it does Colin. It has everything to do with you. I stopped you from killing him; he should be dead, murdered by you. What should have happened by the river is now reasserting itself, the boy will die of smallpox, there can be no other way."

Colin shook his head in disbelief. "So… What are you saying? I did kill him?"

"Yes. But you have been given another chance Colin, use it well."

He watched every detail as the boy slowly died. The father's feeling of desperation, the mother's hopelessness as she cried, the agony the farm boy went through as he battled against death fighting for every breath; Colin saw it all.

"Stop it, stop it," Colin pleaded. "Make him live."

"I cannot, every action has a consequence, what has happened must come to pass."

He heard his Grandmother's voice calling and he opened his eyes. Sweat covered him and his hands trembled as he sat up in bed. He must have been dreaming, but it felt so real to him. He would go to the farm to see if the boy was still alive.

"You're a hungry one this morning," his Gran said as he ate his breakfast in record time.

"I need to go out for a little while, must get a book I need for my school work," he lied, not wishing to tell his Gran the dream and where he was going.

"Well come straight back don't go hanging around with too many people," his Gran stated concerned about the smallpox but pleased he was taking an interest in his lessons and books.

Colin went at once to the farm and saw the farmer and his son walking into the cowshed, he laughed to himself. What a fool he thought feeling stupid to have placed any credence in the dream. He walked back to his Gran's his mind going round in a spin. He had seen his grandfather in the cemetery of that he was certain at the time, but now? He wasn't sure. It was getting all too much for him and dismissed it out of his mind, determined he would never rob that farm again as a concession to his conscience.

Colin returned to his Gran's to find her busy with the cleaning. He went to his room and read for the rest of the day. This pleased her to see him sitting reading and felt a warm glow in her heart for her grandson as she looked at him. Towards evening, his mother turned up with clean clothes and was pleased to see him reading and on best behaviour, a novel experience indeed she thought.

"More reading you should be doing, it keeps you out of trouble," his mother said to him in a kindly tone. "These clothes should last you for a few days," placing them in a cupboard on the wall.

"He's been reading all day," his grandmother stated proudly.

"Let's hope he's turning over a new leaf," she answered hopefully.

For the next few weeks, Colin stayed with his grandmother not going out other than to see Sophie, spending most of his time reading and completing the work the school had set. He was not the duffer everyone thought. He no longer read to help Sophie, but for himself, enjoying the experience, the thrills of the stories alive in his mind.

He had no further dreams and there was talk the schools were to reopen in a few weeks. The worse of the smallpox epidemic was over, there had not been a new case for several weeks, and everyone was hopeful the disease had run its course. It had claimed over fifty lives in total and for the first time in many months, optimism filled the air.

Colin had almost forgotten the dreams; other than the big house, he had shuffled them to the back of his mind. The only blight in his world was talk that school was to commence soon. He wished to leave school for good and detested going back. A week later as Colin was eating his breakfast his Gran mentioned there was another case reported. "Farmer Evans's boy is ill," she stated taking a sip of her tea.

Colin was startled. "What did you say Gran?" unsure he heard correctly.

"The Evans boy from the farm is down with smallpox," she repeated. "The disease is still with us."

Colin stopped eating. The cards in his mind were reshuffling the dream to the front. He felt sick, went up to his room quietly to his bed, his mind going round and round as the dream flooded back. His grandmother knocked the door, entered, and sat on a chair next to him.

She looked lovingly at him and waited a little while before speaking. "What's wrong Colin? Do you want to tell me? I know something is wrong."

"Nothing Gran, nothing," he answered in a low voice.

"Well something has upset you. Is it the farm boy? I didn't know you were friends."

"We're not; but he has smallpox and is going to die."

She placed her arm around his shoulder. "You don't know that, look at those that have come through. The authorities reckon they have all but isolated the strain and it will diminish in the near future," she said softly. "There is a good chance he'll pull through, don't be so pessimistic."

"I do know, Gramps told me, it's all my fault," he replied.

"You must be mistaken. How can you blame yourself for someone catching smallpox?"

"You don't understand Gran the farm boy should already be dead."

"Stay and have a little rest, all this talk of death is too much for you." Death is hard on the young she thought and left him to rest.

Colin curled up in bed and he tried to reason with himself, telling his mind it was not his fault, but kept seeing the farm boy's face as he was hitting him and ducking his head under the water. Then the picture of the family in the farmhouse, it was all so real. He should be dead, dead, he kept repeating to himself and felt angry. I hate him. If he does die why should I care and drifted asleep.

He slept until lunchtime blocking out all thought of the farm boy. He was no good anyway he muttered to himself, trying to justify he didn't care. If he dies, so what, it was only a dream.

His Gran came into the room with a glass of milk and a few chocolate biscuits. 'You're awake then, here they're your favourites."

"Thanks Gran, sorry for what I said earlier."

"That's all right, this dreadful business is affecting us all one way or the other."

"It's just that I get these dreams, Gramps shows me things."

"Yes, yes of course he does love," she answered in placation. "Come now, drink your milk, and eat the biscuits. Get up from bed or it'll be time to go back before you get out."

Colin ate the biscuits, drank the milk and got up, dressed and followed his Gran down the stairs, made himself a jam sandwich and ate it in silence; his thoughts still all a jumble.

Chapter Twelve

The farm boy died two days later, but by now, Colin had divorced his mind from his death, everyone knew he died of the smallpox. He held on to that thought, sure now in his mind everything he saw was only a dream, a coincidence, no more. When the mind won't accept the heart has no chance.

School restarted a few weeks later and the teachers could not help but notice how advanced Colin had become. "It's quite remarkable, his progress, refreshing, and in such a short time," one teacher commented over lunch to another.

To Colin school was still a torture chamber and did all he could to find ways to get round the rules. His reputation as a ruffian was unsurpassed; he was continually in fights with his fellow pupils and avoided like the plague. The only people who associated with him were his gang.

Their favourite pastime was going into shops and taking whatever took their fancy and leave without paying. Shopkeepers had caught a few of his gang shoplifting and the police sent for. On that occasion, they did not end up in court but were given a police caution much to the relief of their parents but warned that if it happened again the shopkeeper would prosecute them.

Several months passed, Colin had no further dreams. At the time, the dreams shook him but now meant nothing, relegated to the back of his mind, no longer even a slight inconvenience to him. He had all the cunning of a fox, the stealth of a tiger taking what he wanted, when he wanted, with little regard for anyone else.

One afternoon, when Colin should have been at school he went for a walk. He stopped after a while, sat near a tree, and he felt himself sleepy and dozed. He opened his eyes and sitting next to him was his grandfather dressed in the same clothes he wore previously, a smile on his face but it was sterner, deep worry lines came down the corners of his mouth.

"Gramps!" he said startled feeling nervous at seeing him so suddenly. "Gran is well," unable to think of anything else to say.

"Yes I know."

Colin's mind shifted back to the big house. "Will I still have the big house and the big cars? I know it's only a dream but it's a nice dream."

"You remember only the cars and the house?" The apparition frowned.

Colin shuddered. "Of course, what else is there? That's what it is all about big houses and cars."

"Yes, if that is still what you really want."

"Of course I want it, more than anything else in the world. Can I see my house again?"

His grandfather held his hand and in an instant they were outside the house, his house, standing in a large garden surrounded by a wall, two cars stood in the drive as previous.

Colin's eyes gleamed at the prospect all apprehension gone. "Why must I wait? I want it now," he cried in delight.

"That is not possible but it will belong to you in time to come, this house is your house in the future but first you must pay the price."

Colin nodded in delight. "Any price; for this any price. The old women can go straight away," he said. "She makes the place look dirty."

"That'll be up to you."

"Can I see inside?"

The next instant they were inside the house, the interior was immaculate, thick curtains hung from the windows, expensive furniture filled every room, large chandeliers hung from the ceilings, and ornate decorations covered all the walls. Colin had seen nothing like it not even in magazines.

In one of the corners rested a wheelchair with a man sitting in it his back turned away, it was obvious he was paralysed from the neck down in constant pain as he tried to move his neck. Two other people were also in the room dressed in white uniforms attending to the invalid.

"Poor chap, how did he end up in the wheelchair?" asked Colin.

"He was shot twice in the back and will be in a wheelchair for the rest of his life never able to move again." His grandfather sadly replied.

Remorse for other people was something Colin did not experience. "He'll have to move out before I move in that's for sure," Colin said jokingly but the words had serious intent. He couldn't have invalids in the house spoiling the look of the place.

His grandfather just smiled at this remark, grabbed Colin's hand and they were in the farmhouse. It was a shabby house, the décor was faded, and the furniture was dilapidated and badly in need of repair. The farmer and his wife were sitting across from each other dressed in black clothes having just buried their only son. The woman was crying, a handkerchief held to her face. The man had been crying but was now sitting in the chair staring melancholically at the fire, a half full whisky glass in his hand.

"Why did they have to take our Robert? He was a good boy," the woman spoke tears running down her face.

"Yes why indeed?" her husband answered taking a sip from the glass and staring into the bottom. "Why anything anymore?"

The woman dabbed her eyes. "I wish it were me in the cold ground not our Robert, a mother should never have to bury her only child," she cried feeling deeply the agony of every word she spoke.

"I was intending to hand over the farm to him in a few years," the farmer said tears falling freely from his face as he took another mouthful of the whisky. A single tear fell into the glass but he didn't notice.

Colin stood unable to move; he looked at these two people trying to look away but his eyes were transfixed on them both. He was staring at sorrow in its most intimate form. What greater loss could there be than to lose a child?

"Why are you showing me this?" Colin asked closing his eyes hoping it would go away. "Can we go back to the house?"

The apparition frowned sternly. "No! I want you to see, to feel, to experience how they are suffering, the smallpox took their child from them, their only child, but it should have been by drowning. How does that make you feel Colin?" his grandfather said, crunching every word as he spoke, each sound ate into Colin's mind, but still Colin felt nothing other than he didn't want to be there.

He looked at the two people, then at his grandfather but was lost for words. He'd placed the incident at the back of his mind but here it was once more forcing him to confront the situation again.

Colin shuffled uncomfortably resting on one foot and then the other in agitation. "But I didn't kill him," he pleaded. "What am I supposed to feel? These people are nothing, mean nothing to me."

The apparition looked directly at Colin, face blank and stern. "No, you didn't kill him but you would have and to further aggravate things you and your gang have tormented this family for years. Yet still you feel nothing, nothing becomes of nothing only emptiness and decay. Listen to what they say."

Colin hung his head in shame forced to listen to these two people talking about their dead son and the plans they had for his future. How they would have cherished their grandchildren but all that gone never to return.

"Gramps take me away from here please," pleaded Colin. As much as he desperately tried not to, he could feel their pain and sorrow and for the first time in his young life felt compassion. The depth and power was too much even for Colin.

Before they meant nothing to him, a farmer, his wife, and a boy he hated. Now he could see them as human beings with feelings, dreams, expectations. This hurt; he was ashamed for the way he had treated these people and resolved to make amends more to placate the apparition than he actually felt himself yet he did feel for them something he had not experienced before.

"Come! It is time to go."

Colin held out his hand and closed his eyes glad to block out the scene he had just witnessed. He felt his grandfather's touch; he opened his eyes and was sitting on the grass by the tree.

He touched his face; a tear fell from the corner of his eye. I must have been dreaming again he thought but it felt real, so, so, real.

The next day Colin went to the farm and stood at the door, took a deep breath and knocked; he could hear his heart pounding inside his chest and felt like running away and had difficulty in holding his ground. A little while later, the door opened. Standing in the doorway was the farmer, bleary eyed and unshaven.

"It's you, what do you want?" He said gruffly, when he recognised Colin, his eyes glazed from drinking whisky.

Colin choked back the phlegm in his throat. "I've come to see if I can be of help."

"Help yourself more like. We don't need the likes of you round here now be off with you before I get my gun."

Colin's knees shook slightly. "I'm sorry about Robert," trying to sound as sincere as possible.

The farmer stared hard at him. "We don't need your sympathy."

"Graham," his wife shouted. "That's no way to behave to someone giving condolences and trying to help."

"You'd better come in, and keep your hands to yourself." he sighed coldly.

Colin walked into the farmhouse; it was exactly like his dream. The chairs were in the same position, even the table the same, yet he had never been inside the house before. He looked on top of the mantelpiece and knew before he looked that there would be a clock in the centre, two brass candlesticks either side with a mirror behind the clock.

"I've come to see if I can help," Colin nervously spluttered feeling ill at ease as they looked at him.

"Were you friends with Robert?" she enquired.

Colin took a deep breath. "Yes and no if you know what I mean," he hesitantly answered.

"A friend," the farmer laughed. "Some friend. He's the lad who was fighting with him; Robert never had a good word to say about him. It's his lot that raided the chicken coops."

"So you are the lad he was fighting," she sorrowfully stated.

Colin bowed his head. "Yes, I'm sorry we fought and I've come to apologise."

"A bit late for that lad, our Robert is dead, gone," the farmer snapped back.

Colin looked to the floor. "Yes sir I know. It's you two I'm apologising to for all the trouble I've caused."

The farmer wasn't convinced of Colin's sincerity, with good reason, thinking him there only to suss the place out to rob later. "As I said it's a bit la…"

"Thank you," his wife butted in before her husband could finish. "We accept. It must have taken a lot of courage to come here and say that."

Colin turned to go and the woman said. "Would you like some tea?"

The farmer looked angry but stayed his tongue.

"No thanks, I'm staying at my Gran's and she'll have food ready for me," he politely replied, said thank you again and headed for the door and walked out feeling glad it was finished.

His thoughts raced as he walked back to his Grandmother's house and felt troubled. If it was a dream, how did he know what the room looked like even down to the mantelpiece? The more he tried to reason the less of an explanation he came up with until in the end he let the subject drop.

An hour later Colin was back at his grandmother's feeling rather pleased with what he had done. "I've been to see the farmer," he stated as he walked through the door expecting to see his Grandmother in the kitchen but to his surprise, she was not there. He called louder but the house was quiet. He ran up the stairs; she was in bed.

He entered her bedroom and said politely, "Gran, Gran, do you want a cup of tea?" There was no movement all remained quiet.

Colin's blood chilled, he had never felt this scared before. He walked over to the bed and lightly shook her shoulder. "Come on Gran wake up."

She moved slightly and he could see she was still breathing, a sigh of relief puffed out of his mouth. "What's wrong Gran? Are you ill?"

She gave a weak smile. "No tired, just tired. I'll be down in a minute."

"I'll help you out of bed," he said anxiously. His hands were shaking, he had contemplated the worse, and the thought shook him to the core. He leaned over, helped her to sit up, and sat by her side.

She held his hand. "I'm all right just need to come round. I'll have that cup of tea now please." Her voice was strained, distant and unfamiliar.

"I'll get the doctor Gran," Colin said concerned.

"There's no need for that unless he can give me back fifty years," she laughed faintly. "Now where's that cup of tea? Let's be having it and I'll be as right as rain."

Colin wasn't convinced; something wasn't right, didn't feel right, and left the bedroom and went to the kitchen. A little while later, his grandmother came into the room and sat down in the chair. She looked frail, as if gossamer would not melt in her mouth. She smiled at him. He brought her the cup of tea, placed it on the table next to her, and sat opposite.

"Are you sure you're all right?"

"Good gracious don't fuss so much love, it's my old bones they need a lot of rest. Where's your tea?"

"I've just had a glass of lemonade," Colin answered feeling so much love for his Gran he could burst. "You're not going to die are you Gran?"

She smiled at his ingenuousness. "We all must some time love, but don't worry your little head over me. I'm happy to go any time," she saw the look in his face and winked at him, "but not just yet hey. Where is Sandy?"

"I've left him with my father he's not well," he answered sadly. "I'm worried about him Gran."

"I hope he gets better soon."

"Hope so to."

Chapter Thirteen

The outbreak of smallpox was at last under control; life was nearly back to normal. Colin was back home with his parents and school was to start the following Monday after being closed for over six weeks. Sandy his dog has sadly died and this upset him greatly. He felt somehow this was a punishment for what had happed to the farm boy, and brooded over this for weeks; any compassion he did have, gone.

The colliery was being dismantled but there was talk the slag heaps were to be moved and washed to extract all the coal; the stones and rubble then used as hard core for roads.

"I've applied to Wilson and Scots as a labourer in Port Talbot," George stated to Henry and Bill over a pint of beer.

"Let me think? Ah! That's the firm that will be washing and moving the slag heaps, if I'm not mistaken," Henry replied.

"I've not heard anything positive, just rumour and talk," George remarked."What have you heard?"

"It's happening, definitely. They'll be looking to start shortly," Henry assured them.

"I'll ask at the interview next week, if that's the case I'll ask to work on the coal tips instead, save travelling to Port Talbot everyday," George remarked.

"If you get in George say a word for me," Henry asked hopefully.

"And me," chipped in Bill not to be left out.

"Let me get the job first boys, there's the interview first," George laughed taking a large drink from his pint.

"We'll give you that George, you were right about the pit closures; best thing that could have happened especially now it looks as if we'll all get other jobs," remarked Henry sheepishly.

"Don't jump the gun, none of us have yet," George reminded them.

"I don't think there's much doubt about that. It's rumoured they'll be using all local labour to wash and move the waste," Bill stated. "With our experience we're ideally suited."

"You two are always counting the chickens before you get the eggs let alone see them hatched. I haven't got the job yet." George laughed lighting his pipe, smoke hitting the ceiling.

George did get the job in Port Talbot. Work started on the tip three weeks later and he was one of the first transferred. A few weeks later, the firm promoted him to the position of foreman and the first person he employed was Henry. They were back working together again.

George was in charge but there was never any conflict between them, they both had their jobs to do and worked to the best of their ability. There was another vacancy two months later and Bill joined them. Wages were not as good as the pit but they could work as much overtime as they needed making the money up that way; long hours never worried them and, of course, they were working, which meant a great deal to their pride.

Things had turned out all right for them in the end and they felt pleased with themselves. They still had their redundancy money and now they were working again bringing in a wage so their little nest egg was safe for the time being, earning interest.

"That lad of yours is doing a good job with our Sophie, she's top of the class in English," Henry remarked to George as they were having a cup of tea together before they started work.

"Colin is getting good reports as well with his school work. What's Sophie now seven or eight?"

"Come on George! She will be ten next month," he answered.

George shook his head. "The years are rolling by."

"Flying more like; your Colin spends a lot of time in our house reading to our Sophie and helping her with her homework."

George looked pleased. "Yes other than school, if he's not at your house he's with the wife's mother."

"They're pretty close those two; he's Gran this, and Gran that when he's with us."

"Between the two of them they keep him out of trouble," George said relieved, "or goodness knows what he'll be up to."

The whistle sounded and they got up to start the shift, "come on you lot," George shouted into the cabin, "let's be having you, the whistle's gone."

Colin was spending a great deal of time with his Gran and Sophie but to say he was out of trouble would be asking too much. He had found a good little earner with coal. His gang were now called the Bulls and was stealing coal from the very site his father was supervisor over and if caught could always say he was there to see his father.

One or two evenings a week they would change into old clothes, sneak past security which was dismal, fill sacks with coal and store it in a secret location until they were able to sell it at the weekend. One of the gang stole an old weighing scale and they sold the coal in little bags around the doors pushed around on an old pram converted for the purpose.

Colin shared the money fifty percent to him the rest among the gang. When they complained, he argued that because his father was the foreman, and in charge of the site, it was only fair that he had half of the money. A spurious argument but it carried the day.

Colin spent his money on books especially the ones Sophie wanted. He kept this from the gang, they never saw this side of him but they could not help notice his schoolwork improved by leaps and bounds leaving them way behind. They put this down to him being naturally brainy not thinking for one moment that he was regularly reading and studying whenever he had the opportunity.

Colin would spend a few hours every week with Sophie and when these two were together an outsider watching would think that butter would not melt in his mouth. He not only seemed a different person, but was a different person. It was as if their souls had touched and already made up their minds that they wished to be partners for life.

When thieving coal one evening, Colin accidentally started one of the belts and it nearly pulled him into the rollers but managed to stop it just in time. The rollers were large steel wheels about as tall and as long as a man; they would go round and round moving the belts forward. There were four of these large wheels. The belts, which transported the waste, would go through the centre of the four around the bottom two wheels and back underneath, crushing any waste or coal into small lumps, dropping out the other end to be sorted later.

If anyone was inattentive and caught in the belt, it would pull him in, moving him round and round inside until it crushed his body into very small pieces. There were signs all about in large, red bold print warning of the dangers and to keep away from the wheels but this meant nothing to the thieves. They were there to steal coal and coal they would steal irrespective. The danger to them was one among many and posed little worry to any of them.

One day when Colin was at the site, he knocked the main lever and the wheels started to move. He was more concerned with the noise than the danger and tried to stop the belts moving forward but was unable; something had jammed in the control box. He could not risk leaving the belt in motion; this would alert the security man that someone was stealing coal and his little profit earner stopped.

He ran behind one of the sheds to the main electrical supply and, without thinking, wedged a wooden log into the box causing a short circuit of the system. Instantly, to his great relief, the belt stopped; the watchman hadn't noticed, mostly he stayed in the canteen. He went back to the rollers and wedged a steel bar he found on the floor into one of them. "Now move," he exclaimed aloud feeling annoyed about what had happened.

A few of his customers were already asking where he was getting his supply of coal but he was able to cover his back by saying his father bought the coal and he was selling it on his behalf. Always careful that his regular clients were far enough away from where he lived in case they bumped into his father or anyone working with him. This was a risk, but a calculated one, everyone knew everyone else in the valley but lately there was a large influx of new families, capitalising on the cheap houses now the collieries had closed and this suited Colin as he smugly hid the coal for later sale.

He was up early the following day, a Saturday and sold all the coal before lunchtime. He intended to spend the afternoon with Sophie and the evening with his Gran, his mother giving permission for him to sleep the night. He purchased strawberries and chocolates to share with Sophie and his grandmother and was looking forward to seeing the surprise on their faces when he produced the goodies.

That afternoon Sophie's dad Henry joined them and even had a few strawberries. Colin liked Sophie's dad; a straight proud man, who said what he thought, out it would come. He appreciated all the books Colin gave Sophie but told him off for spending all his pocket money, not realising he was purchasing the items with the proceeds from stealing and selling coal.

It was late afternoon before Colin left Sophie's house and arrived at his grandmother's, his face beaming as he showed her the strawberries and the chocolates.

"You shouldn't have spent all that money on me," she mildly chastised bright and breezy at his thoughtfulness.

"Yes I should; shall we eat the strawberries now Gran or later?"

"They're your strawberries you decide," she laughed getting two dishes from the kitchen intimating now. "First young man, wash your hands and use the brush."

They ate all the strawberries with fresh cream that his grandmother supplied immediately followed by the chocolates.

"Shall I read to you Gran, I've brought a brilliant book," pulling it from his bag.

"What! Another surprise, this is getting too much for an old lady," she touchingly replied. "I'm such a lucky one."

Colin started reading moving effortlessly from one sentence to another his voice flowing easily over the pages as his Gran listened in glowing delight. She listened for over twenty minutes until she decided to make a cup of tea, stood up and walked to the kitchen as he kept on reading.

"My, my, what a good reader you are, take a break the tea is ready," she shouted from the kitchen.

"Just this last paragraph Gran. What do you think?"

She came into the room with a tray of biscuits and two cups of tea, placed the tray on the table."My, my, you are becoming a little scholar. Put the book away for a minute and take a few of these biscuits they are chocolate coated, your favourites," placing the cup, saucer and plate in front of him.

After tea, they sat together talking until he became tired; he had been busy all day and could hardly keep his eyes open.

"Bed for you, don't forget to clean your teeth and wash your face and hands," she advised.

Colin went to the sink washed and brushed his teeth and went straight to bed feeling pleased with himself. He closed his eyes and was soon asleep. He opened his eyes and he saw his grandfather sitting in a chair next to him.

"Am I dreaming?"

"Come Colin, I've something I need to show you," he said and grabbed him by the hand.

The next moment Colin was back at the site where his father worked and from where he had stolen coal the previous day. He saw the belts and the rollers and there sitting in the shed was his father and Henry. He tried to hide but remembered there was no need. They were part of the picture but not part of the reality; it was a dream or was it? Colin watched them as if they were on a television screen.

"What am I doing here Gramps?" Colin asked thinking his grandfather would tell him to return the coal he had sold and feeling uncomfortable about the fact.

He extended his arm towards where they were sitting. "Wait and watch," his grandfather replied sternly.

His father and Henry were seated at a table talking and drinking tea. Other than them, the place was deserted.

"Come let's start the belts," George stated. "It's nearly time to begin work the others will be here shortly."

They left the shed and Henry went round the back to turn the power on pulling down on the handle.

"It's down George," he shouted, "turn on the switch."

"It's not working try the handle again Henry," George shouted back. "There can't be a lot wrong. It's just a bit stiff from not working over the weekend."

Henry pushed the handle up and back again, walked back to George standing by the rollers, and tried the button himself.

"The power must be down, George," Henry commented. "Damn it, we can do without this on a Monday morning."

"I'll phone down and get the electrician," George stated annoyed at the delay. "Our bonus will be cut if we don't get it sorted quickly."

Suddenly, the button started to spark. Henry had left the handle in the 'on' position. He hurried back to turn the power off but before he could do so the belts started to move sparks flying in all directions around and in between the rollers. They had been jammed and the wheels were trying to go round as the electrical current flowed through them.

George tried to push the emergency stop button but it was not responding. He noticed a bar wedged in between the rollers and reached out to release the obstruction, as he did so the rollers started to move and caught his hand dragging him into the centre.

Colin ran forward. "No! No!" He shouted in desperation.

The spectre turned to him. "You are as air Colin, powerless to stop what is about to happen."

"Do something please. Dad! Dad! No! This can't happen. It's a dream. Stop it, stop it, please, make it stop," Colin pleaded.

"It's as you see Colin."

"Turn it off. Henry! Turn it off. I'm caught, it's pulling me in." George screamed terrified. "For the love of God turn it off or I'm done for."

Henry couldn't turn off anything; he couldn't hear George's desperate calls; he was dead. When he went to turn the handle, the sudden rush in power electrocuted him. Electricity surged through his body knocking him off his feet killing him instantly.

His body lay on the floor smouldering in a contorted heap jerking in spasms in tune with the sparks. The electric current moved his limbs for the final death boogie as it played its last melody on his body as it lay on the floor for the last note.

George was faring no better; the rollers on the machine pulled him into the centre crushing his body as he screamed until he screamed no more, then silence. His body already unidentifiable, squashed beyond recognition dragged inside the drum to be pulverised further into pulp. The sight of the blood sickened, it had painted a picture on the floor, belt, and rollers, one colour, red. The final touches were the Picasso splashes over the shed bulleted onto the side in little dots as the rollers squashed and pulled George into its grip of death to become as one with the dust.

Colin stood next to his grandfather motionless, in shock, shaking as the sickening scene played out before his very eyes. His expression ashen, terror etched into his young face as the realisation sank into him that he was responsible for this carnage. He rubbed one of his fingers over the belt and looked at the blood; his father's blood stained the top of his finger. He felt giddy, sick, nauseated and fainted.

He opened his eyes and was back in his bedroom sweat poring off his head. He jumped out of bed, the picture he had just witnessed clear in his mind. The room was dark, he felt cold, as cold as ice. He rushed down the stairs to get a drink of water physically shaken by the vividness of the experience. It's not real he kept repeating under his breath, he reached for the glass and noticed the top of his finger wet. He put the light on and froze; his finger had blood on the end of it.

Colin turned on the water in the tap and washed it off; quickly he examined all his fingers and hands to see the cut, but there was no cut, not even a slight graze. Where could the blood have come from? His body physically shook. It must be a dream, it can't be anything else, how could it?

He stared at his hands thinking the spot of blood must have come from under one of his nails, yes, he thought, holding that rationalization. That must be it; there could be no other explanation other than… "What is happening to me?" He spoke into his hands, his head hot with perspiration; was it a warning of what would happen because of his actions yesterday? He wasn't sure.

He went back to bed but was afraid to sleep, he just lay there thinking about the nightmare and decided he would go back to the place in the morning and remove the steel bar he had wedged into the rollers and disconnect the electrical supply just to make sure his dream was just that, a dream. He knew deep down it was no dream, it was a warning; his grandfather had come to him to save him from the repercussions of his actions yet again.

The image haunted him as he lay on the bed. The more he tried to block out the picture the more it etched into his brain. He got up as soon as it was light and left the house heading straight for the tip. His whole body ached and felt he was going mad. Reality, actuality and sane logic merged in his mind with fantasy, the mystical magic of dreams. He could not tell one from the other.

The security guard was in the bottom cabin asleep. Colin crept passed and followed the conveyor belt until he arrived at the location of his nightmare.

He went over to the rollers, removed the steel bar he had wedged into the top roller, found the start button, smashed it with the steel bar then threw it away down the mountain side. He pulled at the power lines showing little concern for his own safety until he fully disconnected them from the rollers. He went over to the power box behind the shed, wedged the handle of the electric box in the off position, and used a stone to knock what was left of the handle flat against the box.

To make sure the security guard discovered the damage Colin started to shout and bang the steel rollers making all the noise he could muster in order to attract his attention. The security guard had to discover the damage and report it before his father and Henry started work the following day.

Colin could see the security guard running up the hill to where he was making the noise. Before he got close, Colin high-tailed it over the mountain, cut across the river, and ran until he was safe. He doubled back to see the security guard standing at the rollers shaking his head and returned to his grandmother's feeling much happier.

An hour later, he was at her house and as luck would have it, she was still in bed. He washed his hands and face in the sink, cleaned his shoes, brushed his clothes, and went back to bed. His mind clear, he felt exhausted and soon fell asleep paying no heed to the damage he had done but happy, very happy he had taken enough precautions to stop the nightmare he had experienced from ever happening.

"Are you awake," his grandmother called up the stairs. "I've been up for over an hour. Come on lazybones, let's be having you."

He slowly opened his eyes; was everything a dream? "Down in a minute," he shouted.

He quickly ate his breakfast intending to walk the mountains and thought of Sandy. He missed his old dog and felt sad. Why does everything need to die? It's so unfair he thought.

"Don't be late for lunch," his grandmother shouted as he went out the door.

He walked, trying to come to terms with these strange dreams remembering the farm boy and how what should have happened had reasserted itself to make it so. He tried to dismiss this notion; it kept coming back but each time he tried to think of something else the thought boomeranged.

"I'm not responsible," he shouted to the sky. "Do you hear? Not responsible!" He knew deep in his heart, he was responsible, not by any man made law but by some other force he did not understand. The two sides of his conscience were pulling in opposite directions, one accepting the other denying. The elastic of his mind was tight, very tight, and if it snapped it would propel him into hell and madness but he understood nothing of this, knew only something uncontrollable was happening, which his Gramps was there to try and stop.

His grandfather's words hit him forcefully again and he started to shake violently and sweat. Nature will reassert itself, nature will reassert itself, realising that his father and Henry could go the same way as the farm boy. Get a grip, he thought and sat on the grass to think the process through logically. The farm boy he would have killed, had killed, but a force he did not understand stopped him. This was different he reasoned, he had prevented the accident before it happened, before the time, concluding there was nothing for nature to reassert.

He did not change anything but arranged things differently before the event took place. No one stopped him, he stopped himself before the time it was due to occur; there would be no reason for nature to reassert itself. He was not convinced it was true but needed to hold on to something, anything, and this was the only hope he could grasp.

As the day progressed, Colin went over the event and tried to remember all his dreams when with his grandfather. The big house, the old lady whom he thought grotesque and vile, the man in the wheelchair. What did it all mean? His mind shifted again to his father, Henry and Sophie. He did not want any more dreams the pain was too great. To whom could he talk? There was no one, it all sounded far too complex and unbelievable for his young mind but try as he would, could not shut out these images.

Just think of the big house, the cars, nothing else is important, this is what I should be concentrating on not the bad things in my dreams, he kept reciting, trying to convince himself he was capable of controlling the situation. He arrived at his grandmother's late afternoon and felt exhausted, confused and disorientated.

"You look worn-out, have you a headache? You've missed lunch, shall I get you something to eat?"

"No Gran only tired, I'm not hungry." He washed his hands, he could still see the spot of blood on his finger, knew it wasn't there but he could see it, perhaps he was going mad. He went straight to bed. In a few minutes was fast asleep and slept until the following morning. The gloom of the previous day was gone; he ate a hearty breakfast and felt much better intending to leave the past in the past and look to the future and success.

Chapter Fourteen

The valley was changing, the old way at an end. New people were migrating in taking advantage of the cheap housing after the pit closures. Many of the younger people were moving out looking for work away from the valley and this was having a distorting effect on the population.

Illness was rife; men who worked in the colliery for years were now paying the price. "Living cough bags," was Colin's derogatory remarks. They sat outside their houses unable to walk, gasping for breath. Lungs full of coal dust forcing their bodies to turn them back to dust before their allotted time.

George and Henry were two of the lucky ones; they still had their health and a job. Both had dust, but it did not affect them in any way, life was content as far as they were concerned. Colin's schoolwork continued to improve and he was moved into the top stream proving to all he had ability if applied.

"Colin I'm going out to the shop and to the cemetery; won't be long," his grandmother shouted to him, one weekend.

He stirred, still in bed. "Hold on Gran, I'll come with you," he shouted down the stairs.

She banged on the bottom step with her foot. "Be quick then."

A few minutes later, he was ready to go, a quick glass of milk and a cheese sandwich in his hand they were on their way. The walk took the best part of an hour and after buying flowers, they stood over the grave.

Colin knew to keep quiet when his grandmother was placing flowers on the grave. This was always a sombre moment. He knelt by the side of her and waited for her to complete the task. She closed her eyes, a haze came over her as if her soul had jumped out of her body for just a second, it was brief, but Colin noticed it. When she opened her eyes she looked different, her face glowed, a little more rounded, contented.

She tried to stand. "Good gracious me! Colin, give me your hand I need a help up."

"Yes of course Gran," and held out his arm to act as leverage to pull herself onto her feet.

She turned. "Look! Colin look" she said, "a robin," pointing at the gravestone. A little robin was perched on it, chirped, and flew away.

She tingled with happiness, looked younger, more radiant, her age lines smoothed. She turned and looked Colin directly in the eyes and smiled, his heart melted. It was a deep meaningful smile and he felt its warmth ripple over his whole body.

"What's the happy occasion Gran?" her happiness was infectious.

"It's my time shortly," she answered. "I'm ready."

A shadow fell over his face. "Ready? Shortly? Time? What! Gran? I don't understand?"

"It's not for you to understand only to accept when the time comes, to be happy for me. William is waiting, it is almost time; shortly I will start my journey."

Colin felt uneasy but didn't know why. "Can I come, please Gran?"

She held his arm. "No, this is one journey we must all travel alone. Come on, I have a lot to sort out."

They arrived back home and his grandmother said very little but there was a continual smile on her face, her eyes sparkled like diamonds.

Her words troubled Colin. "When are you going on the journey Gran and for how long?"

She turned and looked at him her face radiant. "The journey will last for eternity and will start soon."

Colin was more confused than ever and thought his Gran was having a funny turn and asked if he should go and fetch the doctor.

"No, I'm just so happy, life has been good to me, very good, and about to get better."

A veil came over Colin's face and he stopped smiling, he felt cold and numb inside, his eyes dropped to the floor and it dawned on him what his Gran was saying. He turned his head away from her and walked into the garden to return a few minutes later. She was sitting in a chair drinking a glass of water still smiling.

"Gran, was Gramps at the cemetery?"

"Yes he was there."

"What did he want?" he asked knowing the answer but hoping he was wrong. Colin was old enough to understand.

His Gran looked happy. "He said it was time for us to be together, we are to be united again, he asked his light to shine on him and be as one again."

"Gran," Colin stuttered tears starting to form in his eyes. "Are you going to die?"

"Dear me is that a tear? No love, death is but part of life. I'll always be there for you just in the next room, it is only ever a thin wall, remember that always, don't be sad, because I'm not, neither must you."

"I like you in this room Gran. Please, stay."

"I told you many times over the years I have no say in the matter. What's to be will be, my wheel has almost completed its turn."

"I'll talk to Gramps, tell him no, I can you know."

She smiled. "Yes, I believe you can, but I don't want you to. I'm ready, you can't deny your old Gran that, come, give me a hug."

They hugged not speaking, lost in each other, one just starting his young life the other waiting to depart.

His Gran pulled away, looked full into Colin's eyes, smiled in a way he had never seen her do before and said. "Remember Colin, I'm only in another room."

"We all love you. You are my friend as well as my Gran. If you go what'll I do?"

"Live your life as your Gramps would wish," knowing as she said the words Colin would have to battle the future without her and whispered a little prayer in her mind he would fight the demon in him and not let the madness win.

"Gramps said I would have a big house, cars, live like a king."

"If that is what he said it must be right, but big houses, fast cars, even being a king must not be the only criteria to measure success. If you have a tormented soul, all the gold on the planet means nothing, think carefully what you want in life, you need to control your temper… just be careful."

"Yes Gran," not really understanding what she was saying.

"Anyway, I have plenty of living to do first so don't worry your little head over me just yet," knowing this was not the truth but did not wish her grandson to worry. "Come it's time you were getting home."

"See you tomorrow Gran."

"Yes I'll see you tomorrow, but remember Colin I am only in another room. You must remember that always."

Colin slept badly that night up long before he was due to leave for school.

"You are an early one this morning," said his mother. "You must have a guilty conscious. What were you up to over the weekend?"

"Nothing," he replied not wishing to speak further. He felt like he had been bitten by a scorpion, and waited for the venom to run its course.

School that day was uneventful, he threatened a few lads, nearly got into a fight with a boy from another class but other than that a dull day. Colin felt something was wrong, as if a mist had descended into his brain with a nagging constant pain in the pit of his stomach tugging at his insides.

His dejection was justified, he arrived home to see his mother sitting in the chair crying, his father sat next to her with his arm around her shoulders, and he knew his grandmother was dead.

Colin fell onto the floor pulsating with pain. All the bruises and cuts he had experienced in his young life through fighting felt as nothing compared to this pain. He trembled to the core of his being banging his head on the floor shouting. "She lied to me, she lied to me, she said she would see me today."

"Come," his father said helping him up off the floor.

He went to his room and crashed onto his bed, the pain was in him, the grief deep. He cried, shouted, banged his head against the wall until almost unconscious, bit his finger until it bled, tears blurred his eyes. His mind went repeatedly over the previous day, the happiness he remembered in his grandmother's face, her sparkling eyes; the words, "my time," kept recurring, winding inside his mind like the ticking of a clock waiting to explode.

"Oh Gran," he shouted seeing her face in his pillow. "I love you, come back, please come back," knowing in his heart that this was impossible. He cried himself to sleep and awoke a while later his eyes crusted over from the tears. He thought first he had been dreaming but the full reality of the situation hit him again, his swollen face moist with tears.

He closed his eyes and could see her face smiling wishing so much he could speak with her again. His eyes opened and his grandmother's face faded as his eyes broke through once more into the reality of the situation. He looked out of his window, a faint smile broke across his face, he saw a robin sitting on his windowsill, "look after her Gramps," he whispered. "She's in the same room as you now," and fell back on the bed to stare at the blank ceiling.

Chapter Fifteen

The funeral a few days later hit home to all the family the finality of losing a loving mother and grandmother. Colin attended the service, first in his grandmother's house and later at the cemetery. His parents buried her in the same grave as her husband. There were flowers in abundance and as he walked past the open grave, threw a single flower onto the coffin and muttered quietly under his breath. "I will always love you Gran, always and forever." He looked up at the rolling clouds. The wind whistled through the grass, the sun hid behind the clouds as if as a mark of respect.

The funeral party started to disperse; Colin felt a few drops of rain on his face just before he entered the car to take him home. His brothers, too young to attend, stayed with neighbours. He sat between his father and mother who broke with tradition to attend the interment; no one spoke; slowly the car moved away from the person they all loved, allowing the dank moist earth to reclaim its own. As the car left the cemetery, Colin looked back and his eyes caught sight of a robin sitting on the wall.

A large part of his life was now empty. He spent more time with his grandmother than he did with his own parents and felt lost and abandoned; time hung heavy on his young shoulders, a dark cloud had descended over him a warning of the turbulence to come.

Colin played out his anguish in the only way he knew. He hated the world, all that it stood for, he was lost inside himself, trouble followed like a dog on a lead. He was on a spiral, the movement downward with every turn.

He had the cunning of a fox the intelligence of a genius and used them to full ability. He would walk up to a shop window just as darkness fell watching no one was near and his getaway clear, a scarf high around his neck and face and hit the glass with a steel rode smashing the glass and running away for no other reason than the glass, and he were in the same place, his actions motiveless. It was a cry for help. The destruction in him was of bulldozer force and manifested itself in an ever-increasing cycle of disruption.

The pupils at his school feared Colin; MD was his established nickname. Tim would go to great lengths to avoid him. He was alone.

The one person still able to produce any semblance of normality in him was Sophie. They spent a lot of time together playing and reading but when away from her he had turned into a demented injured animal. It was not long before the inevitable happened; the headmaster expelled him from school for throwing a stone at one of the teachers catching him on the face. This was the last straw as far as the school was concerned; the headmaster called his parents and informed them Colin was no longer welcome at the school.

"Why do you behave this way Colin?" his father ranted at him when they got home. "You're intelligent, were in the top class so why? Tell me. Answer me that."

Colin had no answer. He shrugged his shoulders and looked at his father in silence. There was nothing to say, he didn't know why himself.

"You'll end up in prison. Do you hear me," his mother shouted from behind him. "You're a disgrace to this family, a disgrace. We have been through enough with you."

He just turned and walked out of the room up the stairs and threw himself on his bed and stared at the blank walls devoid of all emotion. Colin didn't care about what he had done; there was not the slightest remorse and carried on staring at the ceiling. He would run away from the dump that his parents call a home; they would never see him again. His mind went back to Sophie; he would miss her. He was fifteen years of age, almost sixteen, and didn't care about anyone, not even Sophie. This was a lie and he knew it. In his arrogance, the only person he was fooling was himself.

A few streets downhill from Colin's house lived an old lady. It was rumoured that she kept savings under her bed in an old tin. He knew she didn't want for anything and decided to steal her money and run away. He had no idea where but away wherever away would take him, he needed to be out of this deadbeat valley and these down trodden people.

That night Colin called to see Sophie. She wanted to know why he could no longer go to school, "because," he replied and left it at that. Colin read to her, careful not to say anything of his intended plans, just telling her in a casual way he may have to go away shortly intimating because he could no longer go back to school.

Sophie immediately noticed this. "You could find another school," she innocently answered.

He looked at her before replying. "Yes, I could, maybe," realising he shouldn't have said anything.

Sophie was at that age when she was starting to take stock of situations and even though she thought the world of Colin, she knew about his reputation, his bad behaviour and felt sad that her best friend could behave in this way.

"When will you go?" she asked.

"Soon but it's a secret."

"Can I come as well?"

"Look Sophie it won't be for long and not for a while yet, besides, you must go to school."

"So must you."

"I'm older than you."

She said pertinently. "I'll be as old as you some day."

"Yes, then you can go away as well." Colin got up, "see you later."

"Colin," she smiled, "take care."

That same evening Colin was outside the old woman's house watching and waiting. He could see light at the back of the house, reasoning correctly, it was where she spent most of her time. He knocked the door and ran to hide behind a wall and waited, nothing happened. After a few minutes, he went back to the door and knocked again this time harder and quickly retreated behind the wall to wait. Again the door remained shut, she must be a deaf as an old coot he thought. He returned a third time knocked as hard as he could for quite a while and moved back behind the wall. A few minutes passed and the door opened. Good he thought she takes a few minutes to walk to the door more than enough time.

The old woman walked with the aid of a walking frame. She stood in the doorway leaning on the frame; looked both ways, shook her head slowly, turned, went inside and slammed the door. Colin was jubilant, his mind quickly did the calculations; she was slow walking, hard of hearing and needed a frame to stand. He smiled to himself; he could be in and out of the house in a matter of minutes before she had time to realise what was happening. I'm never going to be old it's horrible; all old women should be… but didn't complete the thought blocked by a picture of his grandmother's face coming into his mind.

The old lady slept at the back of the house Colin reasoning that is where she would keep her money. He went round to the back and noticed a drainpipe running from the guttering down the side of the house to the floor. The bedroom window was to the left of the drainpipe and realised he could climb this pipe to get to the window without much difficulty.

Colin returned to the house every night to see if the window was open but each time it was not. He was just about to give up in desperation when he noticed the top was partly open. He smiled; a dark malignant grin replaced the smile; he was at the bottom of the pipe and started to climb.

Within less than a minute he was standing on the window ledge his hand inside the window loosening the latch, it gave easily and he crawled through into the room. He stopped and listened for sound; the adrenaline pumping around his body drugged him with excitement. He calmed himself; he needed a clear head and sat on the inside of the window ledge listening for any sound. After a few minutes he searched the room.

To the right of the window was a wardrobe, he crept over careful not to make a sound and quietly opened the door. The inside was full of clothes; he carefully looked into every pocket finding a few odd coins, which he put in his pocket. He removed the contents of the drawers in the dressing table, found nothing of value only a few old brooches. He decided to take only money, left the brooches, and replaced the clothes very much as he found them.

He searched the room methodically but uncovered no money and was getting angry. He knew she must keep it somewhere in this room, but where? The obvious place was under the bed but there was nothing only a few old pairs of shoes.

Colin looked around the room again, his eyes like radar trying to find the hiding place. It struck him, the floor! He pulled back the mat at the bottom of the bed and noticed one of the boards shorter than the rest.

He manipulated his fingers between the loose boards. He pulled gently, smiling, underneath was the treasure he sought. In the space was a tin box full of papers, a few necklaces, and many rings. They looked expensive but decided to leave them.

He removed the papers; underneath was money, lots of it. He emptied the contents cramming the notes and coins into every pocket. There were thousands of pounds, and couldn't believe his luck. He was rich; it was all so easy.

Colin carefully replaced the board and the carpet and realised he had not put the tin box back and heard a noise, the old lady was moving down below. He stood listening intently, his face turned white.

There was no quick way out; what if she saw him? He looked for a place to hide, initially thought of the wardrobe, but immediately discounted it. If the old lady was in the room all night he would be stuck and started to move to the window but again changed his mind.

He could run down the stairs past the old woman, but she could recognise him and risked the neighbours also seeing him. Panic set in not knowing what to do next. The old lady was at the bottom of the stairs and he could hear her taking the first step. Then she stopped and he heard her mutter to herself. "You're a silly old fool Agnes, you've forgotten the clock," and went back into the room.

Colin gave a sigh of relief, he had the time he needed to execute the getaway without being seen; he pulled up the floor board, replaced the tin, placed back the rug and was out of the window and down the pipe in no time. The absentmindedness of forgetting the clock could well have saved the life of the old woman.

He hid the money in one of his many hiding places and went straight home. He would not touch the money for a few days. The police would be everywhere looking to see if anyone local was spending a lot of cash. A few days passed, still there was no mention of the robbery; all was quiet, which perplexed him.

Colin walked passed the house on several occasions nothing stirred; there was no talk anywhere of a robbery. The old women hadn't realised she had been robbed, he reasoned, and felt safe to go and count the money. There was over £5,000; more money than he had ever seen in his life before and felt he was on his way to the big house and fancy cars and laughed at the stupidity of working hard for a full week for a pittance. He had more money than most of the people in his street, which made him feel grownup and powerful. He was on his way to supremacy and stardom, no dirt encrusted hands for him for only a few pounds per week.

He counted out a hundred pounds and hid the notes in the lining of his coat, the coins he placed into his pockets. He bought Sophie new books and a tennis racket and was ready to spend more money until her mother started to ask questions. She wanted to know from where he got the cash; Colin made the excuse it was his birthday money but she looked unconvinced.

"You shouldn't spend all your money on presents for Sophie. How much have you spent the last week?"

Colin felt on edge, her mother was starting to place him under the microscope. "It's alright, it really is, they weren't expensive books, the racket was in a sale," he lied.

"Well they look expensive to me so no more of this, do you hear," she demanded in mock scolding. "I'll not be having you spend your money like this, if Sophie wants something she can save up her own money like everyone else.

I must be more careful he thought; if her parents questioned the cost of the articles closely, he would have a lot of explaining to do especially if his parents were also involved. There was no way he could justify these costs and when the robbery was discovered the finger would soon point at him.

"Must go," he cried. "See you later Sophie bye Mrs. Lewis."

Sophie called him back as if sensing something was wrong. "This is for you," and handed him a daisy chain her mother helped her to make. "Wear this and it will protect you wherever you are," she said smiling and placed it over his head and gave him a big hug.

"Mind what I tell you now, no more spending or your parents will get to hear about it."

"Yes Mrs. Lewis," he shouted back and was out the door wearing the daisy chain around his neck. He fingered the flowers;

sadness crept over his face. He whispered to himself, "I'm going to miss you Sophie, but it won't be forever, when I am rich, I'll come back and buy you all the books you'll ever wish to read and a necklace, a real pearl necklace."

Chapter Sixteen

A few of Colin's gang were asking where he got his money, word was getting around, and he felt vulnerable. He knew to spend any more locally was risky. The robbery was still undiscovered; the daft old woman hadn't yet realised, but it would only be a matter of time and he needed to be gone before the news broke.

His dreams were now distant memories. The only part he remembered was the promise of the big house and the cars and longed to grow up and take possession of his destiny. His mind dismissed the parts that didn't suit his purpose and retained only what was relevant to his rationale and discarded the rest. In his mind he was already on his way to riches, he had over £5,000 and that was just the start.

By the following week, Colin was ready. He packed his clothes and hid the case under the bed telling his brothers to say nothing, intending to go to London by train early the following morning. He would be there before anyone realised he was missing, by then it would be too late and wrote a note telling his parents he would be away for the next year or so and not to come looking for him.

The early train to London left at 7.00 a.m. arriving in Paddington at 10.30 a.m. Colin was up at dawn that morning and walked to the station in Treorchy. Twenty minutes later the train arrived getting him into Cardiff at 6.30 a.m. with time to spare to catch the connection to London.

Where he would go from Paddington hadn't crossed his mind, excitement, apprehension and melancholy about leaving filled his mind. He had £2,000; the rest of the money he had safely hidden for when he returned, but as the train pulled out of the station, returning was the last thing on his mind. The journey was uneventful, Colin remaining inconspicuous wherever possible; the only person he spoke to was the guard on the train shunning all other contact.

He walked off the platform feeling lonely, scared, thinking that perhaps he'd been too hasty. The surroundings were strange, blank faces passed with no good mornings and felt very much alone. Where he came from everyone knew everyone else but here things were different, movement, animation, noise was there but something was missing, friendliness, warmth. Colin shuddered; his subconscious had picked up the difference and he walked on aimlessly. He turned to look at a notice board and caught the attention of a nearby police officer.

"Are you lost? I've been watching you for the last few minutes. Where are you going?" he stated in a kindly voice.

Colin was taken back he hadn't expected the police officer to speak to him. "No! Not lost," he blustered trying to hide his panic thinking should he run. "Waiting for my aunt," he quickly retorted. "She must be waiting outside the station, must go."

"Go careful. London is a big place. If she's not there come back and I'll see what I can do to help you find her," he said kind-heartedly.

Colin walked quickly in the direction of the exit not looking back but feeling the police officer's eyes were on him as he turned the corner. The weather was overcast, cloudy, rain in the air. He needed to find shelter and starting to panic. He was little more than a child pretending to be a man, lost in a big unfamiliar world.

He walked from one street into another until he stopped at a coffee shop and purchased sandwiches and a hot drink. The afternoon turned into evening; he needed to find a place to stay before it went dark. Insecurity and uncertainty set in, Colin was frightened.

He left the coffee shop, knew he could not just book into a hotel, questions would be asked about him being by himself. He was tall for his age but could not risk the staff calling the police and was at a loss, his apprehension rose as the minutes ticked. He noticed a small hotel just off the main road, took a deep breath, boldly walked in, and stood next to the counter.

A young lady was seated the other side and looked up. "Can I help you young man," she said politely.

Colin smiled disarmingly at her giving off an air of confidence he didn't feel. "I don't think so. No thank you, I'm waiting for my uncle," he lied. "He said to meet here. We are to stay in this hotel for a few days. A special treat because I've done well in my exams at school. He's to take me round London and to a show."

"My you're a lucky one. Has he booked in yet?" the receptionist inquired.

Colin hesitated. "I'm not sure, I imagine so. Phillips is his name." He spoke the first name that came into his head.

The receptionist looked at her reservation book. "There's a Philipton, family of four. It can't be them."

Colin feigned surprise. "No, that's not it. This is definitely the hotel, my uncle has stayed here before many times, that's how I know it's the right one."

The receptionist looked puzzled. "I'm sorry there's no booking under that name."

Colin stood and stared at the receptionist surprised. "That's strange, are you sure," his face blank. "What do I do now?"

"He'll book in when he arrives."

Colin's face beamed. "Yes, that's it. I'll wait."

"Is there any way you can contact him, save waiting," the receptionist said trying to be helpful. "There a phone over there, do you know his number?"

"Yes I have it here?" Colin lied. "I can't see the phone."

The receptionist pointed. "It's over there on the wall, help yourself. I hope everything is all right lucky we are not full."

Colin walked over, picked up the phone, and pretended to dial a number and speak. He waited a good five minutes and walked confidently back to the receptionist and stated casually. "He's still at work, can't make it for at least two hours, my fault I had the time wrong. He told me to ask if I could wait in reception. I could book in I suppose, save hanging around. All the rooms could be gone before my uncle is able to get here."

She grinned at him. "Over excited, hey?" Then her face became serious. "We demand payment in advance I must follow the rules, sorry."

Colin was light hearted. "That's all right I have my own money my uncle can give it back to me later." He booked for one night handing over the correct money for the room displayed on the tariff board attached to the wall above the receptionist's head. He filled in the guest book in the name of Phillips and she gave him the key to a twin bedded room. Colin's cool nerve and quick thinking held the sway. He had bluffed it out with the receptionist and could keep up the pretext for a few days if careful, in that time he would look for something a little more permanent and felt ready to take on the world, his confidence back.

The room had two single beds standing next to each other with a bedside cabinet in between, a large wardrobe by the door, a table with a lamp with one chair next to it. To the left of the table was a large window, each side of which hung long coloured curtains. The window looked out over the road; he could see the hustle and bustle of pedestrians and cars below and for the first time that day felt safe.

He opened the window and to the left a drainpipe ran from the roof to the floor. He leaned out of the open window and grabbed the pipe and tried to move it with his hand, it was solid. Good he thought, my escape if I need it.

He leaned back on the bed nearest the window and felt pleased with himself but lonely. His parents would have missed him by now he thought and the police called. He knew his parents would be worried and felt melancholic as his conscience pricked over what they were feeling, especially Sophie.

Remorse was starting to manifest itself, nibbling Colin's conscience but as time went on the nibble turning into a bite as if a crocodile was snapping at his legs. He could not move; the bed held him frozen in ice as the crocodile came ever closer.

The palms of his hands and face were sweating; fear filled his mind, a blind fear, with nowhere to run. "What have I done? What have I done?" He repeated to himself wiping his face in the bedclothes. Tears formed in the corners of his eyes, a rush of tiredness came over him, and he fell asleep.

Colin slept until early the next morning; the sound of the refuse cart outside the window woke him. It was still dark but he felt refreshed, the crocodile gone. He still had his clothes on from the day before and realised he could do with a bath. Half an hour later, after washing and changing his clothes he felt and looked much better. I need to buy a razorblade to shave, I'm a man now he convinced himself but in reality, his face still had the look of a child, it would be a year or so yet before he need use a razor.

He left his room, strolled down the stairs to the reception desk, and found a different person on duty sitting at the desk.

"Where is the other lady?" he politely asked.

The receptionist was busy and looked up from her work. "Stacy you mean?"

"Yes Stacy," he mumbled.

"She doesn't start for another hour yet, can I help?"

"Yes, my uncle Mr. Phillips sent me down to pay for the room for another three days."

"I can do that for you if you like."

"Yes if you would please." Colin handed over the money for the next three nights and started to walk away when she called him back. He froze and was on the verge of running through the door when she stated he must wait for a receipt.

"Of course, sorry, make it out to Mr. Phillips please."

"All right."

He turned, took the receipt off the counter, and went straight to his room walking calmly not once looking back.

The rush hour traffic was in full swing as he emerged from his room again and casually walked past the receptionist who was the same one as yesterday.

He smiled pleasingly. "Good morning, my uncle left early and said he would sort out the room before he left. I'm to meet up with him later."

She smiled. "Everything sorted then?"

"Yes, everything is sorted."

"Hold on a minute, I'll check for you, I've only just started work."

She looked in the registration book and Colin knew the answer before she replied.

"Yes, he paid this morning for three extra nights. My, you're a lucky one. Wish I had an uncle like that. Enjoy your time in London."

"Yes I will now my uncle has arrived," and walked out laughing to himself at how stupid some people can be, but his bravado was little more than skin deep as he made his way out into the busy street the apprehension back.

Chapter Seventeen

At the end of the first evening, everyone was worried. George looked for Colin in all the usual places but could find him nowhere. Sophie called over to see Colin's parents; her father had told her they had not seen him all day.

"Where is Colin?" Sophie enquired of his mother.

"Your guess is as good as mine, we have called the police but they'll do nothing for twenty four hours so we just wait and hope he turns up," she replied in a down beat voice. "He left a note to say he was running away but not where."

Sophie felt sad. She knew Colin was going but said nothing. She would protect her friend at all costs and left to go back to her house.

A few minutes later Henry and Bill entered the room; they had also been looking for him.

"No luck in the usual places, but one of the lads in the pub said they saw him at the railway station waiting for a train to Cardiff this morning," said Henry.

"Why don't we go and find out the person who was on duty at the station and ask if he saw him," suggested Bill as George turned up.

"That's a good idea Bill," said Henry and George together and off the three went to the train station at Treorchy. Thirty minutes later, they were at the station talking to the stationmaster.

"I was not on this morning but old Paul over there has been here all day, he might know something... Paul," he shouted, "come over here a moment will you."

He walked smartly over to the stationmaster nodding his head at the three people before him.

"George here wants to know if you've seen his boy this morning." The stationmaster enquired in his best voice.

"What's he look like?" he asked inquiringly. We get loads of people through this station."

"Nothing special just an ordinary boy," George answered.

"There was one lad come to think of it, alone, unusual that time of the morning," and Paul went on to describe him and there was no doubt it was Colin. "A ticket to London he asked for, one way, again unusual. Paddington."

"To where?" George shouted in surprise.

"A single to Paddington."

The three men looked at each other their faces said it all. "He's run away to London, that's what he's done, gone, gone to London." George spluttered.

"But where would he get that type of money?" said Bill, surprised.

"He's fried his own chips now without the bacon," Henry stated, not really knowing what he was trying to say, but felt he needed to say something.

"I'm going to the police station to report he has run away to London and ask them to make enquiries... goodness knows what danger he could be in," said a worried looking George.

On the way home, the subdued and preoccupied group stopped at the Stag Hotel Treorchy for a few pints. All were deeply worried, especially George. London was an alien place to all of them. Two of them had never been outside Wales. Bill had once, to Coventry to see his dying cousin.

"Are we off to London then George," Henry said.

"London is a big place where do we start looking?" enquired Bill.

"The local hotels, guest houses around the station for a start," answered Henry. "He wouldn't have strayed far from the station. In all probability he would be sleeping rough, hotels cost money."

"Nothing can be done tonight. But… but London, I'm not sure?" George said puffing his pipe. "Let's have another pint," and trotted off to the bar with three empty glasses. A few minutes later he returned with the glasses filled and placed them on the table. "The Barman said there are six more cases of smallpox in Gelli all in the same street."

"God! Is there no end to this disease it's been with us for years on and off," stated Henry.

"One thing George at least your boy is out of it in London," Bill said half laughing.

"I'd rather him be here, smallpox or no smallpox," George answered.

The whole valley was worried, the fear back; everyone thought they had seen the last of it. Now, six new cases just a few miles away made everyone jumpy, the whole pub seemed to talk in whispers as if by talking in a low voice the disease would somehow pass them over.

A large coal fire burned brightly in the grate at the far corner of the room. It was rumoured if a large fire was kept burning the heat from the coals would stop the spread of the disease. They all knew that it was nonsense but when people are desperate, they will believe anything, no matter how farfetched.

The walk home that night to Cwmparc was a lonely and anxious one. George worried about his wayward son and like the rest of them about the smallpox epidemic, which was sweeping the valley yet again. They all thought the disease had petered out but this new outbreak was as bad as ever and there seemed no end to it. George also dreaded telling his wife, he did not feel shame but sadness, a sense of failure on his part that his son had run away and was now somewhere in London.

There had not been an argument, that's what made it even harder to swallow. Colin had just gone for no apparent reason, this played on his mind, where had he gone wrong. Colin was the eldest and used to spend a lot of time helping his father in the garden as a young child but as he grew up and got older these things meant less and less to him. George knew he was a troublemaker but always gave him the benefit of the doubt, or made some excuse when he behaved badly, always protecting Colin. He regretted not being stronger with the lad in the past, and blamed himself.

"What's to be done about the boy George?" Bill remarked after they had been walking for a few minutes.

"Nothing for the time being. I'll see what the wife says."

"He might well be back in a few days, he can't have that much money and when that goes he'll come running back tail between his legs," laughed Henry. "You know how it is."

"We'll see… hope your right," George answered abstractedly, feeling unsure.

His wife was out of the chair the minute she heard the key in the door and met him in the small passage leading to the back of the house. He shook his head. "London."

"London?" she repeated. "What do you mean?"

"What I say, the boy has gone to London, run away. How clear do you want me to be," he said irritably.

There was silence for a few moments allowing her husband's words to sink in. "What are we going to do?"

"Nothing, nothing we can do, unless you have a magic wand? We could be looking in London for the next twelve months and not find him. I've informed the local police and they will notify the police in London to be on the lookout for him."

"Why would he do this to us? I know he is still upset with losing my mother but to run away…"

"He has always been wayward; we should have been harder on him."

"I just want him back, I want him here with me," she cried in distress.

"Let's leave it to the police for a few days and see if they are able to find him and then decide what's to be done. Have you heard about the new outbreak of smallpox?"

"No, the last were the two cases in Porth but that was a while ago."

"No, there are six new cases in Gelli. Just down the road from here."

"Are you sure George?"

"Of course I'm sure; it's all the talk in the Stag. Why do you keep asking if I am sure all the time, I'm sure," George was irritated and taking it out on his wife.

This was far too close for comfort; the disease had reared its head again. Gelli was a few miles down the road, to make the jump from there to Cwmparc, especially, with the number of people who walked over the mountain road sent a shiver through the both of them.

"At least Colin is out of it," George half-laughed trying to lighten the atmosphere feeling guilty over his sharpness.

His wife was not amused. "Small mercies, I want him here. I'm keeping the other kids indoors and away from school until we know more."

A few days passed, still there was no news. They all felt helpless, George was toying with the idea of going to London to look for Colin when there was a knock at the door. He ran and opened the door to find a police officer standing there and he froze fearing the worse. His wife stood behind him with her hand on his shoulder. Her hand shook.

"Yes officer," George faltered.

"We have had sighting of the boy in Paddington Station; one of the policemen on duty asked him where he was going and said he was waiting for his aunty. He was on the platform for a long time and that is what attracted him to the officer in the first place. Nevertheless, he seemed confident when spoken to, seemed to know where he was going, the officer thought no more of it until he received the enquiry from ourselves. We are searching around

Paddington now as I speak, making enquires in all the local hotels. Do you know how much money he had with him?"

"No not exactly, it can't have been a lot. Where would he have got it from?"

"He may be sleeping on the streets." He noticed the concern in their eyes and was sorry he mentioned this last remark. "Don't worry we'll find him for you," he added, trying to give them hope.

"Would you like a cup of tea officer?" Colin's mother politely asked.

"No thank you must be getting back. When we have further news we'll let you know."

They closed the door both wondering if they would ever see their eldest son again but too afraid to voice these thoughts aloud. The other two children came running in from the back yard to see if it was Colin at the door but found their parents seated each side of the fire staring into the glowing coals.

"When is he coming home, mam?" the elder child asked.

"I don't know love. He's in London and that's all…" her voice faltered.

"Can we go and visit him?" the other asked.

This brought a smile to both their faces and George touched his wife's face with his hand as much to reassure himself as her. The children turned, not waiting for a reply and ran back into the garden oblivious to the worry their parents felt or the uncertainty surrounding their eldest brother.

A few more days passed and there was no further news when Henry came rushing through the door.

"You're in a hurry," George remarked. "What's the rush?"

"It's Sophie, she's not very well. She got up this morning, complained of a headache, not well at all," Henry quickly explained.

"It could be she's caught a cold in the head, give her some honey and lemon and in a few days she will be all right, what about the boy?" George advised calmly trying to alleviate Henry's concern.

"The lad has been at my mother's in Porthcawl these last few weeks, it's Sophie I'm concerned about. Come and take a look George."

They both crossed the street. Sophie was laying on the settee in the front parlour with a blanket over her a hot drink in her hand. As they entered she sat up but it was obvious she was in pain but smiled at them both, despite her discomfort.

"What's wrong, Sophie," George said feeling her head with his hand. It felt hot and clammy. She was definitely running a temperature.

"I'm all right," her voice sounded weak. "Is Colin back yet?"

"He's in London." George answered and immediately knew he said the wrong thing.

Her face went pale, her eyes watery, she lay back on her pillow. "I wish he was here now."

"Come on now, close your eyes and rest there's a good girl," said Henry taking the cup from her hand and pulling the clothes over her tucking them in around her shoulders and neck. They went into the other room and Henry could see the look of concern on George's face even though he was trying to play it down.

"Call the doctor," George stated.

"I'll go now," answered Henry.

"Tell him to be here as soon as possible even if you have to carry him."

Henry's eyes opened wide and took a breath. "What is it George? It's a cold, you said earlier, a cold in the head, that's what you said," he mumbled.

"Has she complained of a backache or been sick." George enquired trying to speak as casually as possible.

"No! Why do you ask?"

"No reason," George lied. "The doctor will know what to do."

"Yes, yes, the doctor, he'll know, there's a lot of flu about this time of year." Henry muttered more to himself than to George.

"I'll tell you what, you stay here with Sophie and I'll go and get the doctor," said George. As he spoke, Sophie shouted from the other room, complaining her back was hurting and had just been sick.

George's face went ashen and turned away from Henry. He walked out of the house and immediately outside the door ran to find the doctor. He knew the symptoms.

The doctor was ready in a few minutes, half pulled, half dragged by George. When they arrived back at the house Sophie was asleep.

The doctor washed his hands and spoke to the three of them. "If this is smallpox we will have to quarantine the whole house including you George, new rules. It may not come to that," he said trying to appease his first remark.

They nodded in agreement; the doctor went into the parlour to examine Sophie. He placed a mask over his face, gloves on his hands and entered closing the door behind him. The doctor was there for over half an hour and returned to the other room looking grave. Removed his facemask and gloves and threw them into the fire.

No one spoke; all watching the flames render the mask and gloves to ash waiting for the doctor to speak. He sat in a chair next to the table, and for a few moments, there was silence. "I have bad news. Sophie has smallpox."

This is what they were all expecting but these seven words now confirmed the worse.

"Will she die doctor?" Henry asked gravely his face white.

"It's early days yet, we'll do all we can; the strain has been identified. I must report the situation and ask you to stay in the house, which includes you as well, George. I need to know where Sophie has been and with whom she has come into contact over the last few days and weeks. It will be out of my hands when I report to the authorities and they may take Sophie into hospital. If they feel the risk of the disease spreading is too great may well leave her here, new guidelines, the house will be under quarantine. I'm sorry but that's how it is."

There was no protest from any of them, they knew what this disease was capable of and realised the gravity of the situation. The doctor got up to go but before he left gave instructions to burn all clothes that had come into contact with Sophie as well as any soft toys, thoroughly wash, boil and scrub their clothes and to wash all the furnishings and floors with hot soapy water.

Sophie was asleep quietly on the settee in the front parlour. The three adults had a light meal and then started cleaning, starting upstairs. George and Henry pulled all the curtains down and stripped the beds taking them down the stairs to be soaked in the large aluminium tub in the back yard already filled with hot soapy water. They washed them and placed them on the outside clothesline to dry.

They went back to wash the furniture and to remove the bed mattress when there was a knock at the door. Anne answered it before the other two came down the stairs. Standing at the door were two people, behind them two policemen. The doctors entered the house, and when inside placed a facemask over their mouth and nose, the two policemen remained outside. One of them would stand guard at the front, the other at the back of the house.

"This house is now under quarantine until further notice," one of the doctors stated in a matter of fact way. No one spoke but all nodded in agreement they understood.

"We've started to wash and remove all the curtains and blankets and…" stuttered Henry.

"All mattresses, blankets are to be taken and destroyed immediately, we have ordered all new, place all the blankets and the mattresses in the bags provided and leave outside the door. We will have them taken away and burned. We have disinfectant in a drum outside the door, all walls and furniture must be washed with it," the other doctor instructed with urgency.

"When will the ambulance arrive to take Sophie to hospital?" Henry asked. Everything was happening too fast.

"It won't, new policy… the infection will be dealt with here, on site, no one is to leave the house until further notice." One of the doctors went to the door and opened it to return with a large drum of disinfectant. "Here! Start upstairs, everything must be cleaned; and redone daily." There was no argument, George and Henry just took the disinfectant and started the task knowing that Sophie's life, and their lives depended on stopping this disease from spreading.

Sophie was now awake and coughing badly, the two doctors in attendance. They removed all her clothes, placed them in plastic bags as well as the blankets, and examined her. It was obvious she was upset; the doctors did their best to try to reassure her that everything would be all right and not to worry. She heard a van pull up outside the door and asked if she was going into hospital. The doctor informed her that she was staying at home and this made her feel better cheering her a little.

They heard a knock at the door and the doctor informed Sophie that her new bed had arrived. The van was delivering new blankets and mattresses; the old ones were in bags outside the door. The deliverymen placed the new ones against the outside wall waiting for the doctors to announce the house thoroughly disinfected before they carried them inside.

The mattress had a tent like attachment where the doctors hung transparent curtains forming a self-contained unit. One side of the unit had a round hole and they placed a tube into the unit attaching it to an oxygen supply on the floor below the bed.

This frightened Sophie at first but the doctors displayed great care and explained that it was to protect her from getting any worse, and how lucky she was to have her own tent all to herself.

Within a few hours, the tasks were completed and they sat down to a well-earned cup of tea. The doctors would sleep on portable beds they brought with them packing them away each morning.

“There is nothing more to do but wait,” one of the doctors stated.

Henry got up and went into the front parlour and when he saw Sophie in the tent tears ran down his face. He so much wanted to hold her, kiss her, touch her, but he knew that was impossible. One of the doctors followed behind, waiting to stop him should he try to hold Sophie in his arms.

Henry stared at her young face, watched her body move up and down ever so slightly as she breathed. He had never been much of a religious man, never saw the need to sing and shout in church but now he felt a burning desire to pray.

“Leave me doctor,” he said. “I know the score, leave me now please. I want to be alone with my baby.”

The doctor was unsure at first, eventually he left the room and closed the door and walked into the other room. The other doctor got up but the first gestured him back into his seat. “They need to be alone for a while.” Anne got up to join her husband but thought better of it.

Henry looked upon Sophie, his only girl, thank God he thought the boy is staying at my mother’s house. She looked so young, helpless, he knelt by her bed and prayed, he prayed that she would get better and offered himself in her place. He opened his eyes and Sophie was looking at him smiling through her tent. He smiled back quickly wiping the tears away not for her to see but she had noticed.

“Am I going to die daddy?” she asked in a way only a child can.

This took him by surprise and for a brief moment stunned him. “Of course not sweet, what makes you say that?”

“I’ve got the smallpox, they say it kills you. I’m not afraid daddy honest. Colin says we all have a special angel looking after us.”

Henry’s eyes filled up. “Yes sweet, a special, special one as far as you are concerned.”

She started to cough and he could see a slight frothing at the mouth but she just wiped it away with her hand. "Can Colin visit me? I miss him so much."

"I know you do. When you are better my sweet."

"Daddy I love you and mammy and Colin and my baby brother," she stated coughing badly again. Her eyes closed and she drifted into a deep sleep.

Henry was distraught, he knew she was only at the start of the disease and things would get worse. He placed his hands together they were trembling uncontrollably. He held them together more to steady them and knelt by her bed and prayed in a way he had never prayed in his life before, imploring God to spare the life of his daughter.

"She's asleep now," he informed the rest of the group when he returned to the other room. The doctors informed them of what to expect over the next few days. George told them they were all well aware of the symptoms of the disease.

That night Sophie took a turn for the worse, she kept mumbling over and over "mammy, daddy, Colin. Where are you?" She then lapsed into sleep and in her troubled sleep cried out again the same words.

Her cough was violent; she was in a lot of pain. The doctors administered an injection; she fell silent her breathing strong. This gave the doctors hope she would pull through but as the night progressed her breathing became laboured and heavy. It was obvious she was fighting for her life.

The morning broke. Sophie's body ran with sweat, the toll of the night etched heavily on her young angelic face. She seemed to age over night, her chest moved up and down as she gulped the air. The doctors worked constantly trying to keep her cool but the delirium was deep inside and held her with vice like brutality.

As the morning progressed, the fever abated somewhat but the night's labours had taken its toll and had weakened her severely. The sheets were changed, bagged, and replaced;

furnishings wiped down with disinfectant, the floors rescrubbed with extra attention to Sophie's room.

The day passed slowly, very slowly; all were weary wondering what the next night would bring. Sophie oscillated between delirium and consciousness getting weaker with every passing minute. Neighbours left food at the door and George brought it into the house, their isolation total. The doctors had a phone, their sole contact to the outside world. George's wife was in communication several times a day, friends came on the phone with encouraging messages still time pressed heavily on them all.

Sophie had a reasonably restful night the delirium still in her. She kept asking where Colin was, why he hadn't visited. "Colin I've read that book you left," she cried. "Why don't you read to me, Colin, Colin," Sophie would whimper in her sleep. Henry, conscious of her every breath, sat in a chair with his wife sitting next to him unable to sleep.

The doctors were constantly attending their patient, relaying messages to the outside of her progress, and taking advice. Sophie seemed to be over the worse but had lost a lot of weight and was in a very weak state. There was optimism, hope in the air for the first time in several days.

The following day saw further improvements consolidating the earlier optimism; she looked to be beating it. The disease had not spread to anyone else in the house and there had been no further reported cases to date in the community. It was still early days but it seemed to be an isolated case; they took every precaution and were to remain in isolation until further notice.

Things were not to last, optimism collapsed, that night Sophie fell into a deep coma, early morning she awoke to heavy vomiting and delirium. As the day broke and the darkness receded, Sophie took her last breath, Colin's name on her lips. The birds outside in the garden sang as morning broke, perhaps, even feeding on the caterpillars at the top of the garden. The air was crisp; the day about to start, but Sophie would not be a part of this day or any day in the future. Sophie was dead, another statistic of smallpox. A young life finished before it had really started.

All was silent save the birds, when death enters a house voices dim. Throats dry, eyes dampen; faces turn soggy. Henry, Anne and George left the death room and went into the kitchen. No one spoke; words irrelevant, redundant, feelings charged to breaking point.

They sat around the fire, faces blank sheets of paper; the writing would come later with the realisation that Sophie was dead, would start to scratch across the blank faces, the mind catching up with the reality. Anne was the first to make a sound, a deep gurgling sound from the back of her throat rising into an agonised roar. "Why? Why my Sophie? Why my Sophie… dear God, why"? Tears burst forth filling her face.

Henry could be of little comfort to his wife, the grief in him rose, choking hope and ran to the sink and was violently sick. The anguish of living through the last few days came pouring out of his mouth, tears streaked his cheeks. George followed him to the sink, stood behind and placed his hand on his back, but Henry, so wrapped up in his own grief, did not even notice him there.

The doctors went back into the room where Sophie lay and cleared the blankets away into bags for destruction, wrapped her body in plastic and placed it in a body bag. They zipped up the bag to her chin and stopped. The regulations stated the body be removed immediately and sealed in a coffin before burial or cremation to prevent the disease from spreading.

One of the doctors went into the other room and asked if they would like to see Sophie for the last time. "I'm sorry," the doctor stated. "In cases like this we must remove the body and seal it in a coffin as soon as possible."

Anne wiped her face and spoke first. "Yes of course… I, come Henry we'll go in together," she faltered.

They held each other's hand and walked along the narrow passage, a moment later they were standing over the body of their only daughter the body still and lifeless. Anne took a deep breath, strange how grief takes people; her first thought was to wonder what Sophie would have liked for breakfast. The thought lasted but a second and reality returned with virulent determination.

The pain, no, pain is not the word, worse than pain, worse than words; they remained silent, two desperate people just staring at the shell of their daughter.

"The pain is over my precious, I send you into God's hands," faltered Henry. "Look after her God, you have taken our most precious gift," he spoke loud.

Anne went to touch her daughter but Henry stopped her. "Come, let the doctors do what must be done," and they walked out of the room.

In what appeared no time, the ambulance arrived and Sophie was gone forever. The house was still under quarantine but a few days after they all underwent a stringent medical examination. The authorities were confident that it was an isolated case and lifted the restrictions and George returned to his own house.

Most of the village attended the funeral. It was heartbreaking to see such as small coffin in the back of the funeral car as it waited outside the house. The top of the coffin covered with white flowers with a card in the centre, which said one word but that one word read as a book, LOVE.

People lined the streets some openly crying as the cortege moved down the street. Anne stayed in the house, as was tradition. George and Bill were in the first car supporting Henry in his darkest hour.

"She was calling for Colin at the end Bill; over and over she was calling his name. I had hoped, you know George, they would marry one day." Henry said in a cracked voice.

"We all did," replied George. "We all did."

They laid Sophie to rest not far from Colin's grandparents; too young to die, yet, not allowed to live.

Chapter Eighteen

Colin was feeling rather pleased with himself over the way he secured a room for a few extra nights and intended to explore London over the next few days. He would worry about what to do next when the time came but for now would live life to the full.

He had another three nights in the hotel and felt confident he could bluff his way to staying another few days without much difficulty. He had money, lots of money; to him it represented the elixir of life. Colin hadn't used much of the £2,000 he had with him. The room was only a few pounds per night so even if he stayed there for a year he would not spend all his money and had another £3,000 hidden back in Wales.

The police, Colin reasoned, would be looking for him by now. Why did I leave the rest of the money in Wales he thought, but at the time it did not seem all that important he had plenty.

At first, walking the streets of London taking in the sights, the hustle and bustle of the traffic, frightened him but after a while got used to the constant movement and the never-ending noise and started to feel more at ease. It was all so strange; back home, he knew everyone, and they him, here it was different. The pace of life seemed so much faster, more urgent, impersonal.

He went into a coffee shop to order a cake and lemonade and sat by the front window. After waiting a while, he returned to the counter to ask how long it would be in coming and returned to his seat.

"Shouldn't you be at school?" the waitress enquired as she brought the order over.

"No, I have finished with school. I'm here to visit my sick aunt."

"Well you look to me as if you should still be there," she said walking off to serve someone else.

He speedily ate and drank his lemonade, paid the money and exited quickly.

The rest of the day Colin walked around London; the more he walked the more alone he felt. No one talked to him to ask how his parents were or what he was up to and was he well. No one cared, for the first time in his life, he felt lonely and lost. He had felt like this before many times but not to such an extent but his pride would not let him admit it even to himself.

His mind drifted to Sophie, and wished he were with her reading to her. He remembered the garden, his father, the happy times spent in helping him. Was it that bad he thought? He passed a bookshop stopped, looked in the window finally deciding to go in; he strolled over to the children's section, without thinking purchased three books for Sophie.

It was late afternoon and he thought it best to go back to his room, he was starting to get bored with his own company and London, but tried not to think about it too much, especially the future. He turned the corner to go into his road and walking towards him side by side were two policemen. He thought of turning and walking the other way, which was a sure way for him to draw attention to himself, so thought better of it.

He noticed an alleyway besides him and promptly turned into it and hid until the danger passed. He emerged a little while later, looked to see if the coast was clear and walked quickly to his hotel.

Someone had noticed his behaviour. Standing on the other side of the road leaning against a wall was a man in his middle thirties dressed in a suit, smoking a cigarette. His eyes followed the boy as he went into the alleyway and watched as he emerged and realised he was avoiding the police. His eyes followed as he went into the guesthouse a few doors down and grinned, "interesting, interesting..."

Colin stayed in the room the rest of the night reading the books he purchased for Sophie. There was also a Gideon's bible in one of the drawers and he started to read the first chapter Genesis. He had never read a bible before and wondered what his friends would make of it, his old friends. "I have no friends now," he muttered and felt depressed.

It was his second night in London, there was no one to fight, no one to care whether he lived, died or ate his meals and longed to be back home. He thought of his grandmother, dead but very much alive in his mind. He wondered where the next room she always talked about actually was and the strange happening with his grandfather. His parents' little house where he lived with his brothers, it made him feel warm, secure, wanted. What would Sophie be doing now?" he wondered and smiled.

His actions came back to him, he was a thief, a robber of old ladies; to go back would mean certain borstal or prison. He lay back on his bed and felt miserable but tomorrow would be another day, and perhaps, he would feel better.

The following morning he was up early, he needed food badly. At 7.30 a.m., he was sitting down to a full fried breakfast with a large mug of coffee in one of the many cafes that were dotted about the street. Breakfast eaten he was still hungry and ordered a toasted bacon sandwich and left eating it and idly walked the London streets not knowing where he was going. He finally ended up outside a museum but it was not yet 9 o'clock. He walked round the building and when he returned to the entrance, it was open.

Colin had never been to a museum before and was dumbstruck by all the paintings adorning the walls. One in particular caught his eye, a man on a large black horse holding a banner in one hand and a lance in the other pointing at a fire-breathing dragon. The man's armour seemed to shine off the picture. He sat on a bench in front of the painting and stared at it for a few minutes wondering who he was and how much he would like to be like him strong and fearless.

"He's Saint George the Dragon Slayer," a voice spoke shaking him out of his reverie.

Colin turned to the direction of the voice, startled; standing behind the bench was a smartly dressed man smiling at him.

"A dragon slayer you say," he said turning and looking directly at the man. "Must go," he said thinking it could be a plain-clothes police officer and stood up.

"Hold on a minute, why the rush? There are many things to see in this museum, I'm here often. I'll show you around. My name is Peter Camp. What are you called?"

He hesitated for a moment, "Colin."

The stranger smiled disarmingly. "Nice to meet you Colin," he said shaking his hand. "Come on! There are many things to see."

They spent all morning together in the museum looking at different paintings and artefacts, Colin not giving anything away. He said he was with his uncle who was at work but Peter suspected this to be a lie. He had watched the hotel since early morning waiting for Colin and followed him to the cafe and to the museum. The meeting was not accidental. He was the man who had watched him evading the two police officers the day before.

"I must be going shortly," Colin informed. "I'm expected back," he lied.

"Let me buy you a cup of coffee first," his companion affably suggested looking innocently at him.

He took Colin to a little pub around the corner from the museum. Colin was apprehensive at first because it was obvious he was under age but Peter assured him everything would be all right and not to worry. They both sat by the window overlooking the road and Peter ordered for him. The coffee turned out to be lemonade and a cheese sandwich. Peter had a beer and a salad sandwich. It all seemed quite harmless. Colin's apprehension disappeared thinking he had made a friend.

A few minutes later, a woman in her early thirties joined them; long hair cascaded down over her bare arms. Her face had firm pleasing features and was easily the most attractive woman in the pub. She smiled through straight teeth, her dark blue eyes looked deeply at Colin and he smiled at her in awe.

She rustled her tight dress covering her full model like figure revealing the top of her cleavage and sat next to Colin. He was totally captivated by her.

"You're a fine looking lad. Where are you from?" she asked showing her teeth as she smiled and winked at him. "Good looking too," touching his arm.

"From Wales Miss," he answered immediately feeling he had made two friends. "Call me Mary," she chuckled, turned to Peter and said under her breath so Colin wouldn't hear. "Whose bed is he going to warm. This one will fetch a good price."

"I'll expect you'll test him first."

"Maybe, they'll pay well for him," and noticed Colin listening.

"Quiet Mary or you'll pay for your own drinks," Peter laughed making Colin think they were whispering over who was to pay for the drinks but Mary's words were lost on Colin.

"Have you just arrived in London? I didn't get your name."

"C...Colin. I arrived two days ago, Miss." He stuttered, his face red with embarrassment.

"Just Mary," she laughed. "You're a raw one."

"We'll soon fix that won't we Colin," Peter laughed winking at Mary.

They spent a very pleasant hour in light conversation; Colin felt more at ease the longer he was in their company. It was now well into the afternoon and the bar was getting full. They were a mixed lot but all seemed friendly, fun to be with, life seemed to be taking a turn for the better with his newfound friends and he didn't feel so lonely. A few customers were worse for drink but

Colin was used to this back in his own town so it seemed quite normal.

As the afternoon wore on the pub got more boisterous. More women mingled with the men wearing clothes that would be quite shocking if worn in his village, but this was London, Colin thought, so it must be all right. The room went quiet suddenly and through the door entered two policemen who walked over to the bar to speak to the barman. A few in the room turned their faces away from the policemen; one woman went out through the back door before they noticed her. This brought reality back to Colin and turned his head towards Mary who jokingly pulled his head between her breasts. Colin was shocked, excited, mesmerised all at the same time. Mary just looked at him and laughed as if it was something she did every day.

The two policemen noticed Peter and walked over to the table, Colin thought they were going to talk to him and turned his face away but they ignored him and spoke directly to Peter.

Then one of the policemen turned to Colin. "What are you doing here?"

"He's my sister's boy, just called to give me a message officer," Mary said. She turned to Colin and said, "be on your way and tell your mother I'll be along in a few minutes," pushing him to his feet towards the door before he could open his mouth.

Colin got up immediately; kept his back turned and left not once looking back. He walked out the door, ran the whole way back to his hotel, and did not feel safe until in his room with the door firmly closed.

"What did you let the boy go for?" Peter snarled at Mary after the policemen had gone.

"He's going nowhere," she barked back. "I didn't want the police asking him any questions; with his accent it could have caused us a problem. They'd have taken him before we had the chance, that young man is mine."

"I know those two," he replied, talking of the policemen. "There'll be no problem with them. They're as bent as a butcher's hook."

"It always pays to be cautious," Mary responded, smiling angelically, "everyone is on the take one way or another."

Colin slept well that night and woke early, refreshed. He looked out of the window, it was still dark; he turned on the radio at the side of his bed as the pips sounded for 6 a.m. "This is early," he mumbled but did not feel so lonely remembering Peter and Mary from the day before and wondered if he would ever see them again. She had done him a great favour in the pub.

He had not eaten for over twelve hours and rubbed his stomach unconsciously. He needed to eat but realised to leave this early, especially alone again, would draw attention to himself from the receptionist. He noticed a sign on the door giving instructions of what procedure to follow should there be a fire and noticed the word back stairs; this gave him an idea.

Ten minutes later, he was out in the street unseen, and made for the nearest cafe. It was dark, the morning cold, far too cold to walk the streets. The loneliness wrapped itself around him and he thought of Sophie.

He left the cafe, walked quickly, and returned to the bookshop where he had purchased books for Sophie. There were all the usual morning papers stacked in neat rows and he slowly moved along the shelf reading the headlines. Daily papers didn't interest Colin and soon lost interest, and moved to the back of the shop.

For the last several years, he had read regularly. This made him feel good about himself and thought of all the times he had read to Sophie and felt sadness, wondering why he could not get Sophie out of his mind, it felt as if she was following him.

A voice behind him brought him back to reality. "What are you looking for young man so early?"

Colin turned. "Just looking for a book to read," he replied to the shop assistant.

"If you need any help let me know."

He just nodded his head and carried on scanning the rows of books with his eyes. A book on anatomy caught his attention and he picked it up to examine further. It was full of diagrams with arrows pointing to different parts of the body full of big words he did not understand. He had an overwhelming urge to know what each of these words meant.

The book was expensive but he felt he must own it and purchased it without further thought. He was on the point of leaving the shop and realised he needed a dictionary and turned and asked the assistant for help.

"You need a medical dictionary for that book she stated and directed him to the right section. He called into another shop to purchase a packet of biscuits, a bottle of lemonade and a bag of sweets and headed back to the hotel, being careful to take the back entrance; it was a little before 8.30 a.m.

Ten minutes later Peter arrived a bit hung over from the night before and waited in a cafe opposite the hotel for Colin to emerge for breakfast. He was not expecting him this early but felt it better to get there and wait. By 10 a.m., Colin had still not shown and Peter was getting impatient. He would not risk going to the hotel and asking after him, that would draw attention to himself, the last thing he wanted to happen. He ordered his fourth cup of coffee and read a newspaper he had brought with him, and as he waited, gave a sigh.

Another hour passed. Peter could not stay where he was he was drawing too much attention to himself; he was already getting funny looks from the staff. He had been in the cafe over three and a half hours so he left and walked over to the hotel. He loitered by the door for a few minutes then for the next hour walked up and down the street waiting for Colin to emerge. By midday, he felt totally dejected. The prize was too valuable to give up easily and decided he would place a watch on the hotel until he knew one way or the other if Colin was still there. He went back to the pub and enlisted one of his cronies to keep a watch on the hotel.

"He must be there," Peter said in frustration to Mary.

"He's by himself, perhaps he's too afraid to go out after the scare he had yesterday with the two policemen. Of course he's still… where else can he go? Eventually he'll show, have faith Peter."

"He must come out sometime, when he does this time there'll be no escape," he said. Mary grinned in response.

Colin was oblivious to his popularity. He was absorbed in the book on anatomy studying every detail, dictionary open on the bed. The biscuits and sweets still unopened where he left them on the chair, the bottle of lemonade half drunk resting by the side of the bed.

It was nearly 2 in the afternoon and Colin noticed the biscuits on the chair and realised he felt hungry. He reached over opened the top of the packet took a few biscuits ate them and resumed his reading after a few swigs of lemonade.

The room was getting dark, he had been there all day, and it dawned on him he would need either to move out or book the room for longer. He knew the hotel staff was getting suspicious because a maid asked yesterday why there was not more luggage in the room. To stay longer risked discovery and decided it would be best to leave, tightness gripped his stomach. He still had one night left, almost a full pack of biscuits and a bag of sweets and went back to his anatomy book.

Peter had one of his cronies watch the hotel for the rest of the day but Colin stayed in the room. He was thinking of going out early evening but decided against it at the last minute. He ate the biscuits, made himself a cup of tea from the facilities available in the room, and lay on the bed. He drifted off to sleep and it was gone 10 in the evening before he woke to a dark room. It disoriented him for a few moments before he became fully conscious.

Apprehension was rising. He lay on the bed listening to the traffic below his window. The room had to be vacated at noon the following day and, with nowhere to go, realised it had been providential to get this far and would be lucky to pull the same stunt again at another hotel. However, he had little choice if he was to avoid sleeping on the streets.

He slept badly that night and decided to stay in the room until it was time to vacate around midday. Just before the allotted time he left the room. As he walked through the foyer carrying his case, he told the receptionist his uncle had booked out early before she started work and thanked her for all her help.

He turned left outside the hotel and carried on walking not knowing where he would end up and felt very much alone. After walking for about an hour, he called into a nearby shop and bought a few sandwiches and a bottle of lemonade. Walking on a bit further he noticed a small park with a seat just inside the entrance, went over, and sat on it to eat his sandwiches. He ate slowly and was just about to get up when he saw Peter walking towards him.

"Fancy meeting you here," Peter feigned surprise. "Where are you going?"

Colin's heart jumped, happy to see Peter. "Just left my hotel… and…"

Peter put his hand up to stop him speaking further. "Why don't you stay with Mary for a few days, she has a spare bedroom if you haven't already booked another hotel," he said picking up the case, already, in his mind it was a fait accompli irrespective of Colin's answer.

Colin felt hesitation creep over him but also a cheerfulness he had somewhere to stay.

"I can pay," he mumbled trying to regain his equilibrium.

"Of course you'll pay," Peter said, smiling, Colin not catching the innuendo.

They walked for nearly forty minutes and Colin was totally lost, they were moving from one street into another, up one alley and down the next until they arrived at a block of flats. The main entrance door was open, they walked up a flight of stairs, turned left at the top, and Peter stopped and knocked on a door even though he had a key.

A few moments later, the door opened and standing there smiling at them both was Mary in her dressing gown.

"He needs somewhere to stay and I thought he could stay with you," Peter said looking at her grinning.

Mary's face beamed with delight. "Glad to have you. Come in, come in Colin," she replied moving aside to allow them both to enter.

"I'll pay the going rate," Colin mumbled as he entered.

"I won't stay long, I have some business to conclude across town and later I'll go home," Peter stated.

"That's alright, Colin and I will get along just great," she answered. "You go and we'll see you whenever, Colin will be fine."

"I thought you lived together," enquired Colin.

"Live together? No, he has his own place, besides, I can't be having men under my feet all day." Mary laughed.

Peter departed leaving the two of them to get acquainted. The flat was immaculate and tastefully decorated, obsessively clean. Across one wall was a large bookcase full of books. This surprised Colin. Mary didn't seem the type to read. The front door of the flat opened into the main sitting room, which was expensively furnished. Thick curtains draped the windows and a large chandelier hung in the centre of the room suspended from the high ceiling. To Colin's mind, this was living; the way life should be lived.

The furnishings matched the curtains; the whole room conveyed a sense of opulence. There was style here, more style than he had ever seen in his life and felt out of place but did his best to look natural. At the other end of the room were large double doors that opened into a dining area. The table in the centre was the best table Colin had ever seen with ten matching chairs arrayed around it. The surface gleamed, reflecting the ornate light above onto the polished wood surface. Each side of the dining table stood two matching sideboards in the same highly polished wood as the table. On the top of each was a five holder candelabra complete with candles. There were paintings on two of the walls, one depicting a hunting scene the other a rose bush full of white flowers.

Off the dining room was the kitchen with matching cupboards covering three walls, a large cooking hob and hood covering half the other wall with a large upright fridge next to it. The room was bright with little lights under each unit shining onto the granite work surface.

There were two bedrooms, one with a large four-poster bed draped with silk, the walls matching the colour, giving the room a warm feminine feel. Off to the side of the room was a bathroom with a sunken bath in the centre mirrors all round the walls giving a sense of space. The other bedroom also had a double bed and a bathroom but not decorated on the same grand scale as the first but a lot better than Colin had seen anywhere back home.

"This will be your room," Mary stated. "Make yourself at home it's not as grand as mine but comfortable, it's all yours, enjoy."

"It'll do fine," Colin replied and meant it. He thought this is the life. The room was considerably better than the hotel room he vacated earlier in the day. He felt adult and important as he surveyed the room.

"I'll leave you now to settle in, please feel free to help yourself to anything you fancy in the kitchen or if you wish you can stay in your room and rest. I'll be taking a bath." With that, she went into her bedroom and closed the door.

Colin felt contented, fetched his case into his bedroom and closed the door, kicked off his shoes and jumped on the bed, in no time he fell asleep. There was a knock on the door and a voice shouted asking if he intended to stay there all evening. "You've been asleep nearly two hours."

"Out in a few minutes," he shouted back.

The following day Mary went out early telling him she would not be back until the evening. Colin didn't mind and spent the morning studying his anatomy book. At lunchtime helped himself to food from the fridge and spent the rest of the afternoon looking over the many books neatly arranged on the shelves. He went to open the door of Mary's bedroom but found it locked. He felt slightly guilty for trying the door but did not dwell on it and went back to his reading.

It was late afternoon and Colin thought he would go out for a walk but found the front door to the flat also locked. This startled him at first but then thought better of it. Mary must have a reason for locking the doors he thought, what else could she have done. At 7 p.m. Mary returned as fresh as when she left in the morning. She asked him if he enjoyed his day and he was going to mention the locked door but decided against it. Why spoil such a good thing he thought not feeling in any way threatened.

Mary unlocked the bedroom door went in leaving the door open, Colin was sitting adjacent to the door and could see her reflection in the mirror. He looked away but his eyes drifted back and watched her remove her dress and stockings. He could feel himself blushing, getting hot, but could not look away. Her sensual, white smooth skin mesmerised him.

She removed her bra and panties and he could see the back of her body in the mirror and felt the heat rising in him. He walked away from the spot and turned away secretly wishing he could see the front of her body but went into the kitchen and washed his face in cold water.

Mary knew exactly what she was doing; she left the door open deliberately knowing Colin could see her as she removed her clothes. By his demeanour it was obvious Colin was a virgin, she would take him to her bed when ready as sport, train him in the art of eroticism, the thought making her tingle.

The sensuality of the moment stirred her, she looked into her mirror and fondled her breasts, laughed at her excitement and returned to the other room wearing an over gown wrapped tightly around her naked body and found Colin in the kitchen. She could see he had washed his hands and had adjusted the front of his trousers before he wiped them; his dripping hands left a wet mark by his fly. This is going to be fun Mary thought and smirked.

That night she discussed the books she had read and Colin realised she was highly intelligent and felt inferior. She knew so much he thought and resolved to read all he could to impress her wherever possible.

Mary kept the dressing gown on all evening and Colin wondered if she had any clothes on underneath. On a few occasions, she moved her legs revealing a flash of white limb. On one occasion when she crossed her legs, Colin could almost see to the top of her thigh the excitement moved him to distraction. She was playing games with him but he was too naïve to realise.

Mary left early the following morning and again locked the door. Colin didn't mind, he would spend the day reading, this went on for a number of days the front door always locked when she left.

Peter had not been near the place and Colin wondered when he would see him again. This did not concern him too much; Mary was now his world and was totally infatuated, under her spell. On some days, they went out together, once to the cinema, many times to restaurants.

She bought him new clothes; when he protested she laughed and said it was because she liked him. This boosted his confidence, spurred him on to read even more to try to impress her with his knowledge as the weeks went by. He was a bird trapped in a gilded cage but didn't know it, her clockwork toy to wind.

Peter did call some weekends and asked Mary if Colin was ready. "In a week or two," she replied.

Colin heard the remark. "In a week or two for what?" he enquired.

"Nothing, nothing, he's talking about something else," Mary replied, staring at Peter. "There are some things that are made to be enjoyed and not rushed."

Peter laughed. "Hurry and have your fun, we need to earn money," and left.

That night when they were together, she went into her bedroom leaving Colin reading. A few minutes later, she called his name and asked him to come into her bedroom. "I'm in the bathroom," she shouted as he entered.

Colin felt nervous. "I'll wait here."

"No need, come through."

He walked through into the bathroom; she was lying in the bath, her face above the water, soapy lather covering her to the top of the tub. No matter where he looked, he could see her face in the mirrors. The bath was sunken into the floor and she asked him to sit behind her.

"I want you to wash my back, please," she grinned suggestively, pulled a sponge out of the water, and handed it to him. Tensely he took it and started to draw it lightly over the top of her shoulders.

She leaned forward and Colin started to wash down her back, he looked into the mirror and could clearly see her breasts above the water line. "Do you like them," she asked taking his hand and placing it over one of her breasts. He nodded satisfaction and took a deep breath.

He felt her nipple, soft yet hard, he had never seen a breast before except in pictures and now he was touching one.

She grabbed his other hand and pulled it round her other breast. "I've two you know can't let the other get lonely. Take your clothes off and come into the bath, we can wash each other." She said motioning him to sit in front of her as she started to unbutton his shirt.

He removed his top and trousers and stood there in his underpants, embarrassed, his manhood on high display. She reached up and dragged his pants down, placed her hands around his hardness and pulled him down upon her. She went wild with passion as he watched in the mirrors; he copied her movements until they were both exhausted. They dried each other off with a towel, moved into the next room, fell onto the bed, made love again and fell asleep locked in each other's arms. He had never known such happiness; he wanted to be with her for the rest of his life.

Colin woke and Mary was lying next to him fast asleep. He looked at her naked body and felt he needed her again and could feel the warmth cascading through his veins. She opened her eyes and said, "my you're a greedy one, didn't you get enough last night?"

Colin smiled. "I love you," he said passionately. "I love you."

She was indifferent. "Yes I know," she laughed and climbed on top of him. "My little horse, my stallion from Wales," she groaned through her passion.

"He's ready now," Mary said to Peter over lunch a few days later.

"You'll leave in three days for France and get him to bring the packages back. We'll sell him on to the Chinese after you've tired of him." She nodded in agreement.

That night Mary informed Colin she had business in France and would he like to go with her, knowing full well he was totally under her spell. They must travel separately she insisted because he would have to travel on a false passport but she would be on the same boat. "We can't be seen together it would attract too much attention especially as the police are after you," she said. This seemed reasonable to Colin and he accepted it without question, naively believing she was doing it only to protect him.

The crossing was uneventful. Mary was always near Colin but never too close to be associated together. They arrived in Calais and Mary got off the boat first and walked through customs keeping a discreet eye on Colin, following behind. They met up a while later and Mary took him to a room in a back street hotel she had previously booked where they made love.

"I must go out for a while, stay in the room, this town is a dangerous place," she lied. "I'll be back in two hours."

Colin busied himself with his books and the two hours soon passed. She returned with two cases placed them under the bed and they went out for a meal. He felt so grown up. If only his friends could see him now, how envious they would be of his good fortune.

They got back late and went straight to bed, the ferry was leaving at noon the following day, and they intended to get up early. Mary packed the two cases under the bed the night before and pretended to lift the two together and fell over. This made Colin roar with laughter and Mary joined in. "You'd better let me carry one of them," Colin said.

She grinned and replied. "Yes, I'm inclined to agree, take the smallest one."

The following morning they left the hotel early to catch the ferry, Colin carrying one case and Mary the other. They also had a small case each, which they brought with them containing their clothes and toiletries. They took a taxi from the hotel, arrived near the port with plenty of time to spare, and went into a nearby cafe for a late breakfast.

"Let's go through it again. What are you going to say if you are stopped by customs?"

"I say I'm from Wales living with my grandmother in London and have been to France to spend a few days with my older sister…"

"No, answer only the question they ask you, no more," Mary insisted. "Stick to the same story no matter what."

This was all a big game to Colin and he eagerly entered into the spirit of the adventure not realising he was being sucked in deeper and deeper. He helped to pack the cases and wondered why Mary was so concerned over customs, then realised it must be because of the false passport and she was trying to protect him.

"What's in the cases if you're asked?"

My clothes in one case, presents in the other for my parents and brothers."

"Good, you'll be just fine, don't act too clever." Colin went straight through customs followed by Mary a few minutes later but this was the easy part; the difficulty would come if he was stopped and searched entering back into his country but the odds were small, besides, if he were, Mary would walk away unscathed.

Colin sat in the upstairs lounge on the journey back with the cases at his side. Mary was also there but sitting a number of seats away. He could not help turning and looking her way, she returned a smile a few times but then sat with her side to him so Colin was unable to see her face. Mary was taking no chances, if something went wrong she did not want anyone to notice a link between them.

The crossing back was uneventful; the ferry soon arrived in Dover. They both disembarked and went straight to passport control. The custom authorities were randomly stopping passengers looking in the cases asking questions of those they stopped. Colin felt uneasy but remained calm. Mary had made him practice what to say and he felt quite sure of himself. Mary went through before Colin; he followed and saw her talking to one of the custom officials, while another looked inside her cases. She looked at Colin and he stopped without thinking, she froze.

"Can I help you laddie," a customer officer asked. "Are you together?"

"No!" Mary exclaimed. "Never saw him before."

"Do you want to look in my cases?" Colin asked unable to think of anything better to say.

"No, come, walk on, you're holding up the queue, let's be having you through quickly."

Mary caught up with him a little while later looking annoyed. "What were you thinking? Why did you stop? You could have been searched." Then refrained from saying more, the danger was past.

"Sorry, I saw you with your cases open and I didn't think," he sheepishly replied knowing he had been foolish.

Mary smiled, "It's for your own benefit, you're on a false passport, I'm concerned you could be caught," she lied feigning concern.

"Yes sorry, sorry. I'll be more careful next time, promise."

"What makes you think there will be a next time," she lied, knowing full well there would be many trips to France before Peter dispatched Colin on his final journey. "These shopping trips are expensive," she laughed.

They got back to her flat and later Peter called to see how the trip had gone. He was all smiles and asked Colin how he enjoyed the excursion.

"Enjoyed!" Mary shouted butting in before he had a chance to reply. "That's the last time; he stopped and asked a customs officer if he wanted to look in his case." Peter's face darkened for a moment then he laughed, a loud rasping laugh that rang around the room.

The cases were on the floor and Mary asked him to take his case into his room and unpack. "Leave the others I'll sort them out later." As soon as Colin was through the door, she walked over, opened one of the cases, and removed the contents. At the bottom was a false compartment from which she removed three packages and handed them to Peter.

"This is worth a bit," he said holding the packages in his hands as if to weigh them. "Must go, my contacts are awaiting delivery, they'll be well pleased with this."

"There'll be a lot more of that from this one," Mary advised. "This one is good, fearless."

"Don't work him too hard on the nightshift, let him have some sleep."

"He's got more energy than most; this one can wear me out, his appetite matches mine."

"A right satyriasis and you a nymphomaniac, the two of you are well matched."

"Takes one to know two, you are a satyriasis in the extreme," she bantered.

Peter grinned. "I'll not deny that. I'll have your cut in a few days," he said and left after covering the packages and placing them in a brown bag.

"Where's Peter?" Colin asked when he returned from the other room.

"He only called in to see if we'd bought him a present. Let's have a bath together." I do have a penchant for young boys she thought and led him into the bathroom.

Chapter Nineteen

There was no further news about Colin and they were all worried. The last person to talk to him was the police officer in Paddington. He had not been heard of since, no letter, phone call, or even a postcard. The local police in Wales circulated his photograph to the police around London but they had hit a blank. He was a runaway and the police paid little attention to these cases.

"He was last seen in Paddington," George said to Bill and Henry in the pub. "If I've heard nothing by next week I have a mind to take a trip up there to search around Paddington for a few days. Someone must know something."

Bill thought for a moment. "I'll come with you."

"Not without me you won't, I'm in as well," said Henry.

"No Henry you have enough on your plate. You only buried Sophie a few months ago. Look you two, I'm taking a few weeks off work without pay. I'm not having you do the same."

Henry and Bill looked at one another and then at George. Bill said. "It's not as if we have no money. We all have our redundancy that's hardly been used as yet increasing in fact with the interest."

George wasn't happy. "That's your nest egg, boys listen, especially you Henry… Sophie…"

Henry didn't allow George to finish. "No, you listen; no one can help Sophie now. I can help to find Colin… I'm coming with you George," he said with finality.

It was pointless putting up a further argument. Henry and Bill had made up their minds and as they sat with a pint of beer each, planned the trip.

The following week saw them on the train to London. They had booked into a small guesthouse just outside Paddington Station and intended to ask around the area if anyone had seen Colin. There was an air of excitement and unreality about the whole thing. George had Colin's most recent school photo in his pocket and was hopeful that someone somewhere around Paddington would recognise the picture.

The hotel they settled on was just round the corner from the station and in no time they were in the one room they had booked. The room was fairly spacious, three single beds, a small table in between each of them, a small chair in the corner, one large wardrobe and an old dressing table with drawers, in the corner. The only disadvantage was that the toilet was at the other end of the landing down a few steps, but the room was comfortable, more than adequate for their purpose.

They had a map of the area but no immediate plan of how they were going to use it. They decided they would visit the guesthouses first and take it from there. They immediately marked off each hotel and guesthouse they visited asking always the same question. "Have you seen this person?" pointing at the picture. This went on for a few days and found no one who had seen Colin; they visited over fifty places and became more despondent as the days wore on.

"We'll keep trying until we find him," Bill said when they were all back in the room feeling worn out and tired.

George shook his head pessimistically. "It seems so futile I… Where could he be?" His voice distressed not knowing where to go next.

Henry turned to George. "We could be looking in the wrong place. Perhaps he's sleeping on the streets; it costs money to stay in a room."

"Room or street we'll find him. He'll have saved some money, he always had some scheme or other going on he thought no one knew about," gestured Bill trying to make George feel better.

"Yes, but he can't have a lot left after all this time," George responded.

"Perhaps he's taken a job somewhere," suggested Henry.

"We'll spend another few days asking in the hotels and guesthouses and then we'll concentrate on the shops and pubs," voiced Bill.

They combed the area for the next week but still no one had seen or heard of him. They had already been to the guesthouse Colin stayed in but a different receptionist was on duty that day. One cafe owner thought he'd seen him a few weeks previous but was far from sure so this information placed them no further forward.

Frustrated, hungry, downhearted, they abandoned the search for the day and decided to call into a nearby pub, depressed with the lack of result.

"Come on, let's grab some food and a pint in here," Bill said and in they all followed.

"The bar please," Henry asked as they walked in not realising they had called in this hotel before.

"You won't find a bar in here this is a hotel, you can have a room if you like," the lady replied from behind the counter smiling. "You all look lost, how far have you come?"

"Wales," Bill replied. "A meal and a few pints we're looking for, where's the nearest place from here please?"

"Just around the corner a few minutes walk. We had a lad from your part of the world staying here a few months ago with his uncle, can't remember what part, same accent as you, that's what made me remember him," the receptionist stated. George pulled out the picture and showed it to her.

She studied the picture carefully. "Yes that's him, yes, definitely quite a good looking lad. Why do you ask?"

"We're looking for him. I'm his father," George mumbled excitedly.

"He was with his uncle," the receptionist replied. "We get a lot of people staying here but I remember he made quite a fuss about his uncle being late, sticks in my mind."

"Uncle, are you sure? What did he look like?" asked Bill somewhat confused.

"Mm, well, can't remember, never actually saw his uncle but I did see the boy on a few occasions. Come to think of it, perhaps the little blighter was by himself all the time, he was smart."

"Is he still here," enquired Bill.

"No, it was a while ago, let me check, he stayed four nights over three months ago, I'd forgotten all about it until I heard you lot speaking, haven't seen him since. He seemed to have plenty of money I remember paid up front in cash.

"Do you know where he moved to?" George asked optimistically.

"I've already said I've not seen him since he was staying here, he could be anywhere: have you asked at the local police station?"

"No, is there any other information you can tell us we haven't much to go on?" stated Henry.

"Only what I've just told you, try the police station that's your best bet. If you don't mind I must get on I'm behind with the paperwork." and started to write making it obvious she had nothing further to add.

They followed her advice and were at the police station in no time. A sergeant was on duty and they showed him Colin's photo explaining the situation. He shook his head, called over a constable sitting in a chair at the other end of the room and showed him the photo, the response just the same.

The trail was cold, but at least they knew where he stayed the first few days after he arrived. Another police officer walked in and George showed the photo to him. He studied it closely.

"His face is familiar," he said scratching his head. "I've seen him before somewhere. I'm sure I have, let me think." They all waited. "I have it, the Lamb and Flag pub. I've seen him around a few times since then. We were together sarg, don't you remember."

The sergeant shook his head. "No can't recall."

"I remember something about being with his aunt; he left and I didn't think anything of it at the time, can't say I've seen him there since. However, I've seen his aunt a real good looker, can't fail to notice her. What's he done wrong sarg?"

The sergeant looked angry. "He's lost, that's what's wrong. Take them round to the Lamb and see if you can find out anything constable." It was obvious from his tone the sergeant was annoyed with the constable for saying what he did. He remembered being at the pub and seeing the boy and had said nothing. Now the constable had opened his mouth he must pretend to cooperate. The last thing he needed was morons from the sticks asking questions and causing trouble.

A little later, they arrived at the Lamb and Flag, the constable entering first. He questioned the barman who couldn't remember the boy but when the constable described the people seen with him, the barman remembered something but wasn't sure. This was the type of bar where people kept a low profile, away from the police, deploying the three-monkey principle.

George told the constable where they were staying, stating they would call at the police station the next day to see if there was any further news and left to go back to their hotel. There was a new feeling of optimism among the men and they decided to go back to the Lamb that night to show Colin's photo around.

Later, they were back in the pub, the place full. They sat at a corner table and started to show Colin's photo but no one recognised him, or if they did, weren't saying. They were not dejected, this was the best lead they had since they arrived in London and felt strongly something would turn up.

Sitting in a corner watching them was a man; he moved and sat at the next table trying to hear what they were saying but was just out of hearing and moved a little closer. He had seen the picture being handed round the bar earlier and had seen the boy a few times over the last few weeks with Mary. Information was money; Peter would pay handsomely for this knowledge.

Henry noticed the man, and nudged George and Bill under the table, moving his eyes towards the stranger; they were being watched.

"There's a large reward for information leading to the whereabouts of the boy." Henry stated just loud enough for the stranger to hear. The stranger shifted again in his seat and they were just about to talk to him when he got up, walked over and started talking to a man standing by the door. The other man had his back to them and they were unable to see his face.

Peter had just walked through the door and after a few moments, the two of them went outside. "What's the game Jimmy?" asked Peter.

"I have information. How much?"

"Depends on what it is, I'm busy so be quick," stated an irritated Peter.

"Three men in there asking about a Welsh lad, there's a reward a big one by the sound of it," he grinned. "How much?"

Peter never liked Jimmy. "So what's that to do with me?"

Jimmy grinned sarcastically. "Shall I tell them the boy was seen with you?"

Peter's eyes flashed fire. "Have you told them anything you little worm?" Angrily pushing Jimmy against the wall.

"Hold on will you, I've said nothing, nothing, honest, I'd never do that. I didn't have to tell you did I," he stuttered.

"Sorry, you're right I'm on edge, a bit hasty. Here have this," placing a five pound note in Jimmy's top pocket.

Jimmy adjusted his coat where Peter had held it. "They are talking in a Welsh accent and were with the police this afternoon asking questions of the barman, showing round a picture of a boy, the boy I've seen with your Mary."

Peter was perturbed, this spelt trouble. "Listen Jimmy, go back and keep an eye on them for me," and added another twenty pounds to Jimmy's pocket. "Find out where they're staying, there'll be another note in it."

Peter was in a panic; Colin had been to France a number of times over the last few months and was proving very profitable smuggling drugs. He and Mary earned more money recently with Colin than they earned during the last two years. Colin was a natural and was so infatuated with Mary would do anything for her which made him ideal for the job.

He had no idea, or if he did, didn't care they used him to smuggle drugs. Colin was a bully, a leader back in Wales, here totally out of his depth in the hands of professionals and would be used until he was of no further value and then discarded as you would an oily rag into the fire.

Peter went straight to Mary's flat, which was a few blocks away from the one he lived in. He needed to warn Mary to keep Colin off the streets.

He let himself in but Mary and Colin were not there. If the Welshmen found Colin and questioned him, the game would be up. They needed a new runner, Colin was getting too hot to handle; it was time for change.

Then he remembered they were not due back from their latest trip to France for another day. He breathed a sigh of relief.

His agitation started again.

Peter has survived because he was careful. He knew Jimmy could not be trusted, give him money and he'd sing like a canary.

Peter had rented the flat for Mary under a false name, but there were several people at the pub that knew the area where she lived. The location of his flat was kept totally secret, if need be they could both go to ground if things got too hot. They were careful with their runners, always picking a runaway. No one asked questions about one before.

He would meet Mary at the port tomorrow but wasn't sure what ferry they would arrive on suspecting it would be the early one. Perhaps the police had shown Colin's picture to the harbour authorities, no, his sergeant friend would have let him know and laughed at his paranoia and overreaction. Mary would not be travelling with Colin; she would have time to get away if customs apprehended him, and he breathed a sigh of relief.

The relief didn't last long; dark thoughts crept through Peter's mind. He would clear Mary's belongings out of her flat and set fire to it; destroy all traces of her ever being there, but thought better of it. He must be rational, yes, must act rationally. Mary is always warning me against overreaction and panicking unnecessarily, he thought and decided to talk to his sister before taking any direct action. She must lie low for a few weeks at the very minimum until it all blew over but the boy would need to go and go immediately.

Colin was the most profitable boy they ever had and Peter would be sad to see him go but the risk was now far too high. He and Mary had done this many times and found there was always a steady supply of homeless children arriving in London with no one asking after them but not all were suitable. Mary was fussy about whom she took to her bed but when she accepted one under her influence, she captivated the youngster who would do anything she asked.

Mary enjoyed the seduction process as much as the money, Peter smiled. They would need to find a new boy to train; profits would fall in the interim but that was unavoidable. They would also have to rent a new flat.

In the past, once they had passed their usefulness, they sold these runaways to the Chinese, who eventually shipped them as sex slaves for rich foreigners, especially the girls. Peter had never had any comebacks from the Chinese, cared little if the youngsters lived or died after they left him but suspected most didn't live that long.

Jimmy went back into the Lamb and Flag and sat by the bar occasionally looking over at the three seated at the other end of the room. Henry noticed him return and beckoned to the other two.

"He knows something," Henry said under his breath. "I'm convinced of it."

George shuffled in his seat. "I'll go and ask him," and was on the verge of getting up to walk over and ask.

Henry placed his hand on his shoulder. "No," he whispered. "Hold on a minute. If he was going to tell us anything he would have when we showed the photo around. Something is not right. He's watching us. Go over now and we'll scare him off."

"He could be after the reward," said George.

"Let's put it to the test. You two leave and head back I'll stay behind and see if he follows. If he does, I'll leave straight after and we'll have him. If not wait for me outside the hotel."

"We don't want trouble Henry," advised George.

"We'll offer him a reward, nothing more."

Bill and George left. Henry stayed stating in a loud voice he needed another pint and would follow later. The stranger got up from his seat as if to go but decided against it and sat back down. Henry waited another fifteen minutes and walked towards the door. No sooner had he walked through the door the stranger left his seat and followed, falling into their trap.

Henry walked slowly back to the hotel stopping occasionally to look in a window and glance back. The other two saw him coming, moved out of sight into a doorway and he walked straight past indicating the stranger was following behind. As soon as the stranger passed George and Bill, Henry turned and walked towards him. Jimmy turned and tried to hurry away only to run into the two following behind.

"Let me go or I'll call the police," Jimmy gasped and was about to shout.

"Yes why don't you call the police? We'll go to the station now and you can tell them what you know and why you were following us," said Bill.

"Following? I was going home."

"Yes of course you were, now, we can do this the easy way or the hard way. What's it to be? We don't want to wake the neighbours do we?" Henry gave a menacing smile. "We're only after a little chat, there's money in it or…" he knocked one of his fists into his other hand.

"Henry please," George said astounded with what he had heard.

"I don't know anything about any boy or Mary. I… only going home," He stammered.

Henry stared him in the eyes, his face contorted in a snarl. "Who said anything about Mary? I think you should tell us what you know, quickly, if you intend to keep your teeth. I'll make it easy; you can start with your name."

He tried to pull away but George and Bill held him firmly.

"Come, come," mouthed, Henry, "your name?"

"How much money?"

"Up to you, information first." Henry raised his hand and started to count to three, but at two he agreed to cooperate.

"Jimmy! How much money?" he demanded.

"A reward, a reward for information and you keep your teeth. Henry raised his hand again. "The boy, where did you see him?"

"The reward how much?" He'd had enough of this intimidation; he had been there many times in his line of work.

"Information first then the money," Henry replied easing off.

"How do I know I can trust you?"

Henry looked him in the eyes. "You can't, take a risk."

Jimmy paused then replied, "in the pub about two months ago."

"And?" Henry mouthed. "Come on, the rest of it. Whose is Mary? Here, have this," pressing a ten pound note into his hand. "There is more where that came from."

"She sometimes comes into the pub… but I haven't seen her for a few weeks."

"That's convenient, why didn't you tell us earlier when we showed the photo round the pub, you were there? Come Jimmy, we're all waiting." Henry whispered.

"Nothing is for nothing."

"You've been paid, here's another fiver, now let's have what you know, last warning or the money is coming back," said Henry.

"The boy in the photo was with Mary that's all I know. I've seen him around a few times with her. She lives locally in a flat but don't know where exactly. Someone in the pub should know."

"Is he still with her?" Henry smiled, the scowl gone.

"I… I don't know, honestly, haven't seen Mary in weeks."

"So you say, so you say, if you hear anything there's a hundred pounds in it for you," informed Henry.

Jimmy's eyes lit up; he was in the money. "Hundred, half now. I'll find the address for you."

Henry's eyes flashed. "You'll get it all with the information."

"I'll keep my eyes open but don't tell anyone I've spoken to you," Jimmy stuttered. "Or I'm a dead man. A hundred pounds mind, that's what you said."

They looked at each other wondering what he was talking about, and put it down to dramatics in order to get the hundred pounds under offer.

"Yes, when we find the flat, nothing before and you must take us there," stated Henry.

"I must have secrecy, you'll keep it quiet."

"Of course Jimmy no one will know you've talked to us we assure you, our secret. We'll be at the pub for the next few days, if you help us to find the boy the money is yours, here's another tenner to show good will. Lead us to the boy, you'll get the money, we'll be gone, no one will ever know, simple as that."

They let him go and he fled without looking back. "You sounded really frightening Henry. I never knew you had it in you," George said shocked at the way he had witnessed Henry behave.

Henry looked at George grimly and replied. "I've lost my Sophie but Colin is alive, if someone knows something one way or the other we'll… Let's get back."

Chapter Twenty

Peter waited at the port for the ferry to dock but they were not on it. Disconcertion set in bordering on paranoia. The next ferry was in six hours; he couldn't wait around the port that long. It would almost certainly draw attention and decided to go to China Town to see his contact and get things started. He wanted Colin taken off his hands as soon as possible.

He knocked the side door of a building. A foreign sounding voice asked who was there. "It's Peter, quick let me in. I have cargo for you."

The door opened; standing there was a short stocky man with his hair in a ponytail halfway down his back. He had a broad nose, dangerous black eyes and large lips. A small pipe was clamped between his heavily nicotine stained teeth. There was a snake tattooed each side of his neck, both arms were covered with tattoos of dragons. He was dressed in a dark short-sleeved shirt and trousers with dirty sandals on his feet.

"I've warned you before Peter not to come here, it's too dangerous. This had better be good," he snarled. "There's an ancient Chinese proverb, people that don't follow rules never live long."

"Cut the lecture and let me in." Peter pushed passed and closed the door. "I've a package that needs to be delivered immediately."

"If it's that hot we don't want it. Go through the correct channels, you know the procedure. The post box is closed for the next few days," the Chinese man answered eyes blazing. "You'll be told when, how, and where to deliver."

"This one is good, strong and as white as they come, male. The parcel is prime in every sense of the word."

"You post when and where told."

"No time, must be done today." He demanded.

"Impossible, the post boxes are full."

"Well empty one, this is urgent," Peter pleaded in desperation.

The Chinaman grinned sardonically. "The price will be halved, and a bit off for the inconvenience. Perhaps you should pay us this time."

Peter's face darkened. "No way, this is a prime specimen; the parcel is top quality and will bring you a good price."

"Not if it comes with a high-risk tag."

Peter knew he was cornered. "Come on," he groaned. "As soon as it's delivered the risk is nothing to you."

"There is always risk Peter. Half price, that's my terms; go through the correct channels if you want a better price, now leave."

"All right, you win, but it must be today that's the deal."

The man nodded, handed Peter a packet and instructed him to dilute the contents in water and give it to the parcel an hour before delivery. "We'll have a van waiting at the usual place after six tonight. If your parcel is not there by eight the deal is off."

Peter was adamant. "It'll be there, count on it."

"Now go, if you break the rules of delivery again you'll be getting a visit from the Triads, count on it."

This made Peter go cold. The Triads never visit more than twice. The second time to deliver the flowers. The Chinaman opened the door, pushed Peter through, and slammed it shut behind him. The Chinese always kept their word, any danger they would ruthlessly eliminate, him included.

He went back to the port to wait the next ferry and spotted Colin waiting for Mary. Thirty minutes passed, still she hadn't come through customs. Then he spotted her and mentally chastised himself for over reacting. Peter waved to attract Mary's attention keeping out of Colin's sight. She noticed him immediately. Her face turned ashen. She knew something serious must have happened for Peter to risk being at the port to meet them and expected the worse.

Customs stopped her, which accounted for the delay, the second time in the last eight trips they searched her baggage, but of course, they found nothing. She worried Peter's appearance had something to do with that and was there to warn her against meeting Colin. She walked past Colin whispering under her breath. "Take a taxi to the flat. I'll see you there later."

Colin stood still. "Go!" She whispered again. They know about the passport, go," she lied and walked on, turned the corner, kept walking and entered the nearest pub followed a few moments later by Peter.

"What's up," looking straight at him and then out the window to see if anyone had followed.

"Where's Colin I saw him waiting for you?"

"Where do you think? I've sent him back to the flat," She whispered.

Peter looked angry. "Back where?"

"You heard. What was I supposed to do?" she snapped. "Now what are you doing here? You only turn up if there's trouble."

He filled her in on the details. "Is that all? Peter, why do you build everything into a crisis?" she laughed.

"Why laugh? What is so funny?" he fumed, mystified by her easygoing response to his anxiety.

"You're pathetic. A few people are looking for him. So what? Colin does not want to be found, he is with us all the way."

"We can't keep him, he'll have to go."

"Stop panicking. Colin will do as I tell him; he's a runaway, stop worrying. I thought we were about to be pulled at the dock, if you feel he's too hot, fine, we'll let him go, train another. I would have liked to keep him a little longer but if you say he goes so be it, now stop worrying."

They went to the flat realising they should not have left Colin out of their sight but the agreement was if Peter was waiting for her she was to get away from the port immediately, alone. When they returned Colin was waiting outside the flat oblivious to what was to befall him. They told Colin they were hungry and going out to eat and to leave everything.

Peter acted upbeat. "We're going out to celebrate tonight."

"What's the rush?" Colin asked intrigued thinking this whole adventure no more than a game.

I'm taking you for a meal," Peter announced smiling.

"I need to change first," Colin protested.

"Change when you get back I'm starving… let's go," Peter impatiently demanded.

Peter put the cases in the flat then they left together, after checking the coast was clear, and took a taxi to a small discrete restaurant that Peter and Mary knew. It was obvious from the welcome they had dined there many times.

They ordered three drinks, Peter insisted in fetching them from the bar. He placed the powder, which the Chinese man had given him, discretely in Colin's coke and walked back carrying the drinks on a tray. A little later, the waiter came over and they all ordered the same meal, steak and chips.

"I need another drink," Mary announced. "Come on Colin your falling behind you've hardly touched your coke. Down in one," she said lovingly smiling at him.

"Three more drinks please waiter," Peter shouted over as Colin emptied his glass. Another three drinks arrived at the table followed by the meals a few minutes later.

"What's wrong Colin?" he heard Mary asking feigning concern.

"Nothing. I'm just feeling a little dizzy. I'll be all right in a minute."

Peter paid for the meal and helped Colin to his feet. The room was going round and he had difficulty standing. They both helped him to the door; the more he tried to walk the worse he felt. The street was ablaze; light and noise seemed to be everywhere. Peter and Mary held him by his arms one each side. Colin had never felt so giddy in his life before. They turned down a lane; he noticed a white blurred object in front of him and collapsed.

Two Chinese men were waiting in the white van, the back door open as Peter and Mary approached almost carrying Colin by his arms. "I've got a parcel for delivery," Peter whispered to the two men.

"In the back, quickly does it. We need to be gone," one of them said and slammed the door shut on an unconscious Colin. The two men jumped into the van and a few seconds later roared off out of sight.

"That was easy. You worry far too much," Mary frowned. They arrived back at the flat a while later and looked through Colin's things. To their great delight, they found over £1800 in a plastic container hidden under a book at the bottom of his case.

"The old devil," Peter grinned. "Perhaps, the three men were after him because of the money this is a tidy sum."

Mary smirked. "He said nothing about this to me even when I was giving him money. Normally they tell me everything."

"You're slipping dear sis," and smiled counting out the money into two piles handing one to Mary. "Colin has been the most profitable boy we've ever had, he'll be hard to replace. The Chinese," he scowled, "ripped me off with the price they gave me for him, but this extra is icing on the cake so all has turned out more than satisfactorily."

"See, I said you worry too much. That last trip to France was also by far the most profitable. I packed more than three times the normal quantity. I would have liked to have kept Colin a little longer though, I was growing rather fond of him, could have taught him a few more tricks."

"Your appetite is insatiable we'll get you a girl next and I can have a go after she's trained."

"I'll miss him, he was coming along nicely, starting to know my little ways. I like to see how far I can go with them. This one, I felt I could do anything with, but there you are, I won't be seeing him again that's for sure, they don't come back from the Chinese."

"I'll play the fiddle if you like, it's best to get rid of them before the attachment gets too great, they're only pets to you anyway for you to play with."

"True but… there are always others I suppose, yes a young girl would be nice. I can have fun watching you, and have a go myself of course."

"Of course, nothing less, back to business. We need to clear the flat and move on. Those men are not about to give up. We need to lie low for a few weeks and let things blow over, they can't stay forever."

Mary packed her clothes and personal belonging within the hour; Peter carried the cases down the stairs. He always rented a garage in case of an emergency, but with all the books his sister had and her belongings, would need to make several journeys.

"I've said to you before you should only take what you need. These books will take us all day to move." Peter moaned. "The less you take to the flat the less when you leave."

"I enjoy reading and need them, so leave it, just pack them so we can be gone, besides, the flat needs to look as if I stay there full time," she shouted. "Leave Colin's clothes, we'll place them in the rubbish bin after we've moved all the books, most are rubbish, the ones he brought with him anyway, cheap to say the least."

Peter hired a van and together with a few of his cronies were busy for the rest of the night and for most of the next day until the only thing left in the flat was Colin's clothes. Mary packed them in black bags and left them inside the door intending to come back the following day to put them out for the refuse collection.

She spent the rest of the day cleaning the flat to remove all traces of fingerprints. She washed down all the windows, doors, walls, light fittings, bathroom, and all other areas that could leave a trace. They would quit the flat leaving nothing that could be traced back to them, taking the low profile option wherever possible, and always meticulous.

It was obvious Mary had done this before and was painstakingly methodical in the way she worked. Peter kept watch in and around the Lamb in case of trouble. There had only been one occasion when they had to leave a flat in a hurry, and had set fire to it destroying all evidence to cover their tracks. Unfortunately, the fire killed an old couple in the rooms above but that didn't worry them, a necessity of the job. The most important thing, as far as they were concerned, was making sure nothing linked them to the flat.

"That's the last of it, we can come back tomorrow for the rubbish, we're out of here all trace gone. See you later at your flat," Mary stated.

"No, wait here 'til I get back. Shouldn't be long I'll look in the Flag to see if the three morons are still there. My flat is in a mess. We can tidy it over the next few weeks and look for another place for you in readiness for the next runaway," and smiled. "A girl."

"Be careful, don't be too long or I'm leaving."

Peter looked in the window of the Lamb, noticed Jimmy talking to the three men, and moved back into the shadow. He stood and watched for several minutes and saw Jimmy take a small packet from one of the men and place it in his inside pocket and they all stood up to leave. He knew immediately what was happening. Jimmy had sold him out; his paranoia had proved to be correct.

He ran back to the flat, Mary was waiting for him. "We must go now they are on their way here," he shouted.

"Come on Peter talk sense. What about all this stuff?" she asked.

"Leave it."

"Burn the flat."

"No time. Quickly, let's go, we need to be away," he shouted. "No!" he pulled her, "not that way, back stairs. They were leaving... They're right behind us, we must get out now."

They were soon in the side alley and could see the three men, with Jimmy leading, walking down the street. They stayed in the alley until the three men went into the building and watched as Jimmy slunk back the way he came. Peter's face contorted into a look of hatred, "you'll pay for this Jimmy, yes, you'll pay," he muttered.

Chapter Twenty One

Henry was the first to enter followed by George and Bill. Jimmy had given them the address and they handed him fifty pounds in the pub saying he would have the other fifty if the boy were still there. George knocked quietly on the door and they waited, he knocked again, harder. Henry pushed George out of the way and knocked loudly a few times, the noise resounding round the corridor; frustrated, he gave a final bang with his shoulder against the door, and at the third attempt, it flew open.

They looked inside the flat; it was spotless and empty except for a few bags of rubbish. Henry looked in all the rooms. It was obvious the occupants of the flat cleaned it thoroughly and left recently.

"There's nothing here, Jimmy's lying, let's go and pay him a visit back at the Lamb," Henry growled.

Bill was angry. "You'll be lucky, he's gone to ground, we should have kept him with us."

George opened one of the several black plastic bags stacked by the door. He went cold with fright, he recognised Colin's coat. He checked every item in the bag and found more clothes that belonged to him, some he hadn't seen before but all Colin's size, without doubt, he was sure Colin had been there.

He examined the contents of the other bags. They found a picture of Colin's grandmother and of Sophie, together with a number of personal items. George knew Colin would never leave these behind voluntarily, especially a picture of his grandmother. Bill went for the police; the other two stayed in the flat combing every inch but there was nothing more to find.

"He's even left his shoes," Henry commented.

"Or forced to leave them," George emphasised.

Two policemen arrived at the door followed by Bill. George showed them the items but they did not prove anything, other than Colin had been in the flat, or at the very least, left his clothes there. One of the policemen agreed he would check out who owned the flat; ask around the area for information. Colin was already on the missing list but he had run away from home voluntarily. The police had thousands of these cases reported to them every year and took little notice.

"At least we know he's somewhere near," stated Henry. "We'll find him George," sounding positive.

"This doesn't fit. I think Colin is held against his will," stated George concerned. "I've a bad feeling about this."

"No, more than likely he left his clothes here meaning to pick them up later," said the police officer. "It happens all the time, leave clothes in an empty flat to collect later, often they squat when the coast is clear," he said unsympathetically. "That's what these squatters do, any empty flat and they're in, know the law better that us."

"In rubbish bags! I don't think so," replied George feeling outraged at the police officer's suggestion.

"Look," said the other police officer. "Place his picture in a few of the local shops and on a number of boards within a few miles radius and ask around if anyone has seen him recently. If he's about these parts, someone has seen him; you can't expect us to go forever chasing runaways."

They asked at a few of the neighbouring flats. A number of tenants said they had seen the boy with the woman who lived there and believed she was his aunt. They kept very much to themselves. The caretaker informed them a Mr. and Mrs. Williams leased the flat; they paid a bond and deposit and as far as the caretaker was concerned they had not given notice and still held the bond. One of the policemen insisted that when they came to collect the bond, or made contact in any way, he was to report the incident immediately to the station.

The other policemen picked up some of Colin's clothes and said. "It looks as if he knew we were coming and left to stay one step…"

Henry spoke over him before he finished. "Or someone is trying to keep us from the boy."

"Let's go back to the Lamb and Flag and see if we can get any further information from Jimmy," Henry whispered to the two of them so the policemen wouldn't overhear.

They left the flat together, the police sealed the door. Henry stated the door was ajar when they arrived. If the police knew they had forced the door, they could take a contrary view and arrest them for breaking and entering. They didn't seem concerned, paying lip service only, not listening half the time.

They went back to the pub; Jimmy was sitting on a stool at the bar, drinking a pint of beer.

"Let me buy you another," George volunteered. "Your information was right but they were gone before we got there."

Jimmy looked pleased. "I always deliver. Do I get the other fifty quid?" he enquired. "The deal was to lead you to where the boy is staying. I was right wasn't I, so I should get the money."

Henry felt like hitting him off his stool, he just smiled, agreed the other fifty pounds should be paid and handed over the money. He wanted further information from this weasel and thought the best way to achieve this was to keep him sweet. George paid for Jimmy's pint, together with three more informing Jimmy there was another fifty quid available if he knew where the boy was now.

"I'll see you here in three days have the money with you," he said. "I'll find him." drank his full pint straight down and left.

"I could gladly throttle him and smile at the same time," Henry growled face red with anger. "I'm glad he went then or I'd have… Let me just say, I'm glad he's not still sitting on the stool," twisting his hands together gesturing what he felt like doing.

Chapter Twenty Two

Colin opened his eyes, his body paralysed, noticed a grey ceiling, one light hung from the centre shining brightly. The light went round and round, he knew the bulb was stationary and wondered why it kept going round. He closed his eyes, locked in a bad dream; his head spun; he wished the motion would stop.

He tried to lift his hands and legs, failed, and drifted back into unconsciousness. He woke again; time seemed an irrelevance. He could see the light, it burned his eyes; he stared deep into the bulb unable to look away, transfixed. The drug given to him debilitated him and froze every limb.

Colin slowly moved his head, one way, then the other, each movement brought agony to his neck. Left, right, left, right he forced his head to move uttering painful noises with every twist. He started to feel a tingle in his fingers, or was it only in his mind; he wasn't sure, and drifted back into oblivion.

Slowly he regained more of his strength, moved his legs and arms trying to kick start his body into action. He turned to his side and noticed he was in a room with no window, lying on a mattress. The rest of the room was empty except for a bucket against the wall; next to that was a wooden door. Fear gripped him. He was in a nightmare and closed his eyes expecting to wake up at any moment.

Gradually, he got to his feet and fell against the wall. One of his legs felt trapped. There was a metal clasp attached to his ankle, a chain led off it into a large steel ring secured firmly into the wall.

He was terrified and pulled against the chain, first with his leg, then with his hands. He shuffled his body towards the door but the chain held him firm and he fell over. He hit the bucket hard with his hand the noise reverberated around the small room.

He shook with fear, regained his balance, and started to shout. The door opened, a short well-built Chinese man walked into the room, dragons tattooed on each arm. He stood in the doorway, arms folded, looking at Colin a broad grin etched across his chiselled face.

Colin ran at him his head down and caught him in the stomach knocking him back through the door. The chain tightened against his ankle and jolted him to a stop, pain shot up his leg. He fell to the floor. The Chinese man laughed. Colin lay face down on the floor.

"Get up," he growled. "You need to be taught manners. You are no good to us behaving that way." He stood on Colin's hand just hard enough to hurt, Colin tried to grab his foot with the other hand, but when that failed tried to bite his leg. He was mad with rage; the speed of his action startled the Chinese man who quickly jumped away. "You are far more dangerous than you look and need to cool down."

He closed the door leaving Colin still in a rage pulling at the chain, returned with a hosepipe and turned it full on him. The cold water made Colin jump; the pressure forced him back against the wall. He turned his back to the water to protect himself. Above the sound of the water, he heard the Chinese man laughing, muttering amusingly to himself. "Plenty of water will make you grow quickly into compliance or drown you, your choice."

He turned off the hose; the whole room a mass of water. Colin turned to face the Chinese man who stood in the doorway grinning and laughing, fire hose still in his hand pointing at him. "Are you cool enough my angry friend?"

Colin ran at him again, before he got half way across the floor he turned the hosepipe back on, catching him straight in the face. He slipped and went down heavily on his back, his body pushed by the pressure of water against the furthest wall. The water kept pounding into him; he couldn't breathe, shielded his face with his hands to protect himself, and tried to stand. He fell, hit the back of his head hard on the wall, knocking himself out in the manoeuvre.

Colin woke to a dark room, his head sore, feeling cold and wet, the floor covered in water. The mattress next to him soaking wet, his clothes dripped. Tears welled up in his eyes and he started to shiver violently. He tried to shout but only managed a whimper. He felt frightened, abandoned, disorientated, fear welled up inside him, a fear he had never known before.

He cowered in the corner, drifted in and out of consciousness. Time dimmed, and felt only the coldness of the room and the hopelessness of his situation. His mind wandered. Mary and Peter, were they prisoners here also? He shouted their names.

He remembered the meal, the drinks, feeling giddy, the noise in the street, the white van, darkness, until he woke, tied and shackled like a bear to the wall of this cell.

The door opened, Colin looked up from the floor, shivering. The Chinese man made a horrible deep sound that echoed in the small room. Colin flinched. He threw a few old towels on the floor and instructed Colin to mop up the water informing him he would be back in a few minutes with a dry mattress. He warned Colin if he did not behave, he would be soaked again and left not just for a few hours but until the following day. Colin nodded his head in agreement; he was too cold, his head hurt too much to disagree. He was a rat in a trap; the Chinese man the cat gloating over him.

He slammed the door and the bolt clanged. Colin stood, picked up the towels, and started to wipe down the room. There were little puddles all over the floor and he used the towels to drain the water into the bucket. He took the full bucket over to the door where there was a small drain and emptied the contents into it.

He did this several times until the floor was dry. The mattress he placed against the wall by the side of the door so the water would not drip back into the room. His clothes hung wet, he removed and wrung them out over the drain, naked and shivering all the while. They were still far too wet to wear so he hung them on the wall squeezing them in between the stones not for them to fall back to the floor, sat down on the cold stone and cried.

Colin waited what seemed to be hours but in reality was nearer thirty minutes. The door opened, the wet mattress removed, the towels taken and left in a corner outside the door. The Chinese man threw a dry mattress and blanket into the corner, telling Colin the room got rather warm when not wet and his clothes would dry in a few hours. Colin wrapped the blanket around himself as if to hide. The man brought a tray of food placing it on the floor. He informed Colin the bucket was for his toilet, and slammed the door closed. A second later a large bolt sealed the door, the light went out, he was in darkness.

He got up as if in a trance feeling his way around the room, the reality of his predicament forcefully swept over him and realised he was in a desperate situation. Wondered why he was here, what had happened to Peter and Mary the woman he loved. His eyes became accustomed to the almost total darkness; the only light a sliver that penetrated under the door. He felt for the food and realised how hungry he was and devoured the bread and cheese quickly followed by a hot watery soup.

The chain rubbed into his leg, his ankle bled, he felt no pain, and wondered why? He was still cold and his head ached. He pulled at the chains shouting to the walls, "hurt me hurt me." His reasoning was starting to be impaired, the only thing that filled his mind was why his ankle was not hurting, he wanted it to hurt, felt cheated he could feel no pain. He fell on the dry mattress and cried like a baby; tears cascaded down his face and he drifted off into a disturbed sleep still willing his ankle to hurt.

Chapter Twenty Three

Jimmy was feeling proud of his business acumen intending to collect another twenty pounds from Peter when he told him the name of the hotel where the three men were staying. At the same time, he would try to find out where the boy was. He reasoned the Welsh men were good for another hundred pounds at least. He would get from them what he could and lie low. They must return to Wales in the next few weeks and there was no way Peter would suspect he was passing on information.

The police returned to the flat more out of duty than to complete their report, and as expected, found no further information. No one collected the bond held by the landlord, which was no surprise. The only lead they had was that some of the clothes found belonged to Colin; the police believed he had cleared out of his own free will and were convinced they were wasting their time.

Jimmy, knowing how Peter operated, believed the boy was under his influence in some way and used for some illegal activity. He was not sure the part Mary played, they always looked out for each other. He knew they were in cahoots over something; he had seen them in the company of young boys and girls before and had on numerous occasions tried to find out what they were up to hoping to get a cut of the action. He never made it to first base but knew there must be money in it somehow.

Jimmy was not aware they were brother and sister, had no idea what type of work they were involved in, all he had was subjective suspicion. They were never short of money, dressed well, always looked tanned, spent lavishly and led an envious life style, which irritated the hell out of him. He wanted the same but was nowhere near as successful.

They would change addresses frequently and kept their movements very much to themselves. Occasionally, no one would see them for months. Jimmy often wondered where they got to over these periods; when he asked no one knew, or if they did, did not tell him.

Jimmy had never done an honest day's work in his life. Always living on the edge earning his money by running illegal errands for minor local crooks, and when he could get hold of them, selling smuggled cigarettes and alcohol combined with petty burglary. He barely made a living wage but always managed to get by one way or another. He resented his lifestyle, jealous of anyone who had more than he did. When he was really down on his luck, he would collect glasses at the Lamb and the landlord would give him a few pints of beer in payment. Today, he had money and intended getting drunk and walked into the pub feeling pleased with himself; he was on the verge of breaking into big time crime, so he thought.

Jimmy sat on his usual stool by the bar. The Welsh men were near the docks chasing a lead, and would not be back until late evening. He was on his second pint when Peter walked in and sat next to him.

"They're staying at the Compton Guest house, it took me hours to find this out," he lied.

Peter did not reply; he knew Jimmy had led the three men and subsequently the police to Mary's flat but did not want him to suspect he knew. He had not realised Jimmy knew where Mary lived, but reasoned, knowing Jimmy for what he was, would have followed her on one occasion. It was always useful to know where people lived. Jimmy was always gathering information selling it to whoever would pay. He did not wish to confront Jimmy in the bar and told him he would have his twenty pounds later that evening and to meet him at the Blue Lion near the river at nine o clock.

"Don't be late Jimmy mate I must be at the other end of town by ten so stay sober, if you're late I'll be gone. Say nothing to anyone, this is between us."

"Why can't you pay me now?" he questioned.

"Tonight, you'll get all that is owed. Besides, I have another job which is worth double," he lied knowing Jimmy would be on the dot when it came to collecting his money.

Peter and two of his henchmen were waiting for Jimmy, staying out of sight under an arch. Peter knew Jimmy would be drunk by the time of the meeting intending to accost him before he had a chance to enter the Blue Lion and be seen. Ten minutes before nine, they saw him strolling on the opposite side of the river; he would need to cross the bridge to get to the Blue Lion.

Jimmy crossed the bridge where Peter and his two cronies confronted him. He ran but was soon caught and dragged under the bridge out of sight.

"Well Jimmy, what have you been saying to the three Welshmen and the police," Peter growled through clenched teeth.

"Noth… Nothing, honest Peter," he answered cowering. "I was only trying to get information for you, nothing else I swear."

"You are good at swearing. Do you think me a fool?"

"No, no, of course not Peter, please I was only…"

"Lining your pockets at my expense and taking me for a fool. How did they know to go to the flat?" Peter's voice was hard and menacing.

"I don't know what you mean. Flat you say what flat?"

"The flat you led them to. Oh my, your memory is bad. Something needs to be done about that, a little prod perhaps, what do you say boys? Shall we give Jimmy a little prod?"

The other two grinned. One said, "as you please boss we're here to help."

"Hear that Jimmy, they are here to help and not tell. Not tell Jimmy. Did you hear that?"

"Please Peter, it was all for you, I needed to gain their confidence. I was leading them off the trail."

"Memory coming back? Off the trail direct to the flat."

"You mean Mary's flat?" he faltered nervously.

"How do you know about the flat?" Peter hit him in the stomach. "You've been spying on her and talking to the three Welshmen, haven't you?" he said threateningly showing his teeth.

"No, no, honest, I was only trying to get you the information you asked, that's all. We'll call it quits over the twenty pounds. I'll give you back what you've already paid me. Let me go, please Peter. I'll find out what I can for you for nothing, I swear." He whimpered. "Honest, I was a little indiscrete and I apologise."

"A little indiscrete and apologise, you say, but with big consequences. You use the words far too much and do them an injustice. Come, come, you know I can't do that. You double-crossed me. What do you think we should do to people like you?"

"Please Peter, give me another chance" he pleaded, "I'll make it up to you, honest."

"Here you go again you insult honesty," slapping him across the face.

"I won't say anything to anyone anymore," he faltered, "give me another chance… here take this money," he cried his voice desperately pleading as he handed all his money to Peter.

"Well thank you Jimmy," said Peter taking the money and placing it in his pocket. "I'm going to take your word for it; I'll even sing you a little song in good faith.

Remember, remember Peter the avenger
He's come to say hello.
Remember, remember Peter the avenger
He'll come to Jimmy no more."

Peter smiled as he sang; without warning stabbed Jimmy in the stomach. "Because you are not going to be around anymore to talk to anyone," and stabbed him again and pushed his body into the river below. Jimmy fell heavily knocking his head against the wall on the way down and was dead before Peter heard the splash. "You're where you belong now Jimmy with the vermin of the river, honest!" and smiled. "Let's get out of here."

Chapter Twenty Four

The room was dark. The sound of the bolt clanked and rattled. The light went on, blinding Colin by the sudden brightness; he shielded his eyes against the glare. Slowly, his eyes adjusted and he saw the Chinese man standing by the door grinning. He stood up, conscious of the chain attached to his leg, shuffled forward until the chain tightened and could go no further.

"I hope the nonsense is over, you're here to stay, get used to it. You are going nowhere."

Colin had spent the whole night in darkness, was frightened, confused, disorientated and could make no sense of it, the fight out of him. He looked exactly what he was; a frightened, very frightened bewildered teenager totally out of his depth and shivered against the inhumanity of it all.

The Chinese man placed a tray on the floor, turned to go out, moved back and pointed to the food and left. Colin ate in silence, rice soup and bread, his eyes still not totally accustomed to the light from the one naked bulb in the room high above his head. An hour passed and the bolt moved. This time a short thin man he had not seen before stood in the doorway, wearing a suit and smoking a large cigar.

Colin stood. "Why am I here, pl…please?" he faltered looking the man directly in the eyes all anger gone.

"Because we want you here," puffing at his cigar. Colin could smell the smoke; in a strange way it gave him confidence.

"Are you going to kill me?" His voice trembled slightly.

The thin man laughed. "Not if you behave, you're far too valuable for that, you'll be put to work, that's what'll happen, put to work," took a pull at his cigar and blew the smoke in Colin's direction.

"What about Mary is she here?"

"Never heard of a Mary," he replied and was about to close the door.

"Wait… am I to stay here?"

"Yes, you'll be put to work to earn your keep."

"Doing what?"

"Serving your betters, being nice to them, slavery when abolished only went underground. Down and outs like you," he took a long pull of his cigar, "should be grateful for the opportunity to pay your way." He laughed.

"What if I refuse?" Colin asked boldly feeling the anger rise in him.

"That's not an option," the thin man grimaced with a half laugh. "They all do what they're told eventually or they end up in acid, that's what will happen to you if you prove to be too much trouble." The door slammed shut leaving the room full of cigar smoke. Colin went to the bucket to relieve himself and sat back on the mattress disconsolate.

In the room above, the thin Chinese man was talking. "I want him ready in six weeks."

The other Chinese man shook his head. "It'll have to be at least eight weeks minimum, six is too soon, he's strong."

"We haven't got the time, delivery must be in six weeks or the buyer will pull out."

"There are other buyers."

"Yes, but they want young girls, a young boy is the exception. Six weeks, delivery must be in six weeks, period."

"Come on be reasonable. We haven't started the treatment yet. If I speed up the process it may kill him, then where will we be?" he forcefully argued.

"I repeat, six weeks! Do what you must do, there's no more time," he was emphatic.

"It's highly probable he'll go mad or die."

"There's an old song, what will be will be."

"I want it known if anything goes wrong I've done my best and there is no come back on me."

He puffed his cigar. "Of course, no comeback and no payment either. We already know the risks and won't hold you responsible but we have confidence you'll pull it off, start the treatment with the next meal."

Chapter Twenty Five

Mary intended to lie low for a while and decided she should go and live in France for a few months. Peter would stay and keep an eye on things from the shadows. The only person who could recognise him was Jimmy, and he had sorted that problem. Peter realised it was highly probable the body would be found but there was nothing linking him to Jimmy. He believed the police would put the incident down as a fight.

A malicious thought struck him; he would direct the blame towards the three Welshmen. If it weren't for the low life from Wales, he'd still have Colin running errands from France.

The meddling three cost him dearly and would pay; he was glad Mary was out of the way or she'd try to stop him from interfering.

The police knew the Welshmen had been talking to Jimmy. Several people in the pub could verify that Jimmy spoke with them on a few occasions and they even bought him drinks. He'd spread a rumour they had a fight; a wry smile passed over his face as he thought how clever he was placing them in the frame for the murder.

Before Mary left he told her of his plan, he hadn't intended to say anything but always seemed to tell his sister everything. "Serves them right."

"Leave it Peter, why create greater risk, let it go, what's to be gained?"

Peter grinned. "Satisfaction, satisfaction."

"That type of satisfaction can get us caught, or killed. It's a perverse risk, it's an ego thing with you, let it rest; there is nothing to be gained. Jimmy I accept, you did right, he's better off out of the way, leave it at that."

"There is little risk, I need to do this."

"As you wish, you should listen to me more, see you in France in a few weeks."

Peter went to the Lamb checking first the Welshmen were not there and ordered a pint. He spotted old Mollie sitting in the corner and walked over. She was the biggest gossip around. He told her confidentially that he heard Jimmy was in a fight with three Welshmen the previous night near the river and knew she would do the rest and left. As a precaution he would stay away from the Lamb until things cooled down.

True to Mollie's reputation it was not long before the word got out, some people even remembered seeing the scuffle. Peter was clever and knew that unless the police found the body would not involve themselves and the odds were well in his favour.

"Three to one it was, that's what I was told, he was given a right belting by the Welsh boys," a customer from the Lamb was talking to his friends who sat opposite.

"Anything Jimmy gets he deserves, he stole my coat a few months ago. I know it was him but couldn't prove it. So good, I hope they gave him a good hiding and a few punches for me to boot."

"Yes, he's a bad one that, but we can't be having people from Wales beating up our boys," came the stark response.

"Look! One of them is looking for his son, if Jimmy knew something he should have told them."

"Well they were together enough, perhaps he did tell them."

"Why give him a hiding if that's the case, that's what I want to know?"

"He took their money and wanted more, Jimmy does nothing for nothing, conned them I expect, good riddance to bad rubbish that's what I say. Jimmy deserved it." Already accepting, a fight took place and Jimmy beaten up.

With that, the three Welshmen walked into the pub and sat at the bar. "Have you seen Jimmy," George asked the Barman.

"I think he's in hiding after what you've given him," he joked. "You only did what many would like to have done."

They were under the impression Jimmy had told the barman about the money and looked displeased the barman had this knowledge.

"He earned it," Henry replied in justification.

"I dare say earned or unearned, he won't be in here for a few days from what I gather," he laughed. The three Welshmen remained impassive. "It's none of my business you understand; keep out of things that's me. Jimmy deserves all he gets, that's my last word on the subject." He placed three pints of beer on the counter took the money and went to the till and then served another customer at the other end of the bar.

"I thought London was a place where everyone minded their own business," said George dispassionately.

"Doesn't seem that way," stated Henry.

"It doesn't matter who knows, it's not against the law. If we want to pay someone it's our business, that's all there is to it," said Bill. "It's no one else's business."

"Yes! Nevertheless, you know Jimmy is a petty crook, that one will do anything for money. We don't want to be tarred with the same brush," responded George.

"The information about the flat was correct, leave it boys. Jimmy earned his money." No one contradicted Henry and supped their beer.

Chapter Twenty Six

Colin lost track of time, one hour, two hours, all hours came and went; one day, two days, night or day meant nothing. The only light he saw was the one light in his room; it was either on or off. On, off, off, on, it was his sun, his night and day. He tried to fight the feeling of loneliness, despair, and abandonment that gripped him. The vice was getting tighter and found it increasingly difficult to focus on anything for very long.

He saw the short fat Chinese man several times a day, or at least he thought it was day, he really didn't know. The light was off, on, a blinding brightness, food tray taken, brought back. Time meant nothing, a space he was filling. The bucket taken, replaced by another; no one spoke, or acknowledged his existence.

He spoke pleadingly. "I'm here, pl… please say you see me," the silence remained. The man gave not so much as a nod in recognition. It was as if he were invisible. The chain around his leg bit into him, the mental anguish far worse.

Colin lay on the mattress shrouded in darkness, his coffin. He tried to focus, thought of his parents, Sophie, brothers, grandmother, a wave of sadness swept over him when he remembered she was dead, but wasn't sure, nothing stayed long in his mind.

He thought of Sophie and smiled. He held her face in his mind, saw her smiling, his pain receded. He heard her voice as plainly as if she were next to him.

She was holding his hand and spoke. "Read to me, read to me," he heard the words over and over, a record stuck in one place tumbling into his ears.

The light went on distracting him, angry it had interrupted his thoughts and shouted, "go away," silence. The bright bulb searing his eyes, the door opened a tray of food placed on the floor, the door slammed, the bolt grated across; silence.

Time a continuum, reference gone. The bulb ached into his brain; the brightness ate at his eyes. He heard the familiar bolt being clinked back, mouth full with food; a pain in the arm, his skin felt drilled, followed by darkness and silence, always the silence.

Colin lost consciousness, he was with his grandmother looking at pictures, and his grandfather's medal glinted bright or was it the bulb, perhaps the sun. That's mine; the medal is mine. His grandmother's voice filled his mind.

"Am I dead Gran?" he whispered into the darkness.

He heard her words clearly. "Death is but another room," he burst into tears.

"Take me away, Gran," he begged. "Take me to the other room," and banged his head violently against the wall.

Darkness turned to colour, red, blood red. His father's blood was pouring over him as the rollers pulled his body through. He gasped for air; every time he opened his mouth it filled with blood, his face red, his eyes shone. He heard a scream, his scream, the blood gone; he was outside his body looking at himself lying on the mattress shackled by the chain, his face bled from the constant banging on the wall of his head.

He heard a voice and turned. The farm boy he had nearly killed and later died of the smallpox stood next to him.

"What are you doing here?" he asked looking at Robert and then watched himself as he talked to the wall.

Robert was silent and stared at Colin's body. Colin stared at his body, turned, and looked at Robert. "You're dead."

A sad smile moved slowly across Robert's face. "Your rage is of no value now. If you are to survive, remove the anger; lock it away in the deep and dark recesses of your brain. Only that will keep you sane. Forgive yourself for what has been; already it is out of your control. Concentrate on what you wish to become in the future. That is still in your control. Take what I tell you as truth. I'm here to help you," he replied.

"Help! Why? I stole from your farm, nearly killed you; did kill you. It's because of me you died. Why help me?" Colin's body screamed back at the wall, both spirits watched. The blood returned; it was all over the room oozing out of the walls, the floors, the ceiling, everywhere. Dripping from Colin's mouth, hair, nose, ears, drip, drip, drip, the sound filled his head as he watched in horror. Robert's spirit transformed into a white haze and started to fade.

"Help, please help, madness is taking over my mind," his spirit spoke as his body below screamed and banged its head on the bloody wall.

The haze solidified, Robert moved back into focus. "You can only help yourself, the answer resides in you."

His body was now screeching at the wall. "I'm a robber of old ladies, a robber of old ladies, a murderer, I killed Robert I killed him."

"How can I help myself?" Colin's spirit replied, tell me.

"I have said."

He felt a sharp pain in his side as if a spear had pierced it; Robert's apparition faded into the blood and was gone. The room was dark, the blood turned back into the stones in the walls. He sat next to his body staring at himself prostrated on the mattress, the madness subdued now by sleep; he had knocked himself out.

He heard the bolt moving, the sound familiar. The door opened, the Chinese man entered holding a needle. He watched as the man pulled his arm, administering an injection near his shoulder. The door slammed shut, the bolt clinked back into its groove, the room silent again. Colin felt his spirit melt back into his body.

His vision went dim, his head ached, his body convulsed, darkness enveloped him. He noticed a white spot on the wall, which started to grow. Thin light beams shot out from its centre filling the room in an ever-increasing circle of brightness. In the centre of the light appeared a silhouetted figure, his grandfather.

Colin felt better. "Help me. What is happening to me Gramps?"

"You are paying the price for your own actions for the greed locked in your heart."

"Take me away from here," he pleaded. "Please take me away."

"Only you have that power."

Colin felt a little bolder. "The big house the cars… you showed me, they are mine. What has gone wrong?"

The apparition filled the room. "That was but one path to your future."

"Can you give me that future? This is torment. I am paralysed tethered by a chain to the floor."

"You are living your future, you will be paralysed, forever in purgatory. Why do you think it'll be any better than this?"

"You showed me."

"No! You were shown a large house that would belong to you."

"You say…" but the apparition's hands went up requesting silence.

"I showed you what might be. Not what will be; that is for you to decide."

Colin's spirit left his body. "I did not decide to be here, the house, the cars, wealth, that is what I want. Why am I here?"

"Your past actions decided for you. This is your choice, paralysed forever locked in your own body. The consequence of past actions, your actions, this is but a taste of things to come."

"This is not what you showed me. I'm going into madness."

"It's exactly what you were shown but your eyes were closed. Madness can also mean oblivion, perhaps, it is better than the other path you were shown?"

"How can that be better?"

The apparition reached out and touched Colin's hand, the walls of the room melted away. They stood outside the house previously shown to Colin. They walked side-by-side towards the house straight through the wall. Sitting in a wheelchair was a middle-aged man; the woman he'd seen when first shown the house fed him.

The woman looked old and weary, deep lines etched into her face, her hair white with care, her eyes sad. The man was unable to move even his hands. The women wiped his mouth and placed a straw into it for him to drink, which he eagerly took.

"This is what you brought my daughter to," the apparition shouted, startling Colin.

"My mother! That's my mother? How can this be?" he shrieked. "She is old, wrinkled worn out."

"This is your future; it is you being fed by my daughter." The apparition angrily bellowed. "You were shot in the back several times, the bullets paralysed you from the neck down, you are in constant pain. Your body is now your prison not stone walls, you have greater freedom in your cell than you do now. Yes, you are rich Colin, but it is a richness earned from other peoples' misery, now you are paying the price."

"Where is my father?"

"There were four of you in the car when you were shot, you the only one to survive."

"My two brothers and father?"

"Yes."

"Dead? This can't be."

"Yes, it will be Colin. This is your other future and will come to pass. You have the big house, the cars, money, but your barn is empty, your body a prison, and will remain so until you die."

"Is there no hope? Madness one way, despair and pain the other. Take me back let me die now. I've seen enough."

The walls returned, he was alone in the room surrounded by silence and darkness and opened his eyes. "Madness it must be, madness it will be," he kept repeating to himself. No, I'd rather die and pulled his body against the wall to give himself maximum slack with the chain and wrapped it around his neck and he tried to strangle himself.

The metal bit into his neck. He pulled harder, harder, but did not have the strength and fell over frustrated; tears ran from his eyes mixing with the blood. He screamed at the floor, banged his head against the wall until his face and head bled further and then blankness; he had knocked himself out.

He awoke; the blood congealed over his face, reality flooded back. There were no more tears left in him, he was past crying, past redemption, past hope. He would go into madness, accept his lot; the big house and cars meant nothing.

For the first time he thought of his father, mother and brothers not of himself. He didn't care what happened to him as long as they were safe. Acquiescence registered across his face, an awakening, he would embrace what lay before him, accept what life would throw at him with a glad and open heart. His family was more important to him than he was to himself and sat back on his mattress with resignation to await his fate.

Chapter Twenty Seven

The police found Jimmy's body a few miles downriver with knife wounds in his stomach. George, Bill and Henry were unaware of this. They were minding their own business sitting at a corner table in the Lamb waiting for him to show when two policemen walked in, strolled over to the bar and started talking to the barman. After a few minutes, they left.

"I bet he's selling out of date beer, this pint's putrid," Bill said grimacing at the other two as he took a drink from the glass and thought no more of the incident.

"It's what I said, Jimmy has taken the money and gone to ground," said Henry.

"He's hungry for money, he's aware there is more, he'll show," answered Bill. George sat on his stool but said nothing. In his mind, he had already given up the search and was thinking how he would tell his wife.

A little later the two policemen returned and stood by the bar occasionally looking over towards them. "Yes officers they're over there," said the barman.

The policemen walked over to the three now seated at a table and asked them to account for their movements over the last few days. This sounded strange, the police already knew they were asking questions around the area but they thought it best to answer. It was easy for them to account for all their movements.

Henry kept a strict diary of where they had been, the times, how long they had been, whom they met, building a picture of their search for Colin, which they freely shared with the police.

"We need to verify this information. Would you please come to the station with us," one of the policemen requested.

They looked incredulous. George was the first to speak. "Are you arresting us officers?"

"No sir, we need you to help us with our enquires."

"You know as much as we do about Colin," George replied confused, thinking the worse. "Have you found him? Is he all right?"

"This has nothing to do with your son, it's about Jimmy, he's been murdered. From the information we have, you three were the last to see him. Shall we go gentlemen," not giving them any choice. "The quicker we can get it sorted the better for you."

They arrived at the police station a while later, taken to the reception area, and instructed to take a seat, the atmosphere to say the least hostile. A few minutes later, a man in plain clothes came through one of the many doors leading off from the reception area. He beckoned them to follow showing them into separate rooms telling them to wait.

Henry was the first interviewed, two detectives alternately asking one question after another in rapid succession. Henry felt intimidated but held his ground.

"How many times did you see Jimmy? When was the last time you saw him? What did you talk about?" The questions went on relentlessly. Henry answered each one honestly. Then they threw a question that flummoxed him. "Why did you beat him up and kill him?"

Henry looked at the two interrogators. "I… we didn't kill him, didn't even know he was dead until you told us. We were paying him to get us information. We had no reason to kill him; our only concern was in finding Colin and that…"

One of the interrogators hands went up to stop Henry speaking and said, "so you thought Jimmy wasn't coming up with the goods so you decided to rough him up a bit but it went wrong, didn't it. Tell us Henry which one of you killed him, which of you killed him?" he repeated louder.

Henry shouted. "Why would we kill him? We had nothing to do with it."

"You beat him up, you must give us that, you've already admitted as much to the barman. Now come on Henry admit it to us." Before Henry could answer, the door opened and a third detective appeared, walked over to the table and whispered something into the ear of one of the interrogators.

"The other two have just admitted they beat him up and pushed him into the river. Which one of you used the knife? We know it wasn't you Henry, tell us, it will go easy on you," moving his face close to Henry as he spoke and then pulling it back and added in a friendly voice. "Make it easy on yourself; tell us what happened, an accident perhaps, a frightener gone wrong. It happens all the time. It'll go worse if you keep lying."

The room was silent. Henry knew they were lying. They were trying to trap him into saying something that was not true by pretending the other two had confessed.

He looked at one and then the other, folded his arms in defiance and said. "You're lying; they wouldn't do that because we didn't kill him."

One banged the table. "You told the barman you beat Jimmy up."

"I said no such thing," Henry strenuously denied.

"The barman said to all of you, and I quote from his statement. 'He's in hiding after what you gave him.' You replied, 'he deserves it.' The barman stated, not realising he was already dead. 'Jimmy deserves all he gets.' Do you refute what the barman said?" The police officer smirked. "Come, stop messing us around."

"No, I'm not denying what I said," Henry answered and realised they were in a lot of trouble. "I was referring to the money we had given to Jimmy, nothing else, nothing else," he protested and saw the triumphant smiles spreading over the two interrogators' faces.

They both stood up one going to the door opened it and shouted to the duty sergeant, "take him to the cells." Turned to Henry and said. "We'll carry on this conversation later."

The other two underwent a similar interrogation but they said very much as Henry. There was nothing else, only the truth. They had detailed records of their movements kept by Henry, the police were able to check this out over the next two days and found every detail tallied to their great frustration, they had hoped to sort this murder quickly.

The police were convinced they had murdered Jimmy and thought they were dealing with sophisticated clever people. When in reality they were ordinary working men, only looking for George's son caught up in something they knew nothing about.

Why else would they produce such a detailed record of their time, the police concluded, if not as an alibi? One of the interrogators wanted to charge them on the information already at hand using the barman as the main witness but they all gave similar stories about the conversation, enough similarity, the other thought for a jury to find them innocent. In any event, it was highly likely the Prosecutors Office would throw it out for lack of solid evidence and had to let them go pending further enquiries.

Back in the hotel room, they took stock. They'd been in police cells for the last two days unable to speak to each other and felt events were running away from them.

"Do you think Jimmy's murder is linked in some way to Colin?" George asked the other two.

"I don't know. I can't see how," Bill replied scratching the side of his head without realising.

"There's a link, there must be, but what it is I don't know," Henry said. "Jimmy took us to that flat and someone didn't want him around to give us more information so they killed him, that's what I think."

"Do you think Colin is mixed up in something against his will?" asked Bill.

"That I can't say, but he's mixed up in something right up over his head. Someone killed Jimmy to stop us getting to Colin. We're dealing with ruthless people and need to be careful."

George was shocked at the suggestion. "Come on Henry I think you're over dramatising the situation. Jimmy was a small-time crook, more than probably it's nothing to do with Colin or us. The police pulled us in because we're the only lead they had and needed to be seen doing something."

Henry shook his head. "I don't think so. There are too many similarities, there's a link, and we need to find it."

"What's our next move?" enquired Bill thinking Henry seemed too positive in jumping to the conclusion.

"Back to the Lamb, someone somewhere knows something. We need to track down this Mary woman, she's behind it somehow," Henry was convinced.

They went back to the Lamb where the reception was rather frosty. A few of the regulars were whispering in the corner as they entered but no one spoke directly to them just innuendo. Keeping quiet would gain them nothing; they needed answers and needed them quick.

They sat on stools next to the bar and Henry asked the landlord for three pints of beer. As the landlord turned George said, "do you believe we had anything to do with Jimmy's murder?"

"I'm called Graham and keep my opinions to myself, that way I'll enjoy my old age."

Henry re-asked the question and Graham shrugged his shoulders. It was obvious they were not going to get any help from the barman.

"Graham, we had nothing to do with Jimmy's murder, we were paying him, and he was helping us. George here is only looking for his boy, we need your help to find him," Henry said. Explaining what he meant when he said Jimmy deserved it. "I was referring only to the money we gave him, nothing more. You must believe that Graham."

He turned and rested his elbows on the bar. "I personally believe you had nothing to do with the murder but there are many here that think otherwise, you three need to watch your backs. Jimmy had enough enemies locally; he didn't need any more from Wales. The fact is he's dead, murdered by all accounts. He got up to a lot of mischief, I'll be the first to admit and I had little time for him, but it's for certain he didn't murder himself and you lot are in the frame."

"He led us to a flat rented to a Mr. and Mrs. Williams, the name that keeps cropping up time and time again is Mary. The flat was empty when we arrived. Moved out in a hurry so the neighbours say, the boy was with her, if we find her we find the boy," informed Henry and took a sip of beer.

"Mary! Yes, I know the name, if it's the same person, been in here a few times always well dressed, a good looker, intelligent, sharp, a rare quality around here. Speaks French and German I've heard, behaves posh, a cut above the rest that come in here. In her early thirties, accompanied normally by a man also well dressed about a few years older than her but I've seen neither lately come to think of it. Why would Mary have business with the boy? Seems strange that."

"Only she can answer that," Bill stated. "Find her and hopefully as I've said, we'll find the boy."

"If I were with her I'd not wish to be found," grinned the barman lecherously.

Henry frowned. "He's still a youngster."

"Is there anyone else here that can help us?" George asked taking a dislike to the barman.

"Following what's happened to Jimmy after he was seen talking to you? You must be joking. You lot are pariahs. You'll get more information talking to that pillar," pointing.

"This other person? Do you know his name? The one you say is sometimes with her," Bill enquired.

"Not sure, but wait, he's often seen talking to that group of women in the cubby hole; hold on, I'll ask." Graham went to the other end of the bar pushed his head through a hole leading into another room. They could hear distant nondescript voices, a moment later, he returned. "His name is Peter. Mary is his sister, he's in here four or five times a month when he's in town which is not often lately, so they say."

"Graham, it's appreciated. You've given us a lot more to go on, have a pint with us," offered Henry.

"Don't mind if I do. They say he's a bad one but well spoken, far worse than Jimmy who would skin a flea for a penny. This Peter would torture the flea just for the sheer fun of seeing it suffer, charming mind, a real gentleman, so the old croakers say; he often buys them a drink."

This new information started them thinking, could it be they have Colin as a prisoner and using him to steal. George and Bill greeted this with a laugh but Henry was serious. George thought it nonsensical, Colin was up to no good, he felt that, and in with a bad crowd, but a prisoner! That was taking things a bit far.

Colin was not just a prisoner, but a prisoner poisoned by drugs, in a few short weeks would either be dead, or if he was lucky, thousands of miles away. Either way, there would be no way back for him; the drugs were slowly, systematically eroding his mind. This was beyond their comprehension, too farfetched to imagine; something you read about in a book, just stories.

George, Henry, and Bill had displayed Colin's picture around the area but nothing came of it. A few said they'd seen a boy like him around accompanied by a well dressed woman, or thought they did, a few weeks ago but were not sure, if they had a fiver for every 'not sure' they'd all be wealthy.

"We are still in the frame over Jimmy's murder; to make a nuisance of ourselves could see us back behind bars. Have you forgotten we were told to report back to the police in three days and that's tomorrow," Bill reminded them.

Chapter Twenty Eight

Peter was worried, extremely worried. The three Welshmen were back on the streets and asking a lot of questions, too many to make him feel comfortable. He could not risk anyone seeing him near the Lamb and had to be careful wherever he went, always looking over his shoulder and this irritated him.

They were combing the area asking after him and getting too many answers. He was quite well known in a few places and reasoned it would only be a matter of time before they turned up something important and he was dragged into it.

Peter thought the few days they spent in the cells would frighten them enough to send them scuttling back home but he was mistaken. It achieved the opposite. They were now far more vocal in their search than before and he needed to do something to get them permanently off his back. He didn't believe for a minute, despite what Mary had said, one was the boy's father believing they were after Colin because he stole their money and they wanted it back.

He thought about following Mary to France for a few months, but that was impossible at the present time. He had a number of deliveries to fulfil, if he went now would frighten away many of his contacts. He needed to keep his head and carry on as normal; some of his old haunts were out of bounds and a number of his connections were avoiding him. A few were already concerned, said in no uncertain terms that he was getting too high a profile for their liking and to keep away. Told to fix the situation or leave the area until things cooled.

Peter took any warning from the Triads seriously. They had seen the posters of Colin displayed and knew any publicity was bad publicity. If the security of any of their operations were jeopardised he would be the one found in the Thames with his throat cut; there were no rules in this game, only survival.

Peter knew they would kill Colin without the slightest provocation; if the situation worsened, the danger would spread to him and get messy. The Triads never gave a second warning, he hadn't had a warning yet just a concern, but knew the warning would come shortly if he didn't bring the situation under control quickly. Followed by retribution if the situation persisted; they were people no one messed with.

An idea struck him. He still had the knife. He was going to throw it into the river after he stabbed Jimmy but was glad he decided against it. He would plant the knife with the Welshmen and tip off the police. Surely, that would do the trick; the problem would be over. The only difficulty was how to plant the knife without them knowing.

He knew where they were staying. He needed to get into their room, plant the knife, and escape without anyone seeing him. He would have to arrange for the police to find it before they did and knew that would be difficult. It was high risk, too high risk; their room was out. Eventually, he hit upon hiding the knife somewhere in the lobby. It was not the ideal situation but the next best thing to convince the police of their guilt and put them behind bars for a long time, problem solved.

He would book into the hotel for one night under an assumed name saying he was from Leicester on business, plant the knife in the tank in the toilet off the reception area, all reception areas had a toilet, and tip off the police anonymously. He phoned the hotel immediately and booked a room for the following night.

He returned to his flat, put on a wig, false beard and glasses. He donned a business suit and carried a briefcase and an overnight bag. He was sure of his disguise and felt even his sister would fail to recognise him. A little later, he confidently strolled into the hotel and checked into reception.

He went immediately to his room, deposited the bags and left to confirm he could get into the lobby toilet without being seen. He could just as easily have walked into the toilet but if the police asked the receptionist questions about who had used the toilet over the last few days it was better not to be in the frame, even though he was in disguise.

He knew the police would ask for a list of the guests over the last few days but felt it unlikely they would check out the false address he had given in Leicester. Even if they did, there was still no connection to the knife, just an anonymous businessman wishing to keep his identity secret, which happens quite a lot and shouldn't arouse suspicion.

The main staircase leading to the rooms was at the opposite end to the toilet, adjacent to the lift in prominent view of the receptionist. He would need to walk past the receptionist to get to the toilet and wished to avoid this if possible. He then noticed a fire door beside the lobby toilet, which led to stairs signposted for emergency use only in case of fire. He would use these emergency stairs, plant the knife in the toilet cistern, and be back in his room, no one the wiser.

He felt so confident he even went into the Lamb and ordered a drink sitting at one of the side tables; no one paid any attention to him. In the opposite corner were the Welshmen in conversation, soon they'd be in deep trouble, and he smiled to himself thinking them fools.

Chapter Twenty Nine

Colin lay on the mattress looking up at the bulb with glazed eyes as it burst into light. The door opened, he was still gazing at the bulb. A man placed a tray of food and drink on the floor and left, slamming the door; darkness descended, silence returned, he just stared, stared at the darkness still not moving. The only motion in the room was a lone tear that ran from one eye; a tear of hopelessness, despair, resignation, Colin had given in to the inevitable.

Outside the room, the two Chinese were in conversation. "He's ready, this has been easier than I imagined. The amount of drugs we gave him to speed up the process should have killed him. At first, he was very stubborn; as it turns out, he's the easiest I've ever encountered. This is the second time he has not touched his food. He just lies there waiting to be told what to do and we still have two weeks to go, this is definitely a record."

"What if he's acting?" the thin Chinese man asked.

"That is no act, he's broken," the other confidently replied. "No one acts that good."

The thin man looked away. "I'm not convinced, he's the most determined one I've seen in a long while and now, in four weeks, ready." He shook his head. "I don't believe it, I have my doubts."

"Look!" the other replied positively. "We've still another two weeks to go, if it is an act we'll know by then, stop worrying. I'm telling you it is no act."

"Carry on giving him the injections, increase the doses. I want no mess-ups; he's too high profile for my liking. I'd rather see him dead than us suffer any comebacks. They're already aware the treatment over six weeks could kill him and have agreed the strategy. Go ahead - do it. The repercussions of him dying will be less than if the treatment was not completely successfully and he manages to raise an alarm. Should he regain his senses and cause trouble, or it proves to be an act as I suspect and he escapes, the Triads will eliminate our cell, you know what that'll mean?" The thin man said and drew his hand across his neck.

"If we carry on increasing the treatment it definitely will kill him, we lose our payment on delivery, and all the work is for nothing."

"You had him cheap in any event; he will remain alive, that should be enough."

"That's not the point. Let me stabilize the treatment not increase, he'll be ready within the week, one week early and compliant, no mistake. Leave it to me."

The thin man was still apprehensive. "But… But!" he spluttered.

"Look! If there's the slightest doubt before we hand him over, I assure you, I'll kill him myself and dispose of the body and say the treatment didn't work."

"Right, but if there are any mistakes over this we are both dead men."

"There won't be I know my job, stop worrying. Let me get on with the work."

The thin Chinese man walked towards the stairs. "If you want me you know where I am. No risk," he emphasised and left.

The Chinese man went back into Colin's room; he was still in the same position staring at the bulb, the food tray untouched. The man asked him to stand; he stood not saying a word. "Sit back down," he demanded. Colin started to sit; the man countermanded the instruction and told him to stand again. He instantly complied with all requests.

He instructed him to sit next to the tray on the floor and eat. Colin immediately walked over to the tray sat down and started to eat the food. He countermanded the instruction again telling him to stop eating and to pour the water, which was on the tray, over his head; once more, he obeyed without question.

Then he told Colin to take his clothes off and go down on his hands and knees and bark like a dog. These instructions went on for the rest of the day the man thinking up ingenious ways of how to humiliate Colin until he was sure he could safely remove the chain on his leg, and would still obey all commands without question.

The next day the man removed the chain followed by further humiliating drills. Once he even had Colin drink his own urine, smother his food with his own excrement, and eat it. Thus making doubly sure his obedience was no act, and delivery of a perfect package to the Triads was beyond question.

Colin was off the chain and for a few hours every day the Chinese man left the cell door open. He was now confident of success, the process fully complete. Colin was no longer human, a machine to be turned on and off at will. An automated toy used and abused at the whim of others for their amusement; to do whatever they instructed; his very life depended upon it.

Colin could see his actions, his mind separated from the deed. His actions and body parted, sliced apart like the two halves of an apple no longer connected but still the same body, his mind the willing instrument of others to instruct as they saw fit.

He locked himself deep inside his mind, afraid to come out knowing the conclusion of the other path. He would accept this path without a fight, without question, his mind would remain closed as a kernel inside its shell holding the reflection of his parents and siblings alive; his mind closed even tighter.

Chapter Thirty

The police arrived with a warrant to search the hotel. They knew exactly where to look; an anonymous caller had given them detailed information; they went to the lobby toilet where they found a knife in the cistern, bagged it, and sent it for immediate analysis. They also searched the room of the Welshmen and a number of other areas in the hotel but found nothing of importance.

They asked the three back for questioning and when they refused arrested them. They were in the police station overnight for interrogation and to await the forensic results of the knife. The police felt sure the forensics on the knife would be conclusive; they were sure they had the murderers and could prove it.

The Welshmen were interrogated for most of the night but the police gained no further information and got increasingly frustrated by what they believed was their lack of cooperation. The knife would be enough they were told so it would go easier if they all made statements. They even tried to bluff them stating, as they questioned each one in turn, that his fingerprints were on the knife hoping one of them would crack.

The police were now convinced they were dealing with a syndicate of hardened criminals and at each opportunity were looking for evidence that would fit with what they believed, not what the evidence actually stated.

Jimmy's body had been in the water for a few days, before they found it; the carcass was bloated to twice its normal size and badly damaged. The forensic test was inconclusive; the knife could have been the murder weapon, they couldn't be sure and there were no fingerprints on it. The evidence again would not stand up in a court of law to the great chagrin of the police. They had no alternative but to let them go the second time, insisting they report to the station every day, still convinced of their guilt.

They left the police station knowing they had been set up. If the knife was the murder weapon, it was pure luck the police were unable to prove it or they would have detained and charged them with the murder.

They were irate. They walked back to the hotel. "Colin's in trouble, big trouble and we need to find him quickly. I'm convinced he's held against his will and someone was prepared to go to any length to keep us from finding him," Henry stated. The other two agreed. There was no laughter this time; they were in deeper trouble than they originally thought. Confused, frustrated, and angry they wondered what they were up against, but knew, whatever it was, it was dangerous.

"Why?" Bill said. "None of it makes any sense. What could Colin possibly be mixed up in which is so awful they'll commit murder to keep us from finding him? It's way past the pale."

"It's obvious the police think we are guilty. Someone is giving them information against us; it's lucky we're not already permanently behind bars. These people won't give up until they succeed, from now on we must be careful, keep our eyes open all the time."

"That's easy to say but what are we looking for Henry?" George questioned.

Bill agreed. "Where do we go from here?"

Henry shook his head. "I don't know, just don't know. There must be something we've overlooked."

They went over everything that had happened, re-examined every little detail, going over all the conversations they had with

Jimmy, the barman, the receptionist at the hotel where Colin stayed but they all led back to Peter and Mary.

"Jimmy knew more than he was letting on that's why he was murdered," Bill murmured.

Henry agreed. "Let's go back to the Lamb, make a nuisance of ourselves, wait for them to make their move. They tried to get us behind bars and failed. They'll now try something else, we need to be ready."

"We're in danger now; to do what you suggest will put us in greater peril. We are dealing with murders and I don't know what else? It'll be us floating in the Thames if we are not careful," said a worried Bill.

"What's the alternative?" Henry barked angrily at him. "To leave and forget about Colin?"

"No but we…"

"Please! Quarrelling will get us nowhere. Bill is right Henry. We are dealing with desperate people; to carry on will mean a knife between the ribs and a swim in the Thames. It's getting too dangerous. Why don't you two go back, I'll stay on a few more days to see if anything turns up?"

"That's not an option George," murmured Bill, "I only said we're in danger and need to be vigilant, and stay together, I never suggested we abandon Colin."

"Bill you're right, sorry to have barked, they're hardly going to attack three grown men together. We're staying until we find your boy George, if it means I end up in the Thames in the process so be it. But I'll take a few of them with me first that's for sure," Henry laughed minimising what he had said but there was a gravity in the laugh indicating his seriousness.

"Henry, Bill, you… ok, thanks boys but…"

"No buts, we are all in this to the end George so let's get on with it," stated a defiant Henry.

George just bowed his head and thought how lucky he was to have friends such as these. Nevertheless, inside he was slowly starting to accept that he would never see Colin again. He tried to suppress this thought, put it out of his mind but it kept creeping back. Colin was dead, and he wondered how to tell his wife.

"Colin's alive George," Henry said as if reading his thoughts.

"I hope so Henry, I hope so," he replied despondently.

Bill placed his arm over George's shoulder. "Come, we'll find him but first we need a good night's sleep."

Chapter Thirty One

Peter was distraught. The Welshmen were back out on the streets. What must he do to get them off his back? He was sure when the knife was found they'd be charged but instead spent only one night in the cells and were released without charge, pending further investigation.

The three were now asking more questions than ever and Peter was on edge. Two unknown Chinese men accosted him informing him the Triads were losing patience, intimating that if he didn't sort things in a few days, it would turn nasty.

There was no need to spell out what this meant. They wished him good day with a grisly smile and walked off leaving him where they stopped him on the street. It was obvious to Peter the Welshmen couldn't be intimidated, if anything, they were intimidating the people they were questioning, throwing their weight around.

They wanted information on Colin and the murder and were asking high profile questions in an open manner. They also had a drawing of Mary and Peter put together from descriptions given them by the regulars in the Lamb. They had difficulty at first but when the customers saw the landlord cooperating they did the same when it became generally known that one of the three had lost his boy and was only concerned in getting him back, nothing more.

They looked as if they could handle themselves; they appeared to be tougher than he first thought and not country bumpkins. Perhaps one pretended he was the father to get information. Colin had plenty of money on him, maybe he had stolen from them, and they wanted to question him and then kill him. Peter had thought all along that they were more than they seemed and each event reaffirmed his belief further.

His first reaction was to get a few men together, beat them up, and get at the truth but that could be difficult. If things were to go wrong, it could make them more determined, who knows how many more were behind them. Besides, where would there be an opportunity to get the three together in such an isolated place. He could kill them and dispose of the bodies but would need help, increasing the risk to himself further. Whatever he did he would work alone.

He thought of shooting them when they left the hotel but there was no guarantee all three would be killed; it would create a media frenzy; Colin's picture would be in all the papers, no, that was definitely out. If the Triads saw Colin's picture splattered over the front page of the daily newspapers it would be the end for Peter. They would brand him a loose cannon, too hot to handle, and would have him killed.

He thought of starting a new life in France away from it all, leave them to it, but his distribution contacts were in London and he would be unable to earn. He had enough savings to last a few years but that was all, besides, Mary had expensive tastes, there was no way she would stay in France permanently so he quickly discounted that option.

He should have killed Colin instead of selling him to the Triads that would have been the end of it and berated himself for his stupidity. The Welshmen wouldn't then have posed a problem, they could ask all the questions they liked and he wouldn't worry. Nonetheless, they were involved and dangerous. He needed to do something quickly. Suddenly, an idea dawned on him.

He would blow the hotel up and them with it, there would be a number of other casualties but he looked on this as a necessity, may even be to his advantage. The media would hardly concentrate on Colin then. If it meant killing another dozen or so people, so what, it would take the heat off him. As long as it protected him and his sister he reckoned it was worth the sacrifice, besides, no one need ever know he was involved, not even Mary, but supposed he would tell her, he told her everything.

There was little chance they would survive a direct blast and the questions would stop. He knew Colin would be out of the country in a few weeks, all trace gone. He would be secure because the Triad would feel safe and things could get back to normal.

Chapter Thirty Two

The door to Colin's cell was open all the time allowing him access to the other basement rooms. Not one of them had a window all were below ground. The rooms had solid walls, not that a window would have made any difference to him. He was totally under their influence, an automaton. He no longer needed the injections, but still received a low dosage; he cooperated fully, eagerly, to the great satisfaction of the two Chinese. All tests were complete, passed with flying colours; the Chinese men informed the Triads the package was ready for delivery at their convenience.

They received a message back to delay delivery until further notice. This annoyed them somewhat, the Triads had insisted that the delivery was to be ready in six weeks even if it killed him, now they were requesting a delay.

They knew the reason, but still, it was frustrating. The sooner the delivery the sooner the payment but knew it would not take place until the danger of the Welshmen was concluded one way or the other. If the press were involved and there was no real news on which to concentrate, Colin's picture could easily be in all the papers. If they thought the risk of delivery was too dangerous, they would kill Colin, and destroy the body without trace. This option irritated the two because they would receive no payment for all the weeks of work they had already completed. There was no question of arguing they had already finished the work, they were just one synod among many controlled and paid by the Triads. If they insisted on payment before killing Colin, they would follow him shortly after.

Colin was a willing servant to the drugs not fighting them in any way. He wanted to be under the influence, the other path too painful to contemplate. Whatever life threw at him, he would accept, without complaint or question.

He remembered his old life but locked all these thoughts deep inside his mind. They came to him in his dreams, as if they were a film played repeatedly on an old screen. The way he treated people, his selfishness, his uncontrollable temper, the theft from the old woman, the fight with Robert and many other things passed through his mind.

His grandmother's smiling face, as she sat by the fire, a cup of tea in her hand looking at him, a tear fell from the corner of his eye. The walks they went on together, the two side by side often holding each other's hand. The many conversations came flooding back to him. The tear turning into a smile, his mind moved to Sophie, saw her face smiling up at him as he read to her.

His father, the many wonderful times they spent together in the garden, he felt happy, contented, feeling his father's love like a cloak wrapped tightly around him. His mind raced on, all this gone, forever gone, because of his actions. Yes, he was the architect of his own undoing; he had finally accepted responsibility that his actions, and his actions alone, were responsible for where he now found himself. A thing he had never done before, another tear rolled down his cheek, darkness shadowed his mind like a veil, his face motionless.

The stout Chinese man noticed the tear in the corner of Colin's eye and a hard look fell across his face thinking he needed to increase the drug dose to eliminate all emotion from him. Then he thought better of it, reasoned it was because of the speed they had to get him ready for delivery. His body had not quite adjusted to the drugs; it was just an automatic reaction and not emotion and the man dismissed it as an irrelevance.

Chapter Thirty Three

Peter needed to ascertain the movements of the Welshmen, to check the times they came and went. Wearing his disguise, he sat in a cafe opposite the hotel drinking coffee, waiting. The three came out just before 9 a.m. and did not return until after midday, stayed in the hotel for the rest of the afternoon, coming out again at 5 p.m. Peter watched the hotel all day and this time decided to follow them, one quality he had in abundance was patience.

They turned left at the hotel and walked for nearly twenty minutes before they stopped at a small guesthouse and he could see them taking out a picture and asking questions. After ten minutes they left and walked to the police station and were there for over half an hour. This worried him intensely and gave him a melancholic feeling. Thinking they had information and were passing it on to the police he decided to check with his contacts at the station. The sooner these meddlers were out of the way the better.

The three were only reporting to the Station as ordered, if Peter had known this he would not have felt so threatened. The reality of the situation was they had no information whatsoever and were repeatedly hitting a brick wall. The police were continually giving them hassle; they were exhausted with the lack of cooperation, frustrated at the treatment received at the hands of the police.

They went directly from the Station to the Lamb and talked to the landlord. Peter, still in disguise, sat in the corner and placed his coat over the chair; he went to the bar and ordered a drink, walking past them. If only he could listen to what they were saying he would have an idea of what they knew, but reasoned it didn't matter. They'd be dead shortly so it made little difference, took a sip from his glass, and smiled.

They stayed at the bar for over two hours talking to people near the counter. A few were nodding but Peter could not make out any words and felt it would be safer if he left and waited outside to follow when they emerged.

Henry noticed it first, "don't turn now, but I think that man in the corner has been watching us since he came in."

To Henry's surprise George answered, "I'm sure he's watching us but didn't say anything. Did you notice Bill?"

"No can't say I did. Shall I go and have a word with him."

"No" Henry replied sharply. "Let's wait and see what happens but stay close when we leave in case there's trouble. We'll stay on the main road."

"He could be with the police," said George. "He looks the type."

"May well be," agreed Henry.

"Look! He is going," George mouthed under his breath. A few minutes later, they started back to the hotel. They noticed the man in the shadows; he retreated further when they walked by but they had already seen him.

"Just walk, don't show we've noticed him," Henry whispered to the others, "but let's keep our eyes peeled in case there are more lurking in the shadows, walk away from the pavement."

They kept a quick pace back to the hotel, occasionally glancing back to see if anyone was following but saw nothing. They went into the hotel and to their room feeling a little shaken.

"There could be more of them, if we show our hand without knowing the numbers we'd end up with a worse hand. You two stay put, I'll go down and sit in the foyer pretending to read the paper and keep my eyes peeled, they expect to see the three of us together and won't be looking for one."

"Don't leave the hotel Henry," said George.

"No of course not."

Peter needed a few days to get all the explosives together, to know what room they were in, and to allow enough time for them to settle for the night. After a decent interval, he entered the hotel lobby and walked to the desk.

The receptionist looked up and smiled. "Can I help you sir."

"I hope so," he smiled back. "Are those three people that just went past from Leicester?"

"Leicester? I remember you; you've stayed here before. When you said Leicester it just reminded me where I've seen you, are you going to stay with us again?"

She's a sharp one thought Peter. "Yes, I think so," he faltered quickly gaining his composure at being recognised. "I'm down on business, left my cases at the station and will pick them up later."

"Would you like me to arrange for someone to collect them?"

"Um…" mumbled Peter pretending to think. "No, that's all right, I think not, thanks for asking. Those men, from Leicester?"

"No, they're Welshmen, one of them is the father of a runaway lad, they're having scant luck from what I can gather."

"A pity, sorry to hear that. There are many runaways in London it's tragic. We need to do more to help these young people. Hope you've given them good rooms they've travelled a long way."

"Yes, all our rooms are good, they're all in one room the largest, overlooking the front. They are nice people."

"Bit noisy there isn't it."

"Not at all. All the rooms overlooking the front are large, and mostly soundproofed."

"Last time I stayed my room was at the back," smiled Peter. "What perfume are you wearing, it smells really nice, must get some for my sister."

The receptionist blushed but told him the name.

"I must write it down before I forget. Do you live at the hotel?"

"Good gracious I should be so lucky. No." she laughed.

"If you did I bet it would be in one of the large rooms," he smiled.

"The largest rooms are on the second floor only. I've stayed a few times but in the box room on the top floor," she smiled; she liked this person, friendly, nice, easy to talk to and wondered if he were married.

"Are all the large rooms full?"

"Hold on a minute I'll check, they are more expensive."

"No matter my company is paying."

She looked down the list in front of her on the desk. "We have two rooms empty on that floor number 210 and 214."

"I hope they're not next to the Welshmen, I hear they're pretty noisy after a night out."

"Noisy, no, they're gentlemen. There's not a word out of them when they're in the room but if you… they're in 209 we'll give you 214."

"No! You're right of course, they're gentlemen. I'll take 210," he smirked. He had the information and the room next to them. A satisfied grin moved across his face. He handed over the money for five nights in advance and the receptionist passed him the key marked 210. He accidentally dropped it on the floor picked it up, grimaced over his clumsiness, and placed the key into his pocket.

"Perhaps we can talk again some time." He shouted over as he waited for the lift.

"Yes I'd like that," the receptionist answered.

The room had one large bed and a smaller one under the window allowing just enough room to stand by the window overlooking the street. He placed his ear to the wall separating the two rooms and could hear them moving around. He placed his ear closer, intently listening; he could hear voices but not loud enough to make out clear words.

He would plant the explosives against the wall next to their room and the blast would rip through and kill them. There would be nothing left of this floor and his troubles would be over; pity about the receptionist he thought, I quite fancied her, if she survives, perhaps, when it's over I'll come back and comfort her.

He vacated the room, headed down the stairs, and left the hotel to get the cases of explosives. He had to go to the other end of town to his flat and needed a taxi, picking it up off the street a few blocks away.

He returned to the hotel with two large cases and carried them straight to his room, placed them on the bed and listened to see if there was noise next door. All was quiet, they were out but then heard the door opening, and talking outside in the corridor, the door slammed, he knew they were back in the room.

He opened one of the cases, pulled out a coil of wire, and cut it into ten equal lengths connecting one end of each to a box that was in the case. He placed the lengths back into the case locked it, removed it off the bed and placed it against the wall and opened the other case.

Inside were ten sticks of dynamite, each stick wrapped up in loose cloth and packed around with rags together with six bags of steel nails. He removed the rags, unravelled the cloth around the sticks, and replaced them in the case securing them to the bottom with masking tape. He placed the bags of nails over the dynamite taping them secure.

He cut another ten lengths of wire and placed one end in each stick of dynamite, closed the case, locked it and placed it next to the wall alongside the other case. The only thing he would need to do later was to attach the two ends of the wires together and set the timer to the detonator. He could not get this until the following day. He would then get the hell out of there and wait for the explosion to blow away his troubles.

Two sticks would have been enough to blow the wall out and do the job. The amount of dynamite in the cases would blow the whole floor, perhaps even the street. The other floors would collapse on top, notwithstanding the damage the nails would inflict on the human body. Originally, he wanted to try to make the explosion look like an accident but thought better of it. It will look as if someone was taking revenge against them for killing Jimmy.

What Peter didn't know was that Henry was sitting in the reception lounge. He watched the stranger going into the lobby, talk to the receptionist and check into the hotel but it struck him as odd that he had no luggage.

He saw him take the key from the receptionist, dropping it. Henry noticed the number 210 the room next to theirs. He went back to the room to report what he had just witnessed.

Henry wasn't sure if the man next door was listening and related the story to the other two in a whisper. They all looked at each other in earnest afraid to speak in case overheard.

"Let's go and have a pint. I've just been out to get some cigarettes," Henry said loudly.

They left the room slamming the door hard but before they left, placed a thin piece of paper between the hinges at the bottom to tell them if someone opened the door when they were away. They returned two hours later but the paper was still where they left it, so they knew, he wasn't there to search their belongings.

This made them nervous and decided one of them would stay awake while the others slept. Henry took the first three hours followed by George then Bill, the night passing without incident.

Breakfast was at a nearby coffee house. Henry spoke first. "We must do something. I feel like a neutered dog. It's not a coincidence. He's not next door for nothing. We need to find out why."

"What do you suggest? You can't break in," stated George.

"Why?"

"He'll call the police that's why, we'll end up back behind bars, we're in enough trouble already."

"Only if we're caught George, that's where you two come in. I have a plan."

Bill shook his head. "Leave me out of it."

"Oh no Henry, I want nothing to do with breaking the law," stated George. "There must be another way, come on, be sensible."

"There could be information that'll lead us directly to Colin. We wait until he's out; you two keep watch. Who's to know?"

"I don't like it one bit Henry not one bit."

"I'm not over the moon about it myself, too much has happened, but this is the best lead we are likely to get."

"It's a dangerous strategy, I'll give you that. The police are already on our backs; to break into the room next door would give them the excuse they're looking for to bang us up and throw away the key."

"Look! Bill." Henry replied irritated. "What if he intends to murder us, someone killed Jimmy? Do we wait around for our turn?"

"What if it turns out the person's a police officer watching us?" said George.

"Could be, there is one way to find out, search the room, do it so he doesn't know we've been there." Henry grimaced. "It's the only way, the only way I tell you."

"We can't break down the door. How do you suggest we get in, fly through the window like a bird?" Bill laughed.

Henry's eyelids went up and he smiled. "Precisely! That's exactly how, in through the window. None of the window catches are secure and easily opened from the outside. I'll move along the sill from our window to his room and get in that way.

You keep watch in the street George, Bill you watch George from our window. If George gives the signal he's coming back, knock the wall and I'll be able to get out and through the door before he's even in the lobby. Don't worry, the risk of getting caught is minimal."

"Famous last words," laughed George.

"You can't go climbing in and out of windows in the daylight you'll be seen, and what if you fall," stated Bill.

"Fall! Height is no problem to me. We'll do it this evening when it gets dark."

"That's a bit like saying we'll land on the sun in the night, day or night, we'll still get burnt, there's a risk you'd be seen, but you're right, we need to know so I'll go along with it."

"Me too! We need Colin back," said George.

After breakfast, they called at a few places to show the photo but their hearts were not in it, thinking of what they were going to do when it got dark. They lunched in the Lamb but did not speak much to each other or anyone else. They were deep in their own reflective thoughts. They were about to commit a crime; even though the motive was honourable they still felt they were doing wrong and this was playing on their consciences, Henry included.

They spent the afternoon watching the next room. The man had gone out early in the morning; they saw him return at 3 p.m. carrying a large black bag over his shoulder. He stayed in the room until just after 5 p.m. and left the room empty handed. George followed him out and saw him getting into a taxi. He took the cab number more from habit than design and placed it in his top pocket. He re-entered the hotel, returning to the room to wait for darkness.

When it got dark, George went into the street and stood on the corner opposite the hotel, looked up at the window and gave the thumbs up to Bill; all was well. Thumbs down meant the opposite and was Bill's cue to knock the wall for Henry to get out of the room immediately.

Henry opened the window in his room and slowly shuffled along the ledge to the other window. Through the closed curtains, he could see a light was on and tried the window. The occupant had locked it. Henry pulled from his pocket a thin screwdriver, pushed it between the sashes of the window, and tried to dislodge the catch but it was stiff. He held the top of the window and tried again; there was a slight movement; the catch moved.

He manoeuvred the screwdriver back and forth under the catch until he heard a click. He pulled up the bottom half of the window and went through making sure he closed it after him replacing the window catch to locked, careful to disturb nothing.

The room was an identical model to their room but there were two beds instead of three, one bed being a double. A lamp in the corner was on and it dimly lit the room making it look warm and pleasant. He went straight to the door and listened for any movement in the corridor. He opened the door and looked out both ways, all was quiet. This was his escape route and needed to make sure he could open the door quickly; he went back to the window, and checked all was well with George.

Henry opened the wardrobe and drawers; they were all empty. The bed was neat as was the room. It seemed from the lack of possessions the man wasn't sleeping there. The only things in the room to show occupation were two cases placed against the wall nothing else. He tried to open one and then the other but found them locked. Then he noticed wires going from one case to the other and he could hear the faint sound of a clock ticking.

He froze momentarily and shook his head in disbelief. Using the screwdriver, he eased the lock of the first case open being careful the whole while; his initial instinct had been correct. He was looking at sticks of dynamite. The other case held the detonator with wires attached to a box with a clock strapped to the side. The time showed there was just over seven hours left on the clock, which registered 4 a.m. when the timer would activate the detonator.

Henry had worked in the pit most of his life, for ten years with explosives. The dynamite sticks were of similar type he had handled many times, there was enough in the cases to blow up the whole street. He was not sure of the timing mechanism but knew the sticks were safe until someone activated the detonator. Without giving it further thought, he removed each wire from the dynamite in turn, separated the detonator and timer, and rendered them safe.

He sat on the bed and breathed a sigh of relief. His hands started to shake uncontrollably when the magnitude of what he'd just accomplished fully dawned on him. He knew that the dynamite, when activated, would not only kill them but most of the other guests, as well as many passers-by. He regained his composure, walked to the door, and wedged it open. The person who planned this atrocity did not intend to come back to the room, secrecy the least of his worries. He knocked on the door of his own room.

"Call George up." Bill just stared at him dumfounded by his openness.

"You're very blasé. Did you find anything?"

"Find! That's an understatement. Yes! You won't believe what, come and look. He won't be back in this room again," walked to the other end of the room opened the window and called to George to come up from the street without any recourse to discretion. He beckoned Bill to follow, went into the other room, and showed him the two cases. Bill's jaw fell open in amazement. George came in and could hardly comprehend what he saw.

"I've made the dynamite safe; it's the same kind we used underground."

"What type of people are we dealing with here? I'll call the police," Bill said shocked. George just stood there shaking his head in disbelief.

"If this went off, a few hundred people would be dead. We must be near to finding something out, something big. There's no length these people will go to stop us."

"There is more to this than just finding Colin," said George. "We've stumbled into something, something big."

"I agree. Our only concern is finding the boy and getting out of it," remarked Henry. "Sooner the better."

"I'll go down to reception and call the police."

"Wait! Hold on a minute Bill. Close the door," demanded Henry. "We need to think this through before the police are called. I've got a bad feeling about the police. They've caused us no end of problems. The dynamite is safe so there are no worries about being blown up, at least tonight anyway."

Bill's face was deadpan. "Don't joke Henry, it's not funny."

"Do you think the dynamite is aimed at us?" stated George.

"Yes of course, who else? We're dealing with ruthless killers."

"What do you suggest then Henry?" George asked still dazed at the revelation.

Henry said. "If we call the police they'll at the very least take us in for questioning, whoever is trying to kill us will go to ground with Colin. We'll be back to square one and they could still kill us later. It's obvious we're near to finding something or they wouldn't go to this length to stop us."

"We're out of our depth here. I still think we should go to the police."

"Then what? Tell me that, then what? Think about it!"

Bill thought for a moment. "The whole place will be crawling with police and the one lead we now have will be gone."

"Exactly!" Why risk it when we are this close. We get Colin and get out," agreed Henry.

"But they'll know. When the bomb fails to go off they'll still go to ground," stated George.

"Not necessarily, there was only one man in the room. If the bomb doesn't go off and there are no police around he'll conclude the timing mechanism has stopped and will come back to check and reset it, we'll be waiting. They are desperate to make sure we are out of the way. When the bomb doesn't go off and there are no police around he'll be back."

Bill shook his head. "But what if he doesn't?"

"We call the police. He'll know the only person to go into the room will be the cleaner and that is around midday so he'll be back some time before then to check. If not, we'll clean the room of our fingerprints and let the cleaner find the dynamite. She'll call the police and we'll be in the clear. Let's get a few hours sleep nothing will happen until the morning," stated Henry.

"I don't like it." George replied. "I don't like it one bit. This is way over our heads. We should go to the p…"

"Look George," Henry interrupted. "To go to the police now and have them crawling all over the place will frighten off whoever is trying to kill us, they're ruthless in the extreme. If we don't find Colin shortly I've a feeling they'll kill him rather than risk exposure.

We have no time to waste. Sorry to be so blunt but look at their track record. If we don't find him shortly, it'll be too late. When he returns to reset the detonator, we'll have it out of him where he's keeping Colin even if I have to kill him and kill him I will if I have to, for what he tried to do here. Make no bones about it, it's now kill or be killed," stated an emphatic Henry suspecting it may already be too late for Colin but kept that thought very much to himself.

George's eyebrows went up. "I hope you know what you're doing. It doesn't seem real what is happening to us."

"I'm with you Henry. George, what do you say?"

George nodded in agreement. "So be it Bill."

Henry indicated he would sleep in the room they were in sending George and Bill to their room to meet again the following day to spring the trap.

Chapter Thirty Four

Peter asked the receptionist to order a taxi to Reading and from there promptly caught the train back into London travelling by tube to his flat. He realised there was a fair chance that after the explosion the taxi driver would come forward as a witness and say he picked up a man near the hotel and dropped him at Reading making the police think he went out of London. He removed his disguise before he caught the train and placed the items in his bag intending to dispose of them later.

It was late evening before he arrived at his flat and went straight to sleep. He wanted to be up early to listen to the morning news and later to go to France and take a few weeks holiday. He turned on the radio but there was no mention of any explosion on the 6 a.m. news. He was perplexed.

The seven o'clock bulletin also failed to mention it so he decided to take the tube to see for himself. An hour later, he was near the hotel; there had been no explosion. His first anxious thought was that someone had discovered the explosives and the police called in the middle of the night. If that were so, why hadn't the police evacuated the area, he wondered. Perhaps the police had been and were lying in wait. The place seemed quiet, too quiet to have had a disturbance of that magnitude a few hours earlier. He called into a coffee shop a few doors from the hotel. He ordered a cup of cappuccino and causally remarked there had been a lot of police around the area the previous night. The waitress shook her head in disagreement and said the cafe had been open throughout the night and she had not seen a single police officer.

This perplexed him further and wondered what could have gone wrong. He reasoned that if someone discovered the bomb the police could not have kept the information to themselves. At the very least, they would have evacuated the hotel and the press would have almost certainly found out about it. No, something else must have happened.

To be sure he walked past the hotel and casually looked in and recognised the receptionist at the desk. All appeared normal. He crossed the busy road, called into another cafe, ordered a cup of tea, and wondered what to do next.

He mentally went through all he had completed when he set the bomb; he conducted everything in sequence and could find nothing wrong with his procedure. He followed the same principle a few years ago at a warehouse in Dover and it blew to the second, the damage exactly as planned. The only thing not planned was the death of the watchman caught in the blast, that was a minor mistake, an accident.

The time was approaching 10 a.m. He was getting more worried by the second. Immediately the cleaner entered the room, she would discover the bomb and would inform the police. They would be crawling all over the place and they would interview the Welshmen. The press would swarm on them; it would make front-page news. Colin's photo would be in all the papers and on the news bulletins before the weekend.

His fingerprints would be found in the room, he never thought to be careful reasoning the explosion would do the job for him. Questions would escalate thick and fast. If the police questioned and fingerprinted him, which was unlikely but a possibility, they may charge him, that is, if he was still alive.

The Triads would kill him and Colin without further consideration. He contemplated getting out of town to lie low until the incident blew over but if he ever came back he would still have the Triads to placate, an impossibility, they would be after him. There was little alternative; as much as he disliked it, he would have to risk going back to the hotel to reset the devise and shuddered at the thought. He remembered his disguise and was glad he had not thrown it away. There was a problem; he needed to go back to his flat get the items, put them on, and be back in the hotel before noon.

His room was half way up the corridor so he felt certain the maid would leave the room until last as he had put the 'not to be disturbed sign' on the door before he left. He hurried back to his flat and was back outside the hotel at 11.30 a.m. He walked around the area hesitantly, still weighing up the different options. If they discovered the bomb, he was finished in London, the Triads would see to that and perhaps everywhere else. In ten minutes he could be in and out and walked towards the hotel reception thinking the quicker it was done the quicker he'd be away and his worries over.

He strolled casually into the lobby smiled at the receptionist and walked slowly towards the lift.

The receptionist called after him. "I thought you were still in your room sir."

This startled him; he was already on edge coming through the front door, turned and smiled directly at her. "I forgot to give the key in when I went out this morning sorry about that. I'm only going back to collect some papers won't be too long."

"Don't worry we often get people taking the key with them, the only problem is their rooms are cleaned last."

This brought a smile to his face, his composure returned. He would remove the timer, lock the cases, place them in the wardrobe out of sight, ruffle the bed to look if he has slept there, and return in the evening with a new timer after the maid had cleaned. It can only be the timer he thought realising he should have tested it first, he entered the lift but still felt on edge; it wouldn't have taken a lot for him to turn and leave things as they were and go to France to be with Mary. There was a risk; if the explosion happened when he was in the building, he would go up with the rest of them. He checked that no one was around, walked smartly to his door and entered.

He woke up on the bed his face looking at the ceiling, his head sore from the crack he received when entering the room, his hands and legs tied with wire.

Henry stood over him a menacing look on his face, the other two near him. "We finally meet," he growled slapping him hard across the face, the false beard gone.

George and Bill winced.

Peter said nothing just spat away the blood from his cut lip. "Why did you try to blow up the hotel?" Henry asked; another slap to the other side of the face. He was playing it tough from the beginning.

"I've just checked into this room," he spluttered. "I don't know what you're talking about," he lied.

"The disguise, the dynamite, following us, come on Peter, we know who you are. Where's Colin?" Henry asked straight to the point.

"Please let me go," he pleaded. "I've just arrived from Leicester. Check with the receptionist if you don't believe me."

Henry grinned. "No, we don't believe you, why wear a disguise? My patience is almost through," Henry stated looking more menacing than ever. The other two looked on in sheer surprise, Henry was really playing the part.

"What are you going to do to me?" he sneered back. "The police are already onto you."

"We could kill you." Henry commented, "or…"

"Then you'll never find the boy or your money," Peter laughed maliciously.

The remark angered George who raised his hand to hit him but pulled back at the last minute.

"I'm the kind one here Peter," Henry whispered. "His speciality," pointing to George, "is skinning people from the feet up."

"Kill me then," he taunted, calculating they wanted the boy more than they wanted him dead.

"Well, you were going to blow up the hotel. Why don't we let you do it? We'll use you as the detonator." Henry stated.

"You're bluffing," he answered still reeling from the blows Henry had inflicted upon him. "You know nothing about explosives."

Henry gave a cold smile. "We'll see about that." He walked over to one of the cases and removed two sticks of dynamite and wrapped them around Peter's waist. He connected the detonator to the dynamite, turned and smiled maliciously at Peter, and packed the other cases neatly under the bed. "Two should do the trick. Don't worry, I'll make sure you are tied to the bed. I don't want you wriggling too much. I'll set the clock before we go, 15 minutes should do it. Is that long enough Peter? I'm quite the expert with this stuff as you can see." Henry smiled evilly. The others knew Henry was bluffing but Peter didn't and that was what mattered.

"You're bluffing," Peter snarled.

"Watch me!"

Peter tried to move and shout but Henry stuffed a towel in his mouth and bound it tight with wire, securing him to the bed unable to move.

"We won't be next door, we'll be long gone. We'll tell the receptionist we bumped into you on our way out and you asked us to tell her you're going to take a nap and not to disturb you until you ring her. I'll tell you what; I've changed my mind about the dynamite under the bed. It's your lucky day, I'll take the rest of it with me no sense in wasting it, two should sort you nicely; soon this place will be a ball of fire. Pity you won't be around to see it, not to worry, there'll be plenty more fire where you'll be going." Henry grinned and slapped Peter across his face.

"You're bluffing," he snarled.

"We'll see," Henry picked up the timer, connected it to the detonator, set it for fifteen minutes, looked over to George and Bill told them to be ready to leave.

"Bye Peter pity you are so stubborn. We only wanted the boy; you could have gone free. But it's too late now," Henry said and they all started to walk to the door.

Peter was going frantic on the bed trying to speak. Henry bent forward. "Do you wish to say something Peter?" He enquired in a matter of fact voice. "Perhaps some last request, maybe? All right, I'll let you have your say. Not long mind, no shouting, we must be going. We don't want to get blown up with you, do we?"

Henry removed the wire from around his neck and pulled the towel out of his mouth.

"You lot are crazy. All right, all right, not the gag again, you win. I'll tell you but stop that timer."

"The timer stays on, you have one minute to convince me. We can't stay any longer. I know you'll understand."

Peter shook and squealed like a pig. A clever pig granted, telling them only half the story but enough for Henry to stop the timer.

He told them about Mary, said she befriended the boy, helped him and he was kidnapped by the Chinese forcing her to flee to France for her life. He told them about the flat, knowing they already knew, adding that Colin had his own room and could have left at any time but chose to stay. Henry asked him many questions but Peter was adamant, he did not know where Colin was only that the Chinese kidnapped him to ship him abroad as a slave or something similar.

"Why did you try to kill us?" Henry asked.

"I was afraid of the Chinese. With you out of the way they would leave me alone."

This did not ring true. Henry carried on asking more questions but failed to get any further information. He then started the timer again and said goodbye, picked up the towel to stuff it back into Peter's mouth.

Peter moved his head from side to side, "OK, stop."

"I've told you the only thing we are interested in is the boy, tell us where he is now, you get to go free. If not, boom," Henry indicated raising both hands in the air as he spoke.

"Wait! Wait a moment with the towel. If you get the boy back how do I know you'll let me go free?" Peter asked moving his head back and forth avoiding the towel as Henry was trying to force it into his mouth.

"No questions asked. We get the boy, go back to Wales, you go free, simple." Henry said shrugging his shoulders.

"All right I'll take you to the boy, it's up to you then?" Peter said.

"No, you tell us where he is and you go free after we have the boy, that's the deal, take it or leave it," Henry demanded. "I'm getting very impatient."

"He's in the Chinese sector or was a few weeks ago," Peter blurted and went on to give the full address and location. He was hoping they would all be killed when they tried to rescue the boy giving him at least a fighting chance of talking his way out of it with his Chinese contacts; failing that France and into permanent hiding, but at least he'd be alive.

The contempt they held for this man was absolute. They knew he was lying and would kill them at the first opportunity without a second thought. He had intended to blow up the hotel to get at them and they had to convince him they were the same. They had little choice but to trust him if they wanted to see Colin again, the problem arose as to how they were to keep him a prisoner until they checked his story.

They searched him before they tied him up finding among other things a bunch of keys, various papers, his wallet, and a 9 mm handgun. Henry looked into the wallet and this gave him an idea. His full address was on the inside. They would take him there and hold him captive until they had the boy back and then decide later what to do with him. There was still the problem of how to get him to the flat without him escaping but they could not leave him tied up on the bed. The room was due for cleaning in a couple of hours, and upon his discovery, he would expose them.

Henry held the gun in his hand and pointed it at Peter's head. George and Bill winced but said nothing. "I've shot a few like you in my time," Henry spoke softly into his ear.

Peter's face was in shock, his eyes opened wide, then closed; he seemed about to shout but Henry rammed the end of the gun into his mouth, any sound he was about to make the end of the gun rendered silent.

Henry looked menacing, Peter was afraid of this man, his body started to shake and he urinated uncontrollably. Henry turned to the other two and smiled so Peter could not see his face. The act was working. He was no more capable of pulling the trigger than the other two but knew that the only language people like Peter understood was total callousness. He needed to convince him that he was more than capable of pulling the trigger without thought as if he had done it many times in the past.

"If you were on my bed and you soiled it, the next would be your blood," Henry said pushing the gun a little further into his mouth. "We are going on a little taxi journey Peter, remember, this is going to be your only warning, if you speak one word out of place or try to escape you'll be fertiliser for the daisies."

Peter nodded his head in agreement and Henry removed the barrel of the gun from his mouth and wiped the end on Peter's shirt before placing it in his belt. "I'll keep this gun. George you get the others from our room, bring the silencers as well," Henry requested loud enough for Peter to hear. There were no other guns but George left the room, returned a few moments later with two bags, and handed one to Bill. They needed Peter to think they were all armed, not just Henry.

"You know about dynamite and carry guns." Peter hesitantly faltered. "Who are you, what do you really want with the boy?"

"Let's just say Italy is not the only place where you find the Mafia, the boy is of value to us," Bill replied before Henry had time to answer. Henry gave him a sharp look as if to say, "don't overdo it."

"I suspected as much, he's got something you want."

"Enough talk," stated Henry.

They untied him from the bed, fetched a dry pair of trousers belonging to George for him to change into, and told him they would be leaving the hotel by the back entrance. He was to walk between George and Bill and just to emphasize the point and to ram it home, Henry hit him in the stomach. They placed the dynamite and detonator into the bags, made sure there was no trace of the explosives in the room and left.

They travelled via the fire escape and once out of the hotel hailed a taxi. Peter was bundled in the centre between Henry and Bill. George sat opposite and instructed the driver to take them to Peter's address. The journey lasted a little over thirty minutes, the traffic being relatively light. They spoke very little alighting from the taxi outside the apartment block.

A few minutes later, they were in the lobby and took the lift to the flat. The lounge was large with expensive furniture. It was obvious Peter lived a luxurious life style. Henry pulled out the gun and told him to sit. There were no illusions among the three. They were dealing with an extremely dangerous person and were taking no chances. They made him sit in a chair, tied his hands behind his back and his feet together, and started asking further questions.

Henry gave him little slaps when he failed to answer, eventually they had the information, and it seemed to be consistent. They informed him they would check it out to see if what he said was correct and dragged him into one of the bedrooms. They tied him to the large four-poster bed, tethering his arms and legs to each corner by a length of wire fed under the bed and wrapped several times around his body. They stuffed a cloth into his mouth, bound tightly, and placed a pillowcase over his head. They were making sure he would be going nowhere;

even Houdini would have had trouble getting off this bed, George thought.

They left the apartment and walked to their destination. The building was as described by Peter, in that at least, he had been telling the truth. The front of the building was a pawnshop selling all manner of items but mainly crammed full with old furniture, except for a pathway in the centre leading to the counter.

"I need to look around the shop," Henry informed George and Bill. "It's unwise to be seen together. They know three Welshmen are asking questions; we don't want to let them know we are on to them. You look around the area especially the back of this building, but do it separately. We'll meet up at the flat in about an hour.

They went different ways. George walking around the building as if casually strolling checking where the windows and doors were, Bill looking in the various shops for anything out of the ordinary. Henry entered the shop browsing through the various items pretending to be a customer.

There were two people in the shop, one carrying a small table to the counter, the other trying to move between several pieces of furniture with great difficulty. The tightly packed furniture looked more for show than for sale. He could hear the customer with the table haggling with the young female assistant over the price, until eventually, the amount was agreed. He walked passed holding the table, a big grin on his face; it was obvious he was happy with the outcome.

"Can I help you sir," a voice called to Henry. He looked round startled; from behind a large wardrobe to his left a short, broad Chinese man walked forward smiling. "Are you interested in that chair," he asked, seeing Henry looking at it.

"Might be if the price is right," Henry answered more in a Cornish accent than Welsh. Henry eyed the man carefully. He was definitely the man Peter described. Henry felt like grabbing him and choking the information out of him but just asked politely, "how much?"

"Twenty pounds, it's one of the best chairs we've had for a long time," he answered. Henry hated the way he grinned.

"That's expensive," Henry answered through a false smile.

"That's the price," he stated "take or leave it."

"I'll leave it thank you. I'll carry on looking if that's alright with you."

"Of course," he answered and walked back behind the wardrobe where Henry could now see a curtain with a doorway behind. The curtain fell back after he walked through disguising the entrance. He browsed for another few minutes and slowly made his way to the counter.

"You must sell a lot of stuff. That last customer seemed happy enough," he asked the young shop assistant casually.

"Not a lot, most of this stuff has been here years, that's the first sale in five days," she innocently answered.

"How do you keep open?" he replied trying to look nonplussed.

"Well they pay me, so here I am," she laughed. "Is there anything I can help you with?"

Henry thought best not to pursue the matter further and left saying he may call back in a few days. It was obvious to him that the business from the shop was not enough to keep it open and was convinced it was a front for illegal activities. He found Bill and George waiting near Peter's flat and went up to discuss the information they had gathered.

"One thing odd about that building is the windows, they have all been bricked up. It must be like the black hole of Calcutta in there but why, unless of course it's being used as a prison." George stated.

"That's just what it could be used for," answered Henry. "The shop is a front for something. We need to find out if Colin is in there and soon. We can't keep this Peter fellow trussed up for more than a few days. We could break in tonight."

The others looked at Henry aghast. "Henry! How can we do that?" George answered rather taken aback.

"If we were… there is no way he'll walk out and meet us; unless… unless one of you two have a better suggestion, I see little alternative."

They shrugged their shoulders.

"All the windows are bricked up. There are two doors in the back leading into the alleyway and look solid wood and will not give easily. There is a small backyard but it is heavily overgrown with brambles and undergrowth." George answered. "There is no way in. There are two windows at ground level but as I said earlier, they have been bricked up."

An idea started to form in Bill's mind. "Overgrown… the yard you say? Could we make a hole in one of these windows big enough to get through?" he stated developing the idea in his mind as he was speaking. "Bricked up windows are weak spots in most buildings."

"We could I suppose, the yard is not overlooked. We could take our time opening up a hole in one of the bricked up windows without a lot of noise," George stated in a doubtful voice and then added. "No, what if Colin is not there and we are caught. We'll be as bad as they are and end up in prison."

"No, come on George, we are not like them, we are doing it to find Colin." Henry answered. "Remember that, we know the shop is a front. We break in and find out what's in there; that's the only way."

They debated the pros and cons of the plan until eventually they talked themselves into it. They would purchase the tools needed, scale the wall to the yard, and try to gain entry into the building. The risks were high, and knew it could land them in a cell but if Peter was correct and Colin was there, they needed to know. If he was not they would just leave the building and take nothing.

Bill went out to purchase the equipment needed for the night's work. Henry and George paid a call on Peter in the next room undoing his bonds giving him some freedom and an opportunity to stretch his legs, eat some food, and use the bathroom. He sat in the chair after going to the toilet, Henry pointing the gun at him the whole time.

They questioned him repeatedly, Henry hitting him once when he was clearly not cooperating. The only other information they had from him was someone lived on the premises full time. They felt much of what he was telling them was lies but they had no way of proving it. They could only carry on asking questions and sifting the information the best way they could but it was difficult. They discounted most of what Peter said but suspected he was telling the truth about someone living in the building.

What they were going to do with Peter after the break-in crossed their minds, but decided one problem at a time was more than enough for the present. It was obvious they could not keep him captive forever.

They retied his hands and feet making him sit in the kitchen; warning him that if he tried anything or shouted he would be back on the bed gagged and blindfolded. Bill returned with the tools in a large bag careful to make sure Peter did not see them. There were two hammers, a few chisels, a small bladed saw with several spare blades, a cordless hand drill with various sized drill bits, a large pair of pliers, small hedge clippers and three torches.

Bill closed the bag and Henry said, "we go after dark, one at a time, leave at least a few minutes in between and hide in the garden until we are all ready to start. We need plenty of cloth to mask the sound of the hammer blows and drill. I'll rip up a few of the blankets into strips and bring them along. We need to be there at least an hour before the pubs close and wait until the streets are clear. To be seen out late with these tools is asking the police to stop us."

They tied Peter back to the bed and donned warm clothes for the night's work. George would go first and wait until Bill arrived to hand the tools over the wall. Henry would wait keeping a watch on the building to make sure no one saw them. The garden was overgrown with brambles, weeds and years of accumulated rubbish. Bottles, cans, papers, old carpets, bits of rotting board and a heap of old window frames filled the small space.

George landed heavily; bottles and tins crunched under his feet. He stood still waiting for the sound to subside and slowly cleared the area around him to give the others a quiet landing. He placed a piece of old carpet on the cleared floor area to deaden the noise further.

He made his way round the wall clearing a path, picking up old bottles, cans, bits of wood and shifting them to the side in order to get round to the bricked up windows. He cut back the brambles and weeds as he went with the small saw he had with him.

It was over half an hour before Bill arrived, handed more tools over the wall to George, and jumped over landing on the area George had just cleared.

"Sorry I'm a bit late, there were a few kids loitering at the other end and I wanted them to move on first," Bill said in a low voice.

"It's worked out all right, I've cleared a path around the edge of the wall and we can't be seen even if someone looks over the wall. How far behind is Henry?" George asked.

They heard a sound the other side of the wall but no one spoke in case it was not Henry until they heard him call. George pulled himself up and told Henry to jump over the wall. A moment later Henry was with them informing them a thin Chinese man had just left the building by the front door leaving a light on in the shop.

They moved around the inner perimeter wall and saw the bricked up windows close up. They studied them thoroughly. Eventually, deciding to take the corner window for no other reason than it seemed the more secluded, the undergrowth was taller there. They arranged the tools and waited until the pubs closed and the night well advanced before they started work. One of them would watch the alleyway to make sure no one was near;

the other two would work on the window, silence being the main priority.

George volunteered to take the first watch over the alleyway and just after midnight, the work started. They found the hammer and chisel far too noisy, and decided to drill out a hole big enough to crawl through in the brickwork. It seemed to take forever, by 3 p.m. they were less than a quarter through the work.

"We'll not finish this work tonight," Bill said to Henry pressing his shoulder against the handle of the drill.

"The outer wall is always the strongest it shouldn't take us this long to get through the inner partition." Henry replied.

"We have at least another three if not four hours to drill, we can't stay here much after 6 a.m. We've got to be back over the wall before it gets too light and the street becomes busy." Bill replied taking his turn at the drill.

George heard a noise and told them to stop work, there was a car in the alleyway. He could see the bottom of the alleyway through a hole in the wall and noticed a black car pull up and stop. No one got out at first and he thought for one horrible moment that the Chinese man had discovered what they were doing. One of the side doors in the alleyway opened and he saw a short stocky Chinese man standing there. The light from the doorway was shining on him and noticed he had dragons, or what he thought looked like dragons from that distance, tattooed on his arms. This must the same man that Henry met in the shop he thought.

The Chinese man beckoned to the car; two people got out, one walked to the front of the alleyway, the other to the back passing George hiding the other side of the wall a few feet away. George looked shocked; he was one of the policemen he had seen at the station. He watched the car closely; out of the back got another person also known to him, it was the sergeant from the station. It all made sense why the police were trying to pin the murder of Jimmy on them and he felt angry but clenched his teeth in silence.

"I've told you before," he heard the Chinese man say to the sergeant, "to use the other door."

"No time," the sergeant answered. He went round to the other side of the car, opened the door and pulled out an unconscious child wrapped in a blanket, the only part showing was the feet. George looked closer unable to comprehend what he was seeing. The only explanation was they had kidnapped the child. He felt like jumping over the wall and killing these people where they stood, but controlled himself and watched as they carried the young child into the building. A minute later, the sergeant returned, got back into the car, the other two followed and drove off, leaving the alleyway empty and quiet again.

George quietly crept over to the others and told them what he had seen.

"Who are these people who kidnap children for god knows what and murder at will if anything gets in their way. Even the police are in on it, no wonder…" Henry was too angry to finish turned and started to drill the wall with renewed vigour.

"We won't finish this tonight," Bill said. "It's just gone 4.30 p.m. I suggest we stop in a little while, clean up, hide the tools in the undergrowth and come back fresh tonight."

"I want that child out tonight," Henry demanded. They both knew he was thinking of his Sophie and said nothing.

It was nearly 6 a.m. and it was obvious they would not complete the work in time. They could have gotten through the wall in a few minutes if they smashed their way in but working silently with the drill was slow laborious work. There was no alternative; even Henry had to accept they had to return to complete the work later that night.

Chapter Thirty Five

They arrived at Peter's flat at just gone 6.30 in the morning, washed themselves, and put on clean clothes. They did not wish Peter to see them dirty, the less he knew the better. They discussed the situation at length over breakfast and knew they were on their own, the police not to be trusted. The sergeant, at least one of the constables and others probably, were in league with these people.

They untied Peter, allowed him time to stretch his legs and to see to his toiletries, all the time Henry pointed the gun at him feeling a great urge to pull the trigger. This was not lost on Peter; he perceived the hatred Henry held for him and felt one wrong move on his part would be his last.

"I'm going to ask you one question Peter," Henry growled. "If you answer wrongly I'm going to kill you." He meant it, his eyes flashed with fury. This was no act on Henry's part, he was angry.

"What policemen are involved in this racket of child abduction?" Henry asked pointing the gun directly at Peter's head. The sweat glistened on the back of Henry's neck. "I'm waiting."

Worry etched into Peter's face, he thought of an answer knowing it may be his last. "I… I'm not sure what you are talking about," he stammered. "Please, please, don't kill me," he pleaded. "Why don't you ask them?"

Henry's eyes narrowed, the gun moved closer to Peter's head. The others were just about to stop him when he hit Peter directly in the face with his other hand. Peter reeled back into the chair and held his face with both hands.

"I'll ask the question once more but before you answer we know who they are but want you to tell us."

Peter stared at the barrel of the gun physically shaking, his bloodied face filled with sweat. "The sergeant, and two constables… there are three, please, I've told you all I know, don't kill me please, don't kill me." He begged.

"The boy, is he still there?" Henry demanded, the end of the gun touching Peter's forehead.

"As far as I know, yes. I know no more, please, I beg you don't kill me," he pleaded again.

Henry hit him with the side of the gun and turned his face away in frustration, his features red with anger, eyes ablaze with fury at the contempt he felt for this man. Hating himself for feeling like this, knowing that if he pulled the trigger he would be no better than the scum prostrated on the chair before him.

George placed his hand on his shoulder. Bill just nodded and smiled meekly at the two of them.

They retied Peter, returned him to the bedroom, and had a few hours sleep. They reported to the police station at midday.

"We are not charging you but if you know what's good for you, pack and return to Wales." George looked hard at the sergeant and the constable next to him; they were the ones he'd seen in the alleyway a few hours before but said nothing.

"Yes," Bill said and smiled. "We will be going in the next few days."

"Glad to hear it. I would hate to have to lock you all up again," the sergeant smirked in reply.

"What for officer?" Henry politely asked, feeling anger underneath.

"Because I can, now go, before I lock you up now," the sergeant barked. "For being disrespectful to the law."

They left the station; Henry wanted to take another look inside the shop to see if he could glean any further information that could be of help before they returned that night. He would pretend to be interested in the chair he had seen earlier.

While Henry was in the shop, the other two waited in a nearby cafe. They would order for him and he would join them later. The same assistant was behind the counter and she recognised him, smiling freely as he slowly ambled towards her pretending to look around. "Have you come for the chair," she asked.

"You remembered! Might be," he smiled. "I'm thinking of making an offer. Where's the other person, the one that jumped out at me from behind the curtain?" he said and laughed.

"Gone out early this morning, he will be back later this afternoon."

"Is he the owner?"

"Yes lives here alone except when his friend stays," she innocently replied.

"Have you any other chairs similar to that one," Henry asked pointing at the chair. "I may want more than one if the price is right."

"Maybe; the back rooms are full of old furniture, you'll have to wait until he comes back."

"Can't you go and check."

"No, I'm only allowed in the shop and the kitchen."

"If all the rooms are full where does he live?" Henry enquired as if making light conversation.

"On the top floor. The building is bigger than it seems. There is also a large cellar I believe, I've never been down there; it's always locked."

"Perhaps," Henry laughed, that's where all the expensive chairs are. Anyway, must go, I'll come back tomorrow sometime and see if he's about. I'm looking for six chairs." Henry lied and left.

He went to the cafe and his lunch was on the table waiting for him. "The cellar, that's where the girl is and if Colin is there that's where we'll find him. The Chinese man with the tattoos on his arms lives on the premises but we might find most of the rooms locked; we need to get large steel-cutters in case we need to cut through any locked doors. The shop assistant informed me he lives on the top floor of the building.

The rooms on the bottom floor are full of furniture; we may need to move some of it to make a pathway to get at the doors. As I said, the only person in the building from what I can gather sleeps on the top floor. We must assume he has a gun and will shoot to kill if we are found in the building so we need to be quiet and listen out for any sound when inside." Henry informed them.

After purchasing the cutters, they spent the afternoon in the flat catching up on their sleep. Later that afternoon they asked Peter once more about the building, the Chinese man with the dragon tattoos, and the three crooked policemen but he gave away little further information.

"We will write a letter to the Metropolitan Commissioner anonymously outlining what we know about the three crooked policemen and this racket with kids, post it first class tonight in case something goes wrong. If we do end up in a cell at least they'll know about the situation and must investigate." Bill said stoically.

Henry disagreed. "If we are caught they will kill us, the police I'm talking about, make no bones about it, we are dead," he emphasised. "However, I see your point Bill, we will write the letter, but wait before posting it. Let's give it to the receptionist with a little money and ask her to post it in a few days."

George spent the rest of the afternoon and early evening writing the letter, Bill and Henry contributing until all the information they knew was included. They were careful not to mention anything that could link it to them. They were fed up with making statements, being questioned and wanted nothing more to do with the police honest ones or otherwise.

If everything went to plan, Colin would be back in Wales within a few days, and no one would be the wiser, mission accomplished. They hadn't worked out what to do with Peter; as much as they felt like killing him they all knew, Henry included, they could not do it, no matter how much they hated him.

That evening saw them at the rear of the shop, everything was as they had left it. There was nothing more to do now but wait until the area was quiet. Just after midnight, they started work. They had already moved the outer wall the previous night and fortunately, the inner wall was of a softer material. It took them less than an hour to make the hole large enough for them to crawl through but as they were removing the last block they heard a sound.

Bill was watching the alleyway but saw no one. A sound was coming from the bottom of the garden someone was walking over the rubbish; the three of them froze, hardly daring to breath; the noise increased. They dared not shine the torch in the direction of the sound and waited, and then they all relaxed and laughed. A cat hissed. It was wrestling with a large rat. The sound they heard was the rat scrabbling through the rubbish, then the cat finally made its kill and the sound died.

George placed the block on the floor and climbed into the room. It was crammed full of furniture. He tried crawling under a table. What he thought was a board but which turned out to be a large mirror resting against the table, hindered him. He tried to move it but it was wedged tightly against the table with other furniture placed in front of it. Henry was correct the whole room was full of old furniture stacked to the ceiling.

He whispered to Henry to stay put until he was able to clear a passage through and crawled around the mirror coming out into a small space in the centre of the room. He saw the door at the other end of the room and started to clear a pathway to it, careful to be as quiet as possible as he rearranged the furniture, shuffling the mirror to the side. Henry crawled through leaving Bill outside to keep watch.

George tried the door out of the room but found it locked securely. Henry went back for the drill and drilled around the lock;

within twenty minutes the door was open. The next room was very much the same as the last full of furniture but a lot larger with a clear passageway to another door, which made their progress much easier.

They were at the other door in a matter of a few seconds but it too was locked and far more robust than the previous one. Henry tried to force the door open with a crowbar, it moved a little but it was obvious it would take a lot more effort and the noise was unacceptable. They decided to drill the lock out and it took over an hour before they could open the door, listening all the while for noise.

They found themselves in a long corridor running the length of the building; George shone his torch along it both ways when Henry motioned him to turn it off. At one end of the corridor was a door, which Henry assumed led into the shop where he saw the Chinese man. The other end of the corridor terminated in a large wooden door where George saw the same man standing the night before and where the police sergeant handed over the young unconscious child into his care.

Half way along the corridor opposite the door they had exited was a steel door with metal bars at the top and bottom traversed across the door locked at each corner. The door looked formidable; they were glad they had the foresight to purchase the steel-cutters but even with these, it would take great effort to open it.

They went to the door that led into the shop expecting to find it locked but to their surprise it was not. A thick curtain hung from the other side of the door. To the left of this door was another, also unlocked. The room behind was large and laid out as a lounge and looked comfortable and friendly, except all the windows were bricked up. In one corner were stairs leading to the top floors where, they assumed, the Chinese man slept. They listened for a few minutes to see if there was any noise coming from upstairs but to their relief all remained silent. They knew there was another separate door leading down to the cellar and it could only be behind the steel door.

They went back the way they came checked with Bill all was well and returned with the steel cutters and hacksaw. The cutters made short work of the four locks one at each corner of the steel door. They were expecting it to be more difficult but then realised there was an integral lock in the centre of the door. They were going to drill around it when George noticed a large key hanging on the wall, tried it in the lock, and heard a familiar click.

George entered the room first and shone the torch around. Cupboards covered two walls with a large table at the end behind which was a heavy wooden door, which led down into the cellar. In the corner, furthest away from them, a wide corridor led to another wooden door, which led into the alleyway. One side of the corridor was neatly stacked with small drums. George walked past these and tried the door at the end. This would be their escape, there were two locks each end of the door, but the keys were hanging on a nail on the side of the wall. George unlocked the door peeped into the alley, relocked the door, leaving the keys in the locks for a quick getaway.

Henry listened intently; all was quiet. Knowing they had their escape route George went back for Bill intending for him to stay and listen for any movement upstairs whilst he and Henry went into the cellar. The only door to the cellar was in this room; it had a large bolt across the centre, with a padlock attached. They used the cutters on the padlock and opened the door. Stone stairs, which led down into the cellar were winding and dark. They shone their torches into this blackness but the stairs were too winding and long for them to see anything other than the walls.

Slowly, they descended the stone steps, Henry first, shining their torches into the blackness. The darkness felt unnatural, eerie and hung heavily on their minds.

They were used to darkness, working in the pit for many years, but this darkness had something evil lurking in it; felt unclean, contaminated. They descend the steps one at a time.

There was a sense of descending into hell, and shook their heads to ward off this aberrant feeling.

At the bottom, the stairs twisted and they entered a large room. They felt oppressed, the darkness squeezed down on them as if trying to squash them into the cold stone floor beneath their feet. They heard a noise, switched off their torches, and moved against the wall, making not a sound and listened, the darkness complete.

The sound was of a young child crying, not loud, low, whimpering, a cry of fear and desperation. They listened for a few minutes; slowly they felt their way along the wall in darkness. The sound got louder. The wall fell away into a door. Quietly they felt around for the bolt, unlocked it, and opened the door.

Henry gasped first as he switched on his torch. In the corner, sitting feet tucked up under her chin sucking her long brown matted hair and shaking with fear was a young girl around ten years of age. The light from the torch frightened her and she was startled.

They both looked upon the scene with horror, spellbound. There were people living in the same world as they who are able to subject young innocent children to this torture. They knew the policemen had handed a child to the Chinese man the previous night, and now seeing her forlorn, helpless, and trembling the full horror came into clear focus.

Henry ran over to the child and she cowered away from him in terror. "Don't be afraid," he spoke mildly. "Please come with us, we've come to take you home," he whispered.

"I have no home," she cried falteringly.

"Where do you live? We've come to take you back there."

The young child just clung to Henry's arm and cried. He smoothed her hair for a few moments and kept saying, "you're safe now, you're safe now, no one will hurt you. I promise."

"Come on Henry, we must move," George said. Henry paused for a moment reassuring the girl she was safe. He picked her up in his arms and stood up. "Come," he said to her kindly and turned to George. "Let's see if Colin's here and get out of this den of vipers."

There was no other sound; George was starting to think Colin was not there. They needed to check two other doors; George went to the nearest one and opened it. The room felt cold, damp, evil, and gave off a repugnant smell. George shone the light around the room, immediately he knew why. In one corner were two naked bodies side by side. He had seen plenty of dead bodies before but did not expect to see them here; as the disgust rose to the surface in his throat, he felt nauseated.

Next to the bodies stood a large drum full of liquid, on the other side a table the same height as the top of the drum; it was obvious what went on here. The drum held acid; the Chinese placed the bodies on the table and pushed them into the liquid where they would dissolve. They were using this room to dispose of bodies. For a horrible second, he thought one of them might be Colin and breathed a sigh of relief when he checked and knew they were not.

Henry followed but when he saw the bodies turned away not for the girl to see. George closed the door looked at Henry blankly, did not say a word in case he frightened the child more than she was already, if that were possible, and went over to the next room and opened the bolt. He shone the torch into the room and there on a mattress was Colin, almost naked, asleep on his stomach.

He rushed over and turned him onto his back. Colin's eyes were open but his mind not in them. "What have they done to you, Colin, my boy," George exclaimed, looking into his lifeless eyes.

"Come George, get him out," Henry said bringing George back from the shock of seeing his son alive but like a Zombie.

He helped his son to his feet. Colin just stood there, eyes staring blankly ahead. George held his arm and beckoned him to walk forward and follow, which he did without question not saying a word. He went up the stone steps leading Colin, Henry followed behind carrying the girl.

At the top of the stairs, they looked for Bill but he was gone. Instinctively they realised something was wrong and stopped. The next moment Henry saw the flash of a large thick bladed sword coming at him. He ducked under the sword turning and holding the girl away from the blade at the same time. The edge of the sword struck the wall, sparks flew in all directions. Henry was helpless; he held the girl and knew the next strike would be lower and would not miss. He braced his back trying to protect the girl waiting for the strike.

George was on the Chinese man before the fatal blow, knocking him into the kitchen table. This gave Henry the time he needed, he rushed to the door opened the two locks and was out in the alley still holding the girl.

The Chinese man regained his composure coming at George sword held above his head, trying to get close enough to strike. George fell back into the corridor and started to throw the small drums at him to try to hold him at bay. It was obvious from the way he held the sword the man knew how to use it.

The sword cut the first drum in two the contents running all over the floor. George moved further along the corridor and knocked over the boxes and drums trying to block his path but still the Chinese man came forward sword in hand, there was no way to stop him. Light shone from the upstairs, enough for George to notice his eyes; they were evil, cold, he threw another drum at him in desperation. He slashed at it with his sword cutting into it like the last, only this time the metal on metal sparked. The liquid was inflammable and the sparks set it alight.

Instantly, flames engulfed him, he screamed and ran back into the kitchen past Colin who was just standing there staring, oblivious to the Chinese man on fire. George ran towards Colin, grabbed his arm, and pulled him forward. He followed without question. The Chinese man was running around the room in panic; tried to get down the cellar where the fire hose was but fell on the steps and rolled down into the cellar, still burning.

The flames were moving round the kitchen helped by the petrol. Henry ran past George into the other room looking for Bill. George pulled Colin out through the door and noticed the girl sitting on the floor leaning against the wall, bewildered, in shock. He tried to re-enter the building to help Henry, the fire was too intense, the corridor a mass of flame. It was impossible, he had to retreat into the alleyway, shutting the door behind him.

George realised when the drums in the corridor exploded they would be in line of the blast. He grabbed the girl with one hand, Colin with the other and ran to the far end of the alleyway, away from the shop. They could not see the flames with all the windows covered. As he had closed the door into the alleyway, the fire was contained within but George knew it would only be a matter of time before the whole lot exploded. All the downstairs rooms were full of furniture and when that caught fire, there would be no stopping the conflagration.

George was frantic, ran back, and scaled the rear wall. He got into the building through the window they had first entered and tried to get to Henry and Bill. He was hysterical with worry, mentally praying as he crawled through. Smoke was quickly filling the room; he crawled on his hands and knees near to the ground as fast as he could move. He found Henry creeping towards him slowly dragging Bill. The smoke was getting to him, his eyes watered. George pushed Henry forward grabbed Bill by the arms and pulled him towards the window. Henry went through first and pulled Bill after him followed by George.

"Quick, let's get out of here, the whole place will go any minute," George shouted not caring who heard. The Chinese man had knocked Bill on the back of the head and blood streamed from the wound. Henry was still catching his breath but they needed to move, to get away fast. George helped Bill over the wall followed by Henry, then he jumped over himself.

Colin and the girl were where George left them. Henry picked up the girl and they were away. Bill staggered a bit still disorientated from the knock to the head. They looked back at the building, could not see any flames but smoke was now billowing out in all directions. They turned the corner. It was still only four in the morning. There was a loud explosion; they carried on walking.

The streets were empty, the sound of a siren heard in the distance. They hurried onwards until they arrived at Peter's flat. Exhausted and dirty, they needed to clean themselves; sleep would have to wait.

Colin stood where put. George gestured for him to sit; he simply followed the instruction. The girl clung to Henry, wouldn't let him go, he didn't seem to mind, sat next to her until she fell asleep. Henry picked her up and laid her on the bed in the second bedroom carefully placing a sheet over her, she was dirty, he knew, but washing could wait.

Colin just stared.

"What have they done to you my boy," his father said laying his hand upon his back.

Colin just stared.

The less Peter knew the better and left him until they cleaned themselves, changed their clothes, and had something to eat. Eventually, they let him out of his room, first hiding Colin in the other room with the girl.

Bill wore a cap to hide his head injury. They told him they stayed at the hotel but returned early to make sure he was all right. Peter sneered. Henry felt like hitting him but instead smiled. They gave him food and a drink, returned him to the bedroom tying him securely, and went into the other room. They accomplished their task, and found Colin but in the bargain, became responsible for a young girl.

There was no way, they reasoned, the police could connect them to the fire but what was to be done with the girl and Peter? As much as they felt like killing him, there was no way any of them would commit a cold-blooded murder. Besides, a letter would be wending its way to the Commissioner of Police in a few days and the crooked officers investigated along with Peter and the rest of his cronies.

They were careful to leave their names out of the letter and not mention Colin but did mention the trade in children and the Chinese building, but after the fire, there would be little evidence to find. Their prime objective was to get the crooked police prosecuted, but with all the evidence destroyed, they were not that hopeful but at least they would try.

Bill went back to their hotel, returning around ten. He told them the police had cordoned off the road where the fire had occurred, the whole building burned to the ground and other buildings damaged beyond repair. The fire service had to keep their distance because of all the explosions. The heat was so intense it melted the road outside the building. It would be many hours before the site cooled and rendered safe enough to investigate.

That seemed the least of their problems; they sat round the table debating what to do next. The young girl was still asleep in the bedroom; they sat Colin at the table next to them but he only spoke when one of them spoke to him. He stared blankly at the wall unable to recognise even his father.

"When we get back home George you need to take the boy to a doctor, they've obviously brainwashed him by the look of things," Henry said stating the obvious.

George looked at his son, compassion filled his eyes and answered, "aye," and added. "The girl needs a check over as well."

"The girl is just plain scared, who wouldn't be with those vermin. We don't even know her name," Henry said; he should have asked her, and felt somewhat ashamed referring to her as the girl. "When she wakes we'll give her a bath and I'll go and buy her some new clothes."

It was obvious to George and Bill that Henry had become fond of the young girl. She was very similar in age to Sophie.

Henry's heart burned in fury that people who should be protecting this child, sleeping in the other room, abused her badly.

The discussion lasted for another hour until they heard her moving. Henry rushed into the room and asked her how she was feeling. "You look quite a sight, do you fancy a warm bath? My name's Henry, by the way, what's yours," he asked smiling.

She hesitated a moment and replied, "Jess--- Jessica James."

"That's a pretty name; after you've had a bath, you can tell me all about yourself and we'll take you back to your parents." Henry knew she said she didn't have any parents but maybe that was because she was too frightened to tell him the truth.

Tears streamed into her eyes. "I haven't got parents, please, don't take me back please," she cried starting to get hysterical.

"You'll not be made to do anything you don't want to, that I promise you," Henry assured and held her tight in his arms. "How long have you lived with these people, we know you arrived at the shop yesterday?"

"I live on the street, they caught me and brought me there yesterday, a kind man gave me a warm drink and some food and when I woke up I was in that room. I was so frightened, it was dark, very dark, and no one could hear me," she whimpered.

"What about school?" Henry stated unable to think of anything else to say.

"I used to go when mummy was alive, since then no, my uncle looked after me but he was horrid, tried to sleep in my bed so I ran away and lived under the arches. There are always other children there but some are very cruel. That is where the kind man gave me the food and drink."

Kind man, Henry thought, feeling his anger rise, hiding the feeling from the girl.

"How long have you been under the arches?" Henry enquired feeling the hurt for what this girl must have suffered.

"I don't want to go back to my uncle. I'd rather go back to the arches."

“The arches is no place for a young girl, you need a warm bed, good food and school in which to learn.”

“My mummy told me I must learn, she used to help me, told me lots of stories.” She blurted out.

“She must be very special,” Henry said in a soft voice.

She started to cry, not loudly, a delicate fairy like cry, a cry of lost happiness. Happiness she had known when her mother was alive. She started to sob, the torment she had suffered over the last six months since the death of her mother came to the forefront.

“I’m sorry,” she replied trying to stifle almost angelic sobbing.

“Your father?” he asked sensitively.

“He died before I was six years old, he was a lot older than my mummy. We all loved him and were sad after. My uncle was horrible to me, said I was a big burden to him and since I had no money I should be nice to him in my bed but I ran away.”

“You can stay with me if you like. I used to have a little girl just like you, she died like your mummy and daddy, and she is now in heaven. I have a baby boy as well; he will be your brother if you let him. My wife likes reading stories and needs someone to listen to her.”

Henry said this without thinking, offering to take this girl as his own, when his thoughts caught up with his mouth he smiled and wondered what Sophie would think of her. He meant every word of it. He knew his wife would be supportive of the decision and wished he had consulted her first but he had asked Jessica, so there was not a lot he could do.

Jessica didn’t answer. The last nice man she took something from she awoke to find herself locked in a dark room, petrified. Her uncle said he would be nice to her if she let him sleep in her bed and not tell anyone, but felt it was wrong, dreadfully wrong, didn’t quite know why, but knew somehow it wasn’t right. No wonder she felt apprehensive.

Henry picked this up and said, "just think about it; don't ever do anything you feel is not right for you. Now a bath, I'll go and buy you some new clothes."

They left the bedroom, one to the bathroom the other to the shops.

Chapter Thirty Six

Peter thought they were as ruthless as he and tried to negotiate a deal, offering large sums of money if they let him go, promising not to tell anyone. They knew it was all lies, immediately he was free, they suspected he would plot revenge, his type always did, there was only one conclusion. They must go to the police, confess all, explain the situation, knowing it would land them in court and perhaps even prison.

They had broken into a building, were responsible for a man's death. He deserved to die, they all agreed upon that, but the law should have dealt with it not them. If they hadn't broken in, he would be still alive. They regretted nothing. They had Colin back and stopped a little girl's suffering. They still had faith in the system. Henry remembered how his friend died on the picket lines when they took the law into their own hands; it still hung heavily on him.

There was nothing else for it, to come clean. They knew going public was a gamble but the other way was too dire to contemplate. To their knowledge, only Peter knew of their existence, the choice was simple, kill Peter, or go to the police. This played on all of their minds; by confessing, they were risking the lives of their loved ones, but what could they do?

The people they were dealing with seemed above the everyday law of the land even had a number of police in their pocket. That aside, they could not accept all police were dishonest, and decided to let Peter go free, go to the police, confess everything and take the consequences.

Jessica was a different story. Henry would do his best to keep her away from her uncle. He had already broken his promise before he had a chance to even get it started, she hadn't agreed yet, and he held on to that.

Henry returned with new clothes for Jessica, her little face lit up when she saw them. Colin remained the same, stared without sign or gesture even when given clean clothes there was not the slightest spark of recognition. George tried to talk to him, tried to make him remember, there was nothing. He would answer back if asked a question; do exactly what they asked of him, no more, other than that, blankness.

Initially, George put it down to shock, now he was not so sure, the important thing was he had his son back, whatever the problems, one way or another they would solve them together. Colin never asked for food. He ate when they gave it to him and told to eat. They were all hungry, none of them had eaten since the day before, and it was now late morning. They had eaten all the food in the flat and decided to go out for breakfast. They were very tired, but none of them felt like sleep, the trauma of the night before still very much on their minds.

After they had eaten, the five returned to their hotel, taking Colin and Jessica in by the back entrance while one of them distracted the receptionist. They booked two other rooms' one for Jessica, the other for George and Colin, saying to the receptionist that they wanted a room each. The large breakfast had made them all tired and it was just after midday. They went to bed and slept until just after eight in the evening. Jessica woke first and Henry told her to stay in her room with the door bolted until one of them knocked.

A little later, they decided to go out for a meal. They all tried to be upbeat, but the gloom hung over the three of them knowing what they must shortly do, no one spoke much. The only person in high spirits was Jessica. Tomorrow they would release Peter and go to the police, who would take Jessica, they would end up in prison, Colin sent home.

Henry and Bill went to check on Peter, the others went back to the hotel, careful to keep Colin and Jessica out of sight. A while later they returned, Henry was about to go into his room, he changed his mind and decided to call on Jessica.

She let him in with a big smile on her face and said. "I love you lots and would like to live with you if you still want me." He still wanted her, but after tomorrow, Henry knew it would not be possible.

"Yes of course, sleep tight Jessica, see you in the morning."

Henry slept badly that night, Jessica on his mind, wondering what was going to happen to her. They went for breakfast all subdued, downhearted and depressed, except Jessica.

George was the first to speak. "I'm sorry it's come to this boys."

"Yes, we all are," Bill replied. "Things are what they are George."

Henry was silent; he looked at Jessica and then Colin and sighed.

"We need to release Peter. Henry, you stay with Colin and Jessica and when we return we'll go straight to the main police station across town." George stated.

Jessica looked up but said nothing suspecting something was wrong. "We'll take a walk and go together," Henry replied downheartedly.

As the two got nearer to the flat, they sensed something was wrong; they turned the corner and knew why. The street was cordoned off, full of police and firemen. Bill heard the words. "It's out of control, move them back."

Flames were shooting high into the morning sky in the two adjoining buildings; there had been a major explosion, the police and fire service were taking no chances. The first thing they thought of was Peter tied to the bed, a shudder went through them both. They waited and watched, could glean no further information and decided to go back and meet up with the others to tell them what had happened.

The three were waiting and saw them approach. Two waved an acknowledgement Colin just stared. George told Henry what they had just witnessed.

"How do you think the fire started?" Henry asked, shocked at this new unexpected development.

"I don't know, Peter was in there, if he's dead we're responsible," George said feeling depressed at the prospect of being accountable for another human death by fire, one day after the first.

"He may have got out," Bill surmised, trying to be positive but not believing it.

"What do we do now?" George asked.

"There's nothing we can do, I think we should wait before we go to the police until we know about Peter, they'll have us for murder," Henry said, talking quietly not for Jessica to overhear.

"Know what?" George asked.

"Know if he's been burnt to death that's what I mean," Henry stated thinking George should have realised first time to what he was referring.

"How long do we wait?"

"If Peter has escaped we'll know soon enough," Henry replied not directly answering the question.

It was not long before the news broke. The first fire claimed three casualties trapped in the basement of the building. The fire was so intense the bodies burnt to a cinder leaving only the teeth. This was the only information the police had to go on, the evidence scant. They hadn't yet ruled out arson but thought it unlikely and were urging people not to keep inflammable liquids on their premises.

The papers the following day were full of the two fires and stated:

'The Police and Fire Service had two very busy nights fighting two major fires within a few miles of each other but do not suspect they were linked. The Fire Service discovered the bodies in the basement of the building, so badly burned only the teeth remained. Three burnt to death in the fire but there may be more. They had very little further information to go on at present and are asking the public to come forward if they were anywhere near the locality that night. They have not yet ruled out criminal activity, alleging the owner, whom they suspect burnt to death in the fire, kept large quantities of inflammable liquid on the premises.

The other fire the following night the police are treating as arson, a full criminal investigation is under way due to the explosions that ripped the building apart and the traces of dynamite found in the charred remains. They believe fourteen people died, but it will take a few more days of rigorous investigation to be sure, and the area will remain cordoned off until further notice. The police are appealing again for witnesses and have set up an incident room and a hotline number to ring through information confidentially.'

"Peter must be one of the dead. There's no way he could have freed himself without help," Bill stated. They knew this anyway; he always had the knack of saying the obvious.

"If he has escaped he may go to the police before we do, it will look worse for us then," George said.

"It's unlikely he got out, impossible I would say; even if by some miracle he did, people like Peter won't go to the police. I've no doubt about that; revenge yes, police no. There is no way the police can connect us to the first fire or the break-in unless we confess, we had nothing to do with the second so we're in the clear there."

"The crooked policemen Henry, what if Peter did survive and asks them to sort us out?"

"What do they know, only that we are looking for a lost boy, that is all? What can they arrest us for, they've already tried to pin Jimmy's murder on us but failed."

"How about kidnapping," Bill butted in quietly listening up until then.

"If Peter goes to the police what proof is there, it's his word against ours. Yes, he'll go after revenge if he's alive, that's certain, but that's a chance worth taking if you ask me, the option is, that or prison," Henry emphatically replied.

"So we must forever be looking over our shoulder for the rest of our lives. That's no way to live. We go to the police and confess Henry," George stated not because he thought it right but could think of no other way out.

"Wait! What if we send Colin and the girl back to Wales? We stay and pretend to look for the boy. That would then leave us two scenarios. The first, we'll be arrested if Peter goes to the police, and arrested if we go to the police, that option counts as one, either way we'll be arrested.

The second, Peter comes for us to extract his revenge, it's better we meet that in London rather than back in Wales. If nothing happens in a few days with Peter, it probably won't happen at all, and he died in the fire, so we know we are safe.

Not totally, but safe enough to know that if he does not extract his revenge on us when we are here on his door step in the next few days it's highly unlikely he'll come to Wales later knowing he will stand out like a belisha beacon. In any event, I'm convinced he is dead. We pretend to give up the search after a few days and go back to Wales empty handed. As far as anyone here is concerned the matter is closed."

George still wasn't convinced. "What do we do if Peter is not dead and he does come for us here, he's hardly going to talk to us first?"

"He'll try to kill us obviously and we defend ourselves, but we've frightened him. He may just leave the matter rest and go to ground, as I said, the chances of him being alive are slim, we are safe boys, nil to nothing I reckon," convinced Peter died in the fire.

"Let's just hope he leaves us alone if he is alive that's all, and that'll be the end of it," George replied. Henry had talked him into the plan and he knew Bill would follow.

George and Henry went back to Wales with Colin and Jessica returning a few days later. Henry's wife accepted Jessica with open arms but was sad her husband had to return to London so soon.

Colin made no response when he met his mother and brothers, still that did not matter they were glad and happy to have him home. There was great change in him. His face was tightly drawn, eyes sunken; he had lost a lot of weight, the main concern was his mental well being. He was dead to the world, himself, and all around him.

Chapter Thirty Seven

Colin was in mental hell. He recognised his surroundings but could not differentiate between reality and his dreams. He had locked his mind so tight against the other life no amount of stimulus his mother and brothers gave him made the slightest difference to his psychological well being. He was inside a prison of his own making and only he held the key.

"Come on Colin you must eat," his mother instructed as she placed a plate of egg and chips in front of him.

"Thank you I will eat," came the automated response.

"What would you like to do today Colin?" she asked smiling.

"Tell me and I will do it," he replied and carried on eating.

"No," she insisted. "You tell me."

"I will eat."

"Yes, Colin eat, but later, after you have eaten, what do you wish to do, come Colin answer me?"

"I will do what you say. I will eat."

His mother looked away in distress and wished, despite all his wicked ways, she could have her old Colin back. "All right," she said trying not to cry. "Finish your food and we'll talk later."

He replied again, "I will eat."

The drugs were starting to wear off and they called the doctor. He was an old-fashioned doctor and failed to recognise that Colin's body was going through a withdrawal process reacting against the drugs. He writhed on the bed in agony and often shouted incoherently. "I'm sorry Robert, sorry… I killed… you are dead… must wash… blood, blood, clean, not clean. What? I've killed them all… my family."

The doctor arrived and after a brief examination came up with nothing more positive than dreams. "He's having bad dreams, keep him warm, and give him plenty to drink. He hasn't been eating regularly with all this nonsense of living away." This was the only explanation he diagnosed and added as an afterthought. "Give him an aspirin twice a day. If young lads will behave in this manner, away from home, running here and there, they deserve all they get."

This period was difficult for Colin; he got worse, his eyes rolled, the dreams intensified, the shouting grew louder, his body always a bath of sweat and then a period of total quiet where he just stared with frightening intensity. His eyes awake, his mind asleep. His mother did as the doctor said; making him drink as much as possible, it seemed to be of little use. His condition got worse as the days progressed.

A few days later, the doctor called again, this time he showed more concern, Colin mumbled continually, but he still put his behaviour down to his stint away from home. He did prescribe a course of medicine that made him sleep even more, which perhaps was what the drug was intended to do, make the patient sleep.

A week passed, Colin started to mumble less and sat for long periods staring at the wall or out of the window. The street might well have been a wall for all Colin noticed. His body was now clear of drugs but his condition stayed very much the same but with less mumbling.

It was not the drugs that were affecting his mind now but a far deeper malady. A crisis of conscience, a deep-rooted malignancy of conscience, which clung to him as moss clings to stone. He had locked himself off from the reality of the world afraid to enter; to enter meant destruction of his family. He did care for them, despite his past behaviour, really care, far more than his life was worth to him and kept his mind locked inside itself afraid, too afraid, to come out to meet the world and what would be there waiting for him.

Chapter Thirty Eight

Peter had escaped. When his hands and feet were re-tied, he held his hands loose allowing enough slack in the binding to wriggle one hand free and then the other. The rest was easy; in next to no time he was out of his bonds and free.

The Welshmen were always careful not to leave anything at the flat belonging to them, but he did find his gun, and to his satisfaction, it was still loaded. This seemed strange to him at first, then realised they would all have their own weapons so why take his and gave it no more thought placing the gun in his pocket.

Peter did not even realise Colin or Jessica had been inside the flat, which was how careful the three were when they left. He achieved his freedom in the middle of the night and thought his captors were back in their hotel asleep and would return early in the morning. He was in no doubt they would kill him, thinking there was no way they would let him live. He knew far too much and longed for revenge; it consumed him as a snake would consume a mouse, bit by laborious bit. The hatred was hot, getting hotter, until it burned the pit of his stomach.

He had told them where they could find Colin; he felt he had no choice in this or he would be dead. He did expect the Chinese to kill them if they tried to enter the shop, but they were ruthless, they may well have come through it he reasoned. He initially thought they may go to the police and the sergeant would handle the situation. Over the years, he had done many deals with him and he had a lot to lose and would do what was necessary to keep them quiet.

He dismissed this immediately, convinced they wanted the boy because he had stolen from them, using one being the father as an excuse to gain support, and probably kill the boy afterwards silencing him forever. Peter believed there must be a lot of money at stake for them to go to the lengths they did to speak with the boy and annoyed he hadn't questioned him before disposal to the Chinese.

He sat on his bed contemplating his next move. He was in a dangerous position, if the Triads knew what he had done, they would find and kill him, if the three Welsh men returned they would kill him. The Triads were near the point of no return, his return in a barrel of acid, or the Thames, he needed to act immediately.

His options were limited; the best he could hope for was for the Triads to kill the Welshmen without them spilling the beans. This would deny him his revenge but at least he could carry on working in London. There was only one way to find out, to wait, and if the Welshmen returned, to kill them himself.

He grinned; he would wait in the room and when they returned, shoot them as they came through the door. They would be off-guard, not expecting an ambush. He was a good marksman and could get the three before they were able to retaliate and use his contacts to remove and destroy the bodies. Alternatively, and perhaps a better idea, leave the bodies and burn the flat with them in it, safer that way. A wry smile passed over his face at the thought of them lying on the floor dead.

The best laid plans of mice and men don't always go as intended and saved the lives of the three men. Peter was not aware of the fire in the pawnshop and settled down to wait for the men to return, gun at the ready a large cooking knife at his side. He heard sirens the night before but put this down to normal night time activity in a busy city. A few hours later, he heard a sound at the front door and hid in a corner of the room behind a lounge chair. He would wait until they were just inside the door and in clear view and kill them before they had time to react and, should he need it, use the knife to finish the job.

They were a long time entering. Peter wondered if they sensed he had escaped and waited for them behind the door but immediately dismissed this thought. There was no way they could know unless they could see through the wall. The adrenalin of the kill was running high through his veins; he fingered the gun as he waited. The sound outside the door was distinct and quiet; the door remained firmly closed. He was nervous, on edge, the back of his neck started to sweat, his hands felt warm and clammy. He had killed before and waited silently in the dark room for the door to open and the three to enter.

He crouched lower behind the chair knowing he had the advantage of light as well as surprise. He was in a dark corner. Their silhouettes would be clear as they entered the door by the light from the window. He would have a clear view at point blank range, whereas he would be in darkness and unseen.

There was a discrete click of the lock, the door opened, a quarter, a half, fully, the actions were quick and sharp. Three shapes appeared; silently one closed the door. The three were in full view, he fired five shots in rapid succession one of them fired back hitting Peter in the left shoulder but each of his bullets found its mark.

Two died instantly. The other groaned on the floor a bullet lodged in his stomach. Blood trickled from Peter's shoulder, his left hand felt numb but he was elated. He had his revenge. He walked over to the one groaning on the floor and kicked him hard in the chest, felt satisfaction course through his body as the man groaned in agony and kicked again.

He switched on the light, his face drained of blood as he stared at the three people. His satisfaction level dropped to zero and started to freeze. The three were Chinese, the thin one he recognise, his contact to the Triads the head of the synod run from the shop. The other two were strangers but he knew they were all from the same organisation.

His mind turned; were they there to kill him? They give a warning first he reasoned, then it dawned, this was the warning squad, they would have slapped him about a bit to make sure the message hit home and left. They were not here to kill him; he'd been expecting the warning for weeks.

He was in trouble and cursed the three Welshmen blaming them for his misfortune. He needed to think, his shoulder ached, he felt nauseated, was not sure when the Welshmen would return. With a bullet in his shoulder he was in no state to tackle one, let alone three, things were more dangerous than before.

"Shut up," he shouted in frustrated rage to the one groaning on the floor and kicked out in anger connecting with the head rendering him instantly silent. The blow was the final death knell to the already dying man speeding the process by a few minutes.

Peter needed to get out of London quickly. He cursed the Welshmen again; he had a good profitable operation, now it was all gone. If he stayed in London, the Triad would kill him. He had other contacts separate from them who were as much afraid of the Triads as he, and would not help when they knew they were hunting him. Hunt him they would, all over the world if necessary and with vengeance for killing three of their own.

His sister was in France too far away to be of immediate help and he needed to see a doctor or at least get his shoulder cleaned. It was only a superficial wound, he believed; he must get out of London but needed medical attention before infection set in. When the men failed to return the Triad would come looking and he was squarely in the frame.

There was nothing else for it, he could not remove the bodies; he would have to burn the flat to render them unidentifiable. This he reasoned should give him the time he needed to get out of London, meet up with his sister, and disappear somewhere in France or Germany. There were other people in the building but that seemed a small price to pay. He needed to buy himself time and gave it no further thought.

He piled clothes and papers around the bodies collected his personal belongings, and set the papers alight staying in the flat long enough to see the fire took hold. He knew dynamite was in the flat. It was only a matter of time before the whole building blew sky high. This gave him the time he needed to get safely away. When he closed the door to leave, flames already covered the ceiling.

Chapter Thirty Nine

The Welshmen were in the Lamb asking questions and showing the picture of Colin to anyone who would listen. They had already destroyed the drawings of Peter and Mary, the less that was said about those two the better. The landlord was now quite friendly and asked how much longer they intended to stay looking for the lad.

"A few more days and we are off home. He'll have to return himself, no doubt he will when his money runs out." George answered shrugging his shoulders as if saying. You know what boys are like. It's been a bit of a holiday really. "We could have done without the questioning over Jimmy and the hassle with the police but I suppose they were only doing their job." He finished on a conciliatory tone.

"Aye, they have a job to do like the rest of us I suppose," and changed the subject. "What do you think of the fires a few nights ago a bad business that?"

"Yes, so I've heard. Where exactly were they?" Henry innocently asked.

"One in the Chinese sector, the other a few miles from here, the following night. That was a bad one though, the paper says they now believe the toll is twenty not fourteen as first thought. It was a bomb you know."

"You don't say," Henry replied looking shocked. "Who would do such a thing?" His eyes rolling in feigned surprise.

"The police haven't a clue. Already been around asking questions, no one here is any the wiser."

"Perhaps they would want to see us again," Henry said, the other two looking at him in amazement.

"I doubt that. What do you know?"

"Less than you," Henry meekly replied. Which was the truth, they knew nothing about the second fire.

"Well I know zilch so you must know less than zilch. No, I can't see the police bothering you three."

"You haven't seen anything of that woman and man we were asking after have you," George asked to the chagrin of Henry.

"No, they seemed to have moved on. Happens a lot around here, they go for months without being seen and then they come in a few times in a week."

"We'll be leaving before long, it looks as if we've reached a dead end but we've enjoyed the break," Bill spoke for the first time.

They were just getting up to go when, to their surprise, in walked the police sergeant and three others. They sat back down and looked away hoping they would ignore them, but hope against hope, they knew this to be an impossibility. The sergeant asked questions around the bar until eventually they stood behind them.

"You three still here. I thought you'd be gone," he growled. "Haven't you had enough taste of the cells yet," he laughed giving a malicious smile.

"We are just taking a few extra days before we go back to the wives. To get drunk a few times, you know how it is. The boy no doubt will find his own way home when his money runs out, other than spending a few nights with you, we've enjoyed our visit to London," Henry replied forcing a smile.

"Did you want to see us for anything then?" George asked trying to create a friendly expression but failing dismally.

"No, unless you know something about the fires a few days ago," the sergeant asked. "I doubt that, so no."

"We were just discussing that," the landlord interrupted. "Twenty dead in one, three the other. A bad business. The papers say one was started by a bomb going off."

"Don't believe all you read in the papers, my superiors think it was a shootout between two gangs, apparently they found a few bullets in some of the dead or what was left of them. These things happen when millions of people live one on top of the other," he sneered.

"I've got my superiors breathing down my neck over this, and a squad of detectives are arriving tomorrow from Scotland Yard to take over the investigation. Well, we can't stay talking all night to the likes of you; some of us have work to do and the four walked out.

"Old sarg is in a bad mood, he's getting pressure from above by the looks of things," the landlord commented. "He's right about work," and walked to the other end of the bar where several other customers waited to be served.

They huddled together so none could hear them. "A shootout between gangs, that doesn't make sense. The sergeant must know Peter lives in the building and one of the casualties. There's something we've overlooked here," Bill commented confused.

Henry was turning a thought over in his mind. "Not necessarily, the last flat that woman lived in was under a Mr. and Mrs. Williams. His flat could also be under a false name, in fact more than probably is, so unless this Peter or whatever his name is, told the sergeant where he lives, which is highly unlikely, knowing the propensity to secrecy they all seem to crave, how would they, or anyone, know?"

The barman walked towards them. "A bad business those fires," George said purely for the landlord's benefit. He nodded and walked back to talk to some of his customers at the other end of the bar.

"We don't know if the fire did start in the flat. I'm more than convinced we are safe; Peter was one of the casualties of the fire. Let's stay another day or so and head home, best all forgotten," Henry said, shouting to the landlord to refill their glasses, offering him a pint at the same time in a gesture of friendship.

"Yes. I never want a repeat of the experience of the last few weeks. We have all had enough excitement to last a lifetime. A few days then boys and we can return home, forget all about the whole sordid episode," stated Bill taking a large drink of his pint shouting "cheers." The other two acknowledged the toast and drank.

"That's the end of it," Henry toasted with his pint and they drank again.

George not to be out done said, "Colin and Jessica," and their pints were empty again.

"Landlord, ale if you please," Henry shouted, placing closure on the incident. A few days later, they returned home, the episode closed forever, or so they believed.

The time they took off work was unpaid, but they still had their jobs. They returned to work the day after they arrived in Wales happy that things were now back to normal.

Peter was able to buy the time he needed but at a terrible cost in human life. The Triads did not realise what had happened until the newspaper reports emerged over a week later and surmised what had occurred. Peter was long gone and they were determined to extract their revenge if they ever caught up with him.

They had already shaken down a few of his known contacts, knew he was wounded but had disappeared, no one knew where. They had lost four good men, and suspected he was responsible for the two fires. The police were everywhere, many drafted in from other areas. The Triad had to curtail their activities, which meant they were losing money and blamed Peter. He had become a pariah, deserted by all.

An investigation into the running of the local police station commenced; senior investigating officers suspended several people pending further examination including the sergeant. They could prove nothing mentioned in the anonymous letter but it did bring into focus a number of other matters. They forced the sergeant and several others to resign but prosecuted no one over the allegations.

The newspaper reports of the fires made national news and the criminal investigation into one was onward going but the police never got very far. Eventually, the whole affair died down, life moved on, the episode moved into memory and forgotten.

Chapter Forty

Jessica settled into a happy and contented life with Henry and Anne; a deep love grew between them. Within a few months, she was calling the baby her little brother. They spread the story she was a distant relative and her parents had recently died, which was half true; her mother had died six months previous and Jessica would be staying for the foreseeable future. Soon it became an accepted fact and received without question she was living there permanently.

The only cloud on the horizon was Colin. George and his wife tried everything, nothing worked. He would sit in a corner and stare. Some whispered 'mentally retarded, should be placed in an institution.' He no longer needed to attend school he was sixteen but behaved as a child of six; someone had to tell him when to go to the toilet.

Occasionally, his eyes would show recognition but quickly close down within a few seconds. He knew where he was, recognised his parents, brothers, house and garden but it was as if he was looking at it all through another person's eyes, he was in a mirror looking out.

Nightmares plagued him constantly; he screamed violently in his sleep and mumbled incoherently. "Wash it… Wash… Off me… Kill… Kill me… I must die. Thief, liar, cheat… I know what you are! Murderer."

None of these words made any sense, even the psychiatrist, who counselled Colin, was dumfounded. He could find no answer suggesting intense therapy to try to break thorough into his mind. He often frightened his brothers when he screamed in his dreams. They were getting darker and darker, the psychiatrist suggested Colin be placed in an institution where there would be constant help.

George opposed this idea. He acknowledged the detrimental effect Colin was having on the other children and eventually agreed, if things did not improve, to send him where he could get constant attention.

One day when Colin and George were in the garden, a robin landed next to Colin's left hand, looked directly at him, and started to chirp. Colin moved his head to look in the direction of the sound; his lips quivered slightly as if trying to communicate with the bird then it flew away. His eyes following until it was out of sight lost in the vastness of the sky.

His father noticed the change, it was small, but there had been a change. Colin reacted to the robin of his own accord. Each day after work, his father took him to the garden and noticed he was looking for something.

A week later, it happened again. A robin flew into a nearby tree. Colin seemed to be talking to the bird; even more extraordinary the bird seemed to be talking back. George watched intently, still and silent. The robin flew down and sat on Colin's shoulder, chirped as if whispering in his ear. Colin's lips moved as if acknowledging what the robin said; quick as it arrived, the robin flew off and was gone.

"Could I have a book to read please," Colin asked. His father turned, dumfounded.

"What did you say?"

Colin smiled. "A book please."

George was ecstatic. "A book! To read you say. Yes of course."

"Yes Aldus Huxley's Brave New World."

His father had never heard of it but would go to the library the following day and borrow a copy.

Colin started reading avidly to the delight of everyone and asked for three or four books a week, reading some two or three times. Even the psychiatrist had to admit he could not account for this behavioural change, at least one point was cleared up, he was far from remedial, he was reading and retaining the information on a grand scale.

This situation lasted a number of months. Even though still locked inside himself he acted like a scanner, taking the information into his brain, and leaving it there for future reference. His reading output even by university standards was impressive but from his background, phenomenal. The psychiatrist tried another course of treatment, taking into account this new development, still it led nowhere, and he was more confused than ever over Colin's behaviour.

After nine months of constant reading, Colin, sitting in a corner of his bedroom, became conscious he was watching himself reading; not through a mirror, but from the ceiling, he was looking down upon himself. He moved from the ceiling and went down the stairs. His mother was in the kitchen humming a tune. He started to talk to her but she ignored him.

"Mam! Hello," he called louder; she carried on humming, he was invisible to her. He went out of the house and stood in the small garden; he walked into the street. He went to his father's allotment and sat down on his usual seat, placed his hands over his face and closed his eyes.

He heard the word, "Hello," the same word he had spoken to his mother moments earlier. He turned, opened his eyes, there standing in front of him was his grandfather.

He smiled at Colin and said; "life has been hard for you of late. It is time to come out."

His eyes widened. "I can't. You know what will happen."

"Tell me what will happen?" his grandfather said in a deep demanding voice.

"You showed me… you know. Why do you ask?"

"I showed you a path, one path. The path you were destined to follow if you didn't change."

"The big house, my brothers and father killed; I killed them; made my mother suffer."

"You talk as if these things have already come to pass."

"I don't want the house, cars, anything. I want them to live, my mother happy," Colin screeched. "What good are these things if it means what you have shown me? The price is too high."

"The value is for you to decide. I have only given you the scales, the weights are down to you Colin; they are your choices."

"I choose to stay, stay locked inside. I want none of it. Let me stay locked up, I choose madness freely, anything but the other."

"You are free to choose, choose what you like, only you can make that choice. Are you not listening Colin? The path I showed you is but one of many, that future has not yet happened."

"I have other choices?"

"Yes! It's time to come out and make those choices, the choices that are truly in your heart."

"I wish to help. The house, cars, wealth are but dust in my hands, I had more all along, a loving family, people around me that cared. A doctor, I wish to help others and become a doctor. Can I do that?"

"It rests with you, the architect there is you. I have guided you for many years, it is now time to take control, to guide yourself."

The shame of his past life started to break, crash over him. He had held these emotions locked away until now, he felt himself slowly pulled back into his body. The gold, wealth, he was looking for had been right in front of him all the time but couldn't see it until now.

His body jolted and shuddered. He was back in the room reading, placed the book on the bed, and went downstairs. He smiled, looked at his mother happily singing and kissed her on the cheek, her hands wet as she washed dishes standing next to the sink.

She wiped her hands on her apron. "Go on… Colin! Get away. What did you just do?"

"I kissed my mother," he replied, smiled, and kissed her again on the other cheek.

"Colin? You're back," his mother screamed delighted.

"Yes, I'm back, and sorry for all the trouble I've caused."

They hugged and hugged again neither wishing to be the first to stop. His father walked through the door wondering at the commotion.

"He's back George, our Colin is back!"

A little later, his brothers returned from school. He grabbed them both and kissed them, to their utter disgust. He remembered Sophie. His heart jumped a few beats. He would read to her forever and ever.

"I'll be back in a little while Sophie should be home from school by now. I'm popping over to see her."

"Colin! No! Come back you'd better sit down," his father insisted. Colin saw the look of concern in his parents' eyes and sat down.

"I have bad news. Sophie died last year," his father said gravely.

"Dead, no… Sophie dead… I don't understand. How?"

"Smallpox a few weeks after you left."

"She was healthy and happy when I left."

"She's buried near Gramps and Gran," his mother said caringly.

A great sadness filled Colin. "I'll take flowers for them all in the next few days."

Chapter Forty One

Peter dared not risk going to a doctor so had an old army medic he knew remove the bullet and patch his shoulder allowing him to travel to France. It was three days before he was fit for the journey; he was very weak but to stay another day in London was far too risky.

He met Mary at Calais and went directly to the flat she rented. His wound wept badly. Mary cleaned and sterilized it but was worried about infection and could not risk him travelling.

"Why didn't you stay in London longer, or phone? I would have come immediately. Look at the state of you?"

"I did not want you anywhere near London. I'm here now so stop the lecture."

Mary was aware of the fires in London but had seen no report about casualties. Peter told her what happened. The Triads had a strong presence in France and they needed to leave, travel to Germany where they would be safer and go to ground.

They had enough money to last a few years. Colin had seen to that so there was no worry in that direction. Once in Germany they would need to be careful in the way they spent and with whom they associated, but other than that, there was no immediate danger.

Peter's condition worsened, his shoulder turned black. In addition, Mary heard from a few of her trusted contacts that the

Triads were looking for them and had a contract out on them both. They were finished in London she knew that but was more philosophical about it than Peter but knew it was bad news.

She could no longer trust anyone, even her most loyal former connections. She had no idea the amount of reward offered but knew when the Triads pursued this course of action previously it was substantial. One of her former lovers ran a side racket in drugs cutting out the Triads, she told them where to find him. They cut off his arms and legs, threw him into the Thames; she collected the reward.

It was a week before Peter was able to travel, the Triads knew they were in France and they needed to leave. They could wait no longer. That morning saw them on the train to Germany.

Mary could speak fluent German but Peter only knew a few words and would need to learn the language fast. They travelled through the night; by lunchtime the following day they were leaving the train to start their new life as Mrs. and Mrs. Grindle. They would have no contact with anyone in London or France, total isolation was the only way to remain safe.

Even with all the precautions, there was risk. The Triad had a number of synods all over Europe; they would distribute their picture to all. The Triads had marked them enemy number one, which meant every synod worldwide would get to know about them with the added incentive of a juicy reward.

They rented a flat in the heart of Berlin. Mary only went out for groceries, Peter staying inside the whole time. Within a few days, he was back to his old self. His arm was still weak but getting stronger every day. After a few weeks, they started going for walks together.

Peter's mind was a wasp's nest that kept stinging him. His heart a burning cauldron of infestation, his body wretched and wracked with malarial revenge that the Welshmen were still alive, he had heard as much. He placed his present predicament firmly in their court, and harboured a maniacal hatred bordering on the fanatical against them.

The time spent in Germany was starting to take its toll. They could not risk working; the Triads controlled much of the illegal activities. They would stand out like a sore thumb, they just idled the days away drinking, looking for things to do to keep occupied. Mary made the most of things, catching up on the many books she had promised herself she would read some day and was quite enjoying the experience, but never told Peter.

"We need to move on," Mary commented one morning over breakfast, knowing Peter got agitated and when in that state could easily give them away.

"Move where? We could go to Wales," he mockingly replied.

She just laughed, but it gave her a thought, a wry smile passed over her face. "Why not, eventually?" Pacifying his impetuosity, not in the least serious for a second, she knew Peter's weaknesses better than her own. "First I've an idea, South Africa. We need to change our appearance."

"What? Plastic surgery!"

She grinned. "Why not? London, Wales, we can go where we like. What do you say?"

I don't know. It will cost a packet."

"We have plenty, no worries there."

Peter tilted his head to one side. "I see where you're coming from. We could go back and work in London."

"It's settled then. I'll make enquiries over the next few days. We'll have new faces and then if you wish you can kill your Welshmen or get someone else to do it for you, why take the risk."

A few weeks later, they were on a plane to South Africa booking into the main hospital in Johannesburg. They were to have extensive facial surgery and after the operations would need a few months to recuperate. New face, new life, new names, Peter and Mary buried forever, killed off under the surgeon's knife.

Chapter Forty Two

Colin's mind was still fragile. The trauma he had suffered, locked away deep in his psyche for so long, was difficult to break. Gradually, with the help of his psychiatrist, he brought the pieces back together. He even mentioned he wished to train as a doctor. The psychiatrist sympathetic to Colin's desires, listened, but tried to steer him away from this idea and not aim at the impossible. He needed qualifications with high grades to make this a reality and he had none. This did not deter Colin in the slightest. Indeed, it had a contrary effect, making his resolve stronger, more determined.

Most of his free time he spent reading. He told his parents he wanted to study to become a doctor; they were happy he wanted to improve himself but did not place much credence in his desire and took the side of the psychiatrist.

He was told he did not have the recognised qualifications required to enrol in medical college; the competition would be fierce, too much for him; he should be more realistic in his expectations. He had achieved no academic qualifications when at school so enrolled in night study classes to obtain what he should have achieved there. He applied for a position as a fulltime student at the local college and they accepted him. He threw himself into the work with the force and speed of a bullet. He had another chance and was determined to make a mark for good in the world.

He remembered the old woman from whom he had stolen; it played on his mind constantly like an out of tune violin. He agonised over what he should do. If he went to the police, it would be highly unlikely he would still be able to fulfil his ambition to get into medical school. At the very least, he would have a criminal record and more than probably end up in prison. He placed the thought at the back of his mind telling himself he was different now, would never do anything like it again. Nevertheless, he had done it in the past, his past, his action, his responsibility, there was no denying it.

The violin rasped, scraped, and kept scratching his mind. The scratch evolved, became infected, it, the only sound he heard. His agony, his burden, and knew he must go to the police and accept the inevitable consequences. The next day with heavy heart, he called at the local police station. It was no more than an ordinary house; the police officer's family lived on the premises, the front room used as the office.

The police officer knew all about Colin's illness and his mental state. George had confided in him of his concern many times over a pint in the local pub, and how it was affecting the family, especially, his other children. He had thought one time that Colin might have to go into a mental institution it was affecting the other children so much.

Colin knocked on the door, waiting like a frightened lamb before the wolf.

"Hello Colin," he smiled opening the door. "I saw you standing there. Come in, come on in my boy," he beckoned.

He walked into the little room and told to take a seat. "How is your father? I haven't seen him in a few weeks been too busy."

"He is good sir."

"Glad to hear it and you?"

Colin swallowed hard. "I'm here to report myself and should go to prison."

"I see," said Gwynfa the police officer smiling. "First would you like a drink of lemonade or tea?"

"No thank you. I robbed an old women of all her money," he blurted nervously his hands shaking holding the corner of the desk trying to steady them.

"And who would this be, may I ask?"

"Mrs. Prosser," Colin submissively answered. "I went into her bedroom and stole all her money."

The police officer knew that Mrs. Prosser hadn't reported a robbery, he would know if she had. She died shortly after Colin ran away, before she found out about the theft. Her son had since sold the house and a young couple with a new baby were now living there.

"Old Mrs. Prosser you say. We've no record of any robbery. When would this be?"

"Not sure, months ago I think."

The police officer looked at Colin sceptically. "Is that so."

"It is so sir. If you don't believe me go and ask her where her £5,000 has gone."

"That's a lot of money Colin you can buy a house for that and have change; where is this money now?"

Colin was confused. "I, lost… gone… some hidden. Haven't spent it… don't think so anyway."

George is right, Gwynfa thought, the boy was two ounces short of a pound making up stories about robbing people that had been dead for over a year, unable to accept the idea that old Mrs. Prosser had anywhere near that amount of money. If she did, she would definitely report the robbery, and if she did not her son almost certainly would have.

"I see, you want me to go and ask her?"

"Yes." Colin innocently replied.

"That's going to be a bit difficult I'm afraid."

"I'll ask her if you like, you'll see I'm telling the truth."

"Of course, I believe you Colin," he answered placating the boy thinking a doctor he wants not a prison cell.

"How long will I go to prison? I need to know. If I'm not too old I still want go to college and become a medical doctor, if I'm allowed."

The police officer looked at Colin with compassion. "A robber and a doctor. Why don't you go home and rest?"

"Rest, what about prison, I should be in prison."

"The police will forgive you and so will Mrs. Prosser I'm sure."

"How do you know? I want to apologise to her, ask for forgiveness," he replied openly sobbing, trying to be brave but the tears fell.

"Just go home Colin that's a good lad, forget all about it. You're not going to prison, go home, rest."

"The robbery what about…?" he spluttered but was unable to find the words.

Gwynfa came round, placed his hand on Colin's shoulder, and gave him a handkerchief. "Here lad, dry yours eyes, forget about the robbery and everything else, just go and get better. We know you're having a tough time of things. Mrs. Prosser and I forgive you; all the police forgive you, there's an end to it. Now off you go."

Colin left the room feeling bewildered, confused, his mind in a spin taking the police officer's advice to go home and sleep. He slept soundly for a few hours, awoke, sat up in bed, and started to read but was unable to concentrate.

He went over the conversation with the police officer in his mind, could make no sense of it. Why did he have all these chances? He confessed, told all, and Gwynfa forgave him. Why? Were his dreams real? He knew he was a different person, more determined than ever to become a doctor, not for the money but to help others, to serve. Holding that thought in his head he fell back onto the pillow and went to sleep.

The following day, Robert the farmer's boy came into his mind, so decided to call on Mr. and Mrs. Evans at the farm. If you asked him why, he couldn't say, he just felt it was the right thing to do.

The weekend saw him at the farm and he noticed how run down and neglected it all looked. Mr. Evans always kept the farm in good order and Colin wondered if the farmer was ill. He knocked at the door Mrs. Evans opened it.

"Well I'll be," she said. "I heard you were ill."

"Yes, I was Mrs. Evans, I'm recovered now thank you," he answered politely. "I've just called…" and then he faltered and said, "to see if… are you both well?"

Mrs. Evans's face took on a serious demur. Colin picked this up and thought he had said something wrong and was just about to apologise. He didn't know what he had done but looking at her face felt he should have known something.

"Mr. Evans died suddenly, without warning, a few months back of a heart attack."

"I'm sorry I didn't know," Colin mumbled and wished at that moment he stayed at home.

"You weren't to know, come on in I'm just about to have a pot of tea and a few biscuits, join me."

They went into the farmhouse, Colin closed the door, and she beckoned him to take a seat. The first thing he noticed was the mirror above the mantelpiece, and the two candlesticks and clock still in the same place.

Mrs. Evans poured the tea, went into the kitchen to fetch the biscuits. Her hair was white, she reminded him of his grandmother and felt warm towards her as she opened the tin and offered him the contents.

"How are you managing with the farm?" he asked, then thought maybe he was being too forward.

"We get by, can't complain," she answered. "I have help a few days a week, labour is so expensive nowadays but I manage."

To Colin it was obvious she wasn't managing. The farm was a mess and now he knew the reason. He remembered his dream, and what his grandfather had said. If something reversed or changed an action that should have happened, nature would reassert itself as soon as it was able. Logic told him he had nothing to do with Robert's death but his heart told him differently. The words kept ringing in his mind "nature will always reassert itself," and felt responsible that Robert was no longer with his mother running the farm. If they had not fought that day by the river Robert would still be alive.

"Could I possibly help? I have a lot of free time at the weekend when not at college."

"Thank you for offering, I can hardly afford the help I have let alone another. I'm already a few months behind with the mortgage payments. Mr. Evans did say he had a little nest egg saved but he died before he told me where he had it hidden, but no matter, it is no good worrying about what I don't have and there is an end to it. Thank you all the same." she replied.

"No, no," Colin protested. "Not for money, for... for nothing."

She smiled at him. "Tell me, why would you want to spend your time on the farm and not get paid? The only thing we have a regular supply of are eggs, but you know all about that don't you?" she said laughing.

This last remark implied he would steal the eggs, which was why he was offering to help. That was the old Colin, capitalizing on someone else's misfortune.

"I promise not to take any of the eggs or anything else. I'm offering because I want to help that is all, I assure you nothing more. Please let me try, if you're not happy I'll go straight away."

Her weather-beaten face cracked into a smile, thinking he would be daunted within a few weeks. "All right you can start by coming on Saturday afternoons."

They stayed talking together the rest of the afternoon and were on their third pot of tea before he got up to go. His parents were expecting him and would worry if he was not back, reiterating as he walked through the front door he would be back the following Saturday and thanked her for giving him the opportunity.

True to his word every Saturday and often after college in the week he was at the farm working as if his very life depended on it. He mastered the more difficult tasks on the farm attacking them with the gusto of youth. Soon the two of them were firm friends; often Mrs. Evans would bring him tea and food on a silver tray as he worked. In a few months, the farm looked much better; it was not quite back to its old state, but Colin felt pleased with himself.

He was doing well at college, one of the top students in the class. He found the night classes hard on top of a full day at college but didn't miss an evening. He ploughed on with determination and resolve, often studying late into the night after arriving home from evening class.

One afternoon when working at the farm Mrs. Evans seemed out of sorts and he asked her if he had done something wrong. She looked at him aghast. "No Colin, you've been an angel. If it hadn't been for you, I don't know how I could have coped this far. You've been a power of help to me. I've been afraid to tell you but I must now, it will become common knowledge in a few weeks in any event," and started to cry.

"I must vacate the farm at the end of the month if the mortgage is not paid. I don't have the money so I'll have to go. I don't know where, re-housed, somewhere local I hope. Can't grumble though I've had a good life, no one is to blame, things happen."

Colin, feeling as if someone had plunged a knife in his stomach, could think of nothing to say. He placed his arm around Mrs. Evans' shoulder and she stopped crying.

"Silly old me crying," she said. "I knew it was coming, it's no surprise. So there you are I mustn't bleat. Come Colin, let's have a cup of tea, the end of the month is over two weeks away. What will happen will happen. I hope you'll come and visit me wherever I am," smiling again.

"Of course I will you know that, we are friends right."

"Right. What a lucky person I am, thank you Colin."

He went home that night feeling depressed then had an idea. Before he went to London, he hid £3,000. He had forgotten all about it until now and wondered if the money was still where he had concealed it.

The following day he was up before dawn. The morning was crisp, dry, and cold, that didn't worry him. Remembered he had covered the notes in plastic, placed the money in a tin box in a crevice near the river. He approached with apprehension, the box was exactly where he had left it, the cash intact and hoped it was enough to pay the mortgage so Mrs. Evans could keep the farm.

Colin was on his way to the farm to give her the money when he realised she would ask where it came from and he had no answer. He would wait until the Saturday and say he found it on the farm, remembering what Mrs. Evans told him previously about her husband having a little nest egg, dying suddenly before he told her where he hid it.

Saturday afternoon he was at the farm as usual and after working for a few hours took the tin to Mrs. Evans and informed her he found it in one of the farm buildings. She opened the tin and her mouth dropped.

"Do you know what's in here?" she asked smiling.

"Yes, money, must be the nest egg you mentioned," he casually remarked.

She counted the money her hands were shaking, it came to just over £3,000. "He said he had some money but this much. I can't believe it. Where did you say you came across it?" she said suspiciously.

"In the cowshed between the top rafters," he stated knowing full well it could not be disproved.

She stared at the money for what seemed an age unable to comprehend the amount of cash before her. "This means I'm able to pay off the mortgage it comes to £2,890," and started to cry.

Colin went over and placed his arm on her shoulder. "Does this mean you'll be staying at the farm?"

"Yes Colin, it means I'm staying thanks to you," she laughed, gave him a hug, and said. "I look a mess, crying all over you, you must think me old and foolish?"

"No Mrs. Evans, I think no such thing. You and my Gran are the kindest people I've ever known." He answered and he really meant it.

"You must take something for this… that's it, a reward," and she started to count out a number of notes.

"None of this money belongs to me," he said emphatically. "I'll not take a penny of it, reward or otherwise, not one penny."

"But… just take…"

"No," he said again. "Please Mrs. Evans I can't, but I'll accept a cup of tea."

"You are very special Colin, thank you again. You don't know how much finding this money means to me," her face aglow with delight.

Colin did know but said nothing just shrugged his shoulders and smiled as if to say, 'you're right.' They spent the rest of the afternoon talking to each other as they supped tea from her best china in celebration. He left her that evening knowing she would be able to stay on the farm for the rest of her life, and felt a warm glow in his stomach. He was sad he had to lie to her but could see no other way, and suspect his grandfather would forgive him for the indiscretion.

His whole life revolved around his studies, the farm and his father's garden and had never felt so happy. The results from his first year exams were excellent, passing all with distinction. He knew there would be another two years of study in order to have any hope of applying to medical college but was not perturbed in the slightest. His mind already saw himself as a doctor, passing the exams little more than catching up with his mind.

He often wondered what had happened to Mary and Peter. He had really loved her, would have done anything for her and hoped wherever she was, she was happy. His father never spoke of what happened in London. Colin often asked but never received an answer. His father's response was always the same. "Best forgotten."

Chapter Forty Three

Johannesburg was a resounding success. Peter and Mary had several operations on their faces over a period of two years costing many thousands of pounds spending months in recuperation, their anonymity complete. The Triads would never suspect their identity. When back in London could start up business again. The time in South Africa had been expensive, depleting their savings; they needed to get back to work quickly.

They arrived in London calling themselves Paul and Susan Grindle a married couple. Mary had rented a flat before they arrived but needed another one in which to ply their trade of seduction and drug smuggling. She'd been living very much as a nun in Johannesburg, she slept with her brother a few times but that held little excitement for either of them, and was looking forward to getting another young boy in harness.

Peter knew enough about the drug scene in London to set up connections quickly, but needed to be careful. His old contacts were out of the question. He doubted if they would recognise him the way his appearance had changed, but still, why take an unnecessary chance; he only needed one to recognise him and all the surgery would have been for nothing.

Their motto of 'any doubt get out' had served them well in the past and would carry on doing so in the future. This philosophy had kept them alive, if it were not for the meddling Welshmen none of what they had been through the last two years would have been necessary.

Mary had tried to persuade him to let the episode rest. "Why take the risk Peter? Let it go."

"They need to be taught a lesson. Have you no heart, look what they have put us through."

"We are new people now, let the old go, move on, get over it."

"I will when they are dead."

"What if they kill you?" she demanded.

"Then I die with honour knowing…" His face turned angry. "Look, that's not going to happen. I hold all the cards; they think I'm dead. I'll do the job; leave no trace and be back in London within a few hours, you worry too much."

"Normally you are the one that worries, and now you take this unnecessary risk; ego Peter, will be the death of you."

Peter was determined; as soon as they re-established themselves in London, he would sort them once and for all. They humiliated him, took him for a fool, no one does that to Peter. He wanted them dead, but first they had to suffer the way he suffered, and he had suffered, blaming the Welshmen for all his woes.

Within six months, Mary had found herself a new boy; Peter developed a new network of contacts. A great deal had changed, a number of his old contacts were in prison, dead or long gone. The police had been active over the period, exceptionally so, successfully cleaning up a large amount of the criminal activity in that part of London. All his old police contacts were gone; the sergeant and a few others forced to resign. This suited Peter; the ground was clear, prime to move into without hassle. The police had done him a favour.

The only cloud left on the horizon was the Triads. They suspended much of their activity until the police action died down but they were still in control and Peter needed to be careful. Soon they would find out a new boy was on the block and pay him a visit, first to encourage him to hand over a slice of the spoils, second to warn if he did not.

This he didn't mind, it was a kind of insurance to keep them sweet and on his side. However, he needed to be careful to make initial contact with a synod where no one knew him personally and offer them a slice of the action before someone contacted him. Normally a synod consisted of three people; one would report directly to the Triad, the only contact they would allow, the organisation was covert to the extreme.

Colin was a few months away from his final exams and providing he had the grades, his application to attend medical college approved. His aim for the impossible had become the possible. He had made it possible by sheer dedication and hard work. His parents walked with a spring in their steps when they knew their son was to train as a doctor. They had no doubt he would achieve the grades required and were already telling whoever would listen their eldest son was to become a doctor.

This had a beneficial effect on the other children and contributed to them doing well at school. Colin, wherever possible, encouraged and helped with their homework. He was still a regular caller at the farm spending almost every Saturday afternoon there; Mrs. Evans was one of his favourite people and firm friend.

The only person from his old school with whom he kept contact was Tim, who often turned up at the farm to give a helping hand. Jessica was growing into a balanced young lady, often Colin would help her with her school work but it was not the same as when he used to read to Sophie. He never let on but often wondered what she would be like had she lived.

Chapter Forty Four

It was raining when Peter arrived at Cardiff Train Station leaving Mary in London with the new boy. She had taken him to France a few times but didn't rate him very highly. She thought of Colin, her best protégé, and wondered if he was still alive. She suspected not as the average life span, once the Chinese sold them, was two to three years. Often they had so many drugs pumped into them they didn't know what day it was, compos mentis not being an option in case they tried to escape. In any event, he would be disposed of as soon as his youthful looks faded; Colin had a few years, tops. She smiled, how enjoyable he was to train, such a willing pupil, a machine in bed, yes, after all this time she still missed Colin.

Peter had other things in mind. He had never been in Cardiff before and had to ask directions to Treorchy. He knew pretty well where they lived from the many conversations with Colin and from what his sister told him. An hour later saw him on the train heading into the valley to extract his pound of flesh.

It was early afternoon before he arrived at Treorchy, the train delayed in transit. He needed a place to stay but first needed to disguise himself not wanting his new identity revealed. He didn't want anyone to identify him. His new face had cost thousands of pounds and much pain. He changed in a public toilet near the Stag hotel in Treorchy. Later he booked a room in the Lion, another hotel further up the main street going straight to his room telling the landlord he was a travelling salesman.

He had to find a place called Cwmparc, knew it was a mile or two from where he was staying but didn't want to ask directions. It would draw attention, the less people he met or spoke with the better.

The following day saw him walking towards Cwmparc, sniggered at the small cramped houses, non-descript and dirty, too down market for his taste. Heaped everywhere over the mountains were numerous black mounds, some so large as to cover a whole mountain side and looking like large carbuncles clinging to its host with leach like tenacity. He knew the first names of the three and was surprised they lived in such a small town believing they were like him, part of the criminal fraternity. Then thought differently, clever he thought, who would think of looking for them in a place like this?

A while later saw him walking through the final street, he could go no further, ahead the slag heaps and mountain. A few people, stared, passed and said good morning. He found this rather disconcerting, grumbled the same back in reply. Where he was from everyone minded their own business and wished they would do the same here.

One old fellow even asked him if he was lost and he realised most of the population knew each other making him stand out like a radio mast. Perhaps Mary was right he thought, the risk was too high and regretted booking into the Lion. Then he remembered the humiliation he suffered leaving only revenge in its place. Many a night the indignity of what they did stopped him from sleeping, but no longer. He would do what he came to do and get out.

The most effective solution was to gun them down and head straight back to London. He believed Henry the most dangerous, the one he hated the most. He would be the first to feel his wrath. It was not long before Peter located where they lived. When he realised they were no more than ordinary working men labouring on the local tip, his heart missed a beat, he felt foolish, even more humiliated to have ever been afraid of such low life. To him they were scum, shovelling dirt, little better than ants; what a fool he'd been, this would be easy.

Mary had told him they were ordinary workingmen, nothing special, Peter didn't accept it and put that down to them keeping a low profile. She could only have had the information from Colin. He was wrong, that is exactly what they were, and hated them even more because common working people had outsmarted him.

As luck would have it, he noticed Bill coming out of the Tremains Hotel and at first was inclined to hide but laughed at his caution and walked straight past him. He watched him turn the corner, followed discreetly and saw him entering his house. It was difficult to loiter in the street. In London no one would take any notice, here it was different. He walked on and caught a bus back to Treorchy to plan his next move.

He discounted the gun, too impersonal. Besides, the only way he could kill the three together would be to gun them down at the same time. This was highly improbable and very high profile. Access in and out of the valley was restricted. There would be little time for him to get out of such a small village, concluding it would be far too risky.

The alternative was to kill and hide the bodies, the problem they had families. He was kicking himself he hadn't brought explosives; he could have blown up their houses killing their families in the process. Caution prevailed, logic overruling passion, he needed to kill them and be back in London before discovery of their bodies.

After he struck his blow, the police would be on the scene asking questions. It would only be a matter of time before they visited all the lodging houses in the area asking for a list of who stayed there over the last few weeks, discovering he stayed at the Lion. As much as he wanted the three dead, he realised he would have to be systematic, and kill them one at a time. The easiest target by far was Bill; if Peter's knowledge was correct, he lived alone. That would be his starting point.

That evening saw him outside Bill's house hiding in the shadows like the rat he was watching as Bill left the house. He followed discreetly and saw him entering the Tremains Hotel. Quickly he returned to the house careful no one saw him. The house was in darkness; he placed gloves on his hands, scaled the back wall, broke a small window in the back door, and entered.

It was a small terraced house neat from a male perspective. It was obvious he lived alone. The furniture outdated. In the kitchen, a fire burned in the grate a guard around the outside to protect the coals from falling out. Recently washed clothes hung from a long rail above the fire. He looked around the house, found money in one of the rooms upstairs and pocketed it. The rest to Peter was junk. His lifestyle was way above their standard, suspecting the others were like Bill. To him they were peasants of the worse kind, and he seethed with anger. How people so low down the social scale had been able to humiliate a person like himself he could not comprehend.

He settled in a chair. Two hours later, he heard the front door click and waited, gun in hand, a switchblade tucked into his belt. Bill clicked the light switch and jumped back in shock to see a gun pointing at his stomach.

"Sit down don't move," Peter harshly demanded. "One false move and I'll empty this gun into your guts."

Bill sat in the chair indicated by the point of the gun. "You won't find a lot to take, you've chosen the wrong house," he stuttered, in shock.

Peter sneered. "No, I've got the right house, definitely, the right house, I can assure you. Bill!" Peter's face glowed evil; the adrenaline rush he so craved was in him.

Bill was frightened. Peter's eyes were cold, watery, devoid of any humanity. "Take what you want you'll get no trouble from me."

"Oh! Yes, it's the trouble you have already caused, that is what I've come to even up. I'll take all right don't worry about that. I have waited a long time for this moment and intend to take it slow." His white teeth sparkled as if advertising toothpaste.

Peter stood, slowly walked the few steps over to where Bill sat and pointed the barrel of his gun directly at Bill's head, and smiled maliciously; he was in control, the master, and in no hurry. The greater the fear, the greater his satisfaction, Peter was on a high.

"Take it all if you like, there's some money in the drawer up stairs, take it."

"Thank you," Peter mocked. "I've got what I want, it's always nice to be paid when a job is done well and done well it will be, I assure you," he stated hitting Bill in the face with his other hand as he spoke.

Bill reeled back in the chair with the force, blood spouted from his nose. He held his nose with his hands.

"I'm strong, hey," Peter grinned. "But... there is always a but isn't there Bill, just to be sure," he hit him with the butt of the gun across the head one way, then the other and sat back down.

Bill groaned in pain. "No! No more please, all the money I have is upstairs in a box under the bed take it and go."

"You still don't get it do you Bill," stood up and hit him again. "Surely you remember me?"

"No, I've never seen you before, never, I'm sure. What do you want of me?" Blood ran down the front of Bill's shirt.

"But you have Bill, shall I beat the brain a bit more, make you remember," he was so enjoying this. "Remember London? Is there light there yet?"

"London! No… What? I don't understand… that was a few years ago," he spluttered his mouth dripping blood.

"At last, the bulb has been switched on, action and consequence Bill. You did the action I took the consequence. Peter at your service, I see the bulb is burning bright now, you remember?" He was manic and hit Bill again in the neck, winding him.

He tried to speak; the punch damaged his windpipe and could only whimper. Bill's eyes were white with fear. He knew in that instant he was going to die, tried to stand and fight back but before he was able to lean forward in the chair Peter drove his knife into his stomach turning it at the same time ripping his insides apart. He removed the knife wiped the blade clean on Bill's hair and grinned. The manic look softened into a smile of contentment.

Bill slumped back; his eyes glazed over, blood pumped from his stomach, the suddenness meant he felt little pain, he knew he was dying. Peter sat back in his seat casually poured himself a drink from the bottle of whisky he found on the windowsill, lit a cigarette and waited.

"Well Bill, you and I will have to part company soon, don't worry the other two will follow shortly, you won't be by yourself for long, I'm kind like that." Peter smiled his face angelic. "You've been a very, very naughty boy and needed to be punished. I will give you a song, an encouragement to help you on your way.

Remember, remember Peter the avenger
come to say hello,
I've dreamed of meeting you for oh so
long, and now my wish has come true.
Pity you are leaving, oh, so soon,
I hope you're enjoying the pain.
I would love to stay to see you
die but sadly, I must go home,
But sadly, I must go home.
Remember, remember Peter the avenge
as he kills two more,
Remember, remember Peter the avenger,
I hope they'll suffer more."

He sang in sickening sadistic delight, drank the whisky, toasted Bill and left the same way he entered humming, "*Remember, remember,*" over and over again.

He knew the discovery of Bill's body would not be until morning at the earliest and intended to be back in London before then. His heart told him to go after the other two without delay and finish the job but his calculating brain knew the risk was too great. They would have to wait until next time. He knew the layout of the place, so there would be no need for an overnight stay and would bring explosives. That night saw him on the train to London still humming quietly to himself, "remember, remember, Peter the avenger come to say hello…"

Bill tried to move. Knew he was dying, his eyes focused on the empty glass of whiskey on the table opposite. His focus hazy, felt himself moving away from the glass; time was short and wrote the letter 'P' on the wall with his own blood slumped back and died.

It was late afternoon the following day before a next-door neighbour discovered the body. She expected Bill for lunch and when he didn't turn up by 3 p.m. she knocked the door, and receiving no reply went round the back of the house muttering to herself that his food had gone cold. She noticed a side window broken and the back door open. She shouted and walked in to find him dead in the chair covered with his own blood. She screamed and ran out the door, soon other neighbours started to congregate in the street, one of them ran for the police.

The first police officer arrived within half an hour followed by others a little while later. They cordoned off the house and a full murder investigation immediately got under way.

The police interviewed Mavis, the neighbour, who had found the body but she was extremely distressed. Bill had been a neighbour for over twenty years and they were firm friends. Twice a week he would call in for his food and for a natter with her and her husband.

By the end of the day, the news was all over the village. George and Henry arrived but denied entry to the house so they called next door to speak to Mavis.

She was sitting in a chair sobbing.

"Where was he Mavis? Take your time," said Henry.

"Dreadful! Blood all… dreadful, Oh!"

"Henry, come back later, can't you see how upset she is, the police have been with her for the last hour," her husband stated none too pleased.

"No! No Mike," She answered. "I'll be all right in a minute, they have a right to know. Henry and George were his best friends. I went round the back, saw a window smashed, the door open, went in thinking he was repairing the glass and had forgot about the time. He was in his chair covered in blood." She sobbed, wiped her eyes in a handkerchief, composed herself, and started again.

"The blood was everywhere, he had obviously been beaten, beaten mind you in the face, and us, little more than a few feet away next door. I could see that from the marks. Who could have done such a thing?" She sobbed again sitting up straight in the chair and taking a sip from the cup of tea her husband made her. "His stomach was hanging out, cold he was; cold as ice. There was a letter P written on the wall, in blood, his own blood, as if he was trying to tell us something before he died," and broke down completely.

George and Henry turned to each other shocked, recognition registering immediately on their faces at what they were hearing.

"Thank you Mavis, you've been very brave, we'll leave you now, you've been through enough, try to get a few hours sleep," George stated and they left.

Outside they walked aimlessly, not saying a word until they realised they were outside the Tremains Hotel. They went in and ordered two pints of beer, still in shock, hardly able to take in what had just happened.

"Bill dead, it doesn't seem possible," Henry stated picking up his pint.

"I've heard about Bill. Murder so they say," the landlord stated. "But who could have…?"

"Leave it Sam not now, not in the mood," Henry interrupted. "Leave us alone, we just need to… We don't feel like talking about it yet," and walked with George to a quiet corner.

"P! He's alive," stated George. "It can't mean anything else."

Henry thought for a moment. "Yes! Alive. Bill was trying to warn us, it's not far off three years. Why so long?"

"I don't know but he'll be coming for us next, this won't stop with Bill."

Henry nodded. "I agree."

"From what Mavis says Bill suffered."

"I'd like to have five minutes with him. I should have killed him in London when I had the chance." Henry mouthed through clenched teeth, his hands tightly closed in anger.

"Someone must have seen him. He can't just turn up here with his fancy voice and clothes, kill Bill and just disappear," George stated.

"He could still be here hiding, waiting for the opportunity to come for us, he's good at the old disguise. We need to be careful."

"He knows no one in the village so he must have stayed somewhere?" remarked George.

Henry wasn't convinced. "Not necessarily he could have come straight from London killed Bill and returned, or more likely hid out in Cardiff. Bill was killed last night by the look of things, Peter could be long gone."

"Not if he's after us, he might be staying locally waiting his chance."

"Unlikely, any strangers the police will interview first, he wouldn't risk that."

"How did he know Bill was alone? He must have been watching the house beforehand. He could only know where we lived by asking someone, that someone we need to find. Let's ask around a few of the pubs and shops if they've talked to any strangers with a fancy voice recently."

"It's not just us George, our families are now in the frame, especially Colin and Jessica. We need to move fast. I'm telling you, if I see him, I'll not hesitate, I'll kill him and sod the consequences."

George nodded in agreement and sighed. "If I don't kill him first."

"You take the shops and pubs from here to Treorchy. I'll start there, work up to Treherbert, and down as far as Gelli."

"Don't forget the Post Offices," George added.

They started immediately, Henry to Treorchy, George starting with the landlord of the pub. The following day the nationals as well as the local papers were full of the story, each speculating the type of person the police should be looking for. Describing the murder as diabolical, dastardly, cruel, merciless and many other gutter adjectives designed to make the reader squirm.

They worked methodically, left no stone unturned. The police were also conducting door to door enquires, interviewed them at length but they gave little away.

No strangers stayed in any of the pubs in Cwmparc; there was a stranger seen on the day of the murder but they could not find anyone who had spoken to him. Henry eventually ended up in the Lion and the landlord told him a stranger with a fancy accent had stayed there for one night. When the landlord described what he looked like Henry realised it couldn't have been Peter unless of course he was in disguise.

That evening when together they shared information. "Perhaps he's paid someone to kill Bill."

"Unlikely, not the type George, he is the kind of person that must do it himself. He needs to feel the adrenalin rush of revenge personally."

Nothing new turned up and they started the exercise again just in case they overlooked something the first time; the only stranger that in any way fitted was the one that stayed in the Lion. Henry questioned the landlord closely again, even buying him a few pints of beer but from the description given it definitely wasn't Peter, but that meant little he would disguise himself.

The stranger stated to the landlord he was a travelling salesman, yet didn't have any wares, only a small case. He stayed one night, the day before the murder, spent most of his time in his room, and did not come down for breakfast, the bar or talk to anyone.

Henry checked at the station; one of the guards remembered a stranger with a nice voice asking for a ticket to Cardiff and how long he needed to wait for the London train. The description matched that given by the landlord of the Lion.

That evening Henry and George met up and sifted through the information yet again. The police had a few leads to follow up but had no concrete information and were frantically looking for a breakthrough, according to Gwynfa.

"I think we should tell the police all we know and ask them for protection for our families," said George on edge.

Henry was anti police. "What can we tell them that will make a difference?"

"The fire in London, how we rescued Colin, the Chinese man, how we held Peter captive and the rest of it."

"What good is that? We'll end up in prison. Where will our families be then? Bill's dead, we'll be locked away, our families defenceless. No George, I'm as scared as you, but if we're around there will be a better chance of stopping him getting to them."

George reflected. "I'm sending the wife and kids to her sister and say they've gone to see her old aunt in Monmouthshire and will be away for a while. The kids can go to the local school there for a few months until this business is sorted."

"I see where you're coming from. Colin will be away shortly in university. You've told almost anyone that will listen. He'll be a sitting duck in Bristol by himself," Henry replied. "How are you going to handle that, it's public knowledge?"

George's face darkened. "Let's make sure we nail him in the next three months. If I knew then what I know now believe…"

"Hindsight George, hindsight, a wonderful thing, we just didn't know. We all thought he was dead. I'll send Anne and the kids to her mother's in Porthcawl, tell everyone they are away at her brothers in North Wales."

"Then what?"

"We wait."

The police intensified the investigation, each lead culminated in a brick wall. With the number of police in the area, it would be too dangerous for strangers to be noticeable. Four weeks later Anne and the children left followed two weeks afterwards by George's family. As soon as they were gone, George told his friends and neighbours Colin was now going to Edinburgh University.

The wives didn't know the whole story but enough to know what they had to go through to get Colin back and one of them was now dead. That was sufficient to convince them to say nothing and go to ground.

The police were getting nowhere. They assumed it was a local person but had no suspect. Bill was well liked; everyone was getting increasingly frustrated as the days past into weeks then into months. Henry and George missed their wives and children and would visit at different times one of them always staying at home, both taking great care no one followed. Always vigilant, never establishing a set pattern, continually on the lookout for strangers.

Chapter Forty Five

Peter followed the story through the papers. 'No suspect. The police are not doing enough. What are we paying our police for? There was a stranger seen on the day of the murder but not traced…' the story died and the press moved on to more recent topics. He knew Henry and George would be on edge, forever looking over their shoulder; they must suspect he killed Bill, giving him great joy to imagine their discomfort.

Mary wanted him to leave the two, arguing the risk outweighed any benefit and he should leave well alone, he had taken his revenge and begged him to place it in the past and move to pastures new. They were making money. Things were very much back to normal.

"Why take further risk?" she pleaded.

Peter was adamant; the others must pay the same price. Mary realised it was futile and let the subject drop but had a bad feeling about it.

Peter had contacted a different synod; they found him profitable, having, of course, no idea of his real identity. He told them he'd spent most of his life in South Africa, married a local girl, and relocated to London.

The Triads were not strong in South Africa due to the constant unrest over apartheid, telling them he wanted out before the whole country blew up in the white man's face. The Triads accepted this explanation without question. The situation was obvious for all to see, and they only made minimal checks with their contacts in South Africa, which matched with their enquiries.

He intended to deal with George and Henry on the one journey. He hated the Welsh with their sickly voices, friendly culture, mocked at their small insignificant houses, hovels for peasants. A repulsive smile moved across his face, a smile of superiority as he thought of himself reading about their murders in the papers, but first, he needed them to suffer.

He knew roughly the layout of the village, had purchased street maps to check for escape routes. There was one over the mountain from Cwmparc and another moving through Treorchy and Treherbert over the mountain into another valley, but were easy for the police to set up roadblocks. The other was down the valley through Pontypridd to Cardiff, making it a little more difficult to organise a roadblock. All three would require a car. Not many of the community had cars so an unknown car would stand out. He could steal one but that meant increasing the risk.

The train was still the best alternative. His preferred option would be to kill them personally and get back to London before discovery of the bodies. He had dreamt many times of how he would feel when he thrust the knife into their guts, especially Henry's, at last the time was near and he snorted like a pig at the prospect.

In case of complications, he would take a few sticks of dynamite, as a last resort. He would miss the thrill of seeing them die in person, but at least they'd be dead and his revenge satiated. He hoped it would not come to that, he wanted their faces in full view as their breath left their bodies.

A few weeks later, he arrived at Cardiff Station; rather than catch the train to Treorchy immediately as he originally intended, decided to book into the Park Hotel in Cardiff firstly donning his disguise.

The following day he changed his mind again and hired a car under a false name and driving licence. He intended to familiarise himself with the exit routes out of the valley in case something went wrong and he needed a quick getaway.

The next day saw him driving round the valley over the Rhigos and Bwlch mountains. He also took the Cardiff road from Pontypridd and up into the valley, getting to know the area and the best route in case of emergency.

He stopped on the Bwlch and looked over into the valley, the danger was obvious. The shortest way out of Cwmparc was over the mountain road he now stood upon and this made him shiver. Roadblocks could be set up at either end stopping all cars. Being a stranger this invited trouble, the inhabitants were parochial, and would know immediately he was a stranger. He was used to working in a large city where it is easy to lose yourself at a moment's notice, not a small little village where to be inconspicuous was an impossibility.

He looked into the valley and watched for some time from his high vantage point the small line upon line of terraced houses moving downwards towards Treorchy. Trains and lorries moved back and forth taking the coal and waste from the tip to some unknown destination.

Coal tips covered most of the valley; ugly black humps wherever his eyes fell. He noticed large conveyor belts starting under the Ragged Mountain moving downward following the contours of the river, the noise reverberating around his ears.

At the bottom of the valley the conveyor belt ended, the slag and rubbish washed and dropped into wagons for onward transport. The coal rubble went into one wagon, the waste into another. The waste used as hardcore in road construction.

After Peter's first visit to Wales Mary recalled Colin had once mentioned his father and his friends, Henry and Bill worked washing the coal tip. Peter wondered if they were somewhere down there with the dirt where they belonged. If that were the case, his task would be that much easier. He noticed the work continued day and night. It was logical, therefore, to assume every few weeks they would be on this mountain overnight. What better time to kill them and hide the bodies giving him the time he needed to get safely to London, but first he needed to establish if that were the case.

He returned to Cardiff and purchased a theodolite with stand. He also bought a complete set of oilskins the same colour the men were wearing on site, a long measuring tape, hard hat, pair of binoculars and wellington boots and returned to his vantage point at the top of the Bwlch. He erected the theodolite on the stand but moved positions every so often to appear as if he were conducting a survey of the valley; all the time watching the activity of the workers below. If Peter had anything, he had the patience of a tarantula awaiting his prey.

It was not long before he spotted Henry half way up the mountain working near a set of large steel rollers crushing coal and waste. His job, from what he could see, was keeping the rollers clear.

A shed stood a little way from the rollers, used, Peter assumed, to shelter from the weather and have their breaks. Adjacent to the shed stood a large steel barrel glowing red with heat as coal burned inside it. A covered bench stood next to the fire and Henry would often sit there watching the rollers in the warmth. Occasionally, someone would join him at break times but mostly he was alone. Peter glowed with delight thinking it would be easy.

The first thought was to shoot Henry. The sound of the rollers would drown out the noise of the bullet, but his lust for revenge overruled this thought. Revenge is sweeter when watched up close and Peter longed to see the whites of their eyes as he killed them.

Two hours after the shift started the foreman would turn up and spend five to ten minutes sitting round the fire talking and move on to the other workers higher up the mountain. It would be at least three hours, sometimes near four before he met Henry again on the way back, to his amazement the foreman was George. This pattern never deviated, repeated every day as Peter watched making sure he never stayed in one place, moving his stand with the theodolite every hour so as to look busy.

There were three shifts, an early morning, a late afternoon, and a night shift. He watched them for two weeks and knew the shift patterns, surmised their next shift would be the night shift. The first night he would watch from the darkness. There were floodlights around the rollers so there would be no problem in making out what was happening. He needed to establish that they followed the same pattern each night and make his move on the second or even the third night. His blood raced with excitement.

He knew if the pattern held he would have a window of three hours to kill Henry, hide the body, and wait for George to return to suffer the same fate. With the two bodies hidden on the mountain, there would be ample time to get out and be back in London before discovery.

He could make out Henry sitting by the fire eating a sandwich the heat shimmering around him. True to form within an hour and a half George turned up, sat with Henry for over fifteen minutes talking. Peter wondered what they were discussing.

"Take one," Henry offered George a sandwich.

"Mine are down the bottom I forgot to bring them with me, I'll have it if you don't mind."

Henry grinned. "If I didn't want you to have it George I wouldn't offer. Hold it in the paper your hands are blacker than mine."

"The weather is set to turn tomorrow; storms and heavy rain for the next few days according to the forecast. It'll be wet and chilly up here; don't forget to build the fire up high for the day shift.

"You state the obvious George. Living without the wife and kids is getting me down. It's been months now and there's been no sign of Peter or anyone. She's asking all the time to return home. I'm running out of excuses."

"Mine's exactly the same."

"We can't keep them away much longer," said Henry. "Even the neighbours are starting to talk asking when they are coming home; they think we have parted."

"That's a blow to the old ego. We should consider letting them home."

"No, he's out there George, as sure as eggs are eggs. He'll come for us and we'll be ready."

"All our mates are on the lookout for any stranger. I can't go on much longer like this, it's driving me mad Henry."

"Can't you see? That's exactly what he wants, until we get him the wives and kids stay hidden. I want the family back as much as you."

The conversation went on watched by Peter high above them in the darkness. Go on boys talk to your heart's delight; you won't be around to see another night through. He saw George rise off the bench and walk alongside the conveyor belt higher up the mountain.

Three and a half hours later George returned, Peter could see them clearly sitting around the fire exactly as expected. It would be dawn in another two hours and he moved back up the mountain to where he had hidden his car off the Bwlch road.

He walked into the hotel in Cardiff just as the light of day was dawning and went to bed intending to check out of the hotel late afternoon. This time tomorrow he would be on the 6 a.m. train back to London.

Chapter Forty Six

Peter woke just after noon, showered and dressed, his case still unpacked. He opened his brief case and unwrapped two handguns; both were loaded. He rewrapped them in the cloth and placed them back in the case in a separate compartment to the six sticks of dynamite that were also there and locked it. He would not be using the dynamite after all.

He checked out of the hotel, placed the two cases in his car, had a late leisurely lunch, and walked around Cardiff window-shopping. In the evening, he called into a Cinema to watch Snow White and the Seven Dwarfs finding the film highly entertaining, remembered he hadn't got a present for his sister and made a mental note to buy one in London in the morning.

An hour and a half later he was on the Bwlch road, his car parked off the highway on an old cart track well hidden from the view of passing cars. The weather had taken a turn for the worse, rain sheeted down. He didn't mind, the worse the weather, the less people were out on the roads; most of the night shift workers would be inside their cabins everything was on target.

In oilskins, cap and wellington boots he looked no different from the other workers. He could be anyone in the darkness, going about his business. He placed his briefcase inside his oilskins and made his way slowly down the mountain.

He waited behind the rollers just out of range of the lights crouched behind a few old oil drums that were randomly scattered about. The cabin's light was on and Peter suspected Henry was in there, but wasn't sure. The fire in the large drum was well stocked with coal and burnt brightly against the night rain, sheltered by a zinc canopy. The flames flickering high as the wind caught it from the side.

He watched sitting motionless, eyes as dark as coal, a mind black as the devil waiting for George to turn up and go before he struck his killer blow against Henry. His lips quivered slightly, his handsome face contorting in a malevolent smile, the excitement electrifying, waiting to deliver the poisoned apple, but there would be no prince to wake them.

He saw a figure approach, rain sheeting off his oilskins. He went under the covering over the seat; He removed his oilskins, hung them in the corner together with his hat. Peter was delighted; it was George.

George ran over to the cabin and went in closing the door. Twenty-five minutes passed. Peter was starting to get anxious, a minute later George came out followed by Henry, and both ran over to the fire. George dressed into his oilskins, said a few words to Henry, and walked up the mountain following the belt. Peter watched and waited until he was out of sight before making his move.

Henry ran back into the cabin and was sitting in a chair as Peter entered, cap down over his eyes as he walked casually over to Henry. Thinking it was one of the workmen Henry was just going to ask what he wanted when he felt a large crack on the head knocking him unconscious onto the floor.

He regained consciousness a few minutes later, hands and feet tied, sitting in the chair, wire round his neck, a stranger stood before him holding a gun. Henry looked through dazed eyes taking a few moments to focus. Peter had at least two, more like three hours, and intended to enjoy every minute of it.

"Hello Henry!" Peter's face beamed. "What does it feel like to be tied and helpless?" holding his smile.

"Who are you? I've done nothing to you," Henry shouted and struggled. Peter hit him with the palm of his hand across the face leaving a welt mark.

"That's for shouting and this one is for asking silly questions," and he hit Henry again with his fist into his stomach.

"You're the one that killed… Yes, you bastard you killed Bill." Henry tried to move; the chair rocked but could do no more.

"That's almost a question," slapping Henry again across the face. "Yes, a most enjoyable experience," he said superciliously. "His whisky was a pleasure to consume. Do you have any here for a little cheer, perhaps?"

Henry's face fell forward as he struggled frantically. "What do you want?" Henry mumbled but knew the answer.

"Let's play a guessing game."

"Piss off."

"Wrong answer," slapping his face. "But it's expected, working in dirt, you're nothing but a common bit of scum, shit on the shoe almost too much trouble wiping off."

"You won't get away with it."

Another slap, "a statement, you're being silly, play the game correctly. Let's try again."

"What do you gain from killing me?"

"At last, it was starting to get tiresome, right question. I'm going to kill you Henry, then George. Simply blot you out so to speak."

Henry tried to struggle and received another slap for his trouble. His nose and mouth bled badly. Peter sat on a chair opposite stretched his arms in the air and said mockingly, "a cup of tea would be nice. Bill gave me whiskey you know, but there again, he was the most civilised of the three, you haven't even made a cup of tea. Shame on you, and I've come all the way just to see you. You must have known I was coming." The smile gone, he hit out again across Henry's face smashing his nose.

"That's for not having tea ready," he sneered. "I must be careful. I don't want any blood in the cabin, can't have them finding you until I'm safely back in London, but there again with this dirt a little blood will go unnoticed."

"How much is he paying you? I'll give you a thousand pounds more if you leave," Henry stated. He saw the hand coming and tried to move his head deflecting it slightly but still taking quite a knock.

"Vulgarity, such vulgarity, the crudeness astounds me. No amount of money can buy this. I'm killing you free of charge, buckshee you could say, but where's my manners, we're not all hobble de hoys.

I'll sing you a lullaby first before I put you to sleep.

Remember, remember, Peter the avenger
come to say hello.
I've dreamed of meeting you for oh,
so long, and now my wish has come true.
Pity you are leaving me oh, so soon,
I hope you're enjoying the pain.
I will stay to see you die before
I must sadly go.
Remember, remember, Peter the avenger
as he kills one more.
Remember, remember, Peter the avenger
there's no time to make you suffer more."

The voice sickened, merciless. Henry knew it was Peter, his end imminent.

"Now a little walk to take in the night air." He slapped Henry again tightened the wire around his neck and kicked him to the floor. "It looks as if you'll have to be dragged outside," and started to dress into his oilskins humming to himself. "Remember, remember Peter the avenger come to say hello…"

George walked to his next call following the belts along the contours of the mountain, rain lashed his face; something was troubling him and couldn't recall what. Then he remembered.

Frequently, people from head office would turn up but would always call into the site office to make themselves known to the foreman and the managers. A few people had commented there was a surveyor taking readings over the mountain by the side of the Bwlch road; he just turned up and started work. This wasn't unusual; there were always people around taking readings and surveys.

George hadn't noticed anyone, a few of the boys living over the next valley travelled over the Bwlch road twice a day to and from work and commented that when they drove past they waved to him but he ignored them, turned his back. One of the men commented about ignorant bosses in the canteen a few days ago.

At the time he took no notice, now it came back to him and was troubled, and decided to go back and discuss it with Henry. He knew no one had reported to the office, annoyed for not noticing the comment sooner about the stranger.

As he walked back he thought about it more, could see the fire burning brightly out of the darkness and the light from the cabin door. A man was standing in the open door dragging Henry along. George crouched down, moved away from the belt, and circled around the back picking up a thin steel rod on the way.

He came up behind the man and saw a gun in his hand. He hit the arm with the steel rod. The gun fell under the belt. George hit him hard with his other hand; the stranger fell backward towards the shed and tried to run for the gun. George stopped him by hitting him across the back with the steel rod. Henry, hands and feet still tied, rolled across the ground trying to get to the gun.

Peter crawled forward toward the gun; George kicked out catching him on the leg both slipping on the wet surface.

"Watch out George he has a knife," Henry said noticing the thin shiny knife in Peter's hand.

George pulled back just as Peter slashed out with the blade narrowly missing his chest and hit out at the knife with the steel rod but missed. They fell about in the sludge, rain lashing their faces, wind piercing. Peter got to his feet first and ran towards

George who rolled away just in time hitting Peter in the leg making him fall over.

He lunged with the knife. George got to his feet, kicked and caught him in the back projecting him forward, and ran at Peter knocking him onto the moving belt.

Peter's arm caught on the belt; he tried to pull back but the belt dragged him towards the large steel drums. They heard him scream, saw him wriggle frantically trying to free himself unsuccessfully. The wheels pulled him in, crushing him completely. The four large wheels moved round and round; capable of crushing stone and coal a body posed no problem. His flat mangled body rattled around inside, in no time it was pulverised.

"Are you all right Henry," George shouted crawling over to him. Henry, other than a badly bruised and swollen face, was unharmed. George untied him and they went back into the cabin and slumped down on chairs.

"That was close; are you all right Henry?"

"Battered somewhat but still alive, I thought I was a goner there for awhile. It was him George, Peter. He intended to kill me and wait for you. He'd changed his face but it was definitely him."

"There won't be much left of him after the rollers have finished. Are there others about?" George asked looking round.

"No, I think it's over now." Henry said.

"We'll have a lot of explaining to do."

Henry placed his hand to his nose; his face was black, the blood mixing with the dirt on his face. "Give me a minute. Let me come round a bit. That sod," pointing to the rollers, "almost knocked my head off, I can't feel my face."

"You look a mess I'll give you that. We're in trouble now that's certain. I'd better stop the belts."

"No, hold on, Let's close the door for a moment keep the rain out and have a cup of tea and take stock."

"What about the body?"

"What body! It'll be little more than mud in a few minutes. We'll deal with that later, let's catch our breath first."

They removed their wet clothes and George made a pot of tea. Henry sat down and George cleaned up the mess to his nose and face.

"You'll have a conk as big as an orange by tomorrow."

"At least I'm alive."

A few minutes passed as they drank the tea. George stood and found Peter's briefcase in the corner of the shed. Inside a handgun, ammunition, sticks of dynamite, string and a length of wire, inside the flap a £1,000. He placed the contents of the case on the table and the money on a shelf where a number of mugs hung.

They dressed against the rain and went to see what was left of Peter. His body had gone between the wheels and crushed before it entered the drums. Blood was visible all over the wheels and floor but already after only half an hour the rain had washed a lot of it away. They found his wellington boots severed off at the knees his feet and part of his legs still inside. Henry went over picked them both up walked to the fire and threw them into the flames.

"What did you do that for?"

"That's the last of him."

They both watched the boots burn until the flesh inside sizzled and fried down to nothing.

"That's for Bill," Henry muttered.

George returned to the cabin and came back with a torch; all the blood had gone; the rain had washed it into the ground and away. The rollers were going round mixing his crushed body with the stones. George found a few pieces of clothing collected them and threw them into the fire, retrieved the gun from under the belt, emptied the magazine of bullets and threw the gun into the fire collected the other gun and did the same.

"We're both thinking the same."

“We’ve little choice, the body’s gone for good. There’ll be little but mud by the morning and that would have washed away with all this rain.”

“I’ll throw the bullets in the river on the way home,” George said.

Henry nodded saying, “leave the dynamite and knife I’ll get rid of them by throwing them down a crevice further up the mountain.”

“No,” George shook his head in disagreement. “Let’s sort the knife now,” picked it up went outside and threw it into the fire. He returned to the cabin, reached up and grabbed the money, Henry looked at him. “It’s blood money.” Walked outside and threw it after the knife. The rain still lashed down, running off the conveyor belt by the bucketful the ground sodden; it had already washed away the marks of the scuffle. The belt continually brought more slag and stone into the drums, crushing it. Peter’s body already turned in pulp.

George went back to the fire removed the two glowing white guns and the knife from the flames, hammered them into flat pieces of metal until they were unrecognisable and threw them under the belt as scrap metal they hissed and sizzled and soon cooled. Went back to the cabin for the brief case and threw in onto the fire.

The following day they phoned their wives and told them to come home. The car stayed where Peter left it until it was vandalised by a few of the local yobs who eventually rolled it over the mountain smashing into many pieces considered no more than an abandoned wreck. The only record of the car was with the hire garage. They registered the car stolen. The police marked it as a car theft crime and promptly forgot all about it.

Mary waited for Peter, growing more anxious by the day, they were a team; she loved him as well as she had loved anyone. When she hadn’t heard from him after a month, knew he was dead and was heartbroken.

She couldn't sleep, eat, even turned off sex; his loss affected her badly and she started to lose it mentally. They had been together all their life, looked after each other, were soul mates, they even on occasions slept together. She was devastated, she lived for Peter and Peter lived for her, they shared the same values.

She still had a young boy, and felt nothing but contempt for him blaming him for Peter's loss. One morning, sitting opposite him at the breakfast table, Mary stared at the boy. In her mind, his face changed into Colin and she remembered. If it weren't for Colin her beloved Peter would be here alive and she hated, with all the intensity of her twisted mind, the face before her.

She stood up, walked into the kitchen, returned with a bread knife, and without thought plunged the blade deep into the boy's neck seeing Colin's face clearly before her. "For my Peter," she calmly cried and cleared the table taking the dishes into the kitchen seemingly oblivious to what she had done.

Her mind had gone; perhaps it was so full of evil it could take no more and burst. Whatever the reason, we'll never know, madness roamed in her eyes where once there was life and a passion to live. The landlord found her a few days later, cowering in a corner of the kitchen the body still in the chair where she had killed it, blood congealed over the floor flies busy at their work.

There was nothing to identify her in the flat; psychiatric specialists deemed her incapable of standing trial and placed her in an institution for the criminally insane. Often, when her ranting started, as much for her own protection as for the staff, they restrained her in a straightjacket. In her quiet moments she would sob the name Peter, and cry, "come to me Peter," over and over again, turn to the wall and carry on an imaginary conversation in French as if the wall was his face.

Chapter Forty Seven

The reunited families were glad to be home at long last. Jessica turned out to be quite a madam, doted on her little brother as a mother hen over a chick. Colin went to see Mrs. Evans telling her all that had happened for the few months he was away, which wasn't much. Most of the time, he was studying. She had two fulltime workers helping on the farm. She completely paid off the mortgage and things were going well for her.

Time drifted forward, Colin entered medical college, and there were no prouder people than his parents. He worked hard and soon became one of the star pupils of that year. Occasionally, in his quiet moments, he thought of his time in London and Mary his first lover and wondered what had become of her and Peter still holding affection for them both.

There was one sad spot in Colin's life, in the second year at college Mrs. Evans suddenly died. He came home for the funeral, a small affair, a few of the local farmers turned up, some neighbours, George and Henry but not many more. The Evans family had kept very much to themselves; there were no brothers or sisters on either side.

Colin cried that day. He had grown to love the old lady over the years; they knew each other really well and wished she could have stayed on this earth a little longer, but it was not to be; he felt a deep sadness over her loss.

A few weeks after the funeral Colin received a letter from a solicitor which asked him to make an appointment to call to see him. His grandmother used the same solicitor so he thought, even though his twenty first birthday was more than six months away, it was to do with the gold medal he would inherit.

He felt there was no rush to make an appointment; another letter arrived before he finally got round to it. Mrs. Evans had left the farm and all its contents to him. It came as a complete surprise. In her will, she said how proud she was to have known him and how lucky she was to have had such a good friend. The final parting words of the will brought a lump to his throat as the solicitor read out. "If my Robert had lived I wish he would have turned out as good as you."

Henry and George's jobs were almost at an end; most of the waste on the tip cleared; they only had a few more weeks left to work. Colin was busy with his studies and could spend little time on his farm. He kept on the two employees, but needed more help. His father and Henry would soon be out of work and this was convenient for all concerned, they started on the farm immediately their jobs finished.

They enjoyed the outdoor life, took to farming as the proverbial duck takes to water, wallowing in the excitement of the work with a gusto that was good to watch. George ordered livestock; Henry and the family would spend most of the summer at the farmhouse the two families together.

A few weeks after Colin's twenty first birthday, another letter arrived from the same solicitor asking him to make an appointment. He knew this time it was about his grandfather's gold medal and rang the morning the letter arrived.

A week later, he saw the solicitor who handed him a sealed package. It was the medal as expected, together with a letter addressed to him directly not by name but as the oldest grandson.

My Dear Grandson,

Life has many twists and turns but things normally work out for the best if you have faith in your fellow human beings. My grandfather won this medal in a war long forgotten and I came into possession of it on my twenty first birthday.

My grandfather also was dead before I received it and so will I be when you read this letter. We, your grandmother and I, decided to do the same, pledge the medal to our first grandson. I cannot call you by name because we have not had our children yet. We are writing this letter on our wedding day, the date is unimportant to anyone but us, but is the happiest day in both our lives. You are a product of the love we have for each other, without our children, you could not be born, but I must pay a price for my love and your grandmother has also accepted the price and believes the story I am to unfold to you.

I spent my early life with my grandfather. I loved him dearly. I was a difficult child, and did many wrong things, in the midst of which he suddenly died. I had no one; my parents died before I was five years of age. I was entirely alone and went off the rails. My life was in pieces. Many times, I nearly killed in anger, but somehow, my grandfather came to me in dreams, helped me back to sanity. I met your grandmother and my life was complete.

I am telling you because you may well have experienced difficulties. My grandfather told me he was possessed by an evil entity which compelled him to wantonly destroy when a child, and so was his grandfather before him, I have no explanation for this; it goes back to our ancestors long gone and forgotten.

I looked upon it as a curse imposed on us since time immemorial, the eldest grandson of the one afflicted, will suffer the torments of no conscience, try to kill another fellow human being before his twenty first birthday. Perhaps, I'm over dramatic, perhaps it is nothing only in my mind, but if you had walked in my shoes, I believe you would think the same. You have come through it, would not be reading this letter otherwise. If you had taken a life in anger, committed murder, it would have pushed you into insanity, permanent insanity so my grandfather told me. He believed it was the price the curse demands, whether you believe is unimportant, I believe, so did my grandfather.

My grandfather came to me in dreams, and I will be there for you if I am able, I cannot promise, it is for time to fulfil, but pledge I will try. You are now through your ordeal. I hope if you have not already done so, found a life partner like your grandmother was to me. The warning I give you is stark and serious, the same as the warning I received. Your first-born grandson will be born without a conscience, and try to kill. That is the price you pay if you have children. You must guard the child against this until he comes of age. It is an unlikely story, granted, whether you believe it or not is down to you, I did, the responsibility rests with you.

Your loving Grandfather.

Colin read the letter many times over; many of his past actions came into focus. The anger he felt towards his parents. He wished them dead on many occasions, the lack of restraint in his behaviour, his blind temper, how he was unable to stop himself when in a rage, wanting, wishing to kill the person responsible. Visions of the two bullies in the schoolyard, all those years ago came flooding back into his memory. He did believe the letter.

Something odd struck him; one of his dreams showed him paralysed; his father and brothers gunned down and killed. Was the invalid in the wheel chair mad as well as paralysed? Perhaps he was mad, the letter said as much. He pondered; maybe whoever gunned him down did so before he killed anyone. Made to suffer, locked inside his body fully aware. There was no answer, whatever the reason, it was now past; he had come through like his grandfather and his ancestors before him. The solicitor told Colin he held a second letter from his grandfather, but had orders to destroy it when he handed over the first. Colin asked the content of the letter but the solicitor was to destroy it unopened.

He was due back in college the next day and spent the morning at the farm helping with the chickens. Henry was in a field, his father near the cowshed. He looked at these two people and wondered what really went on in London, what had they done to protect him from himself and felt a powerful love for them both. His mind jumped again, he remembered a part of the letter that said. "Found a life partner like your grandmother." he thought of Sophie, and wondered if they would be together now if she had lived? He knew they had something special even as children.

He would go to the cemetery this afternoon, visit her grave and the grave of his grandparents. He called into the local flower shop purchased a few bunches of flowers intending to also place flowers on the grave of Mr. and Mrs. Evans and their son Robert buried in the same plot.

The weather was clement, the sun shone, flowers were in full blossom, trees green in full majesty, grass a carpet cut neatly between the graves. The smell of summer filled the air and reigned supreme.

He went first to Sophie's grave, sat on the grass directly in front of her gravestone. He placed the flowers against the stone, pulled a book out of his pocket, and read the story of the Vanishing Mermaid, always in the distance always untouchable. "That is for you," he whispered.

He stayed there for ten minutes, walked over to his grandparents' grave, placed another bunch of flowers on the ground and sat next to them, closed his eyes holding the faces of these wonderful people in his mind.

He stood, his eyes moist, scratched the side of his nose, rubbed the wet from his eyes and found himself standing over the graves of Mr. and Mrs. Evans and their son, Robert. He carefully laid the flowers down on the earth and knelt next to them. The words, nature will always reassert itself, came into his mind. He prayed with all his heart they would forgive him for Robert's death.

"Come on laddie," he heard a voice behind him call. "You've been there long enough, why don't you take a seat over there," pointing to a bench a little way off. The cemetery's groundsman spoke.

"Yes thank you I'll do that," he answered and walked over to the seat. Whilst there he removed the letter from his pocket, read it again, and looked over to his grandparents' grave. The sun blinded him; he closed his eyes momentarily and saw his grandparents holding Sophie's hand.

"Our work is complete, we are leaving you now Colin," his grandfather spoke.

"Wait! Wait!" He shouted as they turned and walked into the sun and were gone. He flicked his eyes as if to refocus, standing before him was Robert. He spoke five words, "your prayers have been answered," and was gone.

"Come laddie, when I said to sit on the bench I didn't mean for you to go to sleep," the groundsman said smiling.

"Sorry," Colin faltered as he focused his eyes. "I was far away. I'll move now."

"That's all right; stay awhile, no problem. It's just that you were rocking about a bit and may fall off and hurt yourself that is all."

Colin stood up to go, a robin perched on the end of the bench and twittered. He watched the bird hop to the side of the bench and jump down to the floor. Colin's eyes followed until the little bird stopped in the centre of a daisy chain to the side of where he sat.

He reached over picked up the daisy chain and placed it over his head. The words of Sophie all those years ago came into his mind. 'Wear this and I will protect you wherever you are.' He whispered, "thank you Sophie. I know you are just in another room."

He smiled and walked towards the cemetery gate fingering the daisy chain around his neck and looked back. The robin was perched on the cemetery gate. Was it all a dream? Were all these visions only in his mind? He didn't know, didn't care, to Colin they were all real. Real as the daisy chain around his neck, and thought thank God for good people and walked out of the cemetery to let the dead rest in peace and into the remainder of his life.